CRYSTAL KEY

Door to a New World

Alexia D. Miller

amiller1009

Alexia D. Miller

{ 1 }

Copyright

Published and Printed in the United States of America
Subjects: Young Adult (YA). Fiction. Fantasy.
ISBNs: 978-0-578-70887-4 (paperback), 978-1-0879-2443-4 (Hardcover)
Crystal Key Book Series. Book 1.

Alexia D. Miller

PLEASE BE ADVISED:

THE FOLLOWING BOOK IS INTENDED FOR THOSE <u>15 YEARS</u> OF AGE AND OLDER. SOME READERS MAY FIND SOME SITUATIONS TROUBLING/TRIGGERING. IF YOU ARE HAVING TROUBLE THROUGHOUT THE BOOK PLEASE TAKE A BREAK OR CEASE READING THE MATERIAL ALTOGETHER. WHILE THE AUTHOR DOES NOT INTEND FOR THE BOOK TO BE TRIGGERING TO ANY OF THEIR READERS, THESE THINGS MAY HAPPEN. PLEASE TAKE CARE OF YOURSELF AND IF YOU ARE FEELING ALONE, HAVING AN EPISODE, OR IN DANGER OF HURTING YOURSELF OR OTHERS, PLEASE SEEK HELP IMMEDIATELY.

Alexia D. Miller

For Tiffany H. who encouraged me and my dream.

For Linda Lee C. Cook, my late grandmother, who never let me forget that I was meant to create and support others.

For my loving pets who dared to combat my sadness and anxiety.

For the family and friends who supported me along the way.

For those who purchase this book which helps me donate to charities.

For the warriors who fight the battles of chronic depression, anxiety, PTSD, and the heap of other mental illnesses which may plague you.

For survivors who have lived every day that you thought would be your last.

For all of those who may not know their true strength.

To all of those who find their escape through the doors of another world through the comfort of a book.

Alexia D. Miller

Crystal Key: Door to a New World

Please check out more of my works, my webcomic and much more on my website at your convenience! You can type www.admcreations.com or use the QR code provided for you below.

Thank you in advance for reading!

Alexia D. Miller

{5}

Crystal Key Book 1

Part 1:

The Beginning...

Alexia D. Miller

Crystal Key: Door to a New World

Alexia D. Miller

{7}

Crystal Key: Door to a New World

Note: Homes not to scale and do not represent exact quantity.

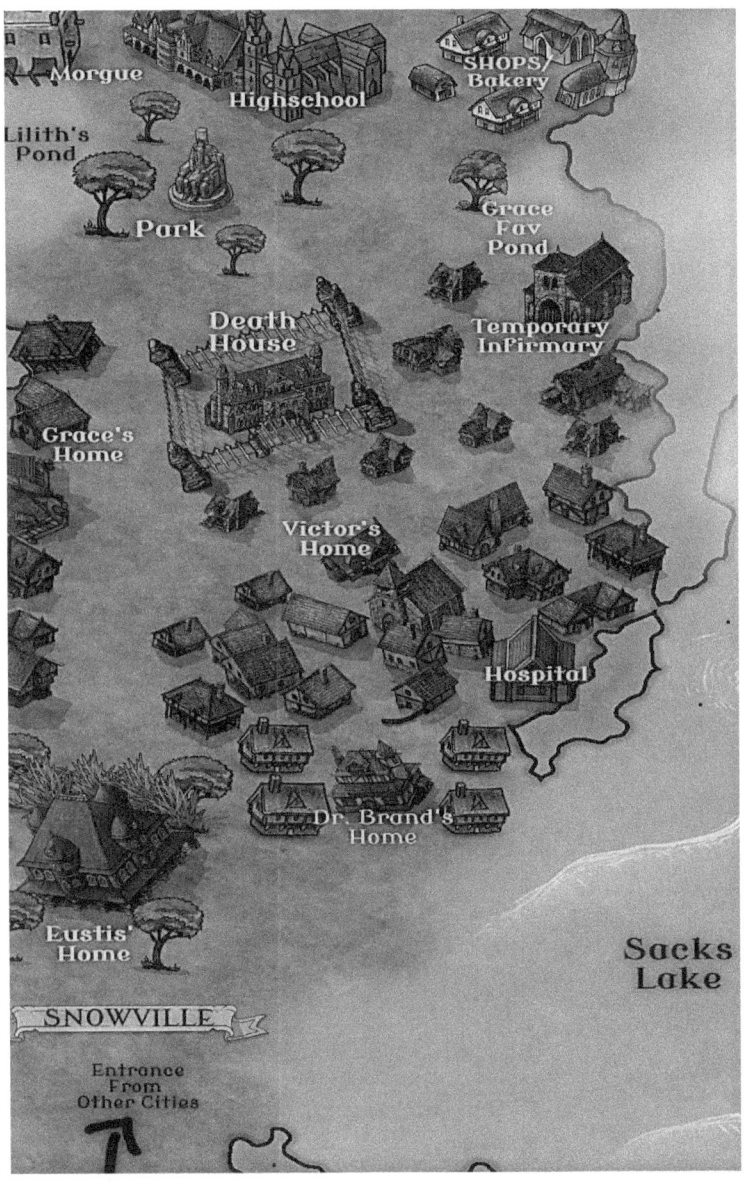

Alexia D. Miller

Grace...

Chapter One: Snowville and the Liars.

Grace *hated* Snowville. She recalled when she'd first moved there two years ago. "Snowville was named after Sir Vildor Sacks. His family built the first homes on the land and organized the people." Her foster mother had boasted. "The winters are sometimes long, but there will be plenty of snow for you to play in. It's small and homely, Grace. Snowville is the kind of place where everyone *practically* knows everyone."

Snowville? What kind of name was Snowville? Grace had thought, though she didn't dare say it. "We have little inside jokes about the town seasons," her foster mother had continued, chuckling to herself. "Because Snowville is a bit strange. One season we call *Sunfall* because of the comfortable weather. Another is called *Midfall* which is pretty much your standard fall days. Then there's *Snowflake*. Oh! I almost forgot! We only have about 5 days of rain a year. Isn't that strange?"

Grace had offered a smile and nodded since her foster mother seemed to be in such a good mood, but if

Alexia D. Miller

she'd been honest, she'd have told her she hadn't wanted to move to a place like Snowville. Long winters were one thing, but small towns were worse. If Grace never lived in another small town to be ridiculed and have her every move announced to the world, it would have been all too soon.

Grace was sure that if there was such a thing as fate, she was horrendously doomed to repeat the same one until the end of time. It was in that moment, as her foster mom continued to ramble on, that she knew she wouldn't like the small town. Thinking back on it now, however, Grace couldn't have known back then just how much she would hate it now. She couldn't have known what she'd suffer.

Grace skipped a rock across the pond ahead of her. She watched as the rock forced ripples into the water with every skid and eventually splashed softly down, swallowed by the water. Her foster parents would tell her, as they always had, that if she tried harder, she would have an easier time. That if she would just give in, she would love living in Snowville.

Grace had been living in Snowville for all of two years and she didn't think her problems had anything to do with how hard she tried. She didn't think it had to do with "giving in" either, because she *gave in* every day. Wasn't it possible that someone else just wanted to make things

Alexia D. Miller

{ 10 }

difficult for her? Wasn't it possible that things were just terrible from the start?

Grace tried to fit in at first, with her new family and all their rules, with the neighbors, the teachers, and the kids at school. Her foster parents just seemed to have the *dumbest* rules for everything in the world and when she didn't understand or didn't like them, she was punished. The neighbors her foster mother labeled "homely" were no better.

She could always hear their whispers. They never failed to mention that she was "wild" as if she was something from a jungle. Grace knew out of every place she could possibly be from, it wasn't from the jungle. She just didn't think it was a crime to run around in a skirt. And her hair? Well, her hair wasn't her fault. Not the color or how difficult it was. It hardly ever stayed neat and in place. At least not without hours of work. Why didn't they understand that she wasn't wild? She was just a kid. But Grace also knew that kids weren't any better.

In fact, kids were the **worst**. At school, the other children didn't seem to have a problem showing her she didn't belong. It didn't matter what Grace said or did, and none of the teachers ever seemed to care how they treated her. She was picked on every day. When she stood up for herself, she was labeled "disruptive" or "bad."

Alexia D. Miller

Crystal Key: Door to a New World

Every day in Snowville was the same as the last. Her days melted together like hot cheese and she was the soggy piece of meat stuck in the middle. Only, it wasn't a very good sandwich. In fact, if Grace were to tell it, it was the worst kind of sandwich; the ones with the brown and green mold hiding away to surprise you until you took a bite.

While her days continued to stretch on for what seemed like forever, today at least, her sandwich seemed edible. She had a new dress and shoes, and even her wild hair had been tamed. Her foster mom battled the thick mess and neatly tied her curls behind her head with decorative brown and white ribbons. Out of all her outfits, Grace thought that she liked this one the best.

She liked that the brown was so close to her eye color and that it stopped right above her knees. Grace liked the small white diamonds that danced along the bottom. She liked how it flowed around her but was still short enough to run in without toppling over. Aside from the dress, she even managed to keep out of trouble in school today.

Grace looked at her skin, a brown itself, as she picked up another stone. As she inspected the rock, needing to see if it was fit for a long fling along the pond, she felt a speck of liquid against her forehead. Another, and then another. She squealed, caught off-guard. Was it really raining? *Snowville's five rainy days already passed this year,*

Alexia D. Miller

she thought in disbelief. It had been 60 years since the last double rain, and before that, even longer.

Grace hadn't experienced that herself, of course. One of the older women on her street always brought it up when it rained. The woman repeated the story so much that Grace could have almost mistaken it for her own memory. As the rain fell harder, Grace took shelter under a nearby tree. It was better to wait it out than dodge the dirt, which was quickly becoming mud, all the way home. *Maybe I'll always carry an umbrella*, she told herself, *and if I don't need it, well...that'd be okay too.*

. . .

When the rain finally seemed to let up, Grace looked at her watch. An entire hour had passed. Grace skipped over the mud puddles as she made her way away from the pond and the last one almost sent her tumbling to the ground. She'd overestimated the length of own her legs and had to quickly jump to the side to avoid the fall. Having recovered from her small scare, Grace chided herself and decided to move much more carefully the rest of the way.

Almost to her house, Grace felt a sharp pain on her right shoulder. Another, harder this time, followed in the middle of her back. She cried out in pain as she turned

Alexia D. Miller

around and a stone smacked hard into her nose. Instinctively, Grace reached up to check it as her eyes teared. When Grace looked up from her palm, relieved not to see any blood, it took a moment for her watery-eyed vision to focus.

To Grace's dismay, standing in front of her were two of the boys from her school; friends of her biggest bully Eustis Schmidt—although Grace always called him Elephant Spit. Eustis was one of the richest kids at school, perhaps the richest even, who got good grades and praise from everyone anywhere. The teachers thought him "nice" and "smart," but his presence for Grace signified impending "mean," and "stupid." Eustis, as far as Grace was concerned, was a monster. So, those boys were monsters too. Even if she didn't know their names.

The boy on the left wearing large aviator glasses threw another stone. This one hit her in the eye, so hard that it sent her right into the mud. Grace tried to hold it in as the two monsters laughed. She tried so hard that she was shaking with effort as they shouted. Through their amused smiles they called her ugly and a freak. If they'd called her anything else besides "a darkie," Grace didn't know.

Their voices were quickly buried by the high-pitched ringing in her ears, the burning in her eyes as she looked down at her dirty, mud-stained dress, and the heat of rage burning in her chest. Unable to hold it in any longer, she screamed.

In a matter of seconds, Grace was on her feet and charging at the boys. Before the other—a boy with his hair pressed to the back of his head by what was likely gel, wearing a blue jacket—could pick up another stone to throw. Soon she wasn't the only one screaming. Grace pounced onto them, shoving them into the dirt. She couldn't stop crying even as her vision was cut in half. Her right eye started to swell, and it hurt, but Grace didn't care.

Grace didn't know how many times she punched them. She didn't count the number of times she bit them. She grabbed hair and yanked it. Who cared whose hair it was? It wasn't hers and that's all that mattered.

In her heat of rage, Grace knew by now her clothes couldn't be the only ones ruined. It felt good to ruin their stupidly over-expensive clothes and that boy's stinky gelled hair. She felt them struggle beneath her. She felt their attempts to overpower her and kept them there as long as she could. Eventually the boys gained enough leverage that they fought their way to their feet, so Grace kicked them where it <u>hurt</u>.

By the time the adults ran outside to the boys' rescue, she'd used a rock to smash the first boy's glasses. He snatched off her watch and even punched her for it,

Alexia D. Miller

unfortunately in the same swollen eye, but Grace thought it was worth it. From behind, a couple grabbed her by the arms and dragged her away from her tormentors. Grace fought to get free. The more she did, however, the tighter their grips became. So tight that ultimately Grace gave up for fear that even her arms would be bruised like the rest of her.

Two other women came along and scooped up the boys. Both pulled them protectively to their chests almost as if they were their mothers. Grace recognized the look behind their eyes, as if they were screaming through the silence to remind her that she was a savage. As if to say that *she* was the dangerous one and the boys were unfortunate souls—two helpless victims to a wild animal's fangs.

It wasn't long before Grace spotted the neighbors watching silently, judgingly, from their windows. She knew none of those people saw her any differently. Even though Grace was the victim, and the boys were manipulative, fight-starting demons. As always, no one would come to her rescue. As impossible as it seemed, no one ever saw how the fights started, and Grace knew that would be no different today. She also knew that it didn't matter.

Already her foster parents were being phoned. Already, the boys were spewing lies and Grace lost her voice somewhere in the back of her throat. It wouldn't matter what she said or didn't. Her words wouldn't do any good. Grace

Alexia D. Miller

looked at the clouds through her good eye. The sky darkened and thunder sounded in the air as the rain began to pour again. *At least the sky cries for me,* Grace thought, *almost as if it were my friend.*

True...

Chapter Two: Girl and The Death House.

*T*rue frowned on the fifth floor as she watched a spectacle down below. Towards the rear of her new house, two boys bullied a girl. She knew how cruel children could be. It didn't look much different than the situations she'd escaped. Would True like living here? If she had any doubts before, she was even less sure now.

Seeing the adults come to break up the fight, True breathed a sigh of relief. At least the grownups could handle things now. Her heart ached for the red-headed girl with the dark wheat complexion. It was as much as she could distinguish about her from where she stood. Not that True could forget such unique features. *Perhaps for that girl too, True thought, it isn't a very good thing.*

Clothes, hair, and skin. They were such small components of a person and yet, in True's experience, not much mattered more to most of the people she met. Being young or old didn't save you from judgement. The red-headed girl stuck out, a rose in a field of white lilies. True

Alexia D. Miller

could understand how it felt, although some days she wished she could forget.

Attempting to keep herself from her more negative thoughts, True distracted herself by looking outside from the other angles of the house. Two-thirds of her view around was filled with dilapidated homes and buildings. Some, she'd seen on her way in, were boarded up or had broken windows with glass still in the yard no one bothered to pick up. To one side of the house, similar to some space a few blocks away from the front door, people bustled cheerfully through their small-town lives.

True studied the abandoned streets from another window on the side of the house. Furthest off from the rest of the buildings, a flickering caught her eye. It almost looked like glass shimmering in sunlight, but True knew that it must have been her imagination. From the looks of dust and grime cacking the buildings, she was sure none of those buildings could be shining. They were unloved buildings after all and when True tried to focus on the building again, she saw nothing.

Still, True thought, *that building looks different than the others do. It may be the only stone building there. That at least deserves extra interest.* Smiling to herself, True turned on her heels and rounded the corner. Her pale feet

Alexia D. Miller

tapped lightly against the dusty stairs. As she went, she could hear her aunts' voices calling out to her.

True watched her dress fall slowly against her legs as she jumped down the final few steps, keeping a hand against the top of the railing to steady herself. She watched silently as her aunts carried boxes inside the doorway and back again. Her Aunt Rose frowned as the rain tapped harder against the van, echoing the quick *Pep! Pep! Pep!* sounds against the metallic roof.

Figuring that perhaps for once her aunts wanted her help because of the rain, True held out her arms ahead of her, ready to accept a box. Her Aunt Rose's gray eyes squinted at her as she stepped back into the doorway, almost as if to figure out just what True was attempting to do. True tilted her head as she looked at her, still waiting patiently. As the two of them stared into each other's faces, True took time to admire her Aunt Rose.

It was unusual to see her aunt's blonde hair. As she often claimed to dye her hair because of her job. She'd said it was to "liven up the place," which always seemed so bleak, black, and white. Normally True's Aunt Rose dyed it a shade of blue, ironic given her name. Today, she was wearing a poncho without a hood, which True thought defeated its purpose. Her long blonde strands were already drenched as

Alexia D. Miller

she cast a disapproving glance towards the water sinking to the floor.

"Ugh. All this water!" She said, sticking out her tongue as she spoke. Coming along beside her, her Aunt Trina shook her head. "As if all of this *dust* wasn't enough." She glanced at True who was still holding out her arms to help before her Aunt Trina squinted her deep brown eyes at her, her brows creased. True, understanding the look, let her arms fall gently to her sides.

Her Aunt Trina, with her long, thick brown waves and large brown eyes, looked nothing like True though she was named after her. In fact, her Aunt Trina had been a close family friend until she married her Aunt Rose—her mother's twin sister. Not that True ever minded it. In fact, she often felt honored to be named after someone so smart and beautiful, though she didn't feel she did her Aunt Trina's name any justice.

"What are you staring at little one?" Her Aunt Trina said, putting down the box in her hands and ruffling her hair. "You didn't *actually* think you were going to be *helping*, did you?" She laughed.

True sighed, lightly pushing her hair back into place. "Oh. I *never* help." True groaned, watching her Aunt Rose place another box in a far corner. "Really. *Never*, you know."

Alexia D. Miller

"Oh yeah? Well get used to it already, kid. You're absolutely *not* helping. The men with the van are here for that," her Aunt Trina spoke over her shoulder as she walked out of the door again. "Go on, shoo." True tilted her head again. She was shooing her, but they'd called her. Had she forgotten?

"Oh. That's right," Trina said suddenly, turning back around. "We were going to see if you were ready to pick a room, but maybe we should save that until after we have everything inside." She sighed as she looked outside, "Before this rain gets any worse."

"I like the fifth floor." True said quickly. "I've picked a room."

"Hmm? The fifth floor? Are you sure you want to be all the way up there alone? Should we move our room to the fourth?" Trina asked, her brows furrowed in thought. True shook her head. "Then I suppose I'll move my equipment to the third floor, and we will room on the second. Luckily for me we have a handy-dandy elevator."

True listened quietly to her aunt's ramblings. She tried to imagine a blueprint of all her aunt's scientific equipment and furniture, tubes, screens, and the like being organized according to some unknown category True couldn't begin to understand. Practically half of all the things being moved into their new house had something to do with

Alexia D. Miller

her work. Even though, as True understood it, her Aunt Trina would be working in a lab close to town.

True often wondered how her aunts' relationship blossomed considering the opposing sides of their jobs in the first place. Her Aunt Rose was a coroner, and literally had death on her table every day. Meanwhile, her Aunt Trina was a biologist with degrees crossing multiple subfields. In True's mind, her aunts were perfect for each other; one serious, with a soft side and the other playful and giddy. It was as if they were a balancing act for the other, in perfect harmony.

Of course, True knew that no one and nothing was perfect but it pleased her, nonetheless. She could only hope that one day, somehow, she would have a relationship with someone that made her a better person. A relationship, though it was perhaps asking too much, that reflected all the best qualities that she witnessed being around her aunts. That was, if such a relationship could exist and not expunge the other.

Suddenly out of her thoughts, True recalled the stone building that had caught her interest. Even if she couldn't help with the moving, she could venture, and first on that list was that stone building. Sure, it was raining but she never exactly disliked the rain. Surely no one despised Rain as much as her Aunt Rose. True was sure it was one of

Alexia D. Miller

the reasons that they'd agreed to move to the small town. Rumor has it that Snowville almost *never* had rain. Perhaps the exact opposite of their last home. Which, True figured would have been a win in her Aunt Rose's book.

. . .

True listened to her aunts' usual chiding about her not wearing shoes outside and of course, she agreed to wear them. At least until she found a safe enough path to use without them. She didn't say so, but True knew just from the looks on their faces that her aunts knew her plan all too well already. It wasn't that she loathed shoes, she simply didn't like feeling the disconnect between her and the earth. That, and shoes weren't particularly comfortable in the first place.

True waited patiently in a dark corner of the room as the men from the moving service fetched her beloved chest. It was an old, thick, wooden thing that she'd had almost all her life. When they gently placed the trunk down in a corner of the room, she wasted no time to rush over. She listened to the familiar light creak of the heavy latch as she opened it and ran her fingers lovingly over the painted wood. She kept her most important possessions inside.

On the top were a pair of blue sandals that matched the dress she wore today. By habit, she normally put her

Alexia D. Miller

shoes inside with her next day's outfit. Underneath this, she found her black water-resistant jacket with the oversized hood. Below that, her new black mask. This mask was a new treasure she'd gotten from a store they passed on the way to Snowville and was already one of her favorites. True loved its oval shape which was slightly pointed at the chin, the moggy ears, and the cat-like triangle painted nose. The eyes were oblong with a most important feature: breathable dark mesh that hid her eyes from onlookers.

Perhaps her personal favorite feature of this mask was the beautiful painted design. Light flower petals rained down both sides from the eyes, almost as if they were a stream of bittersweet tears. Deciding not to rummage through the rest of the chest and her little gems, there would be time enough for that later, True slid on her shoes, jacket, and mask. Slowly, she walked out of the front door and to the side of her house.

Meticulously, True watched the ground as she walked towards the mass of deteriorating homes. She followed the cracked street until it ran out. Soon making her way through the wet grass until she could see the stone structure.

Upon closer inspection of the building, True stood in awe of the golden brown and gray specked stone. Some were chipped, others cracked. As she followed a few of the

Alexia D. Miller

broken patterns in the stone, she made out weeds, thin vines, and flower buds peeking from beneath the stone. Those too, were little gems. True walked the length of the building, circling it to find the front.

In the end, True made her way to the stone steps that led to a slither of a porch and two large wooden doors. Walking up the steps and turning her back to the door, she could just make out modern buildings and tacky colored houses. Disinterested in anything else for the moment, True turned her attention back to the building.

Looking up to the upper left of the door, True could make out an old, rusted metal sign that read *Snowville Temporary Infirmary*. She wondered when the building had last been used as she looked at the dust along the doorway. She wondered why the small town ever needed a temporary hospital in the first place. Perhaps this building was as old as their new gothic styled home.

True didn't know this buildings history, but she could feel it. It was an unmistakable feeling of overwhelming death and faded spots of happiness. It was, to a degree, also what she'd felt entering their new home. She wondered if anyone had ever gone to the infirmary and left happier than they'd come. What kind of joy used to be beyond its double doors? What sort of death? Did any of the people from her home ever make it to the infirmary?

Alexia D. Miller

Their new home, her aunts had told her, belonged to a famous aristocrat family a long time ago. "They threw the most **extravagant** parties! Everyone who was anyone had been to one at least once. Just think about it, True. All that music and dancing!" she exclaimed with excitement. True watched her Aunt Rose put her hands out in front of her as she spoke, imitating dancing around a ballroom floor and took note of her Aunt Trina's playful sigh. Her Aunt Rose pretended not to notice and continued chatting about the décor the house must have had all those years before. Her blonde hair swung towards her face as she moved, talking with her hands again.

True's Aunt Trina butted in mid-sentence, rolling her eyes. "Enough of that already. Let's skip to the good part!" She'd said, throwing her hands in the air impatiently. Her brown eyes seemed to spark with intensity. "The family consisted of the husband, the wife and their young son. They were the Ein-something or other. I can't remember. Apparently, the father was some elite. His father had been a landowner in England and his mother a popularly known woman from Germany. The boy, whatever his name was, was around eight when he disappeared. When he was seen next, he was dead and lifeless! Creepy, right?"

Her Aunt Rose immediately cut-in, lightly shoving Trina out of the way. "Hey. *Dead* is kind of *my* category."

Alexia D. Miller

She smiled, nudging Trina's arm. "You're a scientist who uses the words dead and lifeless as if they aren't the same thing." She laughed, shaking her head. "I think I can take it from here, Trina."

Her Aunt Trina mockingly shook her head, "Oh? Yeah, *no.* I *totally* forgot you were *Queen* of the dead."

"Why yes. Yes, I am—and don't you forget it." Rose laughed, before clearing her throat and getting back on topic. True watched the two of them amusingly. "Ahem. Well, it wasn't a recent occurrence that children died at increased rates. Adults too, had been falling sick and dying. After all, it wasn't as if they had today's modern medicine. However, this was different."

"The boy hadn't been sick, and half of the town had been looking for him. Mainly for the reward the family promised to pay for his return. One day, as Trina so kindly mentioned, the boy turned up at home, completely lifeless. The family called in private investigators and a number of doctors, looking for an answer to the boy's death. While they found evidence that the boy had been murdered— poisoned in fact—they were unable to connect the death to anyone. So, the boy's parents supposedly took to investigating themselves."

True felt bad for the boy and even worse for his parents. Assumedly the boy had been all alone with his

Alexia D. Miller

killer, perhaps even trying to escape. She knew she would have if she were in his position. True couldn't imagine the grief of the boy's parents when his body was returned, lifeless and rigid.

"They invited their own suspects to a party." Her aunt said, completely invested in the tale. "You see, the mother and father had different ideas about who was involved in their son's death. So, they ended up inviting them all. One last party, they'd said, to celebrate the fact that their son had ever lived.

"Every guest, save for a few children who'd accompanied their parents, were poisoned and died. Since they couldn't decide on the killer, they took them all to ensure they'd gotten their murderer. As far as the married couple goes...well, no one ever saw them again.

"It was said that Snowville had their worst Winter, or rather what they call *Snowfall*, in record history that year. Well over half of the year was cold and bitter. People said it was because of the restless souls that became ghosts that night. That the souls of all the men and women became cold-hearted given their untimely demise.

"Years later, the house was sold and one of our ancestors bought it. It's been passed down in the family ever since. Only one person in the family ever lived in it. Years upon years ago now though." Her Aunt Rose said dismissively.

"Does that mean our house will be haunted when we move in?" True had asked. Her Aunt Rose shrugged. "No one's ever said. We have no idea."

Her Aunt Trina smiled, "It'd be pretty interesting if it were, huh? A bunch of dead souls somehow theoretically alive? There's always so much speculation around ghosts and life after death. It would be nice to experience something on our own to make deductions." True wasn't sure in that moment if that was the scientist in her making an appearance or not.

She wondered then if she would like a haunted house or if she'd only feel worse for the dead souls than she felt already. If the story was real, then that meant there would be a lot of sadness and death surrounding their house. She wasn't sure if it was something she could overlook every single day after they moved. It was hard enough to ignore what she already felt anywhere else.

That conversation had taken place a little over a month ago. After her Aunt Trina suggested relocation for her job. She needed to use a facility that was mostly unoccupied, if True recalled correctly. Whatever "mostly" meant. Before True knew it, Snowville was decided on for an old lab in its immediate facility. Of course, her Aunt Rose

Alexia D. Miller

had to verify that she could pick up work in the area first, which turned out to be easier than they'd thought it would be at the time.

When it came to where they would live, her Aunt Trina already had an answer. They wouldn't have to look for a place, her Aunt Trina argued, because *logically* it made sense to utilize the home they already owned. True didn't have any arguments against it. It was a valid point and meant no extra accommodations would be necessary. Besides, True was used to moving around and all it entailed. She was used to being the new girl at school, keeping up with her grades, and transfer documentation.

. . .

After trying to open the large doors, True wasn't surprised to find them locked. She walked back down the stairs and turned around to further examine the building. True was sure she'd seen something on her first trip around. Looking further to the left, True noticed a large square window close to the ground. At some point, the window had been broken. It seemed as if the glass had been picked up or even pushed off into the grass but was never covered or repaired. It made little sense to True why anyone would do

Alexia D. Miller

{ 31 }

either if they weren't going to fix it, but she wouldn't complain. It was her way in, after all.

Without much difficulty, True bent forward toward her knees and made her way inside. Almost immediately, True felt a difference. The air was brisker inside than out, there was a damp, grimy scent hanging above her head, and clouds of dust circled around her as she moved her feet across the floor. Light from the broken window casted uneven light across the room ahead of her.

Looking about, True could see rows of old bed frames along the walls, stained pillows, and tattered sheets scattered on the other side. There were a few old bed frames pushed against a back wall, broken looking machines she couldn't place, and empty I. V's. Closer to her was a long, dark oak table with mostly broken chairs on either side, an intact fireplace with a small pile of old ash around it, and a few documents stacked in another corner of the room.

After realizing that she couldn't make out any of the words on the papers because of some unknowable type of damage, True took notice of a staircase on the far left. She just knew more would await her if she followed the stairs. Something, though she couldn't guess what, was summoning her there. Unable to deny her instincts, True wasted no time to head up the steps.

Alexia D. Miller

Victor...

Chapter Three: Stand and Watch.

*I*t was the second day that it rained. Or rather, the seventh day this year. A second rain in Snowville was so uncommon that people had been coming up with the most outlandish reasons for it. Some were so shaken by it, so sure that it was a bad omen, that they debated even leaving their homes until it was over. Or so he'd heard. As far as Victor was concerned, they were all being overly dramatic for nothing at all. *So, it rained again,* Victor thought, *big whoop. Doesn't anyone in this town have better things to discuss?*

As if the rain hadn't been enough to chat about, there was plenty of other talk flooding the town. Yesterday, a new family moved into **The Death House**; the very gothic mansion on the infamous abandoned street the largest massacre occurred in Snowville history. Victor knew the stories, but the talk of the town never interested him in the slightest. "A small family at that! Three or four people, I heard!" One girl exclaimed loudly in the distance. Three or four?

Alexia D. Miller

Victor had known someone was new, even before the rumors began. He'd caught a glimpse of someone making their way inside while walking to school the day before. Much like now, he'd looked up at the house as he walked past, just as he did every day. Today, however, there were lights shining through a few windows on the first floor.

Students and adults alike avoided this street and those closest to it like it was the plague. Even Victor's mother didn't quite like it given the rumors, but she knew that he would continue to walk his normal path to school no matter what the others said. Victor didn't see any reason to take the absolute longest route around just to avoid a house, unlike the entire school body.

Upon entering the school lot, Victor noticed a noisy scene unfolding. There was an unnecessarily large crowd gathered to watch some sort of drama unfold. Victor slowly made his way through the wave of students, trying to get inside for his early nap, until he caught a glimpse of three teachers surrounding someone. Victor stopped, focusing on the student in the middle of the chaos. Black sandals with pale blue nail polish, an oversized black jacket, and exceedingly pale, slender fingers. A girl?

Two male teachers—Victor recognized both his gym teacher and Zane's old math teacher—and a new female substitute. The woman appeared to be trying to deescalate

Alexia D. Miller

the situation as the girl struggled between the men's grips on her arms. The gym teacher reached out towards the dark mask on the girl's face. "You're making this hard on yourself, kid!" He yelled, "We told you. Masks aren't allowed on school grounds!"

From the moment his hand touched the mask, the girl screamed. Her voice echoed in a loud, broken, emotional shriek. Almost as if every second she spent screaming stole all the air from her lungs. Victor could almost feel her anguish—her fear. It only took a moment to see the crowd taking pictures on their cellphones, whispering, and laughing or shooting judgmental looks her way. It only took a moment to realize that no one was willing to help.

In what felt like a breath, Victor unconsciously closed the distance between them. By the time he realized, he'd pulled the gym teacher's sweaty fingers off the girl's mask—he could be disgusted by it later. He felt the man's index finger crack as he yelled out in pain. Without giving himself the time to think, Victor swiftly kicked behind his knee and watched him fall to the ground.

He took the opportunity to shove the other teacher the moment he was distracted, sidestepping behind him, and kicked him in the crotch. In a matter of seconds, he was on all fours, groaning through clinched teeth. Normally, Victor

Alexia D. Miller

would feel bad for any man in their predicament, but today was an exception. The substitute locked worried eyes with Victor before she stumbled towards the building. He knew the woman was going to alert the principal, but Victor made no moves to intercept her.

By now the girl in the oversized jacket was on her knees, completely silent, with her hands spread over her mask as if to protect it. It was in this moment, when Victor saw the girl knees deep in rainwater, that Victor suddenly felt the heaviness of his clothes and the chill against his face, drenched by the rain. Victor didn't recall the moment he'd dropped his umbrella. He couldn't recall the exact moment he'd rushed to her aid either, but he had.

The crowd was full of shocked exclaims and whispers. A few students, upset that he'd gotten in the way of their twisted entertainment, shouted their complaints his way. Victor burst with anger. "So, what?" He shouted. "All of you were going to just stand there while two grown men roughed up a girl?"

. . .

It wasn't long before Victor's mother was called and he sat in the principle's dreadfully tacky office, next to the girl. "True," Principle Mann said gruffly, as he pulled out his

Alexia D. Miller

office chair, "your aunts will be here shortly. *Your mother* as well, Victor." He said pointedly, almost as if to remind him that he was in trouble. Victor didn't need a reminder but leave it to the principle to emphasize the needless—like he did with his office and his wardrobe.

Principle Mann was a large, overweight male whose tie never matched his outfits. Today he wore a pale-yellow vest and black dress pants. Not too unlike the day Victor caught him checking himself out in inside the boys' bathroom on the second floor. His button-up shirt matched his dark suit pants, but his tie was a dark blue, purple and neon orange splattered monstrosity. Victor couldn't comprehend the reason he decided to accent colors he wasn't wearing as if the rest of him wasn't enough.

Like any other day, Principle Mann's round face was oily. Almost as if he'd rolled it in melted butter before they walked into his office. His nose was plump and red, a steamed tomato without the skin, completely in contrast to his otherwise pale skin. His silver hair was pressed backwards to cover his slowly growing bald spot, though Victor didn't think it was doing a very good job at it, and his sideburns were laid down against his face with a lubricant that left a sizable blue streak near his ears.

Victor could hardly look at the man without getting dizzy. When the two teachers, the girl's—Victor recalled

Alexia D. Miller

Principle Mann calling her True—aunts, and his mother walked inside the doors of the office, Victor was glad for the distraction. After the teachers gave some version of today's story Victor could hardly pay any attention to, emphasizing their "attempt to follow protocol," and how True had been exceedingly difficult after multiple warnings, Principal Mann wasted no time telling them how much trouble he was in. "Victor isn't a *model student*, Principle Mann, but we *never* expected him to assault us." The math teacher whined.

"Just look at what he did to my finger!" The gym teacher cried, holding out his hand to reveal his angled index finger.

"Assaulting teachers is a **very** *serious* offense, Victor," Principle Mann scolded. "**Very** serious." He repeated, as if he hadn't heard.

"Yeah. Well, so is assaulting a woman." Victor countered quickly. "Lying should be too." He said, shifting in chair, crossing his arms over his chest defensively. "They said they were trying to remove her mask but conveniently left out the part about grabbing her. What was I supposed to do? Stand and watch?"

Principle Mann's head quickly shot over to the two teachers as True's aunts rushed to pull up her jacket sleeves. "They did *What?!*" The brunette woman exclaimed loudly. True sat silently gripping the towel Principle Mann offered her, unused. In the space between them, Victor could make out the girl's small, pallid arms. Around her wrists and mid-arms were thick, red pressure marks. So red against her pale skin, that Victor could almost make out the men's entire handprints wrapped around her.

The other aunt—a blonde-haired woman wearing a light pink sweater—wrapped her arms defensively around True, pulling her close. "How *dare* you!" She shouted as Principle Mann's face flooded with embarrassment. His slippery face seemed to almost suit the situation, Victor noted, almost amused.

The brunette took off her glasses, wiping them with a light blue cloth from her breast pocket as she locked eyes with the principle. Victor's own mother looked at the teachers and Principle Mann as if she wished she could leap across the desk. She sat alarmingly still, her hands clenching the arms of her seat, with eyes of fire. Victor could almost see the steam shooting out of her ears.

His mother's face reddened, and her eyebrows creased. Her straight black hair was pulled up above her head as it often was when she had gotten buried in her work and didn't want it in the way, but to Victor it only made her anger more visible. Her blue-jeaned legs were wrapped around the legs of her seat, an extra precaution to keep her from ripping out the men's throats. Just seeing his mother's reaction alone, Victor couldn't comprehend the aunt's calm demeanor.

The air in the room seemed to shift the moment the woman placed her glasses back onto her face, threatening to sue. "Adults abusing children is a much greater offense than a lie or a boy defending a girl via a kick in the nut-sack, Principle Mann." She spoke lowly. Victor could almost feel the room drop below freezing. Already, Victor could see the color dropping from the principle's face, so much so that Victor was sure even the man's nose lost a shade or two.

"In our school, Mrs. Vox, it is still punishable by expulsion." He retorted nervously. Before Victor's mother could say a word, the woman continued, her hand smacking firmly against the desk. Victor thought that maybe the woman hadn't been so calm after all.

"You'll do no such thing!" She snapped. "I suggest, Principle Mann, that you find another form of punishment. If we find that you have not let him continue his education, that our niece has a single issue regarding today's incident, or someone decides to bother her about her attire—let alone suffers another case of abuse at the hands of another of your faculty—we *will* sue! I will bury you in such a difficult legal matrix that the school will be under investigation, you lose your job, and you'll be paying us out of pocket until your

Alexia D. Miller

retirement dries up." Without missing a beat, she turned to Victor's mother. "Do you think that sounds fair?"

His mother did not hesitate to answer. "Absolutely." She agreed with a stern nod. "I couldn't have said it better."

In the end, the teachers were immediately fired. Upon leaving, True's blonde-haired aunt, who Victor learned was named Rose, turned to Principle Mann. "And another thing," she frowned, pointing at him and motioning in a circle at his face, "I don't have a freaking *clue* what's going on with you but I'm thinking you might have a *hyperhidrosis* issue? You know with all that sweating? You might want to get that checked out."

It took all Victor had to keep from laughing as they walked out of the office. When the door shut behind them Victor could make out Principle Mann's sulky voice calling at their backs. "IT'S NOT SWEAT, IT'S OIL! IT'S GOOD FOR YOUR SKIN!!"

. . .

"So, you're suspended for two weeks for misconduct." Victor's mom said as they walked off the school lot. "The Vox's are going to push their niece's start date back to give her a little break."

Alexia D. Miller

Victor nodded, "Yeah but that means--" Victor started. Before he could say more, his mother's arms wrapped around him.

"I am *SO* proud of you, Victor! *Very* proud." She beamed.

Victor knew not to take her statement lightly, but he managed to get suspended from school for the last couple weeks of 8th grade and, somehow, his mother managed to smile about it. The next time he went to school he'd be entering his freshman year of high school. No matter how things happened, Victor didn't exactly feel proud about it. It wouldn't make things easier. If he could have gotten away with it, Victor would have stopped going to school a long time ago. Maybe that would have been better than what the neighbors could say to her now, considering he was suspended.

If he could, Victor would have given up a few years ago when his own mother was suffering at the hands of a man—when his father pushed them to make the ultimate decision. They'd come a long way since those days, but some days Victor felt like they were still stuck in the past. Whatever progress they made hadn't made it any less difficult to look himself in the mirror.

Victor watched True and her aunts walk through the iron gate and up the stairs of The Death House. His mother looked over in awe. "Oh. So, *they* are the ones who moved

Alexia D. Miller

into that house. I wonder why they decided to move to Snowville. Why they decided on that house. It's all anyone has been going on about at work lately. I didn't recognize them. I guess I should have known." His mother said quietly. Victor wondered how True was fairing. She hadn't said a single word in the principal's office.

Victor shrugged. There was nothing he could do about it now. He closed his umbrella as the rain stopped and his mom paused to get another look at the large gothic house. "You know Victor," she said with a smile, "walking past this house probably isn't so bad after all."

"Yeah. It's shorter." Victor said, candidly.

His mother looked at him with a raised brow, chuckling to herself. "Silly boy." She laughed.

"What?" Victor asked, not sure what had his mother so amused.

"Nothing." She grinned as she stepped ahead of him and guided him down the street.

"Tell me." Victor yawned.

"No." His mother said with another laugh.

"Tell me, mom. What did I miss?" Victor asked, puzzled.

"If you try to tell your *mother* what to do again, I'm removing your mattress. The pillows too." She warned.

"No. Okay. I'm sorry mom. Please don't take my mattress." Victor said quickly, worried that she might have meant it.

Alexia D. Miller

{ 43 }

Would she really take the pillows too? He didn't want to find out.

Phelia...

Chapter Four: Sandwiches.

*I*t was the day after Zane's graduation ceremony.

Her brother had gone to Victor's house and their father was working a double shift at the hospital, so Phelia was home alone. She sat quietly in the kitchen, frustratedly glaring at the refrigerator. She was hungry and she was more than tired of waiting.

Both Zane and her father preferred she didn't attempt to make her own meals, but in the moment Phelia figured it couldn't be helped. Zane *was gone* after all. Couldn't exceptions be made? She'd decided not to waste any more hours waiting for his return. Not if it meant starving to death in his absence. Of course, Phelia knew it was an exaggeration, but it is the way she felt anyhow. Zane of all people knew how she despised the growling in her belly.

Phelia attempted to talk herself out of it, imagining that her book sitting alone on the living room table was calling for her. Or, at the very least, warning her that there would be consequences to her actions. This was all jumbled

Alexia D. Miller

nonsense which she knew would mean nothing the end, but Phelia didn't want to say she never tried to deter herself.

Without wasting any more time, Phelia grabbed the stool from the corner, dragged it to the cabinet, and climbed up. She scanned the contents slowly, this one mostly filled with canned goods she had no patience to sift through. She closed the cabinet with a sigh, not bothering with the others, and descended the steps of the stool. Looking back on it, Phelia felt that today didn't feel much different than that day roughly three years ago.

Up until then she'd let her family do just about everything for her. *Not long*, Phelia thought as she opened the refrigerator, *before mother died.* Phelia recalled noticing that other children her age weren't very articulate and not understanding why. Eventually, the answer didn't matter as much as the amount of effort she had to use pretending. Before long, Phelia simply no longer had the energy to mimic them. She had no use for their awkward, childish babble. Of course, she'd stunned her parents. Still, perhaps, not as much as the day she made breakfast. At the time, Phelia remembered thinking she had time to clean up her mess before anyone ever knew she'd done anything at all.

If Phelia did say so herself, she was quite awful at making food. She could hardly reach the low section of the refrigerator back then, though Phelia did not think she'd grown much since then. At the time, she did her best to reach what was in arms-length; there was the spoon and fork on the table, the bottles of jam and peanut butter always in the corner on the floor, bread on the counter, her cup in the living room from the night before, and the terribly heavy jug of milk on the bottom of the fridge.

By the time her parents and Zane made their way to the kitchen, they'd caught her red-handed in the mess on the floor. Milk spilled in puddles around her, she'd managed to fling jam against the cabinets, and a slop of peanut butter was on the floor.

Contrary to her parents' calculated movements and stunned silence, Zane hadn't seemed the least bit surprised. Not staring at her sitting in the center of clutter, taking a bite out of a very messy sandwich or when she'd started speaking sentences on par with someone years her senior. While Phelia was busy mentally chiding herself for getting caught in-between sloppy bites of peanut butter and jam bread, Zane swooped her up into his arms and took her upstairs.

In fact, his only other response was to say "You should have just cried or something. They're gonna argue now." He shook his head and ran her a bath. He'd been right, of course. For days they heard the hushed back-and-forth of their parents' voices from their bedroom or the kitchen. It took weeks before they sat down with her and

Alexia D. Miller

Zane for a "family discussion." By then, at least to Phelia, her parents seemed to come to understand her.

It wasn't until later, however, that Phelia wholly understood that her parents hadn't exactly understood her. They'd simply been trying their best because they loved her. It wasn't because they knew what to do with a three-year-old who could hold intricate conversation with her parents. Even so, it wasn't their fault that their daughter was uncharted territory. It was also in those last few weeks of their mother's life that Phelia realized just how much she loved her family.

Phelia loved that they took time to ask what she wanted and stayed honest with her. Even when Phelia couldn't offer any explanations for her differences her family never complained. Not even when she said she wanted to read something without pictures or wanted to change her room. More than that, Phelia loved that her family didn't push her away when she showed them just how articulate she was. Which was, by her father's opinion, as well-spoken as her 11-year-old big brother.

As well-spoken as Phelia knew herself to be, however, the day that their mother was killed by a drunk driver—something almost unheard of in the small Snowville town because hardly anyone owned cars in the first place—Phelia had been at a loss for words. She couldn't piece together the right words to express such shock and pain.

Alexia D. Miller

Their mother's death made headlines in the local paper for a week and the house was quickly filled with more tears than words.

Following their mother's death, their father did not work a single hospital shift and Phelia hardly remembered the funeral. Immediately after, they were whisked off on a trip to the other side of the world. Zane had said that their father was letting them run away for a while. Even without their mother, Phelia recalled almost liking their trip enough to stay forever. Perhaps if their mother had been alive, they would have.

When they came back to Snowville, their father seemed much less connected to the world. He was overcome with a deep sadness Phelia had never seen. There were many nights she watched Zane attempt to console their father in the dark. Usually, those hash nights ended with Phelia on their father's lap, Zane leaned against his shoulder, and stories about their mother until they all fell asleep.

While Phelia had known that she was sad, she felt worse for her brother and father. Somehow it seemed all too relevant after their mother's death that they'd known her longer. That they'd heard her laugh, felt her warm hands, and been held in her embrace for many more years than she. She'd struggled with the thought of which to feel worse for on many occasions.

Alexia D. Miller

Should she have pitied her father because he'd lost his wife and the mother of his children? A woman that he'd been married to for 15 years and known even longer? Or her brother? A boy who'd lost a mother with a younger sister to look after while he constantly battled the violent waves of his father's sadness--to the point of having to pick up the pieces so his body would not be carried away at sea? Even today Phelia didn't know the answer.

For a year Zane hadn't attended school. In that time, rather than having a sitter, he looked after her himself. Not long after, their father reluctantly returned to work and Phelia was enrolled in daycare. It was only a matter of time before Zane was re-enrolled in school and to have Phelia's "differences" amongst her and the other children cause them trouble before she was unenrolled in daycare.

Eventually, their father pulled some strings to have Phelia enrolled in Snowville's public school system. Unsurprisingly, Phelia was also "different" there. With the help of a teacher, Phelia was moved to a higher grade, a few levels below her brother's. There, Phelia encountered her first bullies; boys and girls who pushed her around, moved or stole her things, and sometimes would force her into a game of monkey-in-the-middle.

Again, her father tried to change things. This time, however, he was met with a dead-end. Phelia would not, they

Alexia D. Miller

were told, be moved up any other grades. Instead of their father quitting his job and moving them away from her brother's school, they settled for home-schooling. Their father spent countless hours on the telephone and laptop each day learning about the process.

In the end, Phelia was to use a variety of textbooks and other materials as a form of research, write her own reports which would be checked by her father and brother, and take a couple national exams to check her progress every year. Zane even suggested bringing back some of his work from school as practice, which she welcomed.

To this day, that process still stands. In fact, she'd just finished an exam and tucked it away in an envelope before her stomach distracted her from her books. As a solution to her hunger, Phelia settled on a ham and cheese sandwich that was wrapped up in the fridge, an apple from the kitchen fruit bowl, and a glass of milk—without the mess. As disappointing as it was, Phelia could hardly manage putting together anything more than a sandwich to this day.

She slowly walked back into the living room and sat down at the coffee table. Phelia looked at her fantasy book, wishing she trusted herself enough to eat and read at the same time. This book, which Zane found tucked away in a small store a few days prior, told a story about knights in metal armor saving a princess. The princess of some broken

Alexia D. Miller

land suffered a serious bout of amnesia and lived away from her people. According to the story, the young girl thought herself a farmhand because of some unexplained happenstance.

Finishing her sandwich, Phelia climbed up her father's thick leather chair, to look out of the window. She looked at the rain fogging the glass and listened to the *plip-plops* against the roof on their white porch. She could make out the thick gray clouds, and rounded puddles towards the street. *How strange* Phelia thought, *that it is the ninth day of rain this year.*

Phelia took note of her sudden urge to rush outside but pushed the thought to the back of her mind. She turned around and slid her body down the leather until her feet touched the floor. Phelia sighed as she took a bite of her apple, wondering what was keeping Zane.

Zane...

Chapter Five: Fresh Baked Rocks.

Zane pushed his drenched hair away from his face with a frustrated cry. He was drenched, shivering, and hating this bizarre rain. He'd been trying to make it home for the last hour, but the rain seemed intent on drowning him where he stood. If he hadn't been protecting the fresh bread he'd gotten from Hellen's Bakery a few minutes before, he wouldn't have minded the downpour. He could almost hear Phelia's groans of hunger as she waited for him. Maybe she was even pacing in front of the door, wondering where he was. If only he hadn't left his umbrella at Victor's place.

Zane reached into his pocket and pulled out the two rocks he'd found in front of the old, abandoned hospital. Although, Zane guessed, he couldn't exactly call them rocks. He'd taken shelter from the rain on the steps of the building. His arms were tired from protecting the bread, so Zane sat the brown bag on the step beside him.

For only a moment he'd thought to take just one *teeny-tiny* bite, but he shook his head, feeling guilty for even thinking it. *It's Phelia's favorite*, Zane said sternly to himself.

Alexia D. Miller

You shielded it this far, what's a little further to the house?
You can't give up half-way! Feeling newly motivated, he
readied himself for his sprint home. When his stomach
began to growl, however, Zane realized he didn't feel nearly
as motivated as he'd thought. *Great*, he thought, I guess
conviction won't keep me from being hungry.

Looking down to pick up the bag, he saw a couple
rocks at his feet. When Zane picked them up, he realized
that what he held weren't rocks at all. One was a familiar
green and the other a transparent blue. The longer he stared
at his translucent blue reflection, the more he wanted to give
it to Phelia. An odd thought, he realized, considering that he
was the one with the blue eyes.

Curious, Zane circled the building looking for more.
He found nothing. No indication of where they came from
or any others in sight. He hoped no one had left them there
by accident, but he also knew that almost no one in town
traveled close to the area anymore because it was too close to
The Death House for their liking. Thinking about it made
Zane remember all the rumors that were going around
school about Victor and a new girl.

Zane himself hadn't seen this new girl, but apparently
neither had anyone else. According to Victor, she and her
two aunts, the Vox's, moved into the house not long ago.
Under normal circumstances, Victor was too disinterested in

people in general to get involved. A girl in distress, however, was completely different. Although Zane wanted to ask Victor about the details surrounding the time they met, he couldn't do it. He remembered the almost dead look in Victor's eyes before he started talking in class. He remembered that Victor had been stuck in a dark place and he was afraid that asking him questions about it would push him there again.

Zane couldn't help but compare it to what he'd seen behind his father's gaze after their mother passed. They didn't seem very different; the dark place Victor had fallen to, and the place he struggled to drag his father out of. He knew better than to think that those dark places completely disappeared. He was certain that the dark place still had a grip on them, because he was really no different himself. He was sure that kind of pain never really went away.

. . .

Rushing in the front door, Zane kicked off his shoes and socks. Looking to his left he saw Phelia in their father's oversized leather chair. She was so small he could almost see the chair swallow her. His eyes shifted to the table where a plate of bread crusts lay awry, then to the bite of apple left in her hand. Next to her was a glass from last night where a sip

Alexia D. Miller

of milk was waiting to be finished off. Zane couldn't believe it. He'd almost dropped the bread.

"You already *ate*?!" Zane exclaimed, voicing his disbelief with emphasis. Phelia's large brown eyes blinked at him from the other side of the chair, guilt clouding her face. "I can't believe this. And why does that look like my sandwich from the fridge?"

"I couldn't wait for you..." She started, her voice fading as she looked at the brown bag in his arms. Zane knew in that moment she recognized her favorite. "W-was that bread for both of us?" She stuttered, coming towards him like a dog ready to devour its favorite treat.

"Not anymore. After I get cleaned up, I am eating *ALL* of it, you little traitor." Zane said as he walked down the hall towards the bathroom. He could hear Phelia's small feet racing behind him.

"No! Zane! Save me a little piece?" She whined.

"Absolutely not," Zane scoffed, closing the door behind him.

"*The Sweet Bread is my favorite!*" She cried.

"That's why I bought it!" Zane yelled from the other side of the door.

"So, you'll share?" Phelia's small voice said gleefully.

"Not even a **crumb**." Zane teased.

"Please?" Phelia sobbed, tapping lightly on the door.

"Zaaaaane."

Alexia D. Miller

Zane's laughter echoed from the other side. "I don't know, Phelia. I got drenched for a traitor. I kinda think I earned it!"

Grace...

Chapter Six: New Clothes, New Friends?

*O*n the tenth day of rain, Grace was having a bad day. She was still being punished for picking fights and destroying "personal property." Of course, Grace attempted to tell her foster parents that the two boys started everything, but they wouldn't listen. They'd explicitly forbade her from going anywhere outside of home and school until next week.

Today, no one had been home after school, so Grace defiantly made her way to the pond, which was much further away than she remembered it being the days she hadn't been grounded. She, nor anyone else in Snowville knew its name, but it was still her favorite. Some time ago, Grace found the rusted sign but the letters had long been worn away. Grounded or not, with every step closer to her favorite pond and further away from home, Grace felt a little bit freer.

Not more than a couple blocks from the pond, however, Grace felt eyes on the back of her head. When she spun around to see, she caught the blurred motion of four

Alexia D. Miller

short figures before they disappeared behind a near-by house. Almost certain that she'd seen Eustis' blonde hair, Grace panicked. Already, she felt the small beads of sweat forming on her forehead. How long had she been followed? For blocks? Since home? Since School? Surely none of the regulars in Elephant Spit's group stayed anywhere near a house like hers, right?

Not wanting to lead the boys to her favorite spot, or rather not wanting them to find out that she had a favorite spot in the first place, Grace quickly turned down the nearest a street. Almost immediately, Grace made out the shuffling at her back. It felt ridiculous.

Grace wanted to turn around and fight them, to throw her fists into one of their jaws, to be sure that she blackened **their** eyes like they had done to hers. She wanted to throw rocks into their pale faces and knock out so many of their teeth they'd be embarrassed to call her another name or laugh in her face ever again. But fighting had been how she'd gotten into this whole mess. Her stubbornness too, she thought bitterly to herself. Because she wanted to be free for one more day before facing her punishment. *If I had went home and stayed there would I even be in this mess?* She wondered.

But wondering wouldn't do anything for her. It was too late now to think about the things she didn't do. Right

Alexia D. Miller

now, she could get away. Still, running made her look weak and scared. *Maybe that's what I am supposed to be*, Grace supposed, *maybe that is the type of child my foster parents wanted. A weak, scared, know-it-all who they could show off. Not the dark girl with the jungle feet and crazy red hair. Not the girl who got black eyes fighting with boys.*

Grace figured that maybe in a way she was weak, and when it came to her foster parents, she was more than a little scared, but she wasn't a know-it-all. Heck, sometimes Grace wondered if she knew anything at all. But no matter what she was, she couldn't be afraid of those boys, her teachers, or neighbors. None of those people cared about her. None of them did anything for her. At least MaryAnne and Duke clothed her, fed her, and even gave her a proper bedroom. At least MaryAnne and Duke seemed to like her—well, *sometimes.*

Suddenly, as Grace zig-zagged down random streets, rain began to pour. Another rain? At her back she heard whines of surprise and disdain. Those boys and their stupid, expensive clothes.

Good! Grace celebrated silently, looking over her shoulder. Amused, she watched them flick water off their arms and hair, shaking like wet dogs. *Ha! I can handle a little rain*, she thought. She'd almost managed a laugh until she realized they knew she'd seen them. They shouted words

Alexia D. Miller

she lost to the sound of the rain, but she knew from their expressions they weren't done with her. So, she ran.

The rain was blurring the vision in her good eye and her right one was useless because of the swelling, but that wasn't enough to stop her. Puddles quickly formed in the streets and Grace didn't bother dodging them. She paid no mind to the splashing nor the water rushing up her ankles with each stomp. Grace didn't know where she was going, but she didn't let that stop her either. She simply ran as blind as she felt. At least she was getting away from them.

She jumped over a broken object in the street, barely seeing it, only to collide with something ahead of her and crash onto the wet, hard ground. A something that turned out to be another person: a petite girl with dark hair. Grace rose to her feet and watched as the girl looked down, wondering if she might try to fight her too. Half of her body was submerged in a puddle, her khaki hat sat to her left, and her open umbrella on the right. Her hair quickly soaked up the rain as her large, cognac brown eyes met Grace's, displeased.

Grace apologized, picking up the umbrella and the hat as the girl stood. Grace rushed forward, awkwardly trying to dust off the dirt, which only sent more water flinging around them. "I'm really sorry. I didn't mean to!" Grace exclaimed, holding out the girl's things. "I will apologize to

Alexia D. Miller

your parents too, you know. If they'll be upset about your outfit!" Grace offered, nervous at the thought of getting someone else in trouble for an accident she caused. She knew how her foster parents tended to react, so what about actual parents?

"My father is at work," the girl replied flatly. "My brother will be here any moment, though another apology isn't necessary. I'm sure they will understand." She said, thanking her as she received her things from Grace's arms. Hearing her small voice speak so formally surprised Grace. She didn't know what to make of it. "How old are you?" Grace asked before she thought better of it.

"I'm seven. I had a birthday recently." The girl spoke without pause.

Realizing that she'd been distracted, Grace swiftly turned around to search behind her. She took a few steps in each direction and stretched her neck silently, looking for any sign of the tyrants. "Those boys are no longer following you." The girl said.

"You've seen them?" Grace asked, her voice coated in disbelief and worry. "Which way did they go?" She asked nervously.

"I did see them, yes. Although I haven't a clue where they've gone. Perhaps I would have been of more assistance had you not rammed into me." She replied, motioning slightly with her arms as she sighed.

"Right. Uh, I'm sorry about that. I didn't see you." Grace said, sucking air in between her teeth as she spoke.

"You had trouble seeing me because I am short? Is that it?" The girl questioned.

Grace's mouth dropped. "No! No, I didn't mean that at all. It's just...I *really* couldn't see you." She said, pointing to her right eye. "I still can't really. Not well. This eye is all swollen up and it's raining hard. Not to mention I was running. See?" Grace tried to explain.

The girl shrugged and Grace stood there in silence. She wondered if the boys were watching, waiting just beyond her line of sight to catch her off guard. Would they attack her as soon as this girl walked away? Would they hurt her too? Should she get away before the girl was caught in the middle of her problems? Grace didn't think she would do well in a fight against more than two of them. Things had been hard enough the last time. She was almost sure all four of them had been chasing her.

A voice brought Grace out of her thoughts. "Phelia, what in the world? I left you for eight minutes." A boy sighed from under his hood. "Maybe someone else finding a way to get drenched while under an umbrella I'd understand, but you?" He chuckled, as he made his way in front of her. He

Alexia D. Miller

shifted his head slowly as he looked over. Grace watched their interactions curiously as the girl turned around, climbed up the boy's back, and held her umbrella over their heads.

"It wasn't my fault, nor my umbrella's Zane. It isn't broken. It was only an accident. That girl there," she said, motioning lightly with the umbrella, bumped into me." Phelia, and Zane, or so they had called one another. Grace thought their names were familiar but couldn't be sure.

"It was *all* my fault! I'm so sorry! I didn't see her! I ruined all of her clothes." Grace cried, hanging her head in front of her. "I don't have any money, but I can make it up to you." Zane walked over towards her and for a moment Grace feared that her apology had not been accepted. She feared that in a few moments, she would face the consequences of her actions. Maybe they were rich like Eustis and she'd made an enemy of them in a single incident—as if she needed any more of those.

Instead of an unwelcomed response, Zane gently placed a hand on her head. "We don't need your money. They're just clothes. Besides, Phelia's fine, right? Just a bit cold and wet. Both are easily fixed. No worries."

"Cold, wet, and hungry." Phelia chimed in and he chuckled. "Right. Cold, wet, and hungry then." They weren't mad at her? When he removed his hand from her head, Grace

Alexia D. Miller

realized she'd been shaking. She didn't know if the cold or her fear were to blame.

Grace looked up at Zane, Phelia sitting up on his shoulders, meeting his blue eyes. She could make out some of his damp brown hair curled against his forehead. Even with the cloudy light from the sky she could see how much the two of them looked alike. "Okay." Grace said finally able to respond, her fear fading.

"I'm starved. Would you like to have dinner with us?" Phelia's small voice asked from above. "You did get me mucky, but you don't even have an umbrella."

Grace wasn't sure how to respond, so she simply said what was on her mind. "Without even knowing my name? You're pretty weird."

"You don't have to accept." Phelia said shaking her head.

"No! No. Of course I will! I could totally eat! A-And I like weird!" Grace blurted out. In the seconds following it, she felt embarrassed for it, but she couldn't take it back now. Even if she could, Grace was sure she wouldn't have. She knew it was probably a bad idea to agree to have dinner with a couple of strangers, but she also knew that she might never get invited anywhere else again. Afterall, no one ever invited her to anything.

More than that, Grace was sure she would rather go just about anywhere but home; grounded or not. She was

Alexia D. Miller

sure she wasn't ready to make the trip all the way home from the other part of town. More than that, Grace couldn't be sure she wasn't still being followed or that those boys didn't have a nasty surprise waiting for her. Maybe, just maybe, they would get tired of waiting on her if she had dinner with them. Maybe, they'd find their way home before she did.

. . .

When Grace made it to their house, she realized why their names sounded so familiar. On their mailbox read the name "Brand." The name of one of the only doctors in their small town. Phelia and Zane Brand, the son and daughter that Grace must have heard someone *somewhere* mention. She couldn't quite recall the reason, but she didn't think it mattered. It seemed fitting to Grace, that a doctor's children would be caring and sympathetic.

Inside, it was warm. Zane brought up the fire in their fireplace and Grace slid off her shoes—as she saw them do— near the door. Zane motioned for her to sit anywhere she wanted and disappeared down the hall to get towels. When he came back, he gave one to Grace and two to Phelia. One, she watched Phelia lay on the couch to sit on and the other she used gently on her hair.

Alexia D. Miller

Grace didn't hesitate to lay on the floor near the fireplace. At home, MaryAnne and Duke had one too. They often told Grace that they couldn't trust that she wouldn't set fire to the entire house, so she wasn't allowed near it. Normally, the only exception was when they had a gathering with the neighbors or a holiday. Grace never said anything against it, it was a parent's job to worry or something anyway, but she disagreed. As much as she loved the warmth of a fireplace or the swaying colors and crisp sounds when the wood burned, Grace wouldn't dare set a fire. Especially one to her own home.

Grace wasn't sure how long she sat there silently, listening to Zane's light shuffling in another room or watching the shades of orange, gold, and red sway in the fireplace casting shadows behind the grate. She saw a flicker of a reddish-brown flame almost the same as her hair. In time, Grace didn't remember the boys who'd chased her through half of the town. She no longer felt her damp clothes or the cold and before long, she fell fast asleep.

. . .

Stirring awake, Grace heard an unfamiliar, male voice. For an instant shrouded in panic, Grace couldn't remember where she was or how she'd gotten there. Slowly

Alexia D. Miller

the pieces came together as she remembered the incident with Phelia. She wondered how long she'd been asleep as she followed the sounds of voices to the kitchen. In the corner, a tall man with dark hair and glasses stood talking on the telephone. He was wearing his doctor's coat, so it took no time for Grace to realize he was Dr. Brand.

Zane stood at the stove, stirring a pot. Phelia climbed from one chair to the next placing silverware on the table. Grace figured it couldn't be ridiculously late yet, considering that they were getting ready for dinner. "Can I help?" Grace asked. Quietly they all glanced her way. Even from a distance, Grace could make out Dr. Brand's brown eyes. Phelia nodded, telling her that she could help set the table if she really wanted something to do.

After the table was set, Zane took his time going around it to fill their bowls then went to the stove to grab rolls of buttery bread. *Stew. Thick, creamy, and smells like heaven!* Grace thought, her mouth watering in anticipation. When her stomach began to growl, Grace was sure they'd heard it. Embarrassed, she quickly asked the first question that came to mind. "Do you always eat together?"

"When we can." Phelia said, drinking a cup of water near the sink. "Father works quite a bit, so most times it's just Zane and I, but when he's home we always do." Grace hadn't been expecting a specific answer, but the one she had

Alexia D. Miller

gotten was different than her own experience. Grace, MaryAnne and Duke almost never had dinner together. With that, Grace excused herself to their restroom, which Phelia directed her to, so she could clean up. It had been an excuse to get over the feeling swirling around inside her. At least until she realized she really did need to get cleaned up.

Looking in the mirror, Grace frowned. Her red curls were a tangled mess, and she hadn't brought a brush. She tried her best to straighten it with her fingers. She looked at her arms, specked with dry dirt and rinsed them well before washing her hands. Her clothes she could do nothing about. Focusing her eyes as best she could in the mirror, Grace couldn't help but stare back at her reflection.

She looked at her dark brown freckles clouded densely around her nose and followed the broken pattern towards her cheeks and ears. Her stupid right eye was brownish-purple and stung to the touch while her good russet brown eye stared back at her on the left. She couldn't fix that. Grace sighed, frustrated. She didn't want to look messy when everyone else seemed so clean and perfect.

Figuring that there was nothing left she could do to fix her appearance, she wiped out the sink, washed her hands again, and left the bathroom. Coming in the kitchen, Grace took the only empty seat, and apologized for keeping everyone waiting. Although Grace didn't detect any hint of

Alexia D. Miller

annoyance in their voices as she sat down, looking up, Grace saw Dr. Brand frowning in her direction. "I'll take a look at that eye after dinner." He said, yawning.

Grace wanted to thank him, but she'd lost her voice somewhere in her throat. Would MaryAnne and Duke get mad at her for having Dr. Brand waste his time on her? Grace felt stupid again. More stupid than usual, for coming back with Phelia and Zane. For sitting at their table ruining their meal, and probably their appetites, with her beaten-up eye.

As Grace's thoughts became more depressing, she felt Phelia's warm hand on her arm. "You're not bothering us. Father's worried about the damage to your eye. Right father?" Phelia said, silently directing Grace's attention to her father. Dr. Brand offered her a reassuring nod. "Absolutely." He said. "Have you seen anyone about that eye? There's a lot of swelling going on there. As I mentioned, I will look at that eye after dinner, if that's alright with you." He spoke quickly. "Oh. Shall we call your parents?"

"No, sir. No one has looked at my eye. I am going straight home after you're finished with me, so I don't need to call my parents." Grace said. The last thing she needed was for anyone to call MaryAnne and Duke. No matter what happens, Grace knew what was awaiting her at home. It was

Alexia D. Miller

never anything good, and today she'd practically run off on her own. Even worse, between the boys from school tormenting her and running into Phelia, Grace never had a chance to see if her foster parents had made it home.

"I could certainly take you home. What was your name, sweetheart?" He asked.

No one had ever called Grace *sweet* anything before. She fought the deepening lump in her throat. "Grace, sir. I don't live far. I am fine with walking. Thank you."

"Are you sure?" He asked, looking worried. "It's getting a little late."

"I'm sure, sir." Grace answered quickly. The worst thing she could do was come home late and involve Phelia and Zane's father in her mess.

"I see. Well then, Grace," Dr. Brand said clearing his throat, "I'm Dr. Philip Brand. It can get a little lonely over here, especially for Phelia. If you'd like, you're welcome anytime."

Normally, Grace never gave an invitation like that a second thought. She knew adults were simply being polite, almost out of obligation, when they offered her something. In her experience, most of the adults she met dreaded her presence. Yet, Dr. Brand's invitation seemed genuine and she, to her upmost surprise, wanted to accept. Grace wanted to get to know Phelia. She wanted to understand the unusual seven-year-old—this girl who took her home after she

Alexia D. Miller

knocked her into the mud, let her sleep in front of the fireplace, spoke such proper English, and almost seemed to read her mind when bad thoughts circled her head. So, she did.

When dinner ended, Dr. Brand went to another room and came back with a brown leather bag. He sat Grace down on the couch, even with her dirty clothes, and opened the bag. He reached inside and slipped on gloves as Grace slowly kicked her feet in front of her. Grace was instructed to open her right eye as wide as she could and blink. After a few times of that, Dr. Brand shined a light into her eye for her to follow. Grace could tell that he did his best to be gentle when he touched her face, even if it still hurt.

In the end, he told her that he wanted to check her eye again soon. He told her that he didn't see any signs to cause concern and rubbed ointment on her eye. When he wrapped it, he advised her not to take it off until she came over again. In truth, Grace couldn't remember the last time someone had been so nice to her. She didn't wonder if the Brands were saying unspeakably cruel things when she turned her back or walked out of their front door.

Outside, Grace found herself in the best mood even when it began to rain again. Maybe even the best mood she'd been in for weeks. It didn't take Grace long to figure out where she was. Grace felt so happy that it didn't even bother

Alexia D. Miller

her that she'd have to go past The Death House. In fact, today she felt braver. So brave that she dared herself to touch it; to prove to herself that she wasn't afraid of the dead. Afterall, Grace knew the unsettling rumors that surrounded the home.

As Grace neared the massive iron gate, she stopped. Had she seen what she thought she saw? As if to confirm her suspicions, Grace saw a shadow cross by a dark window on a higher floor. When a yellow light sputtered on the first floor, Grace bolted. She ran as fast as she could and as far as she could. So far, that she ended up at a large stone building. One that she realized she had seen plenty of times during the day from her no-name pond. Scared that even more ghostly things would occur, she started to run again, opting to go around The Death House instead.

Before Grace could put any real distance between her or any of the creepy buildings around her, however, she fell flat on her face in a thick puddle of muddy water. Frustrated, Grace struck her fists to the ground. She would be in even more trouble when she got home. Grace stood and wiped off as much of the dirt as she could before searching for the culprit—whatever it was that was responsible for tripping her. Instead of a tree-root or a stick, Grace found a fiery red crystal. She turned it over in her hand as it caught the moonlight. Smiling to herself, Grace figured maybe her horrible luck was changing.

In the same moment that Grace thought she'd found happiness she was struck with fear. A voice called lowly out to her from the darkness. At first Grace was convinced one of the boys from school were pulling a prank on her. When she didn't see anyone around her, Grace figured she could lure the boy out. "Who's there?" Grace called, turning to look about her. "I said, w-who's there?" Grace called again, feeling less confident than before. With no answer, Grace ran the entire way home.

. . .

At home, Grace was yelled at. When MaryAnne asked where she'd been, she didn't answer. Grace feared that if she did, she would be forbidden from ever seeing Phelia, Zane and Dr. Brand again. MaryAnne and Duke were in a worse mood than usual tonight, which usually meant that they'd gotten some sort of bad news and Grace had only made it worse. Tonight, Grace would go without dinner, they told her. Tonight, she would go into *That Room*. A room much worse than a ghost's voice...

Alexia D. Miller

{74}

True...

Chapter Seven: Homeroom.

Today, True would go back to school. That had been what she'd told her aunts after she'd gotten dressed. Now that she was on her way, however, she didn't feel up to it. *Today, I go back*, she thought. True repeated the phrase in her mind like a mantra, hoping that it would strengthen her resolve. The truth was, she wished she could have spent another day in Snowville Temporary Infirmary—her new little escape. Back where she'd spent most of her time cleaning for weeks.

True remembered stepping over the tattered staircase the day they'd moved into their new house. She took note of a step that was split and broke away at some point in the past. She listened to the light creeks of the stairs as she ascended until they turned gently to one side to reveal another room. It was an oversized space mostly empty aside from the randomly placed end tables and thick-padded seats. Something about it immediately attracted her to it.

It was almost as if there was an invisible magnet in the air pulling her towards something she couldn't see. True hadn't felt it on the floor below. She wanted to marinate in

Alexia D. Miller

that feeling, wanted it to become some tangible thing that she could look at with her own two eyes, something that she could roll over between her fingers and fully examine.

True knew, however, that she couldn't simply make something she felt become anything other than what it was, but it didn't stop her from wishing. As she made her way through the room, she found herself staring at a remarkably large, empty space on the wall. A space so white that it was almost whiter than the rest of the room. It was almost *too* white.

The room farthest off down the hall had been an office filled with withered papers, pens with dried ink, and a mismatched desk and chair. Figuring that there was nothing more to discover there, she made her way to another room. She walked past another door, which was boarded and nailed shut from top to bottom. Messy painted words read Danger, Floor Caved! KEEP OUT! So, True found no reasons to test it.

Past this, was a small closet-like space which turned out to house a broken toilet and sink. Old towels lay around the floor, which was of little interest to her. The last room she found much more to her liking. True carefully turned the loose doorknob as the door creaked open and a cloud of dust floated up towards her face. In the doorway, she smiled behind her mask as her eyes glided across the room.

Alexia D. Miller

Crystal Key: Door to a New World

There was a large window across from her with a square wooden table beside it. A rusted metal lantern sat at the table's center, aged but unbroken. A thick chocolate brown padded armchair sat to the table's right, slightly angled away from it. Along the walls were a variety of old-fashioned books with thick bindings, although True was sad to see several spewed across the floor in a frenzy. Even more, the worst books looked like they'd been abused by inconsiderate teenagers. Pages of several books were ripped from their bindings and crumbled, pieces of gum were pressed in the corners, and greasy finger stains were streaked across covers under a thick heap of dust.

True took solace in the fact that, given the state of things, whoever came before stopped coming by some time ago. True felt that she'd found a secret treasure hidden away from the rest of the world. She'd found a place where she could disappear from a world that showed her long ago that she didn't belong. True fought the thoughts of the past away just as they attempted to surface, and instead focused on the cleaning she'd need to do before she could utilize the upstairs.

Excited with a sense of purpose, True made her way out of the room, back down the staircase, and out of the window from where she'd come. As she put both of her feet on the ground, she noticed a glimmer nearby. She walked

Alexia D. Miller

closer to it, bent down, and scooped up the object. She rolled it gently against her palm and the rain helped wash away the dirt.

It was a beautiful cloudy-white crystal—a crystal of all things. From the moment she'd held it in her hands True never wanted to part from it again. If it wasn't enough that True had found a little corner of the world worthy of attention her first day in Snowville, surely it meant something to find a rare item that beautiful. She wondered then if she could like Snowville after all? True recalled feeling free as she slipped off her sandals and the rain splashed harder around her. She hardly noticed the lightning strike the sky above her. She stuck her feet firmer into the wet ground as she walked back home and tucked the crystal into her jacket.

. . .

As True neared the high school, she felt anxious and disappointed. She'd finished cleaning with no time to enjoy it and she wanted nothing more than to bury herself within the hospital building. She wanted to let the days pass her over. Now, however, True felt that the opposite would be her reality. She hadn't even managed to step through the door before she was sure her school days would be endless. Again, she wore the black mask and jacket and sighed as she

Alexia D. Miller

wrapped her hand around her newly found treasure. True hadn't been able to leave the beautiful cloudy-white crystal at home.

Until just hours ago True had it sitting in a cleaning solution conveniently found in a book from the temporary hospital building library. Or rather, in a journal. Most of its pages were blank and she hadn't had a moment to read it between cleaning up and house arrangements with her aunts, but on the inner-front cover was a small list of ingredients to mix. The journal had listed it as *Crystal Cleaning Solution (Like New)* in small, neat handwriting.

True brought the journal with her in her metallic gray backpack, hoping to get the chance to read it or her new fiction book she'd received from her aunts during her break. True often found herself intrigued by the thought of magical mythical creatures. So, a crystal was right up her alley. Unfortunately, from what True could see flipping through the pages of the journal, there wasn't another list written out for her use.

Bothered by the thought of possibly losing her treasure, True had spent the morning fastening the crystal into a necklace. It took a couple hours of looking through her things before she found scraps of metal and copper wire she used years ago on a project she no longer remembered.

Alexia D. Miller

Within minutes, she wrapped the wires around the crystal and looped it through an old chain necklace that previously belonged to her mother.

Determined to be completely satisfied with her work, True shook the chain and pulled at it from different directions. When it didn't come loose or fall from its place, True made sure to take it with her. She'd gotten dressed and listened to her aunts' reminders about school. They'd been keen on driving her to school since her Aunt Trina was heading to the lab and would be taking their car, but True wondered if driving her to school had been for their own peace of mind.

. . .

Inside, True could already hear the muddled whispers of students and teachers in the halls. "That's her" they echoed. "Remember what I told you?" As True went to the office to get her schedule from a worker, she felt her stomach drop to her knees. She felt a wave of nausea hit the back of her throat but fought it down. Clearly, the incident before would involve a lot of consequences. Foreseen and unforeseen.

In homeroom a little less than an hour later, True watched her teacher enter the room. He was a tall, thin man with brown glasses and a messy head of thinning hair. He carried a small leather bag over his shoulder and immediately looked in her direction as he walked to his desk in the front of the room. The room itself was a dull off-gray color with a tiled white floor. All the desks, aside from the teacher's, mirrored one another. Each one a similar color to the walls.

From the looks of it, it wasn't just her teacher staring at her. All eyes in the classroom were focused on her as she stood silently nearest the front row of desks. True's homeroom teacher, a Mr. Van-Dayton, awkwardly introduced himself then prompted the students to do the same. Those who already seemed to know each other, which True realized was almost the entire class, chatted away, rudely ignoring Mr. Van-Dayton's instruction.

A few minutes later, True found her way to her seat. It was tucked away in the rear of the classroom beside a small row of windows. A seat she'd "chosen" because everyone else had already selected theirs. The only other desks that hadn't been in the middle of the room—which was filled with clusters of mumbling students—were placed randomly near a wall as if someone simply pushed it to the side. These were also in the back of the classroom beside her. True didn't mind her seat, considering it meant she was

Alexia D. Miller

farthest away from most of the students. Even better, she could catch glimpses of outside from where she sat.

One student, a girl with short black hair and a pink headband, entered the classroom late. Judging by the excitement that filled the room, she was well liked. Mr. Van-Dayton quieted the class and asked True to introduce herself, telling the black-haired girl to wait until she was finished to take her seat. Not knowing what to say, True simply stood up, "My name is True. I just moved here." She said quietly and was immediately met with mockery and snickers. Not sure what else could or should be said, True sat down again in silence.

On the board, Mr. Van-Dayton started to write, not particularly acknowledging True's introduction or her classmates' reactions. True's eyes followed his scribbles as his wrist flowed along the board. *Any comments or concerns involving the new student's face covering or attire are PROHIBITED, and issues are to be handled by the Principle directly* True read.

Another wave of nausea hit her. True had no idea this was the way things would be handled. Did her aunts? Probably not. After all, this would essentially throw a reminder in everyone's face. True could hear the whispering voices

Alexia D. Miller

resound noisily across the room. As if she needed any assistance to begin with, now the words on the board were making a mockery of her too. She shifted her eyes as another student entered the classroom, attempting to focus her eyes anywhere but on the board. Immediately True recognized the boy. She made out his dark black hair and sharp green eyes. He was the one who saved her during the incident before. Principle Mann had called him Victor.

With permission from Mr. Van-Dayton, both the girl with the pink headband and Victor were told they could take their seats. The girl's low heels *click-clacked* against the tiled floor. With every stride she made in True's direction, the room slowly fell silent. Waiting, watching, in anticipation. "What's Sydney doing?" There's no *way* she is going to sit with her." One voice said in a hushed tone.

The girl—Sydney—walked over to True's side, grabbing the empty desk nearest her, and leaned forward. So close in fact, that True could feel her breath against her mask. Her voice sliced through the air harshly. "**FREAK**." She hissed.

In the moments following, Sydney pulled the desk loudly across the floor. All the way to a group of girls sitting with their desks huddled in a corner near the front of the room. Each girl sported a different color bright lipstick. Sydney's desk sat at an angle, cutting the walkway in half, but

Alexia D. Miller

she didn't seem to care. True was stunned as a chain of laughter burst throughout the classroom.

She had been called worse things in the past, but this had been the first time someone had said such harsh words so boldly. Much less, someone who would do so publicly without batting an eye. In that moment True realized that anything negative that could occur in Snowville would rival everything she experienced in the past.

Victor, who had been quietly standing in the same place as Sydney caused a scene, looked over to the teacher. Mr. Van-Dayton didn't say a word. Instead, he cleared his throat, opened the book that sat on his desk, and sat back against his chair. True hadn't expected Mr. Van-Dayton to be any help considering his actions thus far, not to mention his insensitive sentence emphasized on the board, but he'd proved her right in the worst of ways.

True silently watched Victor as Sydney mumbled something in his direction. When he didn't respond, walking forward until he stood silently before her, she rolled her eyes. Without a moment's notice, Victor sat on her desk, swung his legs around to the other side of it, and slid down onto his feet beside her. "You're in the way." He said with a frown.

Sydney's mouth hung slightly agape and a small ruffled noise came from within it. She was dumfounded.

Alexia D. Miller

Immediately, the rest of the lipstick girls yelled at him, what they were saying, however, True didn't understand. Seemingly unfazed, Victor made his way to the last desk beside True and glanced at her before he sat.

True couldn't help but smile, though no one could see it. Part of her was relieved not to re-live the horror of another desk scraping across the floor in the opposite direction. The other part of her was simply amused by his bravado. Even as other students made negative remarks about his actions, he appeared to be completely unbothered. Instead of responding, Victor crossed his arms over the desk and laid his head there, closing his eyes.

True reached her hands back inside her jacket pocket, to feel the crystal against her skin. She breathed in and exhaled in a light sigh. She could do this, she told herself. She *had* to do this. She couldn't repeat her past mistakes. Considering that Mr. Van-Dayton was still flipping through the pages of his own book, True decided some reading was just what she needed herself. Opening her new fiction novel, she began to read.

Alexia D. Miller

Victor...

Chapter Eight: Thank You.

Victor yawned as he took his seat. He wished he'd slept longer the night before. He didn't think he had enough energy to deal with his classmates' stupidity today. His mother had kept him busy rearranging furniture and shopping for knick-knacks to decorate the house. She'd somehow managed to get so excited about finishing everything in one day that he couldn't tell her she'd already warn him out before they'd even begun. Add that to all of the items she'd marked for sell, and hauling off heaps of stuff she decided they no longer needed during his suspension and break from school, there was only one word for it: exhaustion.

With his eyes closed, Victor let his mind wander. The day after graduation Zane came by with his diploma and his mother somehow managed to rope him into helping her with their "cleaning project." Truth be told, even considering how tired he'd been, he was more than happy for his mother. If they were cleaning out the entire house, it had to mean that she'd finally moved on from his father. So, even though he hadn't planned to be stuck helping until almost the crack of dawn, there was some comfort to be had in everything they'd done.

His mother's cleaning spree was one thing but being in this class was something else entirely. Victor wondered if Zane had to deal with any of the annoying crowd in his homeroom or if he'd lucked out and none of them were there to haunt him this year. Somehow, Victor thought, it didn't feel like the first day of high school. It felt like he was still there dealing with immature middle schoolers with nothing better to do but to hand out misery. In a way, considering the all-too-familiar faces in the room, he supposed it really wasn't.

Victor already wasn't a fan of Sydney's. Nor any of her band of make-up witches. Not like most of his 8th grade counterparts had been. In his opinion, all Sydney did was talk about herself or her wealthier-than-average parents. She spoke down to most and tended to be the epicenter of unimaginable drama. Today, she didn't seem any different.

He also didn't like her new haircut, which he could hear her going on about, as if he hadn't heard it enough in the halls on the way to class behind her. She'd apparently found it in a magazine and knew without a doubt that the hairstyle would look "so much better" on her, rather than the "troll in the picture." Sometimes Victor had the urge to

Alexia D. Miller

tell her and practically everyone who liked her off but doing so would always require energy he never had, and time he preferred not to waste on people like them.

And the stunt she pulled on True? He didn't think he'd seen such a disgusting display of arrogance in quite some time. In that department, Sydney could possibly give his own father a run for his money. Even if Victor himself had no clue who True was or why she couldn't take off her mask, he knew a bully when he saw one. Sydney and her friends fit the bill.

Ugh. *Yeah*, Victor thought, *this is going to be another looong year.* He looked up at the board, his mind still racing and interfering with his plans to sleep. So, their homeroom teacher was Mr. Van-Dayton. Victor crossed paths with the squirrely man on a few occasions. Heck, Victor knew that almost all the teachers in the area knew him before he could place their faces.

Victor recalled the long, grueling nights that he and his mother put on their pathetic, thin plastered smiles and took extra care to cater to all the staff's every need. The knots of anxiety and anger that floated around in his stomach when the teachers had their annual end-of-the-year meeting at their house. He recalled the thick spews of hatred and bitter laughter as they discussed their "problem students" and the smiles and cheers when they spoke of their "favorites."

They decided who they didn't want to waste time on or who they did. Which students they'd pass regardless of how they performed in the classroom, either because they were protected like Victor, or they didn't want to deal with them for another year. It wasn't the way it was supposed to work nor did Victor see every single teacher from Snowville attend, Victor knew that, but it didn't stop it from happening. Or bothering him for that matter. By the end of it, Victor was reminded that all of them were rotten fruit and every new and well-meaning teacher who found their way to the meeting, surrounded by drinks, food, and secrecy, would eventually succumb to the mold the others were passing around.

Even without his father, Victor remained on this list. Now, however, the teachers' secret meetings were held elsewhere. He never asked where because he didn't care to have an answer, but he knew better than to attempt to tell anyone else. Instead, he put his energy into acing his exams and quizzes, finishing his worksheets and other like assignments, but he didn't participate in class. Not that many other students did so willingly, but as much as Victor hated to admit it, the fact that he was never forced to do so was a perk of his father's legacy and the list.

Alexia D. Miller

Victor wondered then about True. Considering what Mr. Van-Dayton had written on the board, True would likely be on that list now as well, wouldn't she? Specifically considering the last incident. Maybe the teachers would be afraid to fail her if she did nothing. They'd probably operate under the impression that they'd lose their jobs. *Maybe they'd be consumed with a fear like that*, Victor thought. However unwarranted it would be under normal circumstances, it seemed different not because of the threats her aunts made on her behalf, but more because they weren't following the rules already.

Glancing to his left, Victor saw that True's attention was buried in a book. A book called *A World Unknown*. He'd never heard of it. Now that his thoughts were centered around True and the class, Victor picked up the heavy sound of whispering throughout the classroom. The gossip, unsurprisingly, centered around her.

Mr. Van-Dayton walked around the class, handing out schedules. Victor knew better than to think he heard nothing. Instead of saying anything against it, he mentioned that they'd spend the entire day in homeroom, save for lunch. Suddenly feeling much more tired at the thought of spending the entire day surrounded by idiots, Victor buried his head in his arms to sleep.

Alexia D. Miller

. . .

Eventually, the lunch bell rang and woke him. The room filled with rushed noises and laughter as students zoomed out of the door. Victor took note of the papers beside him. There was a packet of assignments to be finished by the end of the day and his schedule that he didn't pay much attention to. With a yawn, he slipped them into his bag.

Getting up and walking towards the front of the classroom, Victor saw True a few steps ahead of him. He watched as her small, pale hand gently placed her finished packet down on the teacher's desk. He wasn't surprised to see her neat handwriting. He continued to walk silently behind her wondering for an instant about the bruises she'd had on her arms before. When they stepped out into the hall True stopped abruptly, turning around to face him.

"Thank you," She said, her head slightly tilted up as if to make eye contact. Something he found to be impossible with her mask. Looking into what appeared to be an endless black space where her eyes should have been was awkward. Victor shifted his gaze slightly to the left, looking at a group of high schoolers making their way down the hall.

"Thank you...for last time." Her voice was soft and quiet. It sounded even more fragile than what he recalled

Alexia D. Miller

hearing in the school parking lot that day, if that was even possible. What a strange thing to notice, Victor thought. Her voice was completely different now; there were no screams, grating pitches or fearful quivering. Of course, Victor knew that her voice had to be different than what he'd heard that day, but the two hardly compared: this voice, somehow, was perfect.

Realizing that she had nothing else to say and they were standing there in silence, Victor cleared his throat. "Yeah. No problem. Really, someone else should have already helped you before I got there. I'm sorry you even had to go through that." He said, watching her. Victor thought that True would shrink into herself if she could.

As if he'd said something wrong, she took a single step backwards and held her book with her fingers. So tight, that Victor could see her already pale hand turning white at the fingertips. She ceased all movement. As if the smallest change would suddenly make her visible to a devilish animal lurking around the corner, biding its time to make a meal out of her. As Victor was at a loss, he couldn't bring himself to move or say another word until she spoke.

"Rumors are starting because of me. I don't know what they'll say about you. I'm sorry," she said, slowly adjusting her bag with her right hand. She was apologizing to him. About rumors, no less.

Alexia D. Miller

"Don't be." Victor shrugged. "I couldn't care less. People talk. They definitely talk at this school." Without warning, Victor watched as she nodded and walked off in the opposite direction of the cafeteria. So quickly that he hadn't managed to ask if she knew which way to go.

. . .

In the cafeteria, Victor met up with Zane. They discussed their schedules and found that they still managed to have a few classes together. As they made plans to meet up after school at Zane's, they were surrounded by students. Students that included Sydney and her groupies. Victor tried to ignore them as they bombarded him with questions. Sydney was looking for an "explanation" for his actions earlier in class, which quickly turned into wanting to know why he would help the "new *freak*."

Victor sighed in frustration. "I told you, you were in my way. I helped her because I felt like it. Why do you care?"

One of Sydney's groupies quickly chimed in. "So, what then? You're not actually *friends* with *her*?" She exclaimed, making a face of disgust.

Alexia D. Miller

"I don't know her at all. I don't see what difference that makes. It's not worth *moving my desk* over. Who cares who she is?"

Victor suddenly felt the tug of Zane's hand on his arm. "Victor let's get out of here. We'll never finish our lunch like this. You don't owe them any explanation." Victor sighed. Of course, Zane was right. So, they grabbed their trays and headed to Mr. Van-Dayton's classroom for lunch and Victor told Zane about the drama in homeroom earlier that day. When they entered the classroom, Victor pointed at the board.

"Man, that's rough." Zane said, shaking his head. "But it's not like we can report him for writing something dumb on the board." Victor nodded. Every time he looked at it, he wanted to erase it. He had a feeling that True would find their school difficult to attend. Maybe she'd hate it so much her and her aunts would leave Snowville for good. If he'd never met Zane, Victor wasn't sure he'd have still been there himself.

. . .

When lunch was over, Zane tossed their trays into the trash. True was the first to make it back to the classroom, right as the bell tolled. Zane looked over at her with a polite nod and said goodbye to Victor, rushing off to get to his own

Alexia D. Miller

homeroom. When the rest of the class returned, Victor and True had taken their seats and he looked at the packet he took from his bag. He spoke to no one and ignored Sydney's vague, fake apology from across the room. Yawning, Victor picked up his pen and began his work. The faster he finished, the faster he could take another nap.

Phelia...

Chapter Nine: Accustomed vs. Accepted.

*I*t had been a little under a month since Phelia saw Grace. She found herself wondering if her eye had gotten any better. If it was healing properly. Sitting at the dinner table that night, Phelia felt that Grace was much more than she looked. Usually, Phelia went to almost painful lengths to act like a normal seven-year-old, to talk like a seven-year-old would, when she was unsure of how someone would respond to her. Even when her father and Zane said that doing so was unnecessary. Phelia figured that they'd had years to become accustomed to her. Others did not.

With Grace, however, something felt different. In fact, from the moment she lifted her eyes to look at her,

Alexia D. Miller

Phelia knew there was something different about her. It wasn't because of her darker complexion which she'd almost never seen since her time in Snowville, or even her red hair the color of bricks. She'd looked to Phelia like someone had shaped her out of clay and colored her any way they pleased. Grace had brown freckles darker than her skin and eyes a richer brown than her own.

Without ruse, Grace had seemed to accept her in mere minutes. She hadn't made rude comments or showcased some inflated sense of surprise every time Phelia opened her mouth to speak. It felt as natural as speaking to Zane, and yet somehow even more important. Grace was not family. She was a stranger. One who apologized and cared, one who tried to dust the mud off her clothes and took responsibility for her part when it counted.

It was all those things and more. Whatever the case, Phelia felt that maybe Grace was the most capable young person she'd met thus far. Even if she hardly knew her. Even more, Phelia felt that Grace could be a friend: her first friend in Snowville.

Phelia sighed as she rolled the blue crystal Zane gave her between her hands. Zane and Victor were best friends. Surely, he was more experienced in this sort of thing, and both he and their father seemed to like Grace well enough. Would they feel she was rushing things in some desperate search to find someone other than her family to talk to, to spend time with? When Zane got home, she would ask him what he thought.

Zane...

Chapter Ten: She & Her.

When school let out, Zane understood the frustration Victor had been feeling. In one day, by a single lunch period, rumors about True were *everywhere*. No one even used her name. The words "she" and "her" had somehow become synonymous for "True" in a matter of hours. When Victor said he wanted to drop his things off before they made their way to Zane's place, he was even more amazed and disappointed in the way everyone around them were acting.

As if it weren't bad enough that they were starting rumors and calling her anything but True, everyone around them walked on the opposite side of the street from the moment they'd left the parking lot. Of course, they would also take the long way around to avoid passing The Death House, but at least that was a normal occurrence.

For some reason Zane felt relieved that he'd never been treated that way since his move to Snowville. Yet, in that same moment, Zane also realized that True was probably a stronger person than him. He didn't know

Alexia D. Miller

anything about her, but surely it took a strong person to hear the rumors, to see their reactions to her and still not make a scene.

Zane saw the looks on the others' faces and shaking of heads as he and Victor crossed the street and walked a few feet behind her. He heard the disgusted remarks as they turned the corner of another street while they continued towards The Death House. Once near, Zane and Victor watched quietly as True made her way through the thick, black-iron gate and up the steps to the door.

Before she could reach for the doorknob, the door swung open and a beautiful woman with dark blonde hair stepped out to embrace her. "Welcome home sweetie! Sorry we couldn't pick you up. Trina is still at the lab and says it'll be a late night tonight so it might just be the two of us." She exclaimed in a chipper voice, "How was your first day?" She asked as her voice trailed off and they disappeared inside.

Victor mentioned that the woman he saw was one of True's aunts he mentioned before. As they continued walking, Zane couldn't help but wonder what True thought about Snowville and their school. "I figured as much," Zane sighed. "I'd hate it, you know? Having to come back to an aunt so happy for me after all of that stuff at school." Victor nodded in agreement. "You think she'll tell her aunt about the rumors or anything?"

Alexia D. Miller

"No," Victor said quickly. Almost as if he didn't have to think about it. "I don't think so."

"Well, that was a quick response." Zane said airily. "Why so sure?"

"Well, think about what you just said. Would you?" Victor responded as they neared his house.

"Touché."

. . .

"My mom isn't finished with the house yet." Victor said, stopping Zane at the front door. "She's kind of out of control and doesn't want anyone inside until it's perfect."

"Wow. Still? Man...when will she be done?" Zane asked in disbelief.

"Supposedly tomorrow. I hope so." Victor shrugged. Zane nodded as he stood on the porch and Victor disappeared inside.

A few minutes later Victor emerged from the door, shutting it behind him. "Took you long enough," Zane said playfully, jumping down the porch steps in one leap. Victor smiled, walking down the steps. "Wow. I took a *leap* and you *strolled* down the steps. Yep. That pretty much sums up our friendship." Zane laughed.

Alexia D. Miller

"What? Jumping down the steps requires too much energy. It's also potentially unsafe. What if I broke my neck?" Victor retorted, leading the way to Zane's house.

"Are you kidding me?" Zane laughed, "You sound like an old man! What if I was in danger? Would you run to save me?"

Zane laughed harder as he watched Victor look off in thought.

"Depends. When you say danger, are we talking imminent danger or like, I could have lunch, take a nap, and still have hours type of danger?" Victor asked lightly. "I need details. You have to be more specific."

"Oh my God. You really are an old man. You're horrible!" Zane snorted. "*Yeah.* Imminent danger. Like the I'm-minutes-away-from-being-sawed-in-half kind of danger." Zane said sarcastically.

"Tsk. I guess if I had to." Victor sighed, sticking his hand into his pocket, and taking out a smoky, almost black, crystal.

"Maybe this thing would bring me good luck." Victor said with a yawn. Considering Zane's own find, he half expected Victor's crystal to match his bright green eyes. Following his lead, Zane pulled his own out of his pocket, studying the light bouncing off the surface.

Alexia D. Miller

{ 101 }

"It's amazing, but It's totally weird. Finding two of them is one thing, but to think you found one too is kinda insane. I forget. You said you found yours in a totally different spot, right?" Zane asked, trying to recall their conversation a few weeks ago.

"On top of the building." Victor nodded as Zane unlocked the front door.

"Yeah...you never did tell me what you were doing on top of the freaking building." Zane said, not hiding his worry.

"Didn't I?" Victor more stated than asked. "I saw a bird fall."

"A bird? You went on a roof of an old building for a bird? I don't recall you being such an animal lover." Zane sighed in disbelief.

"Well no, I'm not really. The bird just fell right in the middle of flying. Like it had hit an invisible wall and was so stunned that it couldn't move anymore. But when I got up to the roof, the bird wasn't there. Just this." Victor said, looking at the crystal in his hand.

"That's insane. Maybe it was carrying it or something?" Zane wondered aloud as they walked inside and closed the door behind them. "Either way, I think you should steer clear of birds if it means you don't climb up another roof." Zane warned as Phelia walked towards them. With a smile Zane swooped her up in his arms and hugged her tight. "How was your day, Phelia?" He directed at her. She shrugged.

"It isn't a coincidence, you know." Phelia said, holding out the crystal Zane brought home for her for Victor to see, "It can't be. We should look into it."

"Right now?" Zane asked, looking at Victor who only raised an eyebrow. "I don't know, Phelia. I'm not sure these crystals are that important. They probably aren't even real."

"Come on, Zane. I'm curious enough. Besides, it's a little much to ignore and I've been stuck inside all day." Phelia said with a heavy sigh. Her large brown eyes pierced his soul. How could he say no? "Alright, but we aren't climbing on any roofs." Zane sighed.

. . .

Phelia hurried to get changed as Zane bolted up the stairs to find the dark box with the elegant white design on her closet shelf. He glanced at Phelia's blue overalls and white shirt and searched for a matching head piece. It seemed so long ago that their mother spent days ordering bows, headbands, barrettes, and the like for his sister. It was habit now to pick out one of them for her before they left. For Zane, it was important. Every time he placed one on her head, it felt like his mother was there, just out of sight,

Alexia D. Miller

protecting Phelia. He knew it was strange, considering he wasn't even sure what happened to people after they died, but he couldn't help himself.

Seeing that Phelia and her outfit were nowhere to be seen, Zane settled on a white cloth headband with blue flowers as he made his way back down the steps to tie it around her head. He saw Victor waiting patiently near the door. It wasn't simply that Victor watched this sort of thing play out at their house a million times, Zane was sure, but that he'd accepted things for the way they were.

Zane recalled that when Victor first saw their daily routine, he didn't hesitate to ask about it. More specifically, Victor asked about what he coined as Zane's "weird habits." Back then, Victor told Zane he thought he didn't understand because he didn't have siblings. Later, he said he realized that it had nothing to do with that. Rather, it had more to do with Phelia being so different from others her age. She spoke similarly to them—albeit in a more proper way—and seemed, in his opinion, even smarter than most of the families in Snowville. So, why coddle her? Why carry her around like a child? Why pick out her accessories as if she couldn't do it herself?

For Zane, the answer was simple: Phelia was still his little sister. She may be all those things and more, but didn't she still want—still *need*—those things? Did her being

Alexia D. Miller

different than other children mean that carrying her because she was small and cute was ridiculous? Was it inappropriate because she seemed older than her outward appearance? Or was it possible that he was wrong, and she didn't need him at all? Zane didn't have an answer. So, even now, he continued doing it.

"Zane?" Phelia called, interrupting his thoughts. "Is something the matter? What is it?" She asked as she slipped on her jacket. Zane shook his head and opened the door. "Nothing. Let's get going, yeah?" Phelia glanced at him silently before nodding and walking past him, out the door. Zane locked the door behind them as Victor and Phelia started a conversation he didn't hear, walking down the steps. Forcing his previous feelings away, Zane distracted himself with thoughts of the building and the crystals.

He'd never heard Victor say something so strange before. An invisible wall? Was it possible that the bird was hit with something and simply fell? Did all the crystals get dropped by that bird? He knew what Phelia said, but if finding random crystals wasn't a coincidence, then what the heck was it?

Grace...

Chapter Eleven: Minutes.

Grace spent every night since her visit to the Brand house in *That* room. If not for the company of her fiery red crystal, she knew she wouldn't have made it through all alone. The crystal wasn't just beautiful and warm between her hands. It had inspired hope in her when she was surrounded by nothing, and even though there was no light to reflect off of it, she could still make it out in the darkness. Grace felt even her heart warmed at the sight of it.

When the doors opened and closed behind her, when the harsh light flooded her eyes and her face, Grace knew that her foster parents were in a good mood. She tucked the crystal safely in her pocket. Grace could smell the sweet aroma of bread and sausage. She could feel the warmth from the stovetop wrap around her chilled body. She couldn't recall the last time it was warm. She couldn't recall the last meal she'd eaten.

Grace was so hungry that her stomach was in knots. So hungry that she almost felt ill. Her mind was in such a fog. For a moment, Grace thought that she may have been

Alexia D. Miller

dreaming the most wonderful and horrible of dreams all wrapped in one. When she saw the smile that crossed MaryAnne's lips, however, Grace knew that she wasn't dreaming. After all, MaryAnne never smiled in her dreams. Her smile was genuine, or at least as genuine as Grace had ever seen on a good day.

Even those, Grace knew, weren't real. They were in truth, the plastic smiles that sometimes scared her more than their anger. Fearing her foster parents, however, wasn't anything new. MaryAnne was a short woman that Grace thought she might outgrow in a few more years, but every day she also looked the same and Grace found something about that unsettling. Today, she wore her hair down and her colored heart apron. Which, from prior experience, was a sure sign that MaryAnne was ready and willing to *forgive* Grace for whatever she'd done wrong.

Grace watched her pale pink heels click against the floor, her bright red lipstick smile widening as she neared her. "Oh, look at you Grace! You're filthy!" MaryAnne exclaimed, almost as if she were surprised to see it. Something she often did when her punishment had been lifted. She pushed Grace roughly towards the bathroom. "You know the drill, girly." She said, pointing to the tub. "20 minutes." She said sternly. Grace's eyes went from one side of the room to the next, landing on the timer ticking away on the shelf.

Her foster father, Duke, called loudly from the kitchen. "Yes Dear!" MaryAnne called back in an uncomfortably cheerful tone. "If you're a good little chestnut, we'll work hard on your hair tomorrow." MaryAnne said before she went out the door and Grace listened to the sound of her heels receding down the hall. She knew that MaryAnne had used the word "chestnut" to refer, in one way or the other, to the color of her skin.

Grace recalled MaryAnne's words some time ago, as she watched seconds tick away on the timer. "I knew I would take you home," she'd said. MaryAnne told her on more than one occasion that she just *had* to adopt her from the moment she laid eyes on her. Having spent time with her and Duke alike, Grace knew she wasn't wrong in the past.

MaryAnne and Duke spoke about adopting her the same way someone would boast about an exotic pet. Grace was an unusual, unloved animal that should have felt blessed to be rescued. A poor soul who was lucky to be whisked off to a secure habitat for observation and study—at least until she was deemed ready to brave the world on her own.

And Grace had been happy, she had been honored. At least until she realized she'd been sent out into a world she no longer recognized. By then Grace also understood that it was a sure-fire way to kill an animal in the most destructive of ways. If she was from the jungle, then she was a domesticated endangered species. She was, by all intents and purposes, an animal that was confined in a cage. Maybe handicapped even, because she wasn't sure that she could survive outside of it if MaryAnne and Duke weren't there to feed her.

Grace remembered thinking that they'd been fascinated by the way she looked and not who she was. Grace, however, had never been able to object to the adoption. Even if she had been in a position to do so she wouldn't have, and she knew it. Back then, Grace thought she would be able to survive with anyone considering her families in the past. So, why not the strangely normal couple? Afterall, she'd wanted to feel "normal" too.

Grace pulled off her clothes and stepped into the water, looking again at the timer. By the time it finished its countdown, Grace had to be clean, dry, and dressed. She closed her eyes as she lathered her hair and body. When she was somewhat satisfied, she submerged her body in the water. It was hardly warm, but she wouldn't dare complain. She let her face rise and fall until it floated naturally just above the surface of the water.

. . .

Alexia D. Miller

When Grace opened her eyes again, she shot up in fear to look at the timer. Had it already been over 10 minutes? She sighed, at least she still had some time. Standing, Grace drained the water and rung-out her hair. She dried her hair the best she could first since it took the most time. Then she dressed in the clothes on the sink and brushed her teeth. Grace noticed her socks were short today, but again she didn't complain.

She reminded herself of the promise she'd made while she was being punished. She reminded herself that she wouldn't cause trouble or fight with anyone. That she wouldn't raise her voice at the idiots at school. She'd even run away if she had to. Whatever it took to stay out of trouble and not ruin her clothes. Anything and everything so long as she didn't have to go back to *That* room.

The timer struck zero and buzzed in a broken pattern. The sight of MaryAnne's brown hair over her face in the doorway—the result of her rush to peer around the doorframe and into the bathroom—frightened her, but she managed not to scream. "Get your laundry in the basket and come to the kitchen." MaryAnne said with a chuckle, almost as if she enjoyed scaring her. Grace nodded as MaryAnne made her way back towards the kitchen. Grace sighed in

Alexia D. Miller

relief, taking her crystal from her dirty clothes, and sliding it into the pocket of her dress.

. . .

In the kitchen, Grace sat silently at the table. She took slow, cautious bites of her food as she peeked over her fork at Duke. Donald "Duke" Speck was a tall, thin businessman who always wore silver rimmed glasses and whose wardrobe mostly consisted of khakis and tailored suits. His hair line had already begun to recede, and his blonde hair seemed to lose more of its luster every day.

He cleared his throat often as he read his papers, shifting in his seat, and folded the newspapers dramatically every time he took a bite, but never when he sipped his coffee. Grace remembered laughing about it once, until she was punished for that too. Since then, she learned to hold her breath every time she felt the familiar tickle at the back of her throat until she didn't want to laugh anymore.

MaryAnne eventually sat down at the table and she and Duke chatted lightly about having a party to celebrate his raise at the company. Grace never did know what sort of businessman he was, and she couldn't bring herself to ask. After what felt like an eternity, Grace finished her meal. Not knowing what she was or wasn't allowed to do, she sat

Alexia D. Miller

perfectly still at the table. As if feeling her anxiety, or perhaps just simply annoyed with Grace's constant staring, Duke glanced over at her. "Well don't just stand there," Duke said with a scoff. "Go on outside and play or something."

Grace wasted no time to put her dishes in the sink and head to the door, careful not to showcase her relief and joy before she was out of their sight. As she wrapped her hand around the doorknob MaryAnne's voice to her back made her heart race. When MaryAnne came beside her, Grace thought that she'd done something wrong already. That perhaps she'd forgotten something, and they were angry. Maybe she would have to go back because they changed their minds, and her punishment was not over.

Luckily, it was none of these things. Instead of an impending doom, Grace found that cookies and a jacket waited for her. "I baked some chocolate chip cookies. Eat them if you get hungry, okay?" Grace nodded as MaryAnne walked her out of the house and onto the porch. She took them, walking down the porch steps. "Thank you." Grace said politely.

MaryAnne didn't say another word to her. She watched silently as Grace looked over her shoulder at her. Her same bright red lipstick smile decorated on her face. Grace didn't have the courage to continue to look at her. Instead, she walked slowly onwards and listened for the

Alexia D. Miller

familiar sound of MaryAnne's heels on the porch board. She listened to the sound of the door closing and the lock engaging behind her before she started to run. She wanted to get away. She wanted to see Phelia.

True...

Chapter Twelve: Open doors.

*T*rue couldn't believe her eyes. She'd been able to come through the *door* to her "room" twice now. *How strangely magnificent,* True thought. *To find my way through a door that isn't a door, and a room that isn't really a room either.* The door was no physical thing she could reach out and touch. The room was in actuality, an entirely new place where she and other things existed beyond her own understanding. Nonetheless, this space was called a "room" in the journal she'd found. The journal that she'd just recently had time to read.

Unfortunately, it had only a handful of entries, but it led her to the empty wall upstairs in the abandoned temporary hospital she'd made her second home. More importantly, the journal had led her here and explained what she'd felt the moment she found the crystal at her feet: the crystal was so much more than what it seemed to be. The crystal was something beyond the limits of her imagination, and maybe even her wildest dreams. It was, in True's opinion, one of the best of her treasures.

Alexia D. Miller

This crystal could open the door the journal spoke of, which is more than what True could have hoped for. She knew that the entries mentioned that there were others, and they could open doors of their own. To think that there were separate yet linked spaces from her own beyond her reach, waiting to be discovered, seemed as exciting as it did lonely. True hadn't managed to open any other doors, but she wanted to venture. She wanted to gain experience with her crystal to do just that.

Still, she didn't want to get ahead of herself. She had no way to know, after all, if the others would ever make an appearance. Or, for that matter, if they were in Snowville to begin with. *It doesn't matter,* True thought, *this one door is enough. Even if the other crystals never come to open other doors. I have found something else here to cherish. For however long it lasts.*

In the moment that she'd thought to explore, she felt a light vibration. Quickly, True slid on her mask and jacket, flipping to the last entry in the journal as an echo of voices floated around from no specific direction. What was happening? Had she broken the room?

A pressure not unlike gravity itself pushed her to the ground. The space around her bent inwards and outwards in a nauseating wave until she could feel nothing at all.

Alexia D. Miller

Victor...

Chapter Thirteen: Onward.

Only a few minutes after they'd made it to the Snowville Temporary Infirmary—the building beside where he'd found the crystal, but apparently where Zane had gotten his—a young girl in a purple and black dress with thick red hair called out to Phelia. Victor didn't recall seeing her in Snowville although he realized he could hardly distinguish students at school, let alone the blur of people from the rest of town. Still, her outfit was in such contrast to her physical appearance that she looked even more foreign to him. Had there been such a girl in Snowville?

The girl breathlessly explained that she'd been on her way to visit the Brand house when she got a glimpse of Phelia and Zane, so she followed instead. Victor slowly looked her over, his attention centered around the dark bruise around her eye. "I don't know how you keep up with their long strides Phelia!" She laughed, before glancing in Victor's direction.

Alexia D. Miller

Once their eyes met, she quickly cleared her throat. "Sorry. I think I might be intruding. I'm Grace." She said with a smile.

Victor offered a polite smile back. "Hello Grace. You're a friend of Phelia's then?" She looked at Phelia and back to Victor as if trying to solve a puzzle. For the second time, Victor thought he might have said something wrong. Did he always do that when he spoke to girls?

"Uh...well we met in the rain. I sort of knocked her over when my eye was worse." She stated hesitantly.

"Remember the girl who had dinner at our place? I mentioned her during break." Zane chimed in, apparently trying to jog his memory.

"Hmm...somewhat." Victor shrugged. "You said a lot over the break."

Zane scoffed. "Don't mind him. I'm starting to think he's aging three times as fast as the rest of us." Zane said sarcastically.

"That doesn't sound like fun." Grace said, almost as if she'd taken him literally.

Phelia pressed her small hands on Grace's face and directed her head to different sides and angles. "Your eye definitely looks better. I thought father told you not to take off the bandage until you came. You sure took your time coming back." She huffed.

Alexia D. Miller

Grace chuckled awkwardly. "Sorry about that. I was...grounded."

"Grounded?" Phelia started, but Grace carried on with a slightly more upbeat demeanor.

"Boy am I surprised to find anyone else coming here! I was nervous thinking about coming alone." She sighed with a hand lightly on her chest. "Things were a little crazy around here the last time."

"Why would you come here?" Phelia and Zane asked in sync.

"Uh-oh. Is this place off-limits or something?" Grace asked warily. "Not that I'd normally choose to come here by myself anyway. This place is weird." She said, reaching into a pocket on her dress as she spoke. "I was coming here to see if I could find another one of these." She said excitedly, pulling out a crystal almost identical to the others only this one was red. "Isn't it cool? It's a real crystal, I think." Silently Victor, Phelia and Zane each reached into their pockets and pulled out their own crystals. So, there had been more of them after all? "No way! This is so cool!" She shouted.

Victor watched as Phelia clasped her hands behind her back and began pacing. "We all know each other in one way or another. We all have one. Isn't it strange? Why?" She asked. Zane was still in favor of the it's-a-coincidence stance. Victor himself wasn't sure. Sure, four people finding

Alexia D. Miller

similar rocks were easily a coincidence, but four seemingly legitimate crystals? It was something about it that felt different.

Normally, Victor still wouldn't bat an eye over something like this. Not even if it had been a diamond, but considering all the odd phenomena lately like the extra rain, whatever he'd seen happen to that bird, and finding the crystal in its place? It wasn't that Victor thought there was something special happening, but it almost felt like someone wanted them to be found. If it was someone's idea of a trick, they were one heck of a magician. That, or they had nothing better to do than to harass kids and waste crystals. Which seemed unlikely.

Phelia shook her head at Zane, "I'm not certain, Zane...but to say it is simply a coincidence doesn't ring true to me. We have lived here quite some time and it hadn't rained crystals before." Phelia said, her brows lifting. "Zane. When did you say you happened across these again?" "Hmm...I can't tell you an exact date and time per se, but near here. On the steps by the door. One of those days it was raining. During that whole rain anomaly thing. When I brought home that fresh baked bread for a certain someone." He directed at her, squinting his eyes.

Phelia frowned. "I said I was sorry Zane." She huffed. Grace tilted her head, as lost as Victor. What was

Alexia D. Miller

this about fresh bread? He shook his head. That didn't matter. What did matter was that Zane mentioned the rain. Victor remembered that it was raining the day he saw the bird. When he made it to the roof, however, the bird was nowhere to be seen. If it had been hit hard enough to stop mid-flight, then it should have been too stunned or too hurt to just get up and fly away. It hadn't even pulled its wings back to its body when it fell.

"I know. I know. I forgive you." Zane smiled. "Anyway, go on."

Phelia continued. "If the two of you also found them during the extra rainy days then that would be another important detail, wouldn't it?" Victor nodded, rolling his crystal between his fingers.

"Now that you mention it..." Grace said, looking at Phelia, "It was definitely raining. What does that mean?"

Phelia stopped pacing. "I'm not entirely sure. It could mean someone has been leaving them here. It's hard to say." She smiled. "Whatever the case, let's have a look around. If we're lucky, we might find a way in. If we turn up empty handed at least we did what we came to do."

"Do we have to?" Grace whined. "We could get in trouble. We could get caught. It might not even be safe in there."

Grace had a point. They don't know how they'd gotten the crystals or if someone was looking for them.

Alexia D. Miller

Victor never was one to venture into uncharted territory without good reason. Were investigating crystals a good reason? The building was old. Victor knew better, however. If Phelia of all people wanted to get inside there would likely be no stopping her. Zane would surely follow her, and Victor didn't want to wait around not knowing either.

"Well, you can always stay out here and keep watch." Zane said. "You know, if you want to."

Grace looked at Phelia to Zane and back again. As if suddenly on edge, she looked over her shoulders. Her eyebrows creased and she shook her head erratically. "No. No. No. I am *not* staying out here alone. Broad daylight or not." She ran her hands over her face. "But if the place caves in on us or something and we all die, I'm haunting all of you."

"You said if we all die." Phelia said with a smile.

"Fine! I'll haunt your families and annoy each of you for all of eternity!" She yelled, swiping her arms in the air in frustration.

Phelia...

Chapter Fourteen: The Empty Wall.

Phelia was anything but surprised or impressed. They'd found their way in through a low window several minutes ago. Inside, there were withered beds and bulky broken monitoring machines. There was a large table with stacks of meaningless papers, and a relatively clean fireplace. The smell of dust hung heavy on the air but Phelia felt that there should have been more of it. After all, this building sat empty since her family moved to Snowville and even longer, if she had to guess. If she wasn't mistaken, dust was missing from the windowsill as well. Should she mention it to Zane and the others?

Going up the broken staircase, Phelia noticed she'd received hardly any help from Zane on her way up. While she hadn't had much difficulty making her way, she did find it odd that he hadn't swooped in and picked her up as he often did. She knew he'd been a little distracted since they'd left home, but she wasn't able to decipher what was bothering him. Considering she could almost always tell what was on her brother's mind, it was an unsettling thing to

Alexia D. Miller

notice. The more she tried, the more she failed to understand. It was almost as if something stood in the air between them and blocked her view.

As they neared the top of the stairway, Phelia immediately noticed the film of dust was much lighter now than down below. Light shimmered in from a nearby window. As they walked forward, Phelia could see that even the doors were relatively clean. "Someone has been here." Phelia said aloud. "Cleaning, perhaps?"

"Yeah. *Really* recently too, from the look of it." Zane chimed in from behind. He walked into a door to the left, which was a small office with neatly stacked papers and books.

"It doesn't look like anyone has been sleeping here." Victor said from a room further off with books lined beside a chair and even more of them on shelves. It had to have been some sort of study.

Unsettled by a loud crash, they bolted towards the way they'd come. To Phelia's surprise, Grace sat on the floor woven between boxes. "Ow." She grumbled. When had Grace fallen behind? Phelia wondered. "I hope it wasn't loud enough for anyone to notice." Grace groaned.

"Yeah well, *we* noticed." Zane chuckled. "But no one comes here."

"Be careful." Victor said, offering Grace his hand.

Alexia D. Miller

"That's what we believed before all of us ended up here." Phelia directed at Zane, her eyes drawn to the large empty space behind Victor and Grace. Grace's squeals forced her attention elsewhere. "Oh no!" Grace said, pushing the boxes around in a frenzy. "Oh no!"

"What's wrong?" Victor asked as Grace shook her head. "I lost it! I must've dropped it when I fell. My crystal!" She cried.

"It's alright," Victor said, moving boxes out of Grace's path. "If you just lost it then it can't be far. We'll find it." And find it they did. In a matter of seconds Grace was celebrating her reunion, crystal in hand. It had rolled behind her, directly to the middle of the large open space on the wall where no furniture had been piled up nor miscellaneous frames hung, which differed from the rest of the room. The crystal had made it to the exact same white space Phelia found herself staring at not long ago.

"Woah." Grace huffed; her eyes widened in surprise. Phelia and Zane made their way to her side as Grace held her crystal out for them to see. "It's...glowing? This is *so* cool!" She smiled in amazement. "It's never done that before!"

"Okay, but how is it doing that?" Zane asked slowly.

"It's glowing up the same color as the crystal." Victor chimed in, pulling his own out of his pocket. Sure enough, his was doing the same. What exactly was happening?

Phelia wasted no time looking at her own. "Grace? Did you perhaps do or touch something in particular?" Phelia asked curiously, trying to put the pieces together in her mind.

"No way." Grace answered quickly. "Unless you count those stupid boxes. I was trying not to leave fingerprints."

"What?" Zane asked bewildered.

"Well *yeah*." Grace said without hesitation. "In case we got caught. I hoped we wouldn't though."

"Meanwhile, you hoped we'd leave all the fingerprints?" Zane laughed. "How would you explain how you ended up in here? Kidnap?" He asked, amused.

Grace shrugged. "I hadn't gotten that far yet."

"It's an abandoned building," Victor said, shaking his head. "If for some reason anyone came here, they'd find a million people's prints."

"Good point." Grace said, her eyes still on the glowing crystal. "Everyone did say that someone else had been here."

Whether someone had been there or not wasn't Phelia's number one concern. She wasn't worried about police nor any other adult that may find their way inside. What she was interested in were the crystals. What exactly

Alexia D. Miller

were they doing? "These crystals," Phelia began, "It's almost as if...they're reacting to something." She said.

The moment the words fell from her lips, Phelia wondered if she'd come to regret it. A noise—something akin to a single chime—sounded on air, shaking the space around them.

What followed was an immediate warping of the room. Colors swirled and bent on others, the walls became indistinguishable from the ceiling or the floor, and an unnatural heaviness filled the air.

"*Phelia!*" Zane's voice called in a panic as she felt his arms tighten around her. A flicker of light started to take shape in front of her before it disappeared. Had she truly seen a door or was that a result of the dizziness in her head? As the misshapen colors faded into blackness, she could still feel the warmth of Zane's arms. Phelia called out to him, unsure of what was happening, but heard no response. In fact, Phelia heard nothing.

Alexia D. Miller

Zane...

Chapter Fifteen: Mirror.

Zane could feel Phelia still there in his arms as the sensation of falling began. How was it possible that they could fall surrounded by nothing but complete darkness? How was it possible that every time he called out to Phelia, to Victor, or even to Grace, that there was never an answer? He fought away his panic, worried that somehow, he would frighten Phelia. Moments later his body slammed down against something below him.

Something that he could not see in the never-ending darkness. Just the same, he felt the weight on his chest and somehow found himself relieved, knowing that Phelia was still there. What was this place? Why couldn't he see? "Phelia?" he called out again, "Can you see anything? Anything beyond this...this blackness?" Yet again he was met with silence. He did not hear Phelia's voice, or anyone's for that matter.

Zane felt his heart racing, heard the pounding in his ears, and his concern rising to new heights. He wasn't sure anymore. Did he fail to grab his little sister? Had he reached

Alexia D. Miller

out and grabbed something else instead? Did he think he was speaking aloud but he'd just been talking to himself in his head?

No. No. Zane thought to himself. *I grabbed her. Of course, I grabbed her. Right when the chaos started. But did I ever really speak or was it all in my head?* He questioned. As he tried to figure out the answer, the darkness around him slowly began to fade. Eventually, giving way to a midnight sky full of stars. He lay on his stomach, his head tilted back in an awkward position. How could he have been on his stomach? He'd been standing upright with Phelia in his arms before. Even if he did fall, wouldn't he have fallen on his back?

"Phelia? Phelia!" Zane called, feeling movement below him. He quickly rolled onto his back and turned his head to see Phelia. "Phelia!" He exclaimed, as she slowly made her way to her feet, her breathing labored. Following suit, Zane jumped to his feet and wrapped his arms around her only to be shoved. "Phelia...?" Zane started in confusion.

Taking a deep breath, Phelia frowned up at him. "The next time we are sucked into a wormhole-something-or-other, don't grab me. You nearly suffocated me to death!" She snapped. "Honestly, Zane! I'd have been better off on my own."

Alexia D. Miller

Zane couldn't believe her attitude. He'd only been trying to help. Trying to keep her safe. "It was an accident. I didn't mean to hurt you." Still, Phelia glared at him angrily. "I mean it. Don't grab me." Phelia huffed.

"Fine!" Zane hissed, shaking his head. "Whatever."

There was probably some truth to what Victor said in the past, Zane thought. Phelia likely didn't need his help in the first place. In this case, she didn't want it either. The bitterness he'd felt waned as he heard Victor call his name and Zane realized he'd been so wrapped up in looking for Phelia that he didn't notice anything else around him. What happened?

Victor walked up from behind him, Grace by his side. "Glad we're all in one piece." Victor sighed.

"No kidding." Zane said, shaking his head. "What was all of that?" Zane asked only now aware that his crystal was in his hand. "It's not glowing anymore."

"None of them are." Phelia said, looking up at them and holding her crystal out in front of her.

"Guys..." Grace said, her arm raised as she pointed ahead of them. "We are *so* not in Snowville anymore."

Several feet ahead of them was a large white sign adorned with lights around its border. Written in large cursive-like font was the word "Mirror" which overshadowed

Alexia D. Miller

the small ones above it that read "welcome to." Zane looked back up at the star-filled sky then down at his feet.

The grass was soft and green, like standing on clouds. When he ran his fingers through it, he had to fight the thought to tell Victor. If it felt that soft to him, Victor wouldn't hesitate to go to sleep in it. Even in some strange place they'd never seen before. He did his best to focus ahead of them. There he saw a road where lights ran up parallel to one another, following the road.

"Mirror?" Grace said. "This place doesn't look like glass to me. And I thought Snowville's name was weird." She shook her head, her hands on her hips.

"Phelia frowned. "Either we all are having the exact same dream, or...there is some other explanation."

"We're all having the *exact* same dream at the *exact* same time. Yeah, *not* likely." Zane snorted.

Grace tapped her finger against her crystal. "I don't suppose these things can just glow up now, huh? You know, poof us back to where we came from?" She plopped down on the ground and air lightly shuffled her dress. "I don't think that's how they really work, but how should I know? I've never had to deal with voodoo-magic crystals before." She whined.

Alexia D. Miller

"No way." Zane said quickly. "There's no such thing as voodoo crystals. Besides, even if they were it's unlikely that they'd end up in a place like Snowville."

Grace shrugged, "Who knows? Point is, we've got to do *something.*"

Zane nodded in agreement. "She's right. We've got to get back home. We can't just stay here." He continued, throwing his hands in the air. "Though who knows where home is from this place."

"Let's follow the road then." Phelia suggested, already starting to walk towards it. "Someone must be able to help us. There are lights so it won't be so dark, and the road must lead somewhere. A road doesn't simply build itself. Surely someone must have built it."

"And if we're really lucky, we'll get a ride home." Victor yawned, following a few steps behind Phelia.

"You just don't want to walk." Zane scoffed.

"Not wanting to overexert myself isn't a crime. Do you want to walk aimlessly down a road that ends nowhere?" He asked.

"Don't say that." Grace said quickly, jogging to catch up and Zane fell into step behind her. "That sounds horrible."

"There you go talking like an old man again. We don't know that the road ends nowhere. Don't scare people like that." Zane said.

Alexia D. Miller

"Well it feels like it'll never end already." Victor yawned again, slipping his hands into his pockets.

"But we just started walking!" Grace laughed.

Whatever the case, Zane didn't like this. If the crystals had brought them there, Zane had the feeling returning wouldn't be so simple. Definitely not as simple as hitching a ride to Snowville.

Grace...

Chapter Sixteen: Crazy.

Grace couldn't help constantly gazing up at the sky. On either side of the road were the tallest trees she'd ever seen. The sky itself was filled with more stars than she thought existed. Each cluster of stars seemed brighter than the last, following them on the road forever. It was almost enough to make her forget the fear she faced before. Almost.

Grace recalled all too vividly the feeling of the world changing shape around her. She remembered the nausea she felt and the dizziness. Grace even remembered the moment that all the light seemed to be sucked from the room, replaced by a cold void and blackness. It had swallowed her and everything her eyes could see.

It was a darkness that felt very much like *That* room she hated. So similar in fact, that for a moment Grace believed she was still there. That she dreamed MaryAnne and Duke let her out that morning, that she'd never had sausages for breakfast, or been walked out the door with cookies. That she ever saw Phelia and Zane walking and decided to catch up with them, glad to be in the sun again.

Alexia D. Miller

Still, at least in *That* room Grace knew that an outside existed. At least she knew that there was an up and a down, a floor and ceiling, that she and other people existed, even if she felt alone. All those things were just on the other side of her prison—of her punishment. There in that blackness, however, there had been **nothing**.

Grace made many mistakes suspended in that nothingness. At first, she thought she died, or worse, altogether ceased to exist. Then, she assumed that she wasn't alone, which was a costly mistake. Because in realizing that no one could hear her, could see her even, it made everything worse. After that, it didn't take long for her to become consumed with fear.

So, when Grace had been able to open her eyes and Victor was there calling her name, she couldn't believe it. She'd never heard her name sound so beautiful. She couldn't believe she wasn't alone. She was more than relieved.

So much so, that tears begun to rain down her cheeks and Victor did his best to console her. He put his hand gently on the top of her head and smiled in understanding. "Yeah. You were scared, huh?" He'd asked, before telling her that everything was okay. They'd stayed there like that until her tears dried up and she jumped to her feet, suddenly remembering that Phelia and Zane should have been with them.

. . .

Grace didn't know how long they'd been walking down the road. She wished she had a watch. She wished Eustis' idiot friend hadn't smashed the only one she ever had. Still, if she did have a watch would it have worked? She didn't know. She did know, however, that it had been quite some time since they passed the curve in the road and they hadn't seen a single soul. Grace tried not to think about the cookies in her pocket, checking to make sure they were still there. Who knew when they'd need to eat them?

"Look," Phelia said, directing her attention back ahead of them. "There's something there in the distance."

Finally! Grace thought, squinting her eyes to focus. *A Building? Yes. A building of some sort, and buildings meant people.* "Let's hurry up!" Grace yelled, bolting on ahead. She heard the slight protests of the others, but she couldn't stop her feet. They carried her ahead and didn't stop until she could see the building clearly.

It was massive and beige, even larger than The Death House. Something akin to a mansion she was sure. Through each window a dim light shined through and Grace could

Alexia D. Miller

make out the sound of music. Even more than that, she could just make out the sound of voices from somewhere further even though she couldn't understand what they said. Grace didn't care, she was happy enough to hear anything at all.

"See that?" Grace said excitedly as the others caught their breath beside her. "We're close. Someone ought to be able to get us home now." She smiled.

"What's that sound?" Phelia asked looking about.

"A sea of murmurs? Voices...some sort of music?" Victor asked.

"I don't like it. It's sorta creepy." Zane said with a frown.

"How can being saved be creepy? It means there are people, right?" Grace asked. "Hello? Anyone there?!" Grace called, and Zane quickly shushed her.

What was his problem? Didn't he say they needed to get back to Snowville? How were they supposed to get help if they didn't even try to reach anyone? "What?" Grace asked pointedly.

"Grace, we don't even know where we are. We can't just run around screaming at the top of our lungs. We might scare someone."

"Oops." Grace said. "I didn't think about that." She said apologetically.

Alexia D. Miller

The sound of music and voices didn't pause. There weren't any calls from strangers in response to her yelling. *Okay,* Grace thought, *that's a little creepy after all.* As she thought it, Phelia frowned.

"I don't think we should run about screeching, but we certainly can't stay put either. Let's keep going. There's bound to be someone around." Phelia said, taking the lead again.

. . .

"What is this?" Victor said, clearly as surprised as the rest of them. It had taken some time to pass the large house. None of them, Grace was sure, could have expected something like this on the other side. Every building in view were identical save for the numbers on the front. The music they'd been hearing played through a loudspeaker next to the largest clock Grace had ever seen.

Two women, one with bright brown hair and one with neon orange braids, stopped walking feet ahead of them. Each smiled the same smile and offered them a good morning in sync. If not for their outfits, their painted skin and the same smile spread across their face, Grace would say they looked nothing alike.

Alexia D. Miller

As they began to continue walking, the orange haired woman touched the metal chain collar around her neck. Grace took note of the large number four beneath her fingers. "Wear collars. The Catcher." She said, leaving Grace confused as they disappeared.

"Did they just say good morning?" Zane asked, prompting everyone to look at the enormous clock ticking seconds away.

"There's no way it's 10AM." Grace said in disbelief. "Their clock is obviously broken. What's the point of having a huge clock if it doesn't even work right?"

Phelia shook her head, pointing ahead of them. "They said something about collars. Everyone is wearing them." She said. Sure enough, crowds of people walked in every direction ahead of them. Each of them wearing a metal collar on their necks with a number printed on the front.

"Well, what's the catcher then?" Grace asked and the others shook their heads. As far as Grace was concerned, these people—or aliens, whatever they were—and this place was crazy. She also knew that out of all of things, someone else's skin tone wasn't her business, but why were they all green?

"What's with their skin? Are they all sick or something? Is it paint? Why are they green?" Grace asked aloud.

Alexia D. Miller

"Not exactly green. Their skin is teal. Not that it really matters." Victor commented. Whatever it was, Grace had never seen anyone like them.

"They look healthy to me." Phelia said, walking over to the nearest person. "We have to talk to them."

She'd assumed it was paint at first, but was it possible it was their natural skin color?

. . .

According to the clock, they'd gone about for hours, asking everyone they met a series of questions. Feeling helpless and exhausted, they made their way over to a bundle of trees and sat on the ground. "This is impossible!" Grace shouted. "It's like they all just ignore us or give us funny looks! What's their problem?!"

"Almost like they don't want to talk to us." Zane frowned.

Hearing a shuffling from behind them, Grace turned around to see a tall boy with deep brown eyes walking towards them. His skin was the same teal as the rest, and he also wore a collar around his neck. Only, his was a gold leather band with the numbers 0001 at its center. A gold, Grace saw, that matched his hair. Which was a bright, shimmering gold like his eyebrows and lashes.

"They can't speak to you." He gestured towards them.

Alexia D. Miller

"What do you mean?" Phelia asked, seeming completely unfazed by the boy's drastic features.

"I mean," the boy said with a smile that showcased his bright white teeth, "that they are mutes. They can't speak to you. There are a few that may be able to say a few words to you, but that's generally the extent of it." From the sound of his voice, Grace knew that he was likely older than all of them. Older or not, she didn't understand.

"Huh? But you're talking to us." Grace said, puzzled as he sat down in the center of their broken circle.

"Yes." He laughed. "I can, and Mr. One paid top dollar for me too. Well, me and my sister, that is. Gold hair is a rarity, but *two* of us with golden hair also capable of a full range of speech? It's completely unheard of." He shrugged. Grace couldn't understand why he was talking about himself that way. "Then again, so are all of you. Your skin, your hair, and surely you aren't mute. Although your outfits aren't up to code. I'm sure Mr. One would pay top-dollar for you as well."

"Nothing you are saying is making any sense. Mr. One? Up to code? What is this place and how do we get out of here?" Zane asked, irritated. The boy tilted his head and clicked his tongue.

"Mr. One is my owner, of course. The richest of them all. Surely if you don't know that you aren't from here. I've

Alexia D. Miller

already heard the rumors that we had a gang of intruders. This is Mirror. Where might you be from?"

Phelia looked at the boy thoughtfully. "Snowville." She answered. The boy again tilted his head. "Never heard of it." He smiled and clapped his hands. "The way out? I might know...maybe that door is the way to go?"

"What door?" Victor asked.

Suddenly the boy jumped to his feet, sprinting off. "I've got to go tell her!" He looked over his shoulder in their direction, "At night those out and about without their master or their collars are subject to be rounded up by The Catcher. If he catches you, you'll be sold to the highest bidder!"

"W-wait!" Zane called after him to no avail.

In a matter of seconds, the golden-haired boy had zig-zagged his way through trees and buildings and disappeared from their sight. Grace's mind reeled. "Guys? What did he mean sold?" Grace asked warily, the boy's words sinking in.

"I don't have a clue. Honestly, I'm not trying to stick around and find out." Zane huffed, getting to his feet. "We have to find the door he was talking about."

Grace didn't argue. She wasn't planning to meet this Catcher and she wasn't planning on being sold to anyone either. Standing up and looking back towards the clock,

Alexia D. Miller

Grace's stomach dropped. The clock ticked away the seconds to midnight.

When the clock chimed, the ground began to shake. The tremor was so strong that it forced them to the ground. The noise that followed was so loud that Grace was almost sure she'd go deaf by the time it ended.

. . .

When the ground settled, the loud noise vanished, and they had recovered, the people were nowhere to be seen. The loudspeaker no longer played music and the lights faded away one after the other until there was a moment of complete darkness. "Everyone okay?" Zane's voice called from somewhere on Grace's right. "Yeah!" Grace called, followed by Victor and Phelia. They weren't on their way to Snowville, but at least they weren't suspended in nothing all over again.

"What is happening?" Phelia's voice called. She sounded close enough that Grace wondered if she could reach out and touch her. As soon as Grace's fear was starting to resurface, light slowly returned to the sky. A sunrise unlike any other Grace witnessed before unfolded above them. A cloudy swirl of blue hues surrounded a snow-white sun that faded until Grace could almost see through it. It almost seemed to reflect the sky itself.

"So that's why they call it Mirror. Probably...?" Grace said in awe. "Is that even possible?" She asked no one in particular. Maybe this place would drive her crazy.
"It's at least possible here." Phelia replied. It seemed to only take minutes for the sun to rise high in the sky, but according to the clock it had been hours.

"This place is *insane*!" Grace wailed. "Day is night and night is day! Minutes are hours?? Who knows how long it's really been!"

"All the more reason to get out of here." Victor said, though his tone suggested to Grace that he wasn't particularly bothered. Meanwhile, Phelia placed her hands behind her back and began to pace again. "Regardless of the time, we have been warned about roaming at night. Which means we must hurry. The boy—or whatever he may be called— mentioned that he knew of a door. A door that leads out of Mirror. He failed to mention, however, what door and where it is located."

"Well we can't just go around trying the door to every house looking for the way out of this place. That would take forever." Zane sighed, running his fingers over his face. Grace understood how he felt. Especially if minutes were like hours. Who knows how long it would take?

Alexia D. Miller

Grace watched Phelia smile, her eyes glistening as she stopped pacing. *She thought of something,* Grace thought. She could feel it. The moment Phelia had an epiphany.

"We only need to knock on **one** door," Phelia said with a nod. "Considering."

Before Grace could ask, a booming voice bellowed. Grace's attention snapped to the space across from them. In one of the houses, a large creature called out, "Where are your collars? Where are your owners?!" It was a human-like voice deeper than any Grace had ever heard. A voice that came from the belly of a **what**? Grace's jaw dropped.

Was there actually an *elephant* yelling at them?! Its steps shook the ground slightly as it made its way out of the front door and onto the porch. In its hand he held a wooden cane decorated with a green sphere at the top. The elephant wore no clothes, save for a scarf draping around its neck. In her shock, Grace became overtly aware of a myriad of other massive animals standing in each doorway. She could place a good number of them; a racoon, a squirrel with pink-rimmed glasses, and a parrot loudly boasting about something. Too afraid to turn her head and look at any more of them, Grace stood completely still.

The elephant's thick trunk curled into the air as he screeched "CALL THE CATCHER!" The familiar

Alexia D. Miller

juddering sound like a trumpet echoed in the air. Grace nor the others exchanged words or stole a glance in their direction. They simply darted forward as quickly as they could. They carried on running, their hearts racing, hearing the blood rush in their ears until none of them could continue anymore. It didn't matter exactly which way they went or who followed behind who. Grace had only been concerned about hearing their shallow breaths and feet stomping against the ground at her back.

Eventually, they took shelter behind a tree, all of them wheezing and shaken. Even Victor looked strained and tired. Grace coughed through the stinging, sharp pains in her chest. Her lungs practically begged for air, for relief. None of them uttered a single word until they were kneeling beside one another, seemingly recovered.

"We're close." Phelia said. "Very close. We just need to find his door."

"His?" Zane asked, peeking around the tree. "Whose?"

"I don't think his door is the way out itself. The so-called Mr. One that is, but if we were to find his door, we should find the boy from before. The one with the golden hair who might know how to leave." Phelia explained.

"Right and you figure the number on the collar..." Zane started, smacking his fist onto his palm.

Alexia D. Miller

"Yes." Phelia nodded. "The number should be the house number if I'm not mistaken. A number, or address, that tells them who the boy belongs to." Phelia said, seeming to finish Zane's thought.

"So, we are all just going to ignore what she just said?" Grace asked in disbelief. "That boy, these humans or whatever they are, just belong to gigantic animals that talk and walk on two legs?"

"For now," Victor said, putting a hand on Grace's shoulder. "we don't have the luxury of harping on it."

"This place is ridiculous," Grace huffed as she crossed her arms over her chest. "Ridiculous, ridiculous, R-I-D-I-C-U-L-O-U-S." She emphasized.

"We should hurry." Phelia said, this time looking around the trunk of the tree herself. Grace shook her head, stepping beside her preparing herself for another dash. Only, no dash would follow. The ground began to shake more forcefully than the last. An earthquake? Grace wondered, fighting to grab hold of Phelia's hand, the others already interlocking fingers.

"What's happening now?" Zane yelled, his left hand gripping the bark of the tree in front of them. Seconds later a thick, white net pulled them away from the tree and they were carried off. They swayed tangled and shocked in the net, over the shoulder of a gray dog with long, shaggy hair.

Alexia D. Miller

Soon to be stuffed into the back of his white truck. Grace didn't have to see the bolded words on the side to know who the dog must have been. The Catcher. How much more insane could this Mirror place get? Grace couldn't believe it. They didn't just have talking, walking animals, but ones that could drive too?

. . .

The sun was still high in the sky by the time they were driven away. Even when they'd been stuffed into a cage behind a curtain sometime later, Grace could see the platform that the cage sat on, some massive wooden thing that elevated them. She knew it wasn't a comfort that the sun was even visible. It was only a matter of time before it would set, and the light would fade. Only a matter of time before night was present again but would be called morning.

"How do we get out of this one?" Victor asked. Grace wasn't sure if he was really asking. They were locked up alone in a cage, waiting to be sold and she wasn't even sure how it locked. There was no chain or padlock to be seen. There was nothing to try to force open, and the steel bars were too close together for them to attempt escaping through them.

Alexia D. Miller

Grace didn't know what to think. If they couldn't open it, they'd all end up sold. Where would they go? Would they be sold to the same household or would they be separated and never able to escape Mirror again? Grace suddenly hated Snowville just a little less now. At least Snowville didn't capture innocent children and sell them off. Or have gigantic, terrifying animals stomping around and screaming at them.

A flood of voices came from the other side of the curtain, followed by vibrations. Something Grace now knew was the sound of the animals' movement. "The Catcher brought us *extremely* unique gifts today!" A thundering voice boomed. Grace wondered what kind of animal was speaking. "As such, we will have an early auction and give him a percentage of the profits. Four great new gifts!" The voice said excitedly. Followed by the sound of cheers, claps and stomps that shook the entire platform.

"Just how many of those things are out there?" Victor said, irritated. "I don't think it is necessary to be this outrageously loud."

"If I didn't know you any better, I'd think you were so upset because you can't take a nap while we're stuck in this enormous cage." Zane directed cynically at Victor. There was no way Grace could imagine getting any sleep. Not there, and maybe not home either if they ever made it back.

Alexia D. Miller

"As many of them that are interested in owning us forever." Phelia said, gloomily. To Grace, Phelia sounded as if she had given up. They couldn't give up, right? They had to do something. They had to fight, or escape. Anything. They needed her big, smart brain to keep thinking.

"Show them to usssss." Another voice demanded. Passionate voices echoed in agreement. "We want to ssseeeee!" Was it a snake?

"I understand that *some* of you *may* have caught a glimpse of them and others did not have the chance. However, you don't need to fuss. I'll cut you a deal! Tonight, I will showcase them all first! Isn't that a treat?" The first voice boomed again.

"We have to get out of here!" Grace yelled out, kicking the bars of the cage so hard that pain shot up her foot. She instinctively kneeled to hold it with a dry sob. "Stupid cage!" She yelled spitefully. She knew it didn't make a difference, but it still made her feel better to call it names.

"Grace." Phelia called, her face filled with worry. "You can't just kick steel." She said disapprovingly.

"Well what else am I supposed to do?" Grace huffed.

Suddenly, a metallic whirling sounded above them, towards the top of the cage. A few moments of ticking later, the front of the cage lifted, and Grace was so happy that she ignored the throbbing pains in her foot. "Guess I'm stronger

Alexia D. Miller

than I thought!" She celebrated, rushing out of the cage with the others close behind.

"You're welcome." A voice called from Grace's right. Turning her head, she saw the golden-haired boy from before. Only now he had a large white bundle in his arms and there was a girl beside him. Grace figured she must have been the sister he mentioned before. They were nearly identical. Her hair was longer than his, but the same shimmering gold. They shared the same brown eyes, long blonde lashes, and matching leather collars around their necks.

"Huh? You two let us out of there?" Zane asked. "We'd better hurry to the door." The girl said, not bothering to answer his question. She quickly sprinted off, not unlike what they'd seen her brother do before. Putting his index finger to his lips, the boy slowly jogged after her, silently suggesting they follow.

Although Grace was happy to be out of the cage, she found herself a little disappointed she hadn't opened the door after all. Still, she had time for those feelings later, after they made it safely out of Mirror. Even if she didn't know the boy or his sister's name, Grace knew that if she saw them running off, she would do everything in her power to keep up with them, even without the invitation. Losing that boy twice wasn't an option. Luckily for Grace and the others, the siblings seemed to slow down for their benefit as they went.

They were led to an area of trees and bushes not far from the stage where they'd been held against their will. The space was filled with the same lush grass they'd seen when they entered Mirror. Behind a cluster of large trees sat an archway. Looking closely, Grace could see that two trees twisted together, one branch after the other entangled, so much so that she only knew there were two of them because of the trunks at the bottom.

"This is the door?" Grace asked, confused, looking at the space and the other trees beyond it. "That doesn't look like a door."

"The other was a wall before, "Phelia said, "so, I'm inclined to believe it. At least this one looks like something to walk through."

"How do we get it to work?" Zane asked, looking to the golden-haired duo for an explanation.

"Perhaps the same way you opened the other door." They said in sync. But Grace couldn't recall how that had happened. She hadn't meant to fall, or for her to lose her crystal among boxes.

"Ugh. So, I have to fall again?" Grace asked begrudgingly, taking her crystal from the pocket of her dress.

Alexia D. Miller

Zane shuffled through his pocket to take out his own crystal. "I don't even remember putting my crystal away." He said, unsure.

"I hadn't given it any thought before, but neither do I," Phelia said.

Victor shrugged, searching his pocket for his crystal.

"I don't remember. Hard to remember anything after all that chaos."

Grace tried to mimic the steps she'd taken in the building. She even pretended to move boxes with her arms after she forced herself to fall.

"Well that didn't work," Grace said, dusting off her dress. She looked over at the twins who looked at each other silently, not offering an answer. Grace could hear the river of angry voices bellowing from behind them. So loud and unexpected that it frightened her. Her eyes wide, she looked at the others.

"Do you think they know we've escaped?" Zane asked.

"You'd better hurry." The boy said. "They'll be looking for you."

"And they'll call The Catcher again," his sister chimed in.

"We really need to get back home." Phelia sighed.

"Look." Victor said, bringing attention to his crystal. Sure enough, it was glowing. Grace opened her fist, seeing her own begin to shine. Before she could think to ask the questions on her mind, a white light flickered from the entangled trees. Seconds later, the ground seemed to fall from beneath their feet and the sky began to shift.

"Thank you!" Zane's voice called from somewhere in the dizzying space around her. Grace could just make out the boy's smile. "No problem." He said, his voice reaching her too long after she'd seen his lips move. "It's the least we could do."

"We owed you one anyway." The girl said.

What did she mean? How could they have owed them anything? She didn't have the time to ask. She felt a wave of air pulling her through the door and the white light surrounding her almost twice as bright as it had been only seconds before. Slowly the white light faded and gave way to a moment of darkness.

Alexia D. Miller

True...

Chapter Seventeen: Friends-Not-Friends.

True walked to the window, looking down at the others rushing away on the street. The sun was only just setting in Snowville but True felt as if she'd been away for days. When really, it had only been hours since she left home. She wasn't even late enough to make her aunts worry. True could only assume that time really did work differently in Mirror. She'd thought so the moment she saw their night sky.

Looking at the journal in her hand, she touched the crystal around her neck. The journal had been right. There were others with a crystal. "Where the crystals come together, worlds collide and doors will open," True said quietly reciting a phrase from the journal.

Phelia, was the youngest, True recalled. Yet, she'd felt ancient and knowledgeable. More so for being so young. True had gotten the impression that Phelia was like fusing books together to create a person, if such a thing were ever possible. Zane was Phelia's older brother. True had been able to tell from the moment she'd seen them together; *Protective*, True said to herself, *but troubled.*

Though, not so troubled as what Grace seemed to be, True reflected. The very same red-headed girl True saw fighting off her bullies the first day in their new home. She couldn't help but wonder if it was the way she looked that was the root of her issues. Last, but not least, there was Victor. Of course, she remembered Victor. Although True found herself surprised to see him involved.

She didn't understand Victor very well, but knew he was a good person. Only a good person would risk trouble for someone else's sake. Even so, what baffled True most about him was his disinterest in people. How was it possible that he had such a lack of interest in others when he was much closer to normal than she'd ever been, when others seemed so interested in him?

True placed the journal inside her jacket, thinking about the box sitting at home on her desk. Could she manage to make them chains for their crystals as well? Her stomach clenched at the thought of having to approach them, of having to explain why she would be interested in them. Could she even do it?

No, True chided herself, *you must do* it. Afterall, she needed them to go back—she'd need them and their crystals to go through the door which could only be opened

Alexia D. Miller

together. They didn't have school tomorrow. What would she do? True had no way to find them. At the very least they'd all seemed familiar enough with each other. School was probably her best bet.

True took her time re-stacking the boxes along the wall where the door opened before she turned towards the stairway. As she descended the broken stairs, True smiled. When she made it to the bottom floor of the hospital building, she slowly stepped over the window, pulling up the thin board she'd brought to cover it. Walking home, her mind flooded with thoughts of Mirror.

. . .

True looked up at the vast starry night sky, trying to understand what happened. How had she gotten here? And where exactly was here? To make sense of matters amid her confusion, True walked through the events leading up to the warped room and that moment.

The night before, True's Aunt Trina hugged her on her way to her study and a few minutes later in True's bedroom, her Aunt Rose knocked on the door. She quietly strolled in with tea and an assortment of cookies still warm on the plate. She smiled, setting them down on True's end-table as she plopped lightly onto the bed. At that moment,

Alexia D. Miller

True realized that she'd still had on her jacket from her venture a few hours before.

Her Aunt Rose wrapped her arms around her and kissed her cheek. Something she often did when she had something on her mind. "Tea and cookies for the young lady." She joked in an accent. "Your favorite. Your mom's too." She smiled with a look of longing in her eyes, as if she were recalling some moment of the past that she longed to return to. Likely some sweet memory of a time when True's mother was alive and hummed low hymns. A time where the two of them picked out matching outfits for a night out, or even a night in with an endless mountain of snacks and movies. Both undeniably destined to fall asleep before they finished either. Afterall, these were the stories of their time together that True heard most often.

Reaching behind her, her Aunt Rose plucked the black-framed photo from her headboard. "I always meant to ask you why you kept your favorite photos behind your head, instead of on your desk or on the walls." Her Aunt Rose smiled. True watched her aunt quietly as she gently traced her fingers over her mother's smiling face. It was by far her favorite. It was arguably, in True's opinion, the best photo of her mother Nina and her Aunt Rose.

They were twins, identical if not for a few differences. They had the same gray eyes, the same smile, and even

Alexia D. Miller

shared the same height and weight up until the day her mother died. True's mother's skin was twice as pale as her Aunt Rose's, and her hair twice as light and crimped. Aunt Rose, True recalled, had always been the most extroverted out of the two. True's introversion was a trait likely passed down from her mother.

She tried to remember the sound of her mother's laughter, but it faded away long ago. Sometimes, True even found herself pretending that her mother was laughing beside her Aunt Rose whenever she did. That her mother was always in the room chuckling some sweet laughter she couldn't hear. True did recall, however, that her mother's voice was soft like dew after a storm. As she tried to find the words to describe her aunts voice, True realized her Aunt Trina was silently watching her. Waiting for an answer.

"I can still look at it," True said lowly, "whenever I want. It's just...when the photos are by my head, I think maybe I'll dream about mother more." She didn't say so aloud, but True thought that maybe all the things she started to forget as the days passed by were only a dream away. She believed that maybe with her photo near her head, it would attract her memories of her mother like a wish to a well. That if she were lucky enough, every night those photos would make the memories of her mother that much harder to forget.

Alexia D. Miller

Her Aunt Rose lightly grabbed hold of True's hand and kissed the back of her palm. "She loved you more than anything in the world and you did her. Just the way it is supposed to be. She never expected to be gone, you know. She dreamed of seeing you grow up. She was the only person I know that would get excited about growing old. I wish I could tell you that the hurt stops, but I can't. Although, as impossible as it seems, one day it will hurt a little less."

True leaned her head against her aunt's shoulder. She didn't know if she ever wanted it to hurt any less. Not if it meant she wouldn't remember her mother's face or the sound of her laughter anymore. "You and Aunt Trina knew her longer--" True said, and as she often did, she wondered what it would have been like to see her mother grow up, to live years beside her. "—but I still miss her."

"We were born first, and I got to share a womb with her," Rose smiled, "so it's really no competition." She laughed, setting the picture frame back in its place. "Ah," she sighed, stretching her arms above her head. "You remind me so much of her. That's even more of a reason I wish she were here. She'd have been so much better at this. Parenting and getting you to *really* see yourself—she was great at that." She smiled.

Alexia D. Miller

{ 159 }

"Nina could make anyone comfortable in their own skin." She nodded matter-of-factly. True wished for nothing more than to be in her mother's presence. When they moved into the house True thought she might get lucky enough, given the house's reputation, to catch a glimpse of her. Or to at least feel her presence. Just something— anything—to know she was there. Unfortunately, True found nothing of the sort.

"It isn't exactly my skin that has caused me trouble." True sighed.

"Yes, yes." Her Aunt Rose said, getting to her feet. "You're right. I can only hope that one day you'll find the courage you had years ago. You were very optimistic." She smiled, making her way back to the door. "Don't stay up too late. Goodnight my love."

"Goodnight, Aunt Rose." True said, grabbing the cup of tea from her nightstand as the door closed softly.

True hadn't recalled the moment that she fell asleep, but when she opened her eyes it was morning. She dressed and brushed her teeth before making her way downstairs to the kitchen. On the fridge, she found a note from her aunts saying they went in to work early. True wanted to go back to Snowville Temporary Infirmary. She wanted to try and open the door she read about in the journal again. Her previous attempt ended in a weak shimmer before it disappeared. She

Alexia D. Miller

was sure something was there and was determined to do better.

True didn't bother with breakfast. Instead she made tea and put it in a to-go cup, grabbed her jacket, mask, journal, and shoes. She took a moment to fasten her crystal around her neck and went out the door as quickly as she could. She managed her best in school and when it was time to go home, she didn't waste any thoughts on the students staring at the back of her head. She'd went deaf to the sound of their voices and their footsteps.

When she made it home, she was greeted by her Aunt Rose. True did her best to spend time with her before she headed out. By now, she'd been to the building enough times that her body knew its way. She raced barefoot down the streets and cut through the grass until she came upon the window. Without hesitation True dropped the wooden sheet board onto the floor and climbed in.

Upstairs, True stood in front of the empty space on the wall. She flipped through the journal and read through the pages again, just to ready herself. Following the brief instructions, slowly the wall shifted slightly. Eventually, it gave way to a small ball of light that folded into itself and spread out around her. Unlike the day before, it did not shimmer and close. Today, small specks of multicolored light

Alexia D. Miller

glistened all above her and the light formed the shape of a door.

It had no absolute shape or physical knobs. There wasn't a window to look at what may have been beyond it. True wasn't discouraged, however, rather the opposite. The journal hadn't been wrong and that was cause for celebration. Holding out her hand, True felt a warm tingling sensation before air whizzed around her. In a matter of moments, she was pulled in.

What she saw on the other side was magnificent. There were rolling hills of sprouting flowers in every hue imaginable. The sky was a cloudless blue and the sun gleamed down from above. Not far in the distance True could see a pond surrounded by pink pebbles. Her shoes and journal still in hand, True took her time walking towards it. When she could see her reflection flickering on the surface of the water, True slid off her mask and jacket to better enjoy it.

In the distance, on the other side of the water, True could just make out a cabin or similar structure. She grew more excited at the thought of exploring but was determined not to rush through the room. Which to True, wasn't a room at all. Surely, she had all the time she needed to explore to her heart's content, she reassured herself, sitting down to enjoy the cool breeze that was blowing across the hills.

As if in defiance of her previous thought, the space around her shifted. The vibrations surprised her, and True immediately slid on her jacket, mask, and shoes. When the sound of voices echoed endlessly, scattered in the space around her, True found herself anxious and assuming the worst. Not knowing what to do, she flipped through the journal looking for anything that could explain it.

. . .

The next moment that her mind was clear, True felt a heaviness around her and her knees dropped roughly to the ground. It was dark, but a bright sign and lights offered enough light to see ahead, though not enough to block out the dark blue sky filled with thousands of stars above her. Where was she?

True focused her eyes on the sign further ahead. "Mirror." She read quietly to herself, before suddenly becoming aware of the shadows on the ground only feet ahead of her. She understood immediately that these others must have had crystals. It only made sense. The journal had mentioned them, and that when they were together, they could open the doors which she couldn't open on her own.

Alexia D. Miller

The moment True thought to check on them, worried that they were hurt, she heard movement. She quickly searched for somewhere to hide, deciding to bolt to the nearest bush on her right. From there, True watched silently, unmoving. Hearing his voice, True knew who he was. Even before he stepped into the light.

"What...? Oh no." Victor groaned, slowly sitting up. "Did I get lost?" True watched as he slowly made his way to his feet, his green eyes catching the light. He glanced around silently, turning his head in the direction True was in. For a moment, True thought he could see her. When he turned away, True realized she'd been holding her breath. Victor immediately followed the light sobs in the distance, stopping in front of a girl sitting on her knees in the grass.

"Grace?" Victor called cautiously. True realized that she'd seen this girl before too. Her wheat-colored skin and red hair. She was the young girl who wrestled those boys on the street. Without warning, Grace began to cry harder. She attempted to speak, but her words came out in an incoherent, emotional, mess.

"Yeah. You were scared, huh?" Victor said softly, his hand gently stroking the top of her head with a small smile. "It's okay, Grace. It was pretty unnerving." He said as he kneeled in front of her and put a hand to her shoulder. She hadn't imagined Victor to be so gentle mannered. True imagined herself beside them, helping console her.

In some parallel universe, perhaps True could be there comforting them as if she belonged, but that wasn't the reality. As much as she wanted to tell Grace that even she had been afraid, she couldn't bring herself to speak, let alone make her way around the bush and over to them. More than that, True knew, crystal or not, her place wasn't with them. She'd only ruin their lives. Or worse.

Suddenly, Grace wiped furiously at her tears and hopped to her feet. "Phelia and Zane! They should be here somewhere. We've got to find them!" She called, jogging further away. As the two of them rushed ahead, True slowly followed them at a distance. Cautiously, she watched as the two made their way to other silhouettes walking nearby, their faces slowly catching the light.

A young girl and a boy, both of which favored each other. It didn't take True long to understand that they were siblings. Their voices faded away as True ducked behind another bush, keeping as much distance as she could between them as they walked down the road ahead of them. When the bushes disappeared and gave way to vast trees along the roadway, True found herself relieved for more cover. More than that, she was happy that she wouldn't have to crouch the rest of the way. However long or far that would be.

Eventually, following the others lead to immense beige and white houses. Each nearly identical to the last. From what True could tell after the group's encounter with two women, things in Mirror would be interesting. Whether that would be a good or bad thing, True couldn't be sure. Whatever the case, she didn't want to risk being seen by the others and having to explain herself.

Having decided that, it didn't take long for True to make her way to a nearby house on her own. She walked around to the back yard where she found a large white chair. She struggled to get a good footing on one of its legs, until her foot slid onto a ridge and she pushed herself up, holding onto a line of fabric. True's only guess was that a blanket or seat cover with tassels laid over the center. Whatever it was, she found herself grateful for it. Otherwise she'd have never made it to the top. Were they in the land of giants?

True stood on her toes in the seat, which sat against a large glass window, and peered inside. To True's amazement, there were a family of foxes sitting at an immaculate marble table; there was a brown fox she assumed to be male because of its dark brown hat and spectacles, a white mother fox with a floral scarf wrapped neatly around her head, and two young kits with large matching bows in their hair.

The father's deep voice caused the window frame to shake. "Go on and feed your pet, Hilda." He said his brow furrowed. Huffing, one of the kits jumped out of her chair and to the floor. "I hate feeding him," she said as she stopped her way to a corner in the room. There, True could make out a person. He was a man with eggplant colored hair and teal skin that didn't exactly look pleased to have her stomping his way. "More than anything, I hate sharing him with Hilly." She said, grabbing something from a nearby cabinet and slopping it down on an oversized plate in front of him. "Hilly isn't good at sharing and he's *mine!*"

The other twin protested as the father slammed his oversized paw onto the table. True listened to the clinking of their glasses, plates, and bowls as they shook across the table. "That's enough, both of you! Hurry and take your seat." He hissed. "Don't act so spoiled, girls! All of this nonsense you're spouting will sour dinner." True leaned closer to the window, completely in awe of the large animals. Was it strange that even though they were larger than any animals she'd ever seen she still wanted to rake her fingers through their silky looking furs?

"Now, now." The mother fox said, her blue eyes angled slightly. "Let's not fight. We can buy another for Hilly

Alexia D. Miller

at the auction." As she spoke, her white-furred tail gently stroked under the father's chin. "There's bound to be another pet perfect for Hilly, isn't there? Surely we can afford two." Moments later, the foxes sat properly at the table chatting away as if nothing were ever wrong.

Auction? True wondered as she slowly made her way back to the ground from the chair. *But where do they get the people from? Do they change their hair? Paint their skin? Or is that the result of something else?*

True slowly made her way back towards the front of the house. As she heard the others' voices drawing near, True peeked around the corner watching silently. She listened as they went from one person to the next, asking questions and receiving no answer.

Was this place called Mirror because animals ruled it? Because humans were pets? What could a place like Mirror mean for her? For the others? Did these people want to be pets? Were they respected? A swirl of endless questions passed through her mind and True didn't think she'd have any luck finding answers. If the others weren't getting any surely, she had even less of a chance.

Having grown tired of watching the others, True decided to venture onwards. She walked quietly along the houses, careful to stay nearest any trees and bushes she saw along the way. While making her way around a bush filled with small white buds, True heard a shuffling behind her and quickly turned around. In another bush opposite her, a girl shuffled about on her hands and knees.

True took notice of her teal skin and sparkling golden hair. She wondered if it was the moonlight that caused it, or some other unknown occurrence. Seeing the worry flooding the girl's face, True slowly made her way near her and leaned downward. "Are you looking for something?" True asked, quietly.

The girl's eyes widened, and she jumped to her feet, almost as if she hadn't noticed True's presence at all. Seeing her standing, True realized that the golden-haired girl was much taller than she'd looked on all fours. True tilted her gaze up at her as she watched the girl clasp her hands over her throat and shake her head.

"It's alright." True offered, attempting to reassure her, "I'm sorry. I didn't mean to frighten you. Perhaps you don't speak to strangers either?" She more stated than asked, remembering how Victor and the others were met with silence. The girl stared at True for a long moment before a look of thought crossed her face and disappeared again. "They can't speak," the girl explained, "they are mute. Most can't. The more you can, the more you are worth."
"You mean at the auction?" True questioned, curious yet cautious.

Alexia D. Miller

{ 169 }

The girl nodded, pushing some of her sparkling golden hair behind her ear. "You're not from here...your skin..." The girl started, motioning towards True's hands. "No." True answered truthfully. "We have to find the door to leave. Only, I don't know where the door is."

The girl was quiet before she smiled. "There may be a door." She said before pointing at her neck. "I've lost my collar. It slipped off somewhere. If I can't find it the catcher may take me. My brother and I could become separated and Master One would be angry with me. I can't have him pay for me twice." She said anxiously fiddling with her hands.

"The Catcher?" True asked puzzled. "Who is The Catcher?"

"He is the big guy with the net. Anyone out at night without their owner or during the day alone, like now, without a collar gets rounded up and sold at the auction."

"Even if you already have an owner?" True asked.

"Yes," She said quickly. "Especially then. An owner pays more for a pet that they're accustomed to."

True wondered if the girl liked her owner. Or her "master" if she preferred to give him that title. She wanted to know who made the decision that deemed people pets. It was completely different than the way things were in Snowville. How had the animals established dominance over the humans, or whatever it was they were called? Had there been a war? If there had been, True couldn't imagine the humans stood much of a chance against such large animals. Was it possible that animals in their world could all end up as big as the ones in Mirror?

"May I help you look?" True asked. The girl nodded and led the way, retracing her steps. As they went, the girl explained that her brother would be looking for her soon, but she wouldn't dare show up without her collar. She was afraid of what her brother would do to protect her. Her best guess, she'd said, was that he would give up his own to protect her.

At some point during their search, time ticked by and the sun began to rise. A glint of sunlight caught True's eye and she spotted a golden leather band beside a bush. The girl quickly grabbed it and rejoiced as she latched it onto the back of her neck.

With a smile flooding the girl's face, she pulled True by the arm. They raced past clusters of buildings, eventually stopping in front of what True guessed was their destination. It was another large beige and white house, like all the others she'd seen before. The only discernable difference was the 0001 in bold font above her head.

The girl silently motioned for True to wait inside the fenced yard as she slipped away into a small brown door. Indistinguishable noises drifted to her ears from the other

Alexia D. Miller

{ 171 }

side as True's gaze floated to the bright sky above her. It was full of contrasting blue hues, not a single cloud in sight. She recalled that the girl called the night sky day, so this must be night.

Perhaps Mirror was just that. Some strange reflection, some semblance of their own world. Maybe Snowville would be like Mirror with the simplest of changes and she would never have guessed it because she didn't know places like this truly existed. Maybe Mirror was a skewed opposite of everything they knew.

When True heard the brown door open and close again, she met the eyes of the golden-haired girl and a boy she assumed to be her brother. True thought if not for the sister's long hair, the two of them could switch places and no one would be the wiser. True didn't think she could confidently tell them apart otherwise.

Before, True was certain the girl had been wearing a dark pink and black outfit. Now, however, both she and her brother wore long, thick coats made from giant white feathers. The coat itself hung less than an inch from the ground. "Thank you for helping my sister," the boy said offering True a beaming smile. True nodded before a loud boom frightened her, coming from inside the house.

"Quickly." The girl whispered, opening her coat, "Get in. I'll hide you as we walk with Master One." True

Alexia D. Miller

didn't waste time taking her up on the offer. She buried herself in the coat as fast as she could, her heart racing. Was Mr. One dangerous? As soon as her wave of anxiety hit her, however, it quickly faded. Buried in whiffs of fresh air and mint leaves.

Initially, True thought the smell was coming from the gold-haired girl, but she quickly realized the smell came from the large, soft feathers surrounding her. When the girl's feet began to move, True tried her best to match her long strides. Unable to fight her curiosity, True gently peeled back a few coat feathers. She could make out the girl's brother slightly to the left and a mass of white directly ahead of her.

Focusing her attention on it, True thought it was close enough to touch. She could see a long black swirl in the middle of its back as it quivered and turned its head to reveal a short white beak. How beautiful. Mr. One was a white owl. They stopped as a squirrel with a top hat and bifocals handed Mr. One an envelope and a small bag, which disappeared somewhere in his large feathers.

Upon a silent goodbye, True saw Mr. One's deep blue eyes. Specks of white dotted each of them, giving True the impression of a galaxy. He didn't speak, but True had wondered what his voice would sound like if he had. Would his voice echo like ancient bells? Would it be deep like

Alexia D. Miller

currents of the ocean? She allowed her mind to flutter with similar thoughts until vibrations shook the ground. Again, True peeled back feathers to look ahead of her. She strained to get a glimpse of the excitement between movement of animals. Realizing that their attention was towards the sky, True glanced up and her stomach dropped.

The girl's brother hovered closer as True frantically pulled on the inside of the coat to get the girl's attention. "He's...umm! He's umm!!" She tried to think of what she could say, watching as Victor, Zane, Grace and Phelia struggled inside the white net. The large shaggy dog carrying them away smiling as if it was the best day of his life. "He's taking my friends!" True murmured, finally.

True knew that they weren't really her friends, but she needed them to return home to her aunts. More than that, she couldn't watch them be sold off when they didn't belong in Mirror, possibly trapping them all there forever. She couldn't think of any other word to express their importance. Calling them family somehow seemed worse.

The brother's brown eyes seemed to glisten. "Don't worry. You helped us so we will help you." He smiled mischievously and True felt he had something up his sleeve. The boy led them off and away from Mr. One. They'd have to get back to him before the auction ended, he whispered, or they'd be in trouble. True didn't want them to go through

Alexia D. Miller

any trouble on her behalf, but she was happy to have any help at all.

"Everyone who is sold at auction ends up in the cage behind the stage, locked away for safe keeping." The girl began, "We have come so often with Master One that we found the emergency switch. It is somewhat near the cage, and only the top of the sensor is above ground, but it is silent in case the auction ever has to shut down at a moment's notice."

"Has the auction ever been shut down before?" True asked curiously.

"Once or twice." The boy said, swatting a hand in the air dismissively. "Normally, The Catcher would be somewhere nearby by the time the button has to be used. To round up any fleeing merchandise...but..." the boy said with a smile, "...no Catcher means no one is rounded back up. Considering no one has ever escaped, I guess they don't guard it regularly." He shrugged.

"I imagine that anyone who runs off would simply be rounded up a second time. Luck is on our side today." He continued, "Even if the cage did make a little noise, they won't hear a thing over the sound of their own voices. They tend to get rowdy on auction day and today they are more excited than usual."

Alexia D. Miller

Just as they'd said, by the time they'd jumped down on the button and the cage opened, the animals' excited chatter never stopped. There was no way to hear the others' escape over their booming voices. When the two of them made their way back to True, she was hiding inside the stage curtains. "What's wrong?" The girl asked concerned. Her brother tilted his head silently. "Are you alright?"

"I need them to get home, but they..." True hesitated, watching as the others looked around, racing out of the cage. "Well, they don't exactly know me."

"Aren't they your friends?" The girl asked.

"I didn't know what else to call them, but we hardly know each other. I'm sorry, I suppose I should have said that, shouldn't I? Maybe I can just follow you to the door?" Without asking another question, the boy slipped off his coat and lightly tossed True over his shoulder. With his other hand he slid his sister's coat over her. Frightened by the boy's sudden touch, True sat as still as she could. "I can walk." True suggested nervously.

"Sure, you can, but now they won't even notice you." He chuckled. "We can't have you falling behind."

A few minutes later, the siblings were sprinting off with the others close behind. True swallowed her worries and relaxed with the scent of mint leaves flooding her nose. With every step, True felt the light ruffling of the coat

Alexia D. Miller

feathers in the wind. Before she knew it, the boy gently placed her behind a tree. True unfastened her crystal, placed it in between her hands, and waited patiently until the others took theirs out.

"Home." True whispered, holding her crystal to her chest as the space warped around them. She watched calmly as the others were pulled into the light. True walked closer to the doorway and turned to face the boy and his sister, wishing she had words to express the full extent of her gratitude. "Thank you." True said, wishing she asked their names as the door began to pull her in.

The boy nodded. "Of course. Don't mention it. It's the least we could do."

True could just make out his sister's smile as their world faded away. "We owed you one anyway."

Alexia D. Miller

Victor...

Chapter Eighteen: Watching.

Victor was genuinely surprised by what had taken place in Mirror. He'd felt more relieved than ever when they'd found themselves back in the abandoned hospital and that much closer to home. Although he'd initially thought to race home to his mother and his bed, he'd opted for sitting down with Phelia and Zane instead. Grace had hardly given herself time to say goodbye before she shuffled out of the Brand house and Victor couldn't blame her after everything they'd gone through.

Victor didn't know how long the three of them sat around the fireplace. They passed by the hours going over almost every excruciating detail from the time they decided to leave to finding themselves back home. While Victor had been completely unprepared for the turn of events, he couldn't help finding interest in seeing something akin to their own world topsy-turvy. Even so, Mirror was a frustrating place. "There's just too many holes to fill in," Victor said.

"Yes," Phelia agreed with a stern nod. "But therein lies the problem. There are so many unknown variables. How we managed to go through that...whatever it was? What was that feeling of being suspended in nothingness? How was it possible to rematerialize in some other dimension in the first place? How did that boy found us and set us free? Why did he free us from the cage?"

"Should we even really care about how we were found or the whole escape-the cage- and-auction thing?" Zane scoffed. "I'm just glad we got outta there. We could be stuck in Mirror right now, you know?"

"Whatever the case," Phelia said, staring into the low flames of the fireplace, "we can't pretend it didn't happen."

"Can't we?" Zane asked. "Because I think we can."

"I hated it," Phelia frowned, "every second of confusion and worry, but I'd never seen something so...erratically beautiful."

"Yeah. Sure, if you want to call almost getting sold off to the talking animal kingdom and possibly being stuck there forever beautiful." Zane said sarcastically. He looked at Victor, seeming to expect a response.

"Honestly, I think I'll be holding a bit of a grudge," Victor said, "when it comes to Mirror." When prompted he couldn't bring himself to give an explanation. All he knew was that they'd come way too close for comfort to being in

Alexia D. Miller

danger, to being sold off as exotic pets, and he didn't like it. He wished he were able to experience Mirror without having step foot out of bed. Was it too much to ask for their adventures to happen in their sleep and the moment they woke...poof? Things would be some sort of normal again? One thing was for sure. He was starting to rethink ever getting a dog.

. . .

The next morning, Victor sat in class and the relief he felt about being back in Snowville lessened. He struggled with the thought of dealing with his idiot classmates and even more, the fact that he'd have to pretend that things were normal. That just yesterday he hadn't traveled to Mirror. If that weren't enough, Victor couldn't shake the feeling of being watched.

Usually, people's watchful eyes didn't faze him, or he simply never noticed them. Today was different. Maybe, because it was True. The new girl from his homeroom whose aunts had given Principal Mann an earful.

On an average school day Victor could glance over in her direction to find her staring out the small window. Or her attention was buried in some book he'd never heard of. Today, however, she'd been full-on staring at him through

Alexia D. Miller

her mask. Not that he could see her eyes, of course, but he was almost sure of it. Since he couldn't see her face, Victor found himself looking at the dark indentations on the mask where her eyes should have been.

If not that, True would quickly turn her head downcast as he looked up at her. Looking at whatever was on her desk as if she were never looking his way in the first place. Victor didn't know whether he should be bothered or curious. For most of homeroom, his attention was divided between finishing his work and watching her watch him.

After Mr. Van-Dayton announced that the next few days would consist of the class picking a topic and putting together a presentation, they were dismissed. Not knowing what else he could do, Victor tried to shrug things off as him being stressed since their time in Mirror. Feeling silly, Victor headed home.

Over the next few days, however, Victor was sure he hadn't lost his mind. As usual, True disappeared around lunch. Since they didn't have any other classes together, he didn't see her much. Many times in-between classes, however, Victor could just catch her out of the corner of his eye swooping behind something or her mask peeking around a corner.

At their last homeroom of the day, Victor and True were the first to arrive to the classroom as usual. To his

Alexia D. Miller

surprise, True stopped in front of him and tilted her head up at him. They stood there in silence for a moment before Victor opened his mouth, ready to confront her about his observations. Before he managed to make a sound, however, True turned quickly on her heels and made her way to her seat.

As he made his way to his seat, True made no attempt to look up at him, and Victor suddenly lacked the energy to confront her. As the classroom filled with familiar faces, she seemed to work diligently on her presentation poster. Ten minutes before the end of homeroom, Mr. Van-Dayton called True to the front of the class, opting her to be the first to start off presentations. "Come on, now." He directed at True, who had been putting away a pack of markers. "We'll have you present your work today and it'll be someone else's turn tomorrow."

As far as Victor was concerned, Mr. Van-Dayton's tone suggested that she didn't have a choice in the matter. Victor watched as True stood up from her seat and walked towards the front of the classroom. Whispers were already flooding the class as she unrolled her poster. Mr. Van-Dayton, as usual, didn't say a single word in protest.

Victor again took notice of how small and fragile True appeared to be. He watched her pale fingers placing magnets on the board to secure her poster. A portion of her

Alexia D. Miller

thin arms visible as the sleeves of her jacket fell back towards her elbows. He even noticed her tennis shoes. Had he ever seen her wear tennis shoes?

Victor recognized her neat handwriting, like font printed perfectly on paper, almost as if she'd mastered the art of calligraphy. She'd drawn cartoon-like figures across the poster and they weren't bad at first glance. When he looked again, however, Victor was already starting to pity her. It wasn't that the drawings were bad, but rather her presentation and some images she'd drawn were already causing whispers among the students.

Her title was "Death and Beyond," written in large bold letters. The cartoons showed some form of the circle of life. One figure with a rounded stomach smiled and an arrow directed attention to another drawing and another arrow to the next. The same figure, this time holding a baby and the next showing growth and so on.

Eventually, the man who was once the baby, lay dead on his back. True thought it a good idea to draw his bleeding open chest with realistic organs under two flaps. A blob representing his soul floated into the air above him. The final image depicted the man standing with an angel on one shoulder and a small devil on the other. The question "Are heaven and hell literal worlds, like the one we know, just outside the realm of our current existence?" was written out below him.

During her presentation, where she pointed silently at the cartoon boy, to Victor's dismay, True offered up a short explanation about the man's death. She shook her head and said that the man had been ripped open in a car accident, just like a body she'd seen at a morgue. The uneasiness in the air was suffocating.

The class, including Mr. Van-Dayton, were stunned into silence. She'd managed to say one complete sentence in front of the entire class and that was what she decided to say? Victor didn't know whether he should laugh in amusement or pity her twice as much as he had before.

Just as quietly as she'd begun, True removed the magnets from her poster and rolled it back up. She walked to Mr. Van-Dayton's desk and attempted to hand the poster in, but he quickly held up a hand to stop her and directed her to keep it. His explanation was that he didn't need it for grading, but Victor knew from the look on his face that he simply didn't want to take it. Victor wouldn't be surprised if the man were squeamish, but to be so bothered by drawings on a piece of poster board?

Class was immediately dismissed, and Victor watched the others rush out of the room. Many of whom, called True a "freak" as they pushed past her. Victor decided not to

Alexia D. Miller

confront her about staring or whatever it was she'd been up to. Victor lived in Snowville for years now. He knew how vicious their classmates could become when they singled someone out. He couldn't imagine adding to that stress. Even more so if Sydney was at the forefront.

Victor saw Mr. Van-Dayton leave the classroom, but he still decided to put his poster on his desk. He hadn't presented assignments before and he had no reason to start now. Upon exiting the room, Victor saw True with Mr. Van-Dayton across the hall. As he passed them by, he could hear the teacher's nervous chuckle as he told True that her presentation was inappropriate for class, even if it was neatly done.

Outside, Victor met up with Zane and immediately told him about True's presentation. As far as Victor was concerned, her assignment wasn't very conventional, but it had been creative. He'd hardly have called it inappropriate for a high school audience. If only Mr. Van-Dayton knew what normally spewed from the minds and mouths of many of his students.

"She brought up an interesting question though, don't you think?" Victor asked Zane. "Until Mirror, I wouldn't have given it much thought."

"You mean her whole heaven or hell thing?" Zane asked.

Alexia D. Miller

Victor nodded his head. "Yeah. Could heaven and hell be some world like Mirror?" He wondered if they were another world close to their own, some parallel universe where only certain people had access to it via unknown rules or circumstances. It didn't seem so far-fetched an idea anymore.

They'd somehow managed to go to another place none of them knew existed. Even though Mirror was a far throw away from something like the stereotypical heaven or hell, how were they to say it was impossible? A week ago, Victor couldn't dream up a place like Mirror, much less travel to it. He wondered if there was a world out there somewhere filled with people in pajamas, sweet dreams, and oversized pillows. An entire world focused on a good night's sleep sounded much more his style than gigantic animals wanting to make a pet out of him.

"Ugh. I don't even want to think about that. My head still hurts just thinking about Mirror." Zane groaned unhappily. Victor realized that he had even more questions than he'd started with, but Zane was right. Questions *were* tiring. Taking the subject off True's presentation, Victor mentioned that he was relatively sure True followed him around school.

"You're probably feeling paranoid after all those eyes and ears in Mirror," Zane said dismissively. "If she has been as reserved as you say, then she probably hasn't been following you." He laughed. "If I were you," Zane said, slapping Victor playfully on the back, "I'd be more worried about Sydney and her band of lipstick lackeys."

Phelia...

Chapter Nineteen: Tea and a Little Honey.

*P*helia sat quietly watching her father work. He looked desperately in need of a good night's rest. She watched him type away at the keys on his laptop. Almost on cue, every five minutes her father's typing would cease, and he'd jot something down on one of the pages beside him. Phelia watched as time ticked away on the clock above his head, deciding to make her way to the kitchen. There, she grabbed her father's large mug off the counter.

As Phelia grabbed a tea packet from the drawer next to the stove, she recalled the time when their mother passed the hours painting it for their father's birthday. She remembered the soft amused snickering and multicolored paint her mother managed to get onto her cheeks. Phelia wondered if her mother knew that their father used it every single day without fail. If she was in some world just out of reach and visited them often. If she had been there after she died.

Phelia dropped the tea bag into the mug and walked to the bathroom. She turned on the tap and watched it fill slowly before putting it into the microwave. After the beep, she went back to rinse her spoon from the night before and turned off the water. Back in the kitchen, Phelia grabbed the jar of honey from beside the fridge.

She squeezed the bottle until a large swirl of golden honey fell into the tea and watched the water level rise. She didn't bother putting the honey away before stirring it up and sliding the mug onto a tray. Carefully, Phelia made her way back to her father's office.

Seeing that her father was putting a stack of papers into a binder, she slowly put the tray down on the table. When he looked over at her with a smile, Phelia smiled back and gestured at the mug. It had been white before, if Phelia recalled correctly. Their mother painted it a rainbow of colors. She'd written words and phrases on almost the entire outer surface.

Things like "Remember when...?" "Forever," "Happy Birthday," and "Breaks are healthy too, Doctor." Oddly enough, Phelia had never thought to spend time circling the

Alexia D. Miller

mug to read it all. It had always felt taboo to try and find her place between them, even though Phelia knew those kinds of thoughts were silly considering her mother was no longer alive.

"Father," Phelia called quietly, "did you want a cup for your birthday?" Phelia asked, watching her father take a sip from the mug.

"I didn't particularly want anything for my birthday," he said with a smile, "but I couldn't have asked for anything better from your mother."

"Because you don't like other gifts?" Phelia asked curiously.

Phelia watched as he set the mug down on the table and outstretched his arms. Without pause she stepped into his arms and he kissed her cheek. "Your mother knew me better than I knew myself most days. She knew I wasn't one for extravagant gifts. A cup that I could use every day is perfect."

"A practical gift." Phelia said with a nod, lightly taking in his scent. She was never sure how, but he'd always smelled like oranges and cinnamon.

Silently, Dr. Brand lifted Phelia and turned her around gently so that she rested on his lap, picking the mug up again. This time, he took a few sips and held the cup in Phelia's view. Slowly, he tilted the mug so that she could see inside. Directly above the ring of liquid were the words "

Alexia D. Miller

love you." As many times as Phelia handed her father the mug, she was surprised that she'd never known there were words on the inside.

"Yes," her father spoke softly, kissing Phelia's cheek again. "A practical gift. This way I can always remember her. As if she was still next to me speaking into my ear. Only now...I don't hear her voice anymore. Just here," he said, lightly putting a finger to Phelia's chest.

Her father was smiling, but Phelia could almost feel the pain beyond it. A pain that clouded over his gaze no matter how much effort he put in to hiding it. As she watched him stare soundlessly into the mug, Phelia felt that perhaps her father was seeing something else that she couldn't. She resisted the urge to ask.

"I must make the two of you lonely," Her father said suddenly before drinking down his tea in some sort of hurry Phelia couldn't understand, "being away for work so often." After setting down the mug again, he wrapped his arms around Phelia tightly. "Just a little while longer, my dear. If things go as planned, I might not have to at all. Being your father always outweighs being a doctor."

. . .

Alexia D. Miller

{ 190 }

That night as he carried her to bed, Phelia wondered if she should tell her father about their strange experience with the crystals or their time in Mirror. She unwrapped her arms from his neck as he laid her head onto her pillow and pulled up her covers. Phelia questioned if he would even believe it. Instead of that, she asked a different question. "Father, do you believe in other worlds?"

Phelia watched him silently shift on his feet, running his hands through his hair. "Well...your mother was better with abstract questions." He chuckled, scratching his chin. "I don't refute the possibility of other dimensions. I don't have any personal experience with anything like that, of course, but it does interest me. I think most people become interested in the topic a few times in their lives."

Her father looked to the right thoughtfully. "Just because we don't know if something exists—because we can't prove it—doesn't mean it doesn't. I try to think of it like this: at one point and time, one thing or another wasn't proven to exist. Like gravity, for example. It is an invisible force but over time it was still proven to be. So, why shouldn't other worlds be a possibility?"

Phelia nodded with a yawn. Her father's answer surprised her. She didn't know for sure, but perhaps one day soon he would be open to talking about it more. Phelia wondered if she could take her father with them, if she could use her crystal to whisk him away to some other land. She hoped there was another land at least. Anywhere but Mirror.

By whatever means they traveled, Phelia was sure it was because of the crystals. They couldn't have developed some strange ability from nothing. The crystals were the only new variable, the only common denominator. The more Phelia let her mind wander, the more questions she had, and the more she wanted answers.

"Thank you for the tea," her father said pushing away her thoughts. "Goodnight, Phelia."

She sleepily watched her father's figure disappear down the hall, listening to the light sound of his receding footsteps. Slowly, Phelia allowed herself to continue her weary thoughts. Tomorrow, Grace would be coming over. *Maybe,* Phelia thought, *just maybe...I might have a real friend. Or at least someone to spend time with who isn't father or Zane.* She wasn't sure if the thought of it should have made her more worried or excited.

Zane...

Chapter Twenty: Uncomfortable.

Zane found himself spending most of the week distracted. His mind was overwhelmed with their time in Mirror and his little sister. He found himself incredibly upset by the way things went. He'd felt so helpless. Even now he was bitter and confused. He was upset with himself, with Phelia's strange change in attitude while they were there, and every question that popped into his mind about Mirror. They were lucky enough to make it home safe, so why was he still plagued with thoughts of that horrible place?

Safe, he scoffed. *What a joke! How many more minutes away had we been from being separated? From never seeing each other again. Maybe Phelia wouldn't have needed me then either,* Zane thought crossly. *We'd nearly never made it home. Who knows if we'll be swept off to Mirror again? What would happen to dad if we disappeared? It would ruin him. He'd probably never smile again.*

Feeling uncomfortable, Zane reached into his pocket and rubbed his thumb across his crystal. How was it possible

Alexia D. Miller

{ 193 }

that he felt calmer with it near him? How was it possible to feel calm even though he felt like he was carrying a black hole in his pocket? Something that could suck him up without permission and shatter his very existence. The crystal was the reason they'd ever left Snowville in the first place, wasn't it?

Lost in his own thoughts, Zane didn't hear the school bells signaling lunch. Much like he hadn't heard his father or Phelia speaking to him earlier that morning. Vaguely, Zane knew his days were fusing together since their return. So much so, that Zane didn't even remember if he and Victor had been speaking to each other throughout the day or on their walks home.

Zane was brought back to reality at the sound of his name. He looked up silently trying to piece together what he was doing only to see the clock on the back wall. He was in school and it was time for lunch. Had it been that long already? Zane shifted his gaze to the girl on his right.

"Bailey." He said quietly. A girl, one of a very short list, who he occasionally spoke to was trying to get his attention. She smiled at him, pushing a few of her loose brown strands behind her ear. Zane recalled that Bailey had been in a few of his classes every year since he started school in Snowville. She'd even been his lab partner the year before in Science. He looked around the empty classroom and back to her.

"The lunch bell rang almost five minutes ago." She said, flashing him another one of her bright smiles. "Didn't you notice?"

"Right. Yeah, thanks." Zane said looking back at the clock. Bailey chuckled, swinging back on her heels, "Yep. I didn't think anything in the textbook could have *possibly* been that interesting." Zane looked quietly at the book on his desk. He didn't recall opening it, let alone reading any of it. He stood, closing the book, and stuffed it into his bag.

"Are you alright?" She asked, handing him a pen he hadn't noticed he dropped. "You seem a little distracted lately. Did something happen?"

"Have I?" He asked half-heartedly. "Well no. Nothing happened. Umm yeah. I'm fine." What was with him today? Didn't he at least know how to put sentences together? "Thanks," he said, motioning to the pen.

"Sure thing," she said, adjusting the bag over her shoulder.

As he began to walk past her, he felt a tug on his shirt sleeve. "Zane?" Bailey called, blinking her blue-gray eyes. He raised an eyebrow, and she shifted her gaze away from him momentarily. "I was actually wondering if maybe you wanted to go on a date with me?"

Alexia D. Miller

"W-what...?" Zane asked, stumbling over his words. *Did I really just get asked out on a date??*

Grace...

Chapter Twenty-One: Friends and Bullies.

Grace slowly made her way from the Brand house. She'd never had a real friend before and she'd been stunned when Phelia suddenly asked her to become one. She'd said yes, of course. Partly because she'd been excited, and partly because she imagined that what she felt being around Phelia was maybe how real friends felt being around each other. She always wanted a real friend.

Phelia had seemed happy as well. Happier than Grace thought she should have been since she was getting the short end of the stick. Grace had no clue what being a true friend was supposed to be like exactly, but that wasn't her only worry. Afterall, Grace had a bad reputation in Snowville. What would Phelia do if she found out that Grace was, in the eyes of the adults, a troublemaker? She couldn't imagine that being friends with her would make Phelia's life better. She didn't have much she could offer herself, much less someone else.

Alexia D. Miller

Grace looked in the salmon colored bag in her hands. Phelia gave her a gift to celebrate, or so she'd called it. A black walkie that Phelia used to use when she first began homeschooling. Grace hardly heard Phelia's explanation, but she recalled her saying that they had a wide receiving area. According to Phelia, she and Zane had been able to communicate with each other almost to the far side of his school, so there wasn't much reason to believe they wouldn't work from her home to Grace's.

As far as Grace could tell, so long as she didn't turn the knobs on the top, the walkie wouldn't give her any trouble. There was a yellow switch to turn it on or off and a volume adjustment wheel. Phelia had even given Grace her own charging stand to take home. She recalled seeing a similar one in the past. Back when she stayed with a different foster family, but that one had been broken.

At home, MaryAnne and Duke were in a good mood. They hadn't asked Grace any questions about the bag or what was inside it. They hadn't even seemed to notice it. MaryAnne gave Grace a plate of sandwiches and mentioned her lunch in the fridge for tomorrow. If her foster parents' good mood wasn't enough to make her day better, knowing that tomorrow would end the school week did.

Tomorrow would be the last day for the entire week that Grace would have to deal with those horrible boys or

Alexia D. Miller

the mean teachers. Elephant Spit and his band of idiots seemed more willing than ever to pick on her since she'd promised herself that she'd surrender. That she'd stop fighting. Grace could only hope that the good would outweigh the bad if she endured it.

Trying not to ruin her mood, Grace re-focused her attention on her gift. She wouldn't use it tonight, but maybe she'd take it to school with her tomorrow. As she decided to get her things together for bed, Grace stopped in the doorway with a frown. Her room had been redecorated again. MaryAnne seemed to do something different to it every week. It was almost always more excessive than the last. So much so that it worried her.

Today, Grace's room was still white, but the rest was unrecognizable. Her bedsheets were a cotton candy pink, her curtains were dark purple with pink clouds, in front of the bed was a thick, fluffy purple carpet, and an oversized photo of her, MaryAnne and Duke hung on the wall above the bed. It was a photo the three of them had taken their first day together. Grace smiled for the photo, recalling how happy she'd been to be leaving her last foster family.

She'd managed to be hopeful back then, when really all it had done for her was make things worse when everything started crashing down. Grace thought that maybe MaryAnne was right before as she made out the sound of

Alexia D. Miller

rushing water down the hall, likely for her bath. Maybe her problem was just the way she'd been looking at things. Sure, Grace never watched television or sat in front of the fireplace unless her foster parents had company. Sure, she never got any toys or decorated her own room. Yes, she normally ate dinner alone and her every bath ended in 20 minutes, but that was better in every way than what happened if she upset them, wasn't it?

A time when she had to skip meals most days and was shut away in *That* room every day. If she went to school on the days they were upset, she would come home to complete silence and there wasn't ever even a glance in her direction. The baths were freezing cold and MaryAnne would always *forget* to bring her a towel. Of course, as if all of that wasn't bad enough, she still had to deal with everyone in school. All she had to do was stay good, Grace told herself sternly. The next day, however, Grace found that "staying good" was harder than she imagined.

Grace lasted most of the day with Elephant Spit and his idiot friends calling her names, kicking her seat, tripping her when she walked past them or had her arms full. They'd even "accidentally" dropped an open bottle of water all over her classwork, which meant she had to do it over again. All of it, Grace forced herself to swallow. She knew that getting her teacher would do nothing. Eustis was always so "well-behaved" in the eyes of any teacher. Meanwhile, Grace knew they only saw her as trouble.

What they did before lunch, however, was too much to take. It was unforgivable. One of them—Grace couldn't be completely sure who but figured it was likely Eustis—had taken a pair of scissors to her skirt when she wasn't looking. Grace felt the cold steel of one of the blades touch her skin, if only for an instant. They'd snipped a jagged line from the waist down a third of the fabric. Enough to have her skirt fall without warning to her ankles, her powder blue underwear out for anyone to see.

Grace had managed to hold in her screams. She'd been able to pull up her skirt amid the class' outburst and tell the teacher. Ms. Pine confronted the boys, but found the scissors tucked away under papers on her desk. "I didn't do anything." Eustis fussed, crossing his arms. The others whined in agreement.

Grace wanted nothing more than to take the pair of scissors to his stupid blonde hair. She wanted every lie he told to make his nose sprout like a weed. She wanted his head to inflate so much that he floated like a balloon into the sky and disappeared from her life forever. Grace wanted him to suffer at the hands of bullies just like she did.

She felt tears sting her eyes as Ms. Pine gave her a judging look. "She did it to herself!" One of the boys huffed.

Alexia D. Miller

"Or she ripped it on something and wants to blame us again!" Another cut in. With all their voices muddled together, pushing the blame onto her, Grace couldn't say she expected anything less. She couldn't say she was surprised when Ms. Pine shook her head disapprovingly. Or when she heard her tell the boys to hurry off to lunch.

Ms. Pine pulled Grace out of the classroom and down the halls to the lost and found. However, there was nothing that she could use. There was not a single sweater or jacket to tie around her waist. Eventually, Grace was forced to settle for a few safety pins on her skirt that poked her with every stride.

Grace looked down at her skirt which hung unevenly on her waist. She could still make out some of her blue underwear poking through open areas the safety pins couldn't close properly. Not knowing what else she could do, Grace rushed to get her bag and held it to her ruined skirt, embarrassed. She ran out of the classroom again and back to the halls.

If any teachers or staff called to her, she couldn't hear. Grace could barely pay attention to her own steps zooming over the patterns on the floor. She ran so fast that she stumbled rounding the corner to the bathroom. Grace reached inside her bag and felt around for the crystal and the walkie-talkie. With the crystal in one hand and the walkie in the other, Grace lost her energy to fight back her tears.

She cried and cried. Thick, angry, salty tears that stung her eyes until she was tired of crying. When she was able to wipe at the drying tears with the back of her arm, she turned on the walkie-talkie and listened to the static on the other end.

It felt like forever before she could press the button and dare to call Phelia who may or may not have been on the other side. "Phelia?" Grace whispered into the receiver. "Phelia?" She called again, before realizing she'd never released the button to get a response. *She can't answer you if you don't do it right,* she chided.

"Grace? Can you hear me?" Phelia's voice called from the other end. Her voice had been much clearer than Grace anticipated. Almost as if she were standing across the room. So, she tried to lose herself in the comfort of that thought. The thought that she wasn't sitting in a bathroom stall. She imagined herself across from Phelia in the Brand family's front room.

"I can hear you." Grace answered, exhaling slowly after she released the button again. Again, Phelia's voice filled the stall.

"I was thinking...perhaps we should return to the door again. The door in *Snowville Temporary Infirmary.*" Grace hadn't been sure what she expected to hear or say if she did manage to reach Phelia, but somehow that hadn't been it. She wasn't planning on having a conversation about Mirror. "I want to learn more about the crystals." Phelia continued.

Her words evaporated the sense of calm Grace managed to build up. So, against her better judgement, Grace lied. "I-I have to go. I'm sorry." Grace murmured quickly. Phelia seemed to accept it easy enough. She said they'd talk about it later and ended their conversation. Grace turned off the walkie, consumed with a horrible guilt. She hadn't meant to lie. Even less to her first friend, but she hadn't known what else to do.

As much as Grace didn't want to be in school, she was sure she wanted to go back through that door even less. Not back to Mirror to be caught and sold. They'd confirmed that the crystals were magic already. No matter how they worked. Why did the crystals have to take them off to a place like Mirror? Why couldn't the magic from the crystals just do something amazing in Snowville? Like make Elephant Spit and all of his little friends disappear. She could use a little magic like that.

Grace sat in the bathroom stall and ate her sandwiches without much of an appetite. She felt sad, hopeless, and angry. Grace knew that those boys were probably off laughing at her. That they were off celebrating

Alexia D. Miller

their victory. She knew that by the end of the day all the teachers on her hall at the very least, would know about her powder blue undies.

Grace knew that a few more minutes from now she'd have to leave the bathroom no matter how horrible she felt. She knew that she wouldn't be able to walk off and go home. Not just because the school wouldn't allow it, but because MaryAnne and Duke would never give the okay or plan to pick her up. If they weren't in a good mood, they wouldn't even agree to send her a change of clothes.

Grace knew that she would have to walk back into the classroom with stupid, painful pins stabbing at her thigh and her bag held up against her hip. In that moment Grace decided that she wouldn't get out of her chair. Not even if Ms. Pine asked her to come to the board. She wouldn't move a muscle away from her seat until she was sent to the office or school was over and she could go home.

If MaryAnne was somehow in a good mood, Grace might even ask her to mend the skirt. She wasn't sure if either of her foster parents would believe her even if they were having the best day of their lives. Maybe they wouldn't treat her any different than the teacher had. Or worse, they could hate her for ruining things and causing trouble. If she were lucky, she would be able to avoid being hurled into *That* room all over again.

Alexia D. Miller

Crystal Key: Door to a New World

Alexia D. Miller

{ 206 }

True...

Chapter Twenty-Two: Freak.

As class let out that day, True was as relieved as she was disappointed. For the past week she'd been trying to confront Victor. She had a hard time figuring out her timing. She recalled asking herself if it was better to ask him while they were in class or after. If she should approach him silently or by name, even if they weren't friendly with each other. Unfortunately, True had only gotten more nervous any time he'd caught her looking at him. So much so that she wondered if he would decide it wasn't a good idea to sit anywhere near her after all.

When the days went by and he didn't do any of those things, True spent all her free time at lunch building up her courage and practicing what she would say to him. At some point she thought she was confident enough to pull it off, only to stand in front of him, take a deep breath, and freeze.

All the time she had spent talking herself into it, preparing her sentences and approach meant nothing. *It was a waste*, True thought with a sigh. *The moment I opened my mouth, I couldn't even form words.* True criticized herself. If he was going to call her a freak, she hadn't wanted to look him in the face while he did it.

So, the only other thing she could think to do was hurry off to her seat and work on her poster defeated and shamed. A poster, that turned out to be a mistake. She'd been docked points for "inappropriate material" and was given a separate assignment of Mr. Van-Dayton's choice to make up for the grade.

Things hadn't ended there, however. A spike in name-calling and mockery was soon to follow. True couldn't keep count of the students who were calling her a freak. From her homeroom or otherwise. The word attached itself to her like a deformed shadow. From the moment she walked into the door to the moment people shoved past her when they left, True almost heard nothing else. Even her initial spot outside during lunch became compromised when Sydney, the popular girl from homeroom, started to go there.

Yesterday too, things were complicated. In gym, a girl with long brunette hair and green contacts stood beside her putting on makeup and glanced at True from the other side of the lockers. She adjusted her hand-held mirror repeatedly as True put her things away.

Alexia D. Miller

"You want to try some?" The girl asked, tilting the mirror forward in her palm.

Initially, True hadn't known the girl was speaking to her. Not until she walked over and stood behind her, putting the mirror to her mask. "I just *love* this shade!" She exclaimed, pointing a finger to her lips. "Here," the girl said, roughly turning True around to face her, "let me help you."

True took notice of the sound of multiple footsteps closing in around her, looking down at her own feet. As the girl with the mirror reached for her mask, True tried to bury herself in the lockers. When she could see the feet of the other girls and looked up towards the exit, True realized just how small the locker room was. So small, and yet big enough that she could be surrounded. Big enough that the exit could feel like miles away.

As another pair of hands made its way towards her face, True pressed her hands to either side of her mask to keep it in place. "Let us help!" Someone else yelled out. The others laughed and True silently struggled against their yanks and shoves. She struggled just long enough to hear the gym teacher, a Mrs. Burroughs, coming loudly to the locker room.

"How long does it take to get changed? Let's go! Get outta here!" She shouted, clapping her hands together. "We haven't got all day. Move it ladies!"

Alexia D. Miller

True looked at the tall woman, taking in her broad shoulders and the black halfmoons in her ears. Her curly silver hair was pulled tightly into a ponytail and she wore a pale green jumpsuit and thick, dark eyeshadow. True heard enough jokes about the "dusty, gothic tombstone" to know that most of the girls didn't like her. Their mocking nickname for her was enough for True to wonder if they'd call her more than just a "freak" if they ever saw her face.

True didn't want to think about what would have happened if Mrs. Burroughs hadn't come in. The brunette with the mirror clicked her tongue bitterly before slipping into her shorts and rolling her eyes at the teacher on her way out. The other girls, who True didn't bother to distinguish, followed close behind. None of whom missed the opportunity to shove into True's shoulder on their way.

"Not like *freaks* look good in make-up anyway, right?" One girl called out loudly. Moments of laughter erupted somewhere in the middle and True could just make out the voice of another girl saying that she probably looked dead under the mask anyhow. To True's surprise, another girl from the group boldly announced that True, if she liked the dead so much, should just join them. Mrs. Burroughs loudly called out that the girls should shut their traps, or she'd dock their points for class.

Alexia D. Miller

Since then, True decided to skip gym. She couldn't even bring herself to go to the field and make up for some of her missed classes. Of course, this wasn't due to any fault of Mrs. Burroughs, but she didn't want to take any chances; she didn't want to be surrounded in the locker room again. True also made sure to be the last one into homeroom, so she wouldn't have to face Victor alone. She didn't have any hope that Mr. Van-Dayton would help her if anything was wrong, but she thought that maybe other students would be less inclined to try and rip off her mask while an adult was in the room.

When True exited the last homeroom of the day, she saw Victor, Zane and another boy talking on their way out before the stranger walked off in the opposite direction. As she walked across the parking lot behind them, True was careful to keep her distance. After all her time spent trying to speak to Victor, True realized that he often walked home past her house while everyone else avoided it. She'd been surprised to find that on some days, he would walk past her house more than twice a day, coming and going.

True recalled how she'd wanted to ask him why he decided to do it. She wanted to ask if he believed the rumors about the house or if he knew anything about the aristocrat family who lived there so long ago. No matter how much she wanted to ask, however, True knew that talking to him had

Alexia D. Miller

already proved difficult. That and if he hated her too, she wasn't sure she wanted to know.

As they neared True's house, she looked leisurely through her bag to find her key. In doing so, True continued to walk until she suddenly looked up just in enough time to keep her from ramming into Victor and Zane. Victor stood slightly closer to her, his eyebrows bent, and his eyes squinted. "Was there a reason you'd been following me?" He asked suddenly.

Caught by surprise, True dropped her key and hurried to pick it up. When she stood properly back on her feet, she saw Zane's hand on Victor's shoulder saying something she couldn't hear. True's voice was lost somewhere in the space between them. Not knowing how to respond to his expectant gaze, True looked away in a panic.

Swallowing, True recalled the journal tucked away into her bag. She hesitated before reaching inside and holding out the journal in front of her. "Where the crystals come together, worlds collide, and doors open." True recited. As the three of them looked at each other silently, confusion clouding Zane and Victor's expressions, True shook her head and put away the journal.

Searching her jacket and unclipping her chain from her neck, True took a deep breath and held out her hand towards Victor, turning over her palm and spreading her

Alexia D. Miller

fingers to reveal her cloudy-white crystal. In the other, she held one of the extra chains she made.

Zane's eyes widened in shock and Victor frowned. True scoured her mind, desperately trying to find the right words. "You...have one too." She finally managed to say. "What? No way." Zane whispered, stumbling slightly backwards. "Another one?? Not another one. They're sprouting like weeds!"

"How do you know that?" Victor asked quickly, guarded.

"Because you and your friends went through the door too. In Mirror." True said, holding out the loose chain for him. "Here." She offered. Slowly, Victor raised his arm and opened his hand to accept the chain, his eyes shifting to the crystal in True's right hand. "The journal talks briefly about it—the crystals." True tried to explain. "Not enough, but something."

"This doesn't make any sense." Zane said in disbelief. "I don't remember seeing anyone else. I sure as heck don't remember you getting caught in The Catcher's net." Zane sneered.

"I..." True tried to think of the right thing to say, "I wasn't caught by The Catcher."

"I don't get it." Zane said, shaking his head. "That doesn't make sense."

Alexia D. Miller

"I know." True sighed, tired of talking. "I want to go back through the door. I can tell you what I've learned," True said quietly. "If you come to Snowville Temporary Infirmary again." Feeling both nervous and drained, True rushed up to her gate and went through.

"Wait!" Victor called to her back as she ascended the steps to the front door. "Were you the one who cleaned the upstairs of the hospital?" Victor asked.

Without turning to face him, True nodded as she unlocked her door. Rushing inside, True bolted up the stairs and peeked out one of her windows. Below, she saw Victor gaze towards the front door before Zane pulled him forward in a hurry. She couldn't hear them from her floor, but she could tell that Zane was loud, that he was yelling about something.

True stood and leaned her head against the window with a heavy sigh. Somehow, she'd done it; she'd spoken to them. True slid off her bag, still holding her crystal in her hand, and closed her eyes. Wondering if they'd come, she sank to the floor, exhausted.

Alexia D. Miller

Victor...

Chapter Twenty-Three: Curious.

Victor flopped down onto his mattress. It was hard to believe he'd managed to get an answer from True. When they'd left the school and he saw her there not too far behind them, he didn't know that by the time they'd reached her house, he would demand an answer. In his head, things had gone differently. Even then, however, Victor assumed she would silently defy him or even turn on her heels and go home.

It was even harder to believe what she'd said about the crystals. True had spoken more to him in those few minutes than before. Victor recalled the presentation she gave again. Even then True managed not to say much. Had she been watching him to make sure he had a crystal? No. That couldn't be. Victor never removed the crystal from his pocket during school.

Victor wondered if all of the times he'd caught True glancing his way, peeking from around the corner, or facing him just to walk off in the opposite direction were simply her attempts to bring up the crystals. Whatever the case, he

Alexia D. Miller

knew that he hadn't been suffering from a sudden onset of paranoia. He knew that he hadn't been overreacting.

So, when things seemed different and he no longer felt her glance from the corner of the classroom, when she walked past him and was the last one to homeroom, Victor had taken notice. It wasn't as if he'd seen her spend her time with anyone. He hadn't even seen her hold a conversation with any other student since she'd started school, but now it seemed like she steered away from everyone completely.

Her books that generally occupied her free time after she finished her classwork were nowhere to be seen. In the back of his mind, Victor had spent a great deal of time wondering if he'd done something to bother her, or if something was wrong. He hadn't realized just how much of his routine in homeroom started to revolve around little things she did until now.

Victor had quickly grown used to her presence. He expected to see her the moment he walked in late, knowing that she was always the first to arrive. He was fascinated by how quickly she finished her work, somehow still with perfect handwriting. His eyes often drifted to her books while he put his head down on his desk for his next nap. Victor would read the title and try to guess what the book was about and imagined what part of the story she was reading before he drifted off to sleep.

Alexia D. Miller

Even when homeroom was over, he took his time gathering his things and watched her gently place her work on the teacher's desk before going back to her chair. Victor found himself unable to break the habit of watching her small hands go across her desk and pick up her things as if grabbing them too quickly would cause them to break apart. Unlike other students, True never rushed to put her things away or dropped something from her desk.

So when, just hours ago, Victor called himself confronting her and she fumbled around in her bag, Victor felt as if a taboo had been committed when her key fell to the ground. He immediately regretted asking her anything at all. When Zane put a hand to his shoulder and told him to just let it go, he rolled the thought over in his mind. Even if he decided to do that, he didn't know the most appropriate way to do it. He couldn't take the words back after he said them.

Victor wasn't sure what he thought she would say, but he never expected to hear about the crystals or Mirror. How had she been there that day? They'd searched the used floors and the only way to go up to a higher floor in the building was blocked off. No matter how many times he ran through their actions or the building in his head, he couldn't understand where she was or how she ended up in Mirror

Alexia D. Miller

with them. Even if it were possible that True lied, Victor couldn't imagine it. Why would she?

As far as Victor could tell, True didn't have a reason to do so. He sighed, taking out his crystal and the chain she'd given him. One like the one housing her own, as he recalled. Her crystal looked like the others, a different color of course, but the same in any way that mattered. Victor inspected the chain and eventually pressed his crystal in-between the two coils. Had she made it herself? Victor shook his head. Even trying to imagine True talking to a clerk about jewelry seemed futile.

For the first time, Victor found himself wondering what she looked like as he stared up at his white ceiling. Was her face as pale as her arms and feet? He wondered what kind of eyes stared back at him from behind her mask. Without it, she probably wouldn't leave the house, Victor assumed. After all, the fuss he'd gotten suspended for was due to that mask in the first place.

Had True been in some sort of accident? Had she had some sort of horrible encounter with chemicals? Had she had reconstructive surgery or something? Similar questions flooded his mind before he became frustrated with himself. *What the heck am I doing?* Victor thought. *Stop making up wild stories just to satisfy yourself.*

Alexia D. Miller

Victor knew his questions arose from genuine curiosity, but it didn't make it excusable. He'd never even seen a single strand of her hair. As far as he was concerned, it took someone extremely meticulous to keep others so far at bay. Even he slipped up from time-to-time. Even a few people at school knew one thing or another about him besides the clothes on his back.

Victor didn't know what to say to the others. They'd likely have as many questions as he did. Maybe Phelia even more so. Laying there on his bed wasn't doing him any good. With a frustrated sigh, Victor stood up and dragged his fingers through his hair. He had to call Zane.

Phelia...

Chapter Twenty-Four: Questions and Answers.

Phelia was more than interested in this girl called True. While she couldn't say she trusted her, she did want whatever information she'd acquired about the crystals. She wondered how many more people came across the crystals and if any of them had also made their way to Mirror. What was all of this about a journal? Phelia wasn't sure how much it mattered that the girl didn't show her face.

Grace was on her way thanks to their walkie-talkies and Zane and Victor were already sitting down at the table eating breakfast as their father left out the door. As Phelia made her way back to the kitchen, she recalled that Zane had the crystals on his brain too. In fact, they'd been the only thing to pique his interest as of late, which was uncommon.

Phelia was sure that something happened with him, but he'd been spending more and more time away from the house and even less time alone with her, so she never knew exactly when to ask. Zane, to Phelia's disappointment, also stopped asking about spending time together. Phelia knew,

Alexia D. Miller

however, that there would come a time when Zane found other interests and wanted little to do with a baby sister, but she hadn't expected it to be so soon. Was it because he was now in high school, or was it simply because he had grown tired of living like he was the one without friends because of her?

Phelia climbed into her seat and bit into her toast. As she chewed, she tried to change her focus to True and the crystals again. She recalled what Victor said the night before. Was it possible that this girl had been there, and no one had caught a single glimpse of her? Where was she when they first opened the door in the wall? They'd searched the building and while there did seem to be signs that someone had been moving things around, possibly even cleaning, they hadn't seen her.

Phelia wondered if it was possible that she climbed out one of the windows when they weren't looking and make her way back in later. It seemed like too much work for one person just to hide because they didn't want to be seen. Did the fact that she had a crystal automatically mean that she traveled to Mirror? Was it possible hers was a fake? How would they discern a fake in the first place? Phelia shook her head, taking another bite. *Victor seemed convinced, and he saw it up close,* Phelia thought.

Alexia D. Miller

{ 221 }

"Should we meet her?" Phelia asked aloud as Zane went to get the door. Grace sprinted into the kitchen, her hair bouncing lightly above her head.

"Hello everyone!" Grace said, smiling to Phelia.

"Am I going to have to explain it all to you too?" Victor directed at Grace as she wiped her hands on one of the kitchen towels and sat down across from him.

"Nope!" Grace said cheerily as Phelia motioned for her to help herself. Grace grabbed an empty plate on the table and scooped up oatmeal and eggs. Phelia watched quietly as she took a banana from the fruit basket and peeled it. "Phelia told me last night." Grace explained.

Zane raised an eyebrow in Phelia's direction, and she explained that she'd given Grace the other walkie-talkie. If he had any questions, he didn't ask. "We should at least see what True has to say," Victor chimed in, bringing them back to the topic at hand. "I don't know her well or anything, but she did come up to me and try to say something before, I think. I don't know why she'd do that if she wasn't being honest."

"I'm not so sure we should even go back," Grace said, finishing her banana.

"That's exactly why we should see what she has to say first." Phelia said, watching Zane finish his breakfast and put his plate into the sink.

Alexia D. Miller

"She didn't say when." Zane chimed in, turning around to face them. "She never said what day."

"Well it couldn't hurt to go today." Phelia said, recalling the upstairs of the infirmary. "We all noticed that someone had been there straightening up. In fact, things were almost too clean for a building no one else had been visiting. So, she must frequent the place often. Especially if what she said to Victor was the truth. If she was the one who had been cleaning." Phelia said, finishing her toast.

"I guess we could always decide what we want to do after we talk to her, together." Zane said with a sigh. "We can afford to go a few times and see if she turns up." Phelia nodded in agreement, looking over at Grace whose face flooded with worry. Phelia placed a hand lightly on her shoulder, "It's alright Grace. No one is going off alone and we are going to talk things out."

"A unanimous decision." Victor said with a nod, "We all agree, or we don't go anywhere."

"Besides," Phelia said, taking a sip from her glass, "we couldn't even get the crystals to work in Mirror. So, we probably couldn't leave if we tried." Phelia tried to reassure her.

"Okay." Grace said with a groan, "Okay."

Phelia smiled with a nod. She wasn't sure herself if she truly wanted to return to Mirror, however, she at least

Alexia D. Miller

wanted to know if there was more they could learn about the crystals. If the masked girl weren't being honest, it would only be a matter of time before they found out. For her own sake, Phelia hoped Victor was right. She didn't want to waste time. Quickly, they finished their breakfast and Zane washed dishes before they left.

Zane...

Chapter Twenty-Five: Tomorrow.

Zane shook his head as they walked, his eyes following Grace and Phelia a few feet ahead of them. "What did you tell her?" Victor asked, raising an eyebrow. Zane finally managed to tell Victor that Bailey suddenly asked him out on a date.

"Honestly, I didn't say anything." Zane answered truthfully. "I wasn't even sure she actually asked me." Zane said, watching Victor clear his throat to keep from laughing. "Don't laugh," Zane said quickly, shoving him.

Victor stumbled forward, thrown off-balance, before he stood upright and shrugged. "What?" Victor asked mockingly. "Why not? What's better than laughing at your friend's expense?" He joked.

"You're such a jerk." Zane laughed.

"Okay." Victor said with a snicker, "Noted."

"She gave me her number." Zane said, walking again.

"You should just say yes." Victor said following close behind.

Alexia D. Miller

Zane couldn't understand Victor's sudden urge to ship him off with Bailey. Was he messing with him? "If it was Sydney, would you?"

Zane watched as Victor stuffed his hands into his pockets and scrunched up his face.

"No. Absolutely not. But we aren't talking about Sydney. Please, let's **never** talk about Sydney. Anyway, we are talking about Bailey. They're nothing alike."

"I know they're different." Zane scoffed.

"Good. I was starting to wonder if you knew anything." Victor said with a sigh.

"What's that supposed to mean?" Zane asked pointedly.

"You've just been...spacy. That's all. Kind of out of it." He retorted with a shrug. "So, when did she want to go out?"

Zane was quiet a moment. Even he knew that he had been distracted. He wanted to ask Victor what they'd been talking about lately but wasn't sure if it would upset him. He wanted to ask if it was that obvious, but he didn't. Zane turned his gaze back to Phelia and Grace. They were talking intently about something as Grace flung her arms out in front of her, mouthing words he couldn't hear.

"Uh...tomorrow." He responded, noting that Grace seemed to talk with her hands often.

"Well that's the rest of the day to make a decision." Victor said, lightly patting him on the shoulder, mocking

Alexia D. Miller

Zane's normal habit. Without another word, he sped up to walk beside the girls. Zane followed suit, stepping into stride alongside Grace who was talking about some elephant with blonde hair. Zane guessed she must have meant a character on tv.

Grace...

Chapter Twenty-Six: Dumb.

*I*t felt good to rant to Phelia. She hadn't judged her or made disbelieving faces while she spoke, even though Grace hadn't given a completely detailed explanation. When she referred to Eustis as Elephant or Elephant Spit, Phelia didn't question that she was talking about a boy from school. When she mentioned that he and his idiots picked on her, Phelia asked if she told the teachers or some other figurehead.

"It doesn't matter who I tell. The teachers don't believe a word I say because they think Elephant Spit is a Saint. So, I am the devil in every classroom. Apparently, I am *always* picking fights. Everyone is convinced that *I'm* the bully!" Grace said, waving her arms in frustration.

Phelia shook her head. "Father took me away from people like that when I asked. I'm beginning to think that homeschool is better. Especially if that is still all I'm missing out on."

Grace sighed, "MaryAnne and Duke would *never* let me do something like that. They don't trust me with my own clothes, let alone to stay home and do schoolwork. They probably think I'm too dumb anyway."

"MaryAnne and Duke?" Phelia asked curiously. "They're my foster parents," Grace said flatly. "I'm adopted." When Grace looked at Phelia she couldn't place the expression on her face. If she was feeling sorry for her, Grace didn't like it. Grace scratched her head. She could just make out the old hospital building in the distance.

"You don't think you're dumb, do you?" Phelia asked. Grace met the sad look in her eyes. Frowning, she fidgeted with her crystal tucked away in her pocket. "Well— no it isn't that I—I mean, I'm not as smart as some people, but I don't think I'm dumb." Grace stuttered, feeling guilty again. Not for just assuming that Phelia was immediately pitying her, but also for not being completely honest.

She hadn't outright lied like before, but it still felt the same. She still felt the nerves bubble up in her chest and her saliva turn to dust. Grace didn't particularly feel dumb in that moment, but she wouldn't go so far as to say she didn't ever believe it. The truth was, she did feel dumb and worthless almost every day. She didn't think she was particularly smart, but she thought that if she kept going, if she was really lucky, she just might make it out of Snowville.

Alexia D. Miller

True...

Chapter Twenty-Seven: The Journal.

True breathed a sigh of relief. They'd made it, and sooner than she thought. As they stood quietly in front of her, she could see their faces flooded with a multitude of emotions, but at least they were present.

While she didn't feel comfortable reading the journal entries to them herself, she could make the journal available to them in person. As short as the journal entries were, True had come to value what was written. She read them so many times by now, that she had them committed to memory. Perhaps the others would value them too.

"So, if we read these—this journal—we will know what you know?" Zane asked as he turned the journal over to inspect the covers. True nodded silently as he cleared his throat. "Well uh...I can read them aloud if that's alright with you?" He asked hesitantly.

It was only then that True wondered if Zane assumed the journal was her own. She wanted to tell him otherwise but decided to offer another nod instead. She watched as Zane flipped through the book one page after the other. He looked at her quizzically. "This is...*really* short."

"Yes," True nodded again.

"The entries are practically a paragraph or two." He mumbled in disbelief. Victor walked over to peer over his shoulder.

"Well we should judge it after we read it." Victor shrugged. "I'm pretty sure it isn't her journal. It isn't even her handwriting." He said dismissively. So nonchalantly that even True had been surprised. Zane shot a skeptical look his way.

Victor turned his head to see that everyone was staring at him and looked in True's direction. "What? We have homeroom together and she presented a hand-written poster. It's not that weird." He said defensively. Zane laughed only to receive an elbow to the rib. "Shut up and read." Victor demanded.

"You don't have to be rude about it," Zane laughed again. He said something under his breath that True didn't hear, causing Victor to shoot a disapproving glance in his direction.

True stood silently in the corner as Victor sat next to the others as they made their way to the floor. "Hurry Zane. The information is what matters, not length. Although, I would have preferred something more." Phelia's small voice

Alexia D. Miller

said, crossing her legs on the floor. "We must make do with what we have."

"Alright, alright already." Zane said, flipping to the first entry.

"One. There's so little I know of them—these crystals. I've decided to start writing things down so that you can have them too. Mind you, I am not a great writer and I have no clue what order to go in. Still, safekeeping, right? Anyway, the first thing I learned is that the crystals all come from the same stone. Something called the Master Crystal. As I understand it, the crystal is a large, multicolored mass. I don't know how many crystals have come from it or how it came into existence.

"Two. I've learned that this crystal opens something called a door. An entryway to another place, invisible to the naked eye until it is activated. I have gone through the door twice now, both times to the same place. I believe I know how to open it now. It is a matter of wishing, so to speak, to pass through. Deep breath. Closed eyes. Wish, wish, wish. It is becoming easier, faster, after every attempt.

"Three. There's another person from the area here today. He has a crystal too. His name is Mathew. I asked if he had ever seen or heard of the Master Crystal. He said he had no idea what I meant. He mentioned that he went through a door too, to some place completely different from

Alexia D. Miller

the one I described. He said it was the perfect place. As if it was a room made just for him; the exact words that had crossed my mind before. I don't know how it is possible. Maybe the crystals all open different doors?

"Four. Nothing happened yesterday. Mathew and I tried to open a door together, but no matter how long and hard we wished, we couldn't do it. I don't know if that means we aren't doing it right or if it's because we were strangers trying to imagine the same thing. Or maybe it's not possible to open a door together. It probably doesn't matter, but I had a dream last night that we could. That Mathew and I had watched the light fill the room and we disappeared and walked through another door. Maybe I pushed too hard.

"Five. It's been weeks since our attempt to open the door together and, in my disappointment, I couldn't bring myself to write anything since. We'd been learning more about each other. I've found Mathew to be a wonderful person. Some part of me has been hopeful that we could force the door to open for us if we grew closer.

It was today, however, when I was flooded with those feelings again, that the door opened for us. A door leading to a place of pink hues and warmth. A place outside our own "rooms"—as I have decided to call them. I don't have the words to describe what we saw. I never even knew if the place had a name.

Alexia D. Miller

"Six. When we'd left that room the other day we struggled for some time. We were stuck in the room, suddenly aware that we didn't know how long we'd be gone. We must remember next time: every entrance has an exit. The crystals will eventually lead us there.

"Something else was interesting too. Time flowed differently there than at home. Once we returned, we realized that it hadn't been nearly as long as what we'd assumed. I almost never wanted to leave. Isn't that strange? I'd never felt so delighted.

"Seven. There's someone new again. A girl this time, like me. She seemed to know something about the crystals already. I don't know why, but she seems to hate me, though she's taken a liking to Mathew. We haven't been able to open our rooms or any other door since her arrival. I don't understand what's happened, and I understand Brilla even less. If she has been to her own room at least, she hasn't said anything about it.

"Eight. We met twins today. The eldest, a girl named Vale and her brother Vick. I have already come to like them. They are quiet but straightforward, and they have the warmest smiles. Even their crystals match each other. Brilla didn't seem to take much of a liking to them. As horrible as it is, I've found myself relieved at the thought of it. I thought, at least I wasn't the *only* one that she disliked.

Alexia D. Miller

"Best of all, the most amazing thing happened! The door opened for us all. As far as I understood it, no one wished for anything. I can't help but wonder if it was because it was meant to be. Brilla thinks I am an airhead. She believes I am only making things more complicated by conjuring up my own reasons for us to disappear to unknown places. Is it so bad that I believe things happen for a reason?

"Nine. We're chosen? That's what he'd told us. Chosen for something beyond ourselves, something amazing. Given everything we've already seen, I can't imagine there being something more. In just a month everything in my life has changed. We have keys. Crystal keys...that open doors to worlds beyond our own. I have so many questions burning inside of me, but he said we will have to see for ourselves. He said that he doesn't have much time to explain. That something more is coming, and we have to be ready."

"Ten. Brilla wants to run away now. She doesn't want the crystal. She wants to go back to her life. We were told it was our destiny. We don't have long to prepare. Things have changed. Things are harder now and I don't know what will happen in the future. Still, we can't just turn back, can we? How could we leave things the way they are? We can't simply ignore all that we've learned.

Alexia D. Miller

"We were supposed to have so much more time. That's what we were told. I don't think it matters anymore. I'll be alright. We all will, won't we? If Mathew is lending his support nearby, so long as Vale and Vick continue smiling, we will change everything.

"Once Brilla accepts things for the way they are, we can begin. Uriel, Brilla, Vale, Vick, and Mathew. We couldn't have guessed in a million years that people like us would be traveling to different worlds. Where the crystals come together, worlds collide, and doors open."

As Zane finished reading his voice trailed off and the room fell silent again. True withdrew into her own thoughts, still vaguely aware of the others' voices. "Why did the end sound so different from the other entries? Who was the "he" she mentioned?" Victor asked aloud.

"I have many more questions than answers." Phelia said with a hint of annoyance. "How had the two of them—Uriel and Mathew—managed to open a door alone? Is it a fact that everyone can open a door that leads to a room just for themselves? If so, why is that? If these people were so-called chosen, what does that entail? Does Uriel's journal mean that the others also lived in Snowville before us? Are they still here?"

Zane sighed. "No kidding. I'm definitely worried about the way those entries went. I don't know the first thing

Alexia D. Miller

about these crystals, but I don't like the sound of being chosen for anything. That last entry gave me a horrible feeling. Sorta like something terrible was happening to them all of a sudden."

Grace nodded. "Yeah! I have some too. Like, why didn't Brilla like anyone? What's her *problem*? Did Uriel and Mathew like each other or were they just friends?" She asked, motioning with her hands as she spoke. "I need more information!" She huffed, suddenly falling silent and looking embarrassed. Victor, Zane and Phelia blinked at her. "What?" Grace chuckled.

"Why are your questions completely unrelated to the crystals?" Zane questioned in disbelief.
"I don't know. I thought they were kinda related." Grace laughed awkwardly.

True watched their interactions soundlessly from the corner, not sure if there was anything she could offer. She too had been drowning in questions since finding the journal. However, True was determined to find comfort in ever being involved in anything outside of her own life. In being someone singled out for something better than being a "freak." Was it supposed to matter why?

Victor...

Chapter Twenty-Eight: An Understanding.

Victor agreed with both Phelia and Zane. He had more questions than answers. He didn't have a clue why Grace was so caught up on Brilla's behavior or who liked anyone. However, she did mention something that formed another question in his mind. Does their relationship to each other change anything about the crystals? Afterall, Mathew and Uriel had begun to build their friendship before they went through a door together.

Grace called to True. True didn't move from her spot or answer. She didn't even turn her head in Grace's direction. So, Grace called her again, louder this time. Victor took note of the slight raise in her shoulders before she turned towards her, walking closer. Had Grace startled her? "Don't you know anything? You did have the journal." Grace said. True was quiet holding her hand out to Zane, who returned the journal.

"I know that the crystal opening private rooms must be the truth." True said quietly. Victor took notice of True's

Alexia D. Miller

pale feet, her toes painted a shimmering silver. How had she managed it? Every day it was getting colder in Snowville and inside the abandoned building wasn't any better. With every word he could make out thin whisps of their breath in the air. Wouldn't she get sick? He could see the fabric of her light blue dress touching her ankles and wondered if they could use the fireplace. Was it still functional? Would it attract attention?

Phelia's suspicious tone brought him out of his thoughts. "How can you be so sure? Have *you* been inside this room?"

True nodded slowly. "Yes. The day we visited Mirror I was inside." Victor could see the moment that Phelia's suspicions faded, giving way to a curiosity she could hardly contain. Victor could almost measure it as if she had a meter above her head.

He couldn't blame her. Every explanation Victor conjured up before somehow paled in comparison to the truth. True had been on the other side of the door? So, they'd went through the door with the crystals and weren't aware of her because she really couldn't be seen.

"So," Phelia said thoughtfully, "when we arrived in Mirror you would have been the first or the last person there."

"Yes." True nodded. "I was first. I think."

Alexia D. Miller

"It was pretty dark in Mirror. That could explain why we didn't see her." Victor said with a shrug.

"Okay but where were you the rest of the time?" Zane asked.

"Yeah!" Grace chimed in with a whine. "Where were you when we got captured??"

"With the twins." True responded slowly.

"You mean you were at Mr. One's place? The *exact* place we were trying to end up. No way!" Zane exclaimed.

"Before the rescue we hadn't met the sister, that's for sure. When did you meet them?" Grace asked.

"The girl lost her collar and I helped her find it. She took me home and I met her brother there." True answered lowly, taking a step towards the wall. Victor frowned, watching her silently. Was something the matter?

"What was Mr. One?" Phelia asked quickly. Victor wasn't sure if she was asking simply out of curiosity of if she was asking to test her. If he had to guess, he would have said it was the latter. Phelia made no attempt whatsoever to explain what she meant by the word "what."

True took another step back.

"He was an animal. A snow owl of some sort, I believe." True said, shifting on her feet.

"Oh! *That's* what he meant!" Grace said, smacking her fist against her palm. Victor and the other's turned to look at

Alexia D. Miller

her. "When we went through that tree, or door...whatever it was, the boy said he owed us anyway. I guess he must've meant you."

"But I thought that only people that didn't have owners or collars were rounded up." Zane frowned.

"Not having a collar is all that matters." True said, shaking her head.

"Even if they already have an owner." Phelia said disapprovingly. "That's horrible."

"Then why did you help us?" Grace asked. "You didn't even know us." Victor could see True's feet, slowly inching back towards the wall with every word they said.

She looked like a mouse cowering from a predator. Did it even matter why? She didn't have to help them, but she did. After a few moments of silence, Victor understood that True had no intention of answering the question.

"Why didn't you speak to us? If you had gotten there before us, why didn't you walk with us? Why didn't we see you with the twins? Even when we all returned to Snowville, you would have had to leave with us somehow." With each question True took a step back towards the wall.

Victor took to his feet, his mind reeling. He didn't know what he could say to her, but he knew that he hadn't been wrong. Victor thought back to her quick and awkward introduction on the first day of class. He thought of all the times in class she could have spoken but didn't.

He recalled True's silence as she stood a foot away in the doorframe of homeroom before turning on her heels. Even the day before when he'd confronted her, and she dropped her key. The quick, short sentences she offered them to explain before rushing to her door. Suddenly, as if by the wiping of a lense, Victor understood.

"She was afraid." He said, looking at the others who were also back on their feet. "Zane," Victor said, looking towards him, "I told you how quiet she was—is."
"Yeah." Zane said, nodding, "So?"
Victor looked at True, not sure if he should close some of the distance between them or if she'd take off without warning. "I think she just...has trouble being around people. She always seems so tired afterwards, like she's using up energy with every word she says."

As Victor tried to explain, he wondered what kind of expression True hid behind her mask. Even this was speculation. Was he helping or making things worse?
"That's why you followed me and then disappeared before we ever got the chance to talk, right?" Even from where he stood, he could see her shaking. Victor could almost laugh at his stupidity. *How hadn't I noticed? Why did it take this*

long to get it? How stupid could I be? He asked himself bitterly.

. . .

Half an hour passed before anyone could find their voices. True had since sat down with her back against the wall. At some point, her shaking stopped, and she rested her hands in her lap gently. Grace was the first to speak, slowly walking towards True. "Gosh. I'm sorry if we were making you uncomfortable."

Phelia nodded in agreement. "Perhaps I was also demanding too many answers from you. Even if you have the journal, this is all new to you as well," she said apologetically.

"We're all sorry, actually." Zane chimed in. "I think it's safe to say that we don't have any more questions for you today."

"Yes," Phelia said with a stern nod, "but if you happen to have questions for us at some point, please ask them."

. . .

Before long, they were all climbing out of the window and out into the street again. True wanted to go through the door again, and it was the only way they could

Alexia D. Miller

get any answers. It didn't seem like much of a choice, as Grace quickly pointed out, but it had to be better than nothing. Tomorrow, they would go through the door again, together this time.

Victor couldn't imagine what True expected when she asked to meet with them, but he hoped they didn't give her a bad impression. Thinking about their behavior back in the building made Victor question True's life at school. How had she been fairing? Even more than that, Victor wasn't sure why it mattered so much to him.

He allowed his steps to fall behind until he stood adjacent to True. There was something else he had to ask. "True?" He called. "Umm...are you alright? I wanted to apologize. I don't really know if everything I said was totally accurate or anything, but if I embarrassed you back there, that wasn't my intention." Victor said, scratching his head. He walked alongside her, wondering if she was too tired to speak to him or if her silence was the price he had to pay for making her uncomfortable.

"Maybe a little." She answered finally. "But...no one outside of my family has ever done something like that for me before."

"Done something like that?" Victor asked curiously, "What? Embarrassed you?" He didn't notice that they'd stopped walking. "I think that's probably a good thing."

Alexia D. Miller

"No." She answered quietly.

"Hey Victor!" Zane shouted from up ahead, "Are you coming home with us today?"

Victor put his thumb in the air, feeling too lazy to yell back. When he looked back to his side, True slipped a small bag onto his wrist and walked off in a different direction. "Thank you." She said as she disappeared around a corner.

Victor tilted his body forward to see if he could catch another glimpse of her. When he realized she was gone, he peeked into the bag. Inside, he saw chains that mirrored the one she'd given him before. Was he supposed to hand them out to the others? "I guess it makes sense if I do it." Victor said, shaking his head as he stuck his hands in his pockets. He took his time walking towards Phelia, Zane and Grace.

"Hurry up old man!" Zane laughed. "You're gonna get left behind slow poke!" He teased.

"Why are you calling him old?" Grace asked.

Phelia took Grace by the hand, leading her towards the Brand house. "That's just something he says." Phelia giggled.

Phelia...

Chapter Twenty-Nine: The Need for Answers.

When they'd gotten home Phelia, Zane and Victor sat down around the fireplace and spoke to Grace on the other end of the walkie-talkie. It was important that they were certain they would go through the door again. Again, Grace was reluctant, but decided that if everyone else thought it would be worth it, she could stand to go through the door one more time.

After dinner Phelia sat a plate in the fridge for their father, hearing Zane and Victor's voices carrying over from the front room. Something about a date with a girl from class? "Does this have anything to do with you not wanting to leave your sister for the day? If Grace can't make it, I don't mind stopping by and spending time with her." Victor offered.

"That doesn't sound like a bad idea or anything but that's not it. Why are you so in favor of me going on this date anyway?" Zane huffed. "As long as we have known each other, you've never been so quick to ship me off."

Alexia D. Miller

"Bailey's a nice enough girl. Probably one of the only nice girls at our school who isn't on her way off to college. If you going on a date will get you back to your old self, then it's worth a shot to me. That, and it was always sort of...obvious that she liked you." He sighed.

Phelia peeked around the corner to look into the front room. She didn't know if she should walk out of the kitchen and interrupt them or stand there, an unwilling participant. "I've never heard you say she was nice before. The one time I do, and you still sound like an old man." Zane said, shaking his head. "Wait...what do you mean it was obvious that she liked me? You never said a thing!"

Victor shrugged. "I didn't exactly think it would matter. It's not my fault. Besides, if I told you that, then every time you spoke to her that's all you'd remember."

"You're my best friend. I'm pretty sure you're not allowed to insult me." Zane replied sarcastically.

"Whatever you say. So, what's the issue? Do you just not want to go?"

Phelia watched Zane scratch his cheek, a nervous habit. "It's not that. It has very little to do with Phelia and a lot more to do with not knowing what is gonna happen tomorrow. I mean...we barely made it back to Snowville. Much less by sunset. We could have never made it back. Not to your mother or our father."

Alexia D. Miller

"I'd thought about that too. My mom, your dad...they'd have been devastated." Victor said gloomily. "But we do have something going for us."

"Oh yeah? What's that?" Zane asked, skeptical. "We've been to Mirror before. We know how some of it works, right? We'll spend a whole lot less time trying to figure things out. Maybe even speak to those twins again. Best thing is, we know exactly where the door is."

"That's true!" Zane said, patting Victor's back. "So, you think we will make it home?"

"Stop hitting me." Victor said, pushing Zane's arm away. "Anyway, I'd bet on us." Victor nodded with a smile.

Phelia decided to tip-toe out of the kitchen and around to the stairway. She changed her clothes upstairs and brushed her teeth before tucking herself into bed. It was something she had been doing when their father wasn't home, as of late. While Phelia felt she had no reason to complain about Zane not seeing her off to bed, it had been a change she wasn't used to.

Lately, there'd been a lot of that, things and people she would normally understand now felt confusing and left her with questions. Normally she could feel and empathize with strangers, like True. She wasn't sure if it had been because she was overzealous when it came to the crystals, but even that didn't explain enough.

Alexia D. Miller

From the moment things with Zane started to fog, all her sense of understanding seemed to be beyond her. As if someone was pulling a thread and unraveling her second by second. Phelia wasn't sure if her brother's date had anything to do with the wall she felt between them. Frustrated and tired, Phelia forced herself to sleep.

. . .

In the morning, Phelia dressed in red overalls and a black sweater her father had bought a duplicate of his own and Zane's, with white snowflakes on the ends of her sleeves. It was almost that time again, Phelia thought. The time that their father took them shopping to find matching outfits and took a family photo to show their mother for her birthday.

Of course, Phelia understood that their mother could never receive the photo. She knew that the graveyard cleaner would simply come and swoop up their photo for another year. The same as he had done the year before, and the one before that. Later after they return home, her father would pull out the family photo album and slide a copy of the polaroid in, speaking words neither her nor Zane could hear.

Once, Phelia thought to ask him if he knew the fate of the photo he placed at their mother's grave, and if he did,

Alexia D. Miller

why he would leave it there to be thrown away. She thought better of it, but some days she still found the question coming to mind anyhow. Still, she wasn't sure she wanted to see the hurt behind her father's gaze. Whatever the answer was, it couldn't have been anything particularly happy. After all, no matter the circumstances, it was about their mother and her father's new habits since she'd left them.

As Phelia grabbed a small black bag and made her way down the stairs, Zane stopped her. He disappeared around the corner and came back with a black headband with a white snowman on the front. Without a word, he slid it over her hair and inspected it, when he was satisfied, he nodded and the two of them went down the stairs together. There, Phelia took note of his damp hair. "You should wear a hat," she directed at him.

"I will." He said flatly, going into the kitchen.

"Victor left already?" Phelia asked, hearing shuffling in the kitchen.

"Yeah. Uh...he went to have breakfast with his mom. We are meeting up in a couple hours, so I figured the two of us could head to the bakery."

Phelia felt a relieved that he wanted to go anywhere with her at all. Still, she wasn't sure what to make of it. First the headband. Now, the bakery. Was Zane in a better mood? She watched him put on his shoes and followed suit.

Alexia D. Miller

As they walked out of the door and onto the porch, Phelia reached her hand into her bag, feeling around for the crystal.

"What are we getting?" Phelia asked, making her way to the sidewalk. She looked up at the sky, the sun beaming above them.

"Anything really." Zane yawned. "We can get whatever you want."

Phelia watched him tuck his hands away into his pockets. "So, Victor is going to meet us at the building too. You're not too busy today?" Phelia asked, recalling his conversation with Victor the night before.

"Nope. I don't have any plans today." He answered with another yawn. So, he had canceled his date after all. Phelia wasn't entirely sure about dates. She'd been on a date once, with their father. They'd gotten ice cream and walked through the park. Of course, Phelia was certain that her brother's date would require something different.

Phelia recalled the slew of them she'd seen in movies. She knew that both parties dressed up. She knew that in the movies, the woman usually wore an elegant dress and held the man's arm as they strode along. Surely Bailey wouldn't be wearing an elegant dress in the cold. Phelia wasn't even certain that Zane had any particularly "classy" clothing. Phelia recalled his suit and tie from their mother's funeral, but that hardly seemed appropriate for something like that.

Slowly coming out of her thoughts, Phelia was startled by her brother's blue eyes, peering down at her. "So, you haven't been replaced by an imposter then, I take it?" He asked sarcastically.

"I'm sorry Zane," Phelia said, understanding that Zane must have been speaking to her while she was lost in her own head.

"Yuh-huh. I was trying to ask if you knew what you'd want from the bakery. *More specific than* something sweet." He emphasized.

Phelia thought for a moment. "Actually, a doughnut sounds delicious."

"Hmm...so it does." Zane smiled, leading their way to the bakery.

At the bakery, Phelia and Zane sat outside on a bench, waiting for their order, drinking tea. Phelia fought the doubt clouding her mind. While Zane didn't seem to be completely himself, he did seem closer today. She wanted to ask if something had happened. Even more, she wanted to know if there was something she could do. Still, she couldn't bring herself to ask.

"Are you ready for today?" Zane asked, grabbing their order from a server at the door.

Alexia D. Miller

"I suppose I am," Phelia said, watching him take his seat again. "I'm ready to figure out something more at least."

"For answers," Zane nodded.

"Yes," Phelia said, watching a swirl of steam from her cup disappear into the air. "Although I realize it is possible that we won't receive any. I know better than to force answers from thin air. Those will always be the wrong ones, but I also don't want to sit and do nothing."

"Honestly, I'd just settle for opening the door and getting back home in one peace—getting home without being captured again." Zane sighed.

"True. I'd like to avoid that if possible." Phelia agreed. "Victor seems to think that we will do better in Mirror this time around."

"Do *you* believe it?" Phelia asked, reaching into the white paper bag to grab a doughnut.

"I think he made good points. I just don't know what to think. About anything, really." He sighed, leaning back against the bench. "But I plan to do things better this time around, that's for sure."

Alexia D. Miller

Zane...

Chapter Thirty: Not Mirror??

*I*t wasn't long before Zane and Phelia made their way inside the abandoned building and up the stairs. On the lower floor he could make out True sitting in a crooked chair and Grace standing nearby. Immediately upon seeing each other, Phelia and Grace exchanged quiet greetings. Not more than a few minutes later, Victor arrived.

Zane sighed, for a moment wondering what they were doing there. Were they really going to go back through that door and into Mirror? He didn't want Phelia to be disappointed, but maybe as her older brother he should have told her there was no way they would willingly go back. Or was that inappropriate considering who Phelia was? Zane didn't know the right thing to do or if there was ever a right thing in the first place.

Victor's hand on his shoulder snapped him out of his thoughts. "Didn't you hear me?" Victor asked, his eyebrow raised. Zane shook his head. "We should go on up. Unless you need to sleep in or something? I'm not opposed to a nap." He yawned.

Alexia D. Miller

"Of course, you'd love it if I said yes, wouldn't you?" Zane asked sarcastically. He knew Victor's answer before he opened his mouth.

"Yes, please. I would love it if you did." Victor smiled playfully.

"Sorry to disappoint, but there's no way you're taking a nap right now." Zane laughed, pulling Victor him behind him. He ignored all his exaggerated sighs and any complaints about wanting to be back in his bed. In truth, Zane wanted to be fine. But even Victor's playful mood didn't make him any less anxious.

What Zane preferred was to put a stop to this insanity altogether. Still, Zane couldn't deny that he had questions. He just wasn't sure there were any answers to be found in Mirror. Last time they went they'd been lucky enough to know anything at all. Even if there were other ways for them to get answers, he didn't know if he wanted them bad enough to go back again.

Upstairs, Zane took out his crystal and stepped near the empty wall beside the others. He did his best to swallow his nerves. They'd all decided, and they were there, so there wasn't any going back now, right? He looked down to his left, seeing Phelia's determined face, all her attention on the wall. Zane had to stop himself from reaching out to her. Stop himself from trying to grab hold of her hand or pull her into

Alexia D. Miller

his arms. He remembered the words she'd said. He remembered her angrily demanding that he not offer any help.

Zane could just make out Grace's voice on the other side of her, saying something he couldn't hear. He saw Phelia look over in her direction and open her palm to Grace, who slid her fingers between hers quickly. Zane sighed, feeling a small sense of relief. Even if he hadn't been the one, it was far better knowing that she and Grace wouldn't be separated.

"Wish to go through the door." True's small voice instructed. So, Zane closed his eyes, took a deep breath, and wished. If Victor was so sure they could handle it, if they already had a plan to see the twins in Mirror, then maybe things wouldn't be so bad. If they'd get answers and hopefully *never* have to see Mirror so long as they lived, Zane was fine going back one more time.

Before he knew it, bright light forced Zane to open his eyes. Everything that was anything seemed to bend and swirl in a broken pattern, folding in onto itself. The echo of light chimes sounded, ultimately fading.

Again, anything he recognized became indistinguishable from the rest of the space around him. Zane tried to look down to see himself, to hold out his arms in front of him, but he couldn't move. The light dissolved

Alexia D. Miller

and an overwhelming darkness filled every corner of his vision. He felt a heaviness on every part of his body until he wasn't sure he ever had one at all.

There was nothing but darkness and complete silence. Zane couldn't be sure which bothered him most. From their last experience traveling through the door, Zane knew that if he were to speak, he wouldn't have a voice. Just as there would be no one to hear him.

This time felt longer and the weight against him felt heavier than he remembered. In a matter of seconds, Zane struggled to breathe. He didn't know if he was panicking, or if the moment he'd found himself surrounded by blackness, oxygen became scarce. Zane couldn't help but wonder if Phelia felt what he had. If she was surrounded by this horrible darkness and was suffering.

By the time Zane started to sink in his fear, thinking that he was going to be rendered unconscious or worse, the darkness around him receded. He felt the sensation of falling until his back pressed hard against a surface. Colors began to fill his blurry vision and he inhaled a gulp of fresh air.

As he recovered from his scare, he could make out something soft and plush beneath him. His nose soaked up the scent of wildflowers and something sweet he couldn't place. Quickly, Zane propped himself up to see the softest,

Alexia D. Miller

most luscious green grass he'd ever seen. He saw no lights in the ground or leading to a stretch of road.

In fact, there was no road at all. No large sign with a name or the sound of strange music nearby. In every direction, Zane saw flowers of every shape and color. Most of which were some odd variety that he'd never seen. It was beautiful.

Coming into view from his right, Zane could make out Grace, Victor and Phelia. "We are *so* not in Mirror people!" Grace yelled, bouncing around excitedly. Zane watched her thick, red hair sway rhythmically in her ponytail and her orange ribbon drifting through a bout of wind. Zane smiled, feeling a load lift off his shoulders.

He watched Phelia smiling quietly, looking at Grace prancing around in circles. They really weren't in Mirror after all. Zane made his way to his feet as Victor walked over to him, looking over his shoulder. "What's up?" Zane asked with a smile.

"Where's True?" Victor asked, and Zane realized that he hadn't seen her either.

Moments later, with Grace and Phelia at their side, Zane and Victor walked over the hill ahead of them keeping a look out for True. Over the hill, they saw another. At its peak, a figure stood with their back to them. Catching a

Alexia D. Miller

glimpse of the dark hooded jacket and pale feet, Zane called out to True.

She turned her head in their direction at the sound of her name. Her hands were clasped behind her back, holding her flats with two fingers. Today, Zane realized that True hadn't been wearing her usual dark gray mask. She was wearing a white mask with intricate swirled vines. It was oval shaped with a pink pair of lips painted on that matched two dots above the eyes where the eyebrows should have been.

At the top of the hill, Zane stood in awe of what was before him. Down the hill led to a large bridge that seemed to be woven from tree branches and vines. Under the bridge was a stream of clear water. So clear that even from the distance, Zane could clearly see the bottom.

On either side of the bridge were small hut-looking houses. These too looked as if they were masterfully woven from branches. An oversized leaf was tied onto each roof. No matter where he looked, Zane found more flowers in bloom and the same quality of grass as where he stood. "*Amazing!*" Grace shouted, flinging her arms out wide. Zane could feel himself smiling. He didn't know how they'd managed to escape going to Mirror, but he'd been happy they had. He felt the breeze drive away his negativity.

True was the first to start down the hill. Her pale feet slipped effortlessly through the flowers, cradling her shoes to

Alexia D. Miller

her chest. Not long after, Zane watched Phelia slide off her shoes and tuck them into her bag before running down the hill.

Grace wasted no time to follow, kicking her shoes down the hill as she ran after them, laughing. One shoe she'd kicked so hard that it flung over Phelia's head and rolled down the rest of the way. Zane looked over at Victor who shrugged before they both bolted down the hill, racing in silent competition. They flew past the girls, Victor jumping over a large stone further ahead.

Zane listened to Victor's voice in the expanding distance, noting the hint of mockery in his tone. "Oh yeah?" Zane yelled, squinting his eyes at Victor before plopping down onto the ground. He raised his arms above his head and rolled his body as fast as he could, laughing until he rolled past him. Dizzy, Zane struggled to his feet, catching the look of surprise on Victor's face before he raced behind him to catch up.

Without warning, Grace thunder bolted past them both. She turned her head to look over her shoulder, smiling from ear-to-ear. As she made it to the bottom of the hill, she raised her fists above her head, celebrating her victory.

Grace...

Chapter Thirty-One: Free.

Within a matter of minutes, Grace, Zane, Victor and Phelia all lay on the floor of the bridge. They suffered through the sharp pains in their chest and struggled to fill their lungs with air. Grace laughed through a wheeze. She couldn't remember the last time she had so much fun. She couldn't remember the last time she'd felt so happy—so free.

As Grace watched the rise and fall of her chest, she was struck with a realization anew: they *somehow* managed to avoid going back to Mirror. There had really been a different place on the other side of the door. Grace didn't know where they were or what to call it, but she thought that if this wonderful place had food, she wouldn't mind staying forever.

Even though Grace knew how unreasonable that was, how impossible it would be, she still allowed herself to imagine it. *Just for a moment,* she thought, *and then I will have to face reality again.* She tried to imagine her and the others sitting around a table or on a blanket, sharing stories and food. She even imagined that with every day she spent

Alexia D. Miller

her time happily running through the flower-filled fields *That* room at MaryAnne and Duke's would break apart until it no longer existed.

Almost recovered from their races down the hill and again to the bridge, Grace looked over to True. Who Grace realized, unlike the rest of them, took her time going down the hill and walking onto the bridge. Grace watched her standing on her toes, peering over the side of the bridge. A moment later, she began walking past them all gliding her hand over the intertwined branches and vines, as small white buds peeked every so often through her fingers.

As True walked quietly ahead, Grace and the others slid on their shoes. A few minutes later, Phelia mentioned that they should figure out where they were. "Although there was no sign like we saw in Mirror," Phelia commented. "There must be a way to know."
"We still need to find the door too, wherever it is." Victor said, leisurely putting his hands into his pockets.

As they neared the turn on the bridge, Grace could see the bridges' end. Not far ahead of them the bridge thinned and met the ground again. *Almost like a slide*, Grace thought. *A very bumpy, vine-y slide.* Focusing her eyes as they got closer, Grace could see figures moving ahead of them.

Alexia D. Miller

"People?" Grace wondered aloud. Walking off the end of the bridge, Grace gasped. Not people exactly? As far as Grace could tell, they were beings someone had drawn and breathed into life.

"So, you guys see them too?" Zane asked.

"Yes." Grace answered breathily. "Definitely."

Men and women of some sort, adorning the purest of white hair and...wings? Each one of them the same height as the last, bustling to one direction or another. They wore light gray robes with loose sleeves. As Grace continued studying the sea of white, she could just make out differences in their facial expressions, eye colors and hairstyles.

Seeing Phelia walking by, Grace rushed up to her side.

"We can't just waste time. Who knows when things will change?" Phelia said, matter-of-factly. Grace nervously followed her to the nearest woman. She had the same snow-white hair and wings, but bright blue eyes that matched a pawprint mark on her cheeks.

"Hello." Phelia said politely. The woman blinked quickly, looking as surprised by Grace and Phelia as they were of her.

"My goodness!" She exclaimed, her hands covering her mouth as she leaned forward to look at them. "Human guests?" She said, looking up at the others as they came

Alexia D. Miller

near. "We haven't had one in such a long time. What a *SPELNDID* day it is, indeed!" She said cheerily, before she dropped her head with a frown. "Yes. Yes. Splendid and yet bittersweet."

"What is she talking about?" Grace whispered to Phelia who shook her head. "Is she okay?" Grace wondered aloud.

"Where are we?" Phelia asked, tilting her head to the side at the woman.

Suddenly, as if she hadn't been discouraged before, the woman's face lit up and her wings fluttered quickly, lifting her into the air. "Well you're in *FlareWing* of course!" She laughed, circling them before hovering in front of them again.

Grace smiled as she watched her, in awe. Her wings were real, *and* she could fly? *I love this place! Who knew we would end up in a land full of real-life fairies!!* Grace thought giddily. Her excitement withered as the woman's eyes widened and she quickly placed her feet on the ground. "Oh! I must be going! The Princess! Father—Father Wing!" She stuttered. "I can't afford to diddly-dawdle! It's almost time!"

"Almost time?" Phelia asked.

"Yes, yes." The woman answered. "Father Wing will be reborn, and the new Princess will arrive! Oh, I *must* finish in time!"

"Father Wing? New Princess?" Grace wondered aloud. "What does that mean?"

The woman's wings fluttered again, faster this time and she teetered side-to-side in front of them. She spoke quickly, her eyes shifting in one direction to another. "Soon." She spoke almost too quickly for Grace to hear, pointing further ahead of them. "At The Grand Tree." She said.

Following her finger, Grace realized that she'd been so distracted by the fairy people that she hadn't seen the humongous tree towering over everything nearby. A tree, easily over 40 feet high, made the huts seem even smaller. Huts that Grace also realized were hardly larger than the fairy people around them. Just what was that tree?

The Grand Tree, as the woman called it, held leaves greener than the grass they stood on. The leaves themselves, seemed to have brims etched in gold. Almost as if someone had taken a liquid brush to each leaf and traced it perfectly. The longer she stared, the more aware Grace became of the shimmering particles of light floating in the wind. Almost as if the tree itself rained glitter.

Alexia D. Miller

When Grace peeled her eyes away from the tree, the woman was nowhere to be found. Grace willed her eyes to find her in the crowd to no avail. She quickly realized it would be practically impossible to find her again. So, Grace and the others split up to find someone else to speak to. To their surprise, they were met with silent glances.

"Is there anyone else having a serious bout of Deja vu?" Phelia asked, frowning as she looked towards the sea of people.

Zane frustratedly ran his fingers down his face. "I know I am."

"Can we all agree to take a nap now?" Victor asked, yawning.

"Have you lost your mind??!" Zane yelled, taking Victor by the collar, shaking him. Victor groaned, not bothering to put up a fight. "We are in the middle of a crisis!" Zane shouted, shaking him harder. "You idiot! Pull yourself together!"

True...

Chapter Thirty-Two: Not a Fairy.

"Everything is a crisis with you. What do you want to do then? If we are just going to go around repeating what happened in Mirror, then I have plenty of time to take a nap." Victor grumbled.

"We can't just stand around, Victor. We have to try something!" Zane replied angrily. "Do you want to get stuck again?"

True wasn't sure what to do. She didn't have experience deescalating trouble, let alone getting between the argument of two friends. She looked at Grace and Phelia, thankful that they were asking them to quit fighting. True wasn't sure what to do either, but she did know that Victor had a point. Although True didn't feel like she or the others were in any particular danger, they couldn't go around hoping to force someone to answer their questions.

"I wouldn't try too hard if I were you." A voice called. True searched for a sign that someone in the crowd was looking to help them. When she didn't see anyone, she dismissed it as her imagination. At least until she spotted

Alexia D. Miller

movement beside Zane. Seeing Phelia point towards Zane's shoulder, True was certain that she wasn't the only one who noticed.

A ball of light laid itself to rest on the middle of his shoulder before fading, giving way to a small figure. *A boy?* True wondered. He sat cross-legged on Zane's shoulder before fluttering to Victor, then Grace. "It's not their fault really." He said, his wings fluttering quickly as Phelia leaned in close to study him from behind. "They have a one-track mind right about now. If you'd come at any other time, you humans would be the focus of FlareWing." He said matter-of-factly.

"What an interesting face you have." He directed at Grace with a smile. "Interesting indeed."
She frowned. "Interesting?" Grace mumbled.
"Well you're the first to look exactly like a fairy." Phelia said lowly, her fingers resting under her chin.

He turned around to face her crossing his arms. "I resent that." He said displeased. "Besides, you humans know very little about us Faeries. And it is Faeries, *not fairies!*" He huffed.
"There's a difference?" Grace asked, her face showcasing her confusion.
"Of course, there is!" He cried, moving erratically through the air in front of her.

Alexia D. Miller

"A Fairy is the product of human imagination—the pseudo version of us Faeries." He said, throwing his hands in the air. "As if we have no depth, no reason or will—fairy is a name for a skewed belief in what we are."

As he made his way to True, she found herself mesmerized. Only when he was in her direct line of sight did she truly register her surprise. His hair was long and white, tied low down his back. He wore the same gray robe she'd seen on the others, but his sleeves were wrapped to his wrists with a brown fabric. Around his neck was a bright rainbow-colored scarf, and his ankles were covered in thick, sheer cloth.

Most remarkable for True, however, was his face. His left eye was a sea-green hue. The other a clouded white, not unlike her crystal. Underneath his mist-colored eye was an intricate pattern of green leaves and a swirled flower. As she continued to stare at him from the other side of her mask, his voice trailed off and True was overcome with the feeling that he could see her. That his mismatched eyes looked beyond her jacket and mask—that he could see exactly what she was hiding.

For only a moment, or perhaps even an eternity, True felt completely and utterly naked. Like he'd seen the very depths of her entire being with a single glance. As if to confirm her rising suspicions, an amused smiled crept across

Alexia D. Miller

his face. "Well now..." he blinked slowly, "aren't *you* interesting?" He more stated than asked. In the moment True could feel the watchful eyes of the others as he spoke. When he offered his small hand, True hesitated to take it.

He gently wrapped his palm around a couple of her fingers. "T-True." She stuttered, attempting to greet him appropriately.

"Twister," he smiled again, showcasing his bright teeth. Without warning, he turned around to face the others. "And you are?"

"That's Grace, Victor and Zane." Phelia answered placing her hands behind her back, "I'm Phelia. Zane is my brother."

"Nice to meet you all." He said with a nod. "Come. I suppose I'll be your guide. Not that I've done it before." He laughed. The others shared glances silently before following into step behind him. It wasn't as if they had any better ideas. It didn't hurt either, to True at least, Twister seemed friendly.

"So, why are you so small?" Grace asked suddenly, motioning with her hands. "Everyone else is practically giants in comparison to you. Not that any of them are very tall. Even I'm bigger than them!"

"Grace!" Zane whispered, "You can't just ask people why they're small!" Grace's mouth dropped.

Alexia D. Miller

"Oh! I can't?" She asked, wide-eyed. Phelia attempted to apologize on her behalf.

Twister shook his head. "It's a natural question. I used to be asked the same thing every day in FlareWing, believe it or not." As he spoke, he hovered slightly ahead of them, his wings flapping slowly, leading the way to wherever they were headed. "I was born this way. Or at least, I've been this way since soon after my birth."

"I thought fairies were all tiny their entire lives, but it's only you." Grace said, tapping her chin in thought. True watched as Zane shook his head disapprovingly in her direction. She cupped her hand over her mouth. "I'm sorry. I'm doing it again, aren't I?"

"It's alright. It's unfortunately a common misconception in the human world." Twister said, shrugging. "When Fae are born, they are small. Like a human child...but smaller? It is difficult to explain."

"There are some infants born prematurely, which would cause them to be much smaller than average. Perhaps you mean something like that?" Phelia suggested.

"Perhaps." Twister answered thoughtfully. "In any case, it is an important tradition to expose young Fae to the outside world soon after birth. It's not uncommon for our families to travel to the human world to spread positivity,

Alexia D. Miller

light, and love. Perhaps just as important, we also do good deeds for humans." He smiled.

"It's normal for Fae to shrink in size when they pass through the veil. So long as they have already started their growth process or in the case of the adults, reached maturity. The veil—it's like a wall of energy that surrounds our world—cloaks us from humans. That is of course, unless a human has the gift of sight."

"Gift of sight?" True asked inquisitively.

Twister looked over his shoulder. "Sure. The gift of sight. You know, seeing spirits, Fae, demons, and angels, for example. Some humans are born with it. Others acquire it through different means."

"I never believed in that sorta thing." Zane said dismissively.

"Well you needn't believe in it for it to be true. Just as you didn't have to believe in our world to arrive here." Twister said, looking over his shoulder at him.

"So, there's a such thing as demons and angels? As spirits?" Phelia asked, her face shrouded in thought.

"Of course," Twister responded, "Humans often develop a strange sense of superiority over everything in the universe. As if they are the only intelligent forms of life that could exist."

"Nuh-uh!" Grace shook her head, creating an X out of her arms. "No thanks. I never want to see *any* kind of ghost!"

Alexia D. Miller

True wasn't sure she agreed. If she could see spirits, perhaps she would be able to help the souls that supposedly linger in her home. More than that, she might have been lucky enough to see her mother again.

True never recalled a time that she hadn't believed in other worlds, ghosts, and demons. She often dreamed of experiencing parallel universes and seeing extinct beings with her own two eyes. As far as she was concerned, the crystals had given her just that and more.

"Well, Grace," Twister continued, "children tend to have a natural ability to see us. The older they become, the more likely they are to push the gift away or lose it altogether. If you see us, it is likely that you at least have the capability to do so somewhere inside you. Though it may please you to know that anyone that passes through the veil and enters FlareWing can do so while here. Considering they are in our home, of course. Luckily for both you and I, the veil wards off evil."

Grace interlocked her fingers. "Any way I can take it home with me then?" She pleaded. True couldn't help but wonder if Grace was desperate for change. She thought back on the scene she'd witness from home. Did Grace suffer through those types of spectacles every day? She could imagine that if she had, it was likely True knew what potentially negative forces she wanted to ward off.

Alexia D. Miller

Twister laughed; a sound analogous to soft windchimes. His wings fluttered musically as he leaned forward, his fingers spread over his face. "I don't believe there is, but if I could I'd let you borrow it. If you *truly* needed it."

"That's too bad." Grace said, "Thanks anyhow." She smiled.

"You're the only person I've met that wouldn't bat an eye at asking for an entire piece of a world." Victor said, shaking his head.

"Hey. It's not my fault you didn't think to ask." Grace chuckled.

"True. It sounds like something to wrap up in." He uttered looking off into the distance. "Like the perfect recipe for a nap."

"I'm starting to get why Zane thinks you're an old man." Grace said, shaking her head.

As the others laughed, True found herself looking from one to the other. They were warm. Not unlike the feeling she had surrounded by her aunts. As beautiful as it was, True also knew that their warmth often accompanied another feeling: loneliness. She felt like she was on the other side of a window glass, staring at something she could never obtain.

Alexia D. Miller

"So, what happened after you went through the veil?" Phelia asked.

"Well," Twister sighed, "After the visit everything seemed fine, according to my family. I was born with these eyes, so it wasn't as if that changed, but something had. Somehow, I was stuck. Unlike other Fae, I didn't return to my original size after crossing back into our world."

"You couldn't change back?" Grace asked, shocked.

Twister nodded, "I grew older in other ways, physically and mentally in all ways that matter, but I stayed like this. The same size I would be on the other side of the veil. My parents tried everything they could think of." Twister sighed.

"They took me back through the veil and even spoke to Father Wing. He told my parents that something happened to my magic. Something even he couldn't undo. So, nowadays my parents haven't had another child. Not that I can blame them. I'd feel worse for a little sister or brother that ended up like me."

"Or they could've been taller than you." Grace chimed in, causing Zane to run his fingers down his face with a groan.

"I suppose there's that too." Twister spoke sadly. "It wouldn't be honest to say that I was like everyone else. Or that I wasn't isolated, but I at least chose that for myself. I try

Alexia D. Miller

to stay away from my parents. If I can stay away," Twister said, clutching his fists at his sides, "maybe they won't be afraid. If I stay away long enough, they could forget about me and try again..."

There was a heavy silence as they continued to follow Twister. True couldn't imagine it. The thought of Twister living with such a burden made her heart ache. She wanted to wrap her arms around him and tell him that things would be alright. She wanted to say that she would be his friend. That he didn't have to go through it alone.

Giving True the impression that he could see through her once again, Twister turned around and looked in her direction with a small smile before clapping his hands together. "Enough with the sad stuff, yes? Look. You've all been so engrossed in a small Faerie's tale that we've made it all the way here and none of you have so much as looked about!"

Victor...

Chapter Thirty-Three: Follow the Twister.

Twister's hut was the definition of isolated, as far as Victor could tell. It wasn't that the area surrounding his home was somehow less beautiful than the rest of this world or that his house was lacking in comparison to the others they'd already seen. In fact, Twister's roof had flowers interwoven in leaves which descended to the doorframe, unlike the others he recalled seeing before.

What gave Victor the feeling of seclusion was pure distance. Twister's hut was pushed off to the side on a hill. No other Faeries crossed their path as they walked. There was an absence of voices and chatter. Inside his home, which Victor compared to a studio, there was a small replica of the hut they stood in on a bench beside the door. A smaller-scaled home that Twister apparently built for himself since he could do nothing in the original.

Victor hadn't decided if he should be amazed at his craftmanship or filled with pity. He walked slowly throughout the hut, taking note of the branched furniture, a

Alexia D. Miller

stone stove, and a floor mattress in a room off to the right. He wondered how soft it was. Going back to the other side, Victor watched the others peek out of the windows as True gently touched the flowers blooming on the walls.

"Come! There's so much more to see than my small place!" Twister said, standing on the oversized bench next to the replica. "Today, you are my guests. We will come back later." He said, making his way to the air. "We have time before the ceremony. Why don't we go to the market?" Twister suggested happily, clapping his hands in front of him.

"Ceremony?" Phelia asked. "What do you mean?"

"Sure. You know, the thing Aqua-Fae mentioned before." He said, flying out of the door.

Victor followed him, Phelia at his heels. "Who is Aqua-Fae?" Victor asked curiously.

"Why the Faerie you were speaking to earlier, of course." He said quickly, turning around and pressing his index fingers to his face. "With the birthmarks here." He said, tapping his cheeks. Birthmark? Victor wondered, thinking about the marks under Twister's eye. *They are born with those marks...?*

"Wait." Grace called, pointing at the door. "Aren't you supposed to lock it?"

Twister chuckled. "Lock it? Of course not."

Alexia D. Miller

{ 278 }

Grace's jaw dropped. "No way! You don't even lock your doors? You must not have any bullies or bad Faeries then." Twister shook his head, "We are far from being without them in history, but we have been 'bad or bully' free for some time now. We Faeries have no reason to lock our doors. We value each other more than the things we own. Everything that lives must honor and care for their own species, else they'd become extinct.

"Well I wish Elephant Spit would become extinct. Him and his idiots." Grace huffed. Victor didn't want to waste energy figuring out what she meant. However, he caught the quick movement of Phelia's fingers, pinching Grace, whispering something he couldn't hear.

"So, you haven't lived with your parents since you went through the veil?" Victor asked, his mind cycling through Twister's story again. He couldn't imagine leaving his mother forever.

Twister appeared amused. "I was just a pair of wings then. I wasn't ready to leave home for some time. Even when I did go, I wouldn't say I was exactly...prepared. It felt like the right thing to do, so I did it. Nowadays, my parents lead the Fae Army—not that we have needed the army for a long time now. Still, it is an important job."

Victor could hear a sort of pride when he spoke, as if he looked up to his parents, even though his eyes conveyed a

Alexia D. Miller

sadness he hoped to never understand. "It's an important and stressful job. Even when it isn't being actively used. Things were difficult. It felt like seeing me was reminding them of some great failure. A burden that they began carrying into their workplace. Which could be very dangerous if they had to battle."

As they walked, Victor could see the blurred buildings in the distance gaining focus with every step. From Twister's hut, he hadn't been able to distinguish one thing from the other. He didn't know why, but it seemed like bad form for a Faerie to speak so woefully. Victor watched as they walked past rows of trees and flowers blowing in the wind.

A few yards ahead, Victor could make out a large fountain with a statue made of stone at its center. A large white and gold flower, incased in what He assumed to be glass, sat in the middle of two infant Faerie figures. On either side of the two young Faeries were two pregnant mother figures with their hands resting on their bellies and eyes downcast towards the children and the flower. Further to the side, beside each woman, were males. Both mirrored each other, holding out a hand that gently rested on the woman's shoulder.

As they passed it, Victor saw that both the children and mothers had large wings on their back, but one of the men had nothing. He wondered if his pair of wings had fallen off. For a moment he thought to circle the statue to satisfy his curiosity, but realized the statue was larger than he anticipated. How long would it take him to get to the other side?

"It's beautiful." True said softly. Victor nodded. "Beautiful, yet ancient." Twister's voice chimed in from behind. "It was constructed a long time ago now, but since you've arrived today of all days, you will understand why this statue means anything at all." He pointed back in the direction that they'd been walking. "First, however, we should get some food from the market. There will be plenty of time for stories later."

. . .

At the market, soft humming filled the air. Unlike in Mirror, there were no loudspeakers to be seen, so Victor couldn't discern where the music originated from. White-haired Faeries zoomed past them in multiple directions, some carried baskets, some held bundles of flowers, and others carried bags of odd trinkets Victor couldn't place. To his surprise, some Faeries carried nothing at all. Their things floated in the air behind them, almost as if pulled along on an invisible rope.

Alexia D. Miller

Victor stepped to the side as a Faerie holding a small bundle in her arms, flew past him, a large wooden wagon floating above her head. If almost every Faerie he saw were adults, Victor and Zane still had over a foot of height between them. Even True, who was shorter than him, looked relatively tall among them.

Victor was just starting to compare Grace and Phelia's heights to the Faeries as a swirling ball blocked his view. Twister stood in front of him, handing him a flashing sphere. "These are for you." He said, tossing more of them to the others. He watched the blue liquid spin slowly before curiously poking it with his finger. Shocked, Victor watched his finger press against the cold liquid which bent loosely one way and then the other before returning to its original shape. Water?

"Explore until to your hearts' are content. Try anything you'd like. Remember to tell the Fae that I've sent you, no payment required. When you've finished, those will lead you back to me. The closer you are to my location, the more they will flash, like now." He smiled, putting his thumbs up. "Please stay within the bounds of the market. I can't have human guests getting lost all on their own. Sound good?"

Before anyone could open their mouths to form a question, Twister disappeared. He could hear Graces

Alexia D. Miller

excitement and see Zane's shock as they looked at the liquid sphere. Phelia inspected hers from below, seemingly more interested in the ball than Twister's disappearance.

Minutes later, Grace and Phelia had gone off, arm in arm, through the market, disappearing from Victor's sight. "He's not here to explain so I guess we'll have to figure things out ourselves. I don't know about you, but something smells amazing over here. I'm going to find something to eat. You coming?" Zane asked, patting him on the shoulder.

Victor glanced to the left, seeing True at a nearby stall. "I'll catch up with you," he answered, watching Zane walk off towards a far stall with a nod. Victor made his way to True's side. "Well, well!" Boomed the Faerie. A bald man, the first Victor had seen, with thick white eyebrows and a silver hoop in his left ear. Unlike Twister, he didn't have any markings on his face. *Surely, he must be able to grow hair,* Victor thought, *considering his eyebrows.*

"Leave it to Twister to have such a **beautiful** guest!" The Faerie continued. "Please, help yourself." He smiled. Victor looked over to True. Was he flirting? How old was this Faerie, exactly? How did Faerie ages work anyhow? Did he even want to know? Was the man simply being polite? Afterall, True was wearing her mask and jacket. He hated being curious. Questions were difficult to manage.

Alexia D. Miller

Victor wasn't sure if she was beautiful, but he did know other things. He knew that when she spoke, he listened. Not simply because she didn't speak often, but also because when she did speak, it never seemed to be for her own benefit. More than that, he knew that he liked the sound of her small, silvery voice.

Victor quietly watched as True picked up a flower from one of the boxes on the stand. "Go ahead and try one!" The man insisted.

True looked to Victor and then back to the flower.

"*Eat* the flowers? Victor asked, astounded.

Victor watched the silver hoop dance lightly in the Faerie's ear as he nodded. "Feel free to try one of them all!" He said cheerfully. Victor frowned, watching True's small fingers pick up a pale brown bud. Victor studied it, unsure. He noticed the pale-yellow strings sticking out of the center and the white specks going down the green stem.

True held out her hand, holding the flower close to his lips. She wanted ***him*** to eat it? Victor looked at her mask, feeling expectant waves from her direction. He willed his brain to find an escape. Unfortunately for Victor, his effort was pointless. Unable to come up with an excuse and thinking he'd feel guilty if he refused, Victor reluctantly agreed.

Alexia D. Miller

He closed his eyes, assuming that not being able to see the flower would keep it from tasting disgusting. He held out his hand, hoping if he were lucky, the flower would just taste like grass. When the seconds ticked away and Victor didn't feel the flower against his palm, he opened his eyes only to see True standing on her toes, pressing the flower to his lips.

Victor opened his mouth in surprise, stumbling slightly back as the flower made its way into his mouth. He looked at True, feeling slightly skittish. A strange feeling to have, he thought, considering he couldn't see her face. Victor chewed the flower slowly before he snapped his head to the left, looking back at the Faerie. "It tastes like honey." He said, shocked.

The Faerie smiled widely, his wings fluttering behind him. "They're all delicious!" He laughed. Victor looked back to True. As if she'd been waiting to hear those exact words, she grabbed a small basket from the side of the stall and picked a handful of the small buds, placing them in front of the Faerie.

"Well that's not very many at all. Feel free to put them in the basket. I will keep track of them. Why don't you try a few more, at least?"

True turned her head towards Victor and he realized that things were about to get out of hand. He'd already

Alexia D. Miller

counted over 20 different flowers on the stand. Unable to refuse her, he quietly allowed her to give him one flower after the next. The red one that looked like a ladybug's wings was spicy, the pink one with the black petal tasted surprisingly like syrup, and the silver one with the blue dots tasted like toasted marshmallows.

Victor couldn't recall them all the further down the list they went. He ate flowers until he was sure his tastebuds couldn't take it anymore. Somehow, to Victors relief and dismay, they worked their way through them all and True tucked them away into the basket. To Victor's surprise, True managed to write them all down in a small notebook during his "sampling." Though Victor thought of it more like agony. Would he even be able to eat anything else?

True thanked the Faerie as he laughed, clutching his stomach. "It's almost payment enough to have seen those faces! *Please*, come back again!" The Faerie snorted loudly. As much as Victor wanted to be upset about the man's light mockery, he couldn't. He'd found the Faerie's happy laughter to be an unusually comforting sound. *I don't know if I like him*, Victor thought, *or hate him*. Victor shrugged watching True tuck her notebook back into the folds of her jacket, Still, *I guess it wasn't all bad.*

"Thank you, Victor." True voiced quietly from his right. Before Victor could reply, however, True strode off in

Alexia D. Miller

another direction and disappeared between the space of another stall. Victor shifted on his feet with a yawn, sticking his hands into his pockets. He shook his head, amused. "I'd better catch up with Zane then." He said to no one in particular, heading off in the direction he last remembered seeing him.

Phelia...

Chapter Thirty-Four: Frightened Animal.

Phelia found herself amazed by the Faerie market. Every stall was filled with colorful, exotic-looking plants, fruits, vegetables, and trinkets. At every stop, Phelia relished the challenge to figure out what one thing did or was versus another. To her benefit, not one of the Faeries at the market seemed to mind her questions.

While Phelia wasn't surprised given the lack of animals or insects, she quickly understood that Faeries did not consume meat of any sort. The variety of fruits and vegetables, however, took some adjustment. Not just the random shapes they were sold in, but also the strange patterns and colors.

One stall had bowls of powder—seasonings as she understood it. Once she tasted the dark gray one that Phelia could only say was spicy charcoal, she wanted nothing more to do with the table. Meanwhile, Grace had been laughing in-

Alexia D. Miller

between chews of a brown and black striped stick. A sample, Grace explained, from two young Fae.

"It tastes like caramel and cinnamon." She smiled, offering one to Zane and Victor as they made their way near. As they walked away from the stalls, Phelia peeked into the boys' baskets, determined to decipher what was inside. As Zane bit into an oblong star-shaped fruit, Phelia scanned the crowd.

"Have either of you seen True?" Phelia asked, knowing that she was too tall to lose in the sea of white-haired Faeries. Not to mention, she was wearing a dark jacket almost the exact opposite of everyone she saw. Zane shook his head and Grace shrugged.

"You don't think she got lost, do you?" Grace asked, biting down on another stick.

"I saw her earlier but not since then," Victor said with a frown.

"Should we look for her?" Grace asked waving her stick around in the air. "Shouldn't be too hard to find considering...well, you know."

Phelia narrowed her eyes at Grace. "Are you trying to say something specific?" She directed at her. Afterall, Phelia was hardly any taller than any Faerie there.

Grace laughed tapping the stick against her cheek. "Nope. Nothing at all."

Alexia D. Miller

Splitting up, they each went in search for True, finishing the food in their basket before meeting back up again. Not one of them had any luck finding her. One Faerie selling jewelry recalled seeing her recently but couldn't point them in any particular direction.

Seeing the flickering in front of her, Phelia was reminded of the twirling mass Twister had given her. She'd forgotten it was ever there, floating around just out of sight. "Why don't we ask Twister?" Phelia asked, pointing in front of her. "He provided these to find him, so perhaps he can also find one of us with it."
"It's worth a shot." Victor nodded.

Each of them took a few steps in opposing directions, testing the ball of liquid before Zane called out to them. "This way!" He yelled, waving an arm in the air. Making her way beside him, Phelia watched both of balls flash. Once. Twice. Three times. Following Zane's lead, Phelia looked ahead of them.

"It's leading us out of the market," Phelia said, watching the water roll through the air ahead of her. As they continued to follow Twister's magic circles, though Phelia didn't have a clue what to call them, she was vaguely aware of Faeries putting away their merchandise. Phelia looked up to the sky. The sun was shining high with no sign of setting. She

Alexia D. Miller

didn't know much about FlareWing, but weren't they closing the market early?

Eventually, Phelia realized that they were heading back the way they'd come. The spheres flashed quicker with every step closer to the fountain in the near distance. Phelia squinted, trying to focus her eyes ahead of her.

"Isn't that...True?" Grace asked, her voice besieged with uncertainty. Only as they walked closer did Phelia understand why.

Beside the feet of the statue, True's jacket lay on the ground. A girl, who Phelia could only assume to be True, sat with her back to them. Phelia could just make out her shoulders on either side of long platinum blonde hair styled in a braid. She seemed to sit with her knees tucked to her chest and as she shifted, the end of her braid lightly slid across the grass.

The flowers, which seemed to be plucked from the grass around her, had been woven into the braid. Phelia thought they almost appeared to have blossomed there in-between the strands of her hair. Floating in front of her was Twister. He fluttered from one side to the next placing flowers in her hair and making framing motions with his hands. Phelia could just make out the sound of his voice chattering away excitedly.

Alexia D. Miller

At the sound of cracking, True stiffened. Like a frightened animal, True slid on her mask, tucked her hair into her jacket and bolted towards the fountain, disappearing in a matter of seconds. Twister whizzed forward, rushing towards them, dropping the flower in his hand. As he did, the liquid ball beside Phelia swirled, increasing in speed until it burst and rained sparkling particles of water to the ground.

"Oh, now look what you've done!" Twister huffed. "You've terrified the girl! He said disapprovingly. "To think I just managed to get somewhere with her." When True emerged from behind the fountain, Grace immediately threw her hands into the air.

"True! Your hair is *beautiful!*" She shouted.

Grace's compliment was met with silence. Undiscouraged, she continued to talk. Phelia looked to Zane who stood almost frozen in place staring directly at True. Victor, to Phelia's surprise, was looking at no one. He faced a nearby tree with his back turned in their direction. Whatever was he doing? Phelia wondered.

True shuffled around silently picking up the items that dropped from her basket. Phelia could just make out a bundle of oddly colored flowers and a lavender fruit she recalled seeing at one of the stalls. She watched True closely, looking for any strand of hair spilling out of her jacket. When she didn't find any, she was disappointed. How could

Alexia D. Miller

someone be that quick and efficient in the heat of the moment when they had such long hair? To not have missed a strand even with flowers in her hair. What did she do, change outfits for a living?

"Ahem." Twister coughed into his fist, clearing his throat. "We ought to get going. We need to get to The Grand Tree. It's almost time." He said, the other liquid spheres quickly bursting, raining down more shining droplets.

"For the ceremony?" Phelia asked, turning her Gaze to Victor who hadn't moved from his spot against the tree.

"Yes." Twister said, dropping lightly onto True's shoulder. "The greatest and cruelest of times for us Faeries. Even I found myself particularly fond of this Princess." Twister frowned. Phelia couldn't help but wonder what he meant. Just what was it about this ceremony?

Zane...

Chapter Thirty-Five: Ceremony.

As they made their way to The Grand Tree, Zane's brain was occupied with thoughts of True. The events from earlier played on a loop in his mind. No matter how much Zane tried to pause on True sitting on the ground with her hair decorated in flowers and the sun beaming down on her, he couldn't. Which left him with no choice but to let the entire episode cycle through his head.

Since the moment his eyes focused on her Zane was speechless. With each second, he wondered how close they'd been from seeing her face. *If only I'd been careful. He thought. If only I had watched my step!* He scolded himself bitterly. Zane couldn't place the upset feelings flooding through him. He hadn't even realized he was so curious in the first place.

Zane tilted his head slightly to get a glimpse of True. Wherever the curiosity had come from, he wanted to satisfy it. Feeling a light tug on his clothes, his gaze was forced away from True. Zane looked down at Phelia who was directing his attention ahead of them.

Alexia D. Miller

At the center of The Grand Tree, a flickering light appeared. When the light faded, two figures emerged. One was a woman, a Faerie roughly a foot taller than any that he'd seen. The other, a male even taller than her. "The Princess and Father Wing, I take it?" Phelia directed at Twister.

"Yes. In the flesh," Twister smiled, guiding them closer through the crowd.

The Princess curtsied beside Father Wing, who lightly bowed his head. Father Wing was dressed in layers of red robes, decorated with curved golden patterns along the hems. His butterfly shaped wings mirrored the others, only larger with a deep, red pattern on each side. Even his eyes were the color of flames with hair to match. He stood confidently by the woman's side, guiding her along a path that was building in front of them with every stride.

The Princess shared the same blazing eyes. She wore a layered silver and red robe that exposed her back. Her hair was white and fell loosely past her shoulders. Unlike the white hair she shared with the other Faeries, her wings were vast golden colored orbs gently flapping against her back.

"Why are her wings like that?" Grace asked.

"Every Faerie is different." Twister said with a smile. "Princess Yuu is no exception. She was gifted with wings FlareWing has never seen."

Alexia D. Miller

"She's pregnant." Victor said, drawing Zane's attention quickly back to the Princess. Beyond her layers of white and silver fabrics, Zane could see her protruding belly. As she made her way forward, she gently rested her left hand on her stomach.

"Not for long." Twister nodded. "In a matter of minutes, we will welcome the new Princess."

"How do you know it's a girl?" Phelia asked.

"Every birth is a girl." He said flatly. "Each of them, the next Princess."

"She can't have boys?" Grace asked with a hint of skepticism.

"It is our understanding that the Princess must be a girl, but that is simply the way it's always been." Twister quickly clapped his hands. "They're coming this way. Bow." He instructed.

As Princess Yuu and Father Wing crossed the field of Fae, line after line kneeled slowly and bowed their heads in silence. Those closest to The Grand Tree circled around behind them, putting Zane, Twister, and the others only a few rows behind. Moments later, a soft hymn filled the space between them.

Zane looked around amazed. Large iridescent specks from The Grand Tree flowed behind Princess Yuu as if beckoned by her presence. As far as Zane could tell, no

Alexia D. Miller

Faerie seemed surprised by the ocean of gleaming lights swirling about them. Not even as they continued on, getting further away.

As they walked past Faerie huts and the fountain, Princess Yuu and Father Wing bowed speaking words Zane couldn't hear. Past Twister's home in the distance to the right and more huts, they came upon the Bridge. Over the rolling hills and past any area they'd seen when they arrived in FlareWing, they were led to a large crater in the ground.

Zane watched apprehensively as the Faeries lined up around the edge of the crater. What were they doing? Was this safe? He wondered, as Father Wing and Princess Yuu flew to its center without hesitation. Gradually, they dropped silently to the dark ground below. Not caring if Phelia would complain, Zane took hold of her hand.

In the heart of the crater, Father Wing waved a hand over the ground, causing a ripple of red bolts to dance below their feet. To Zane's surprise, Princess Yuu did not flinch or step away. As they faded, an unusual red and gold flower rose from the ground beside the Princess. Zane watched intensely, unsure of what was happening.

Princess Yuu smiled, and the flower's petals folded onto itself until they shaped hearts on the stem. With another wave of Father Wing's hand, the flower shook and broke apart, swirling until it looked like liquid glitter. "What

Alexia D. Miller

the..." Zane muttered, watching Father Wing guide the glittering substance through the air with his arms until it disappeared into Princess Yuu's belly.

"What is he doing to her?" Zane asked, worried.

"Completing the process." Twister answered back. "Initially, the Princess only has a single petal inside of her belly, which slowly matures. Father Wing must complete the process so that Princess Yuu's pregnancy enters its final stages. Then she gives birth."

"Wait." Grace said, smacking her hands against her cheeks. "You mean she's giving birth to a *flower*?!"

"Shh." Victor said, shushing Grace, as a light surrounded Father Wing and Princess Yuu down below.

"Sorry." Grace said, covering her mouth with her hands.

"I don't understand," Phelia said quietly.

"Let me tell you," Twister said lowly, "the reason the ceremony matters. The beginning of today's Faerie world— one of the most important stories of FlareWing's history."

. . .

"FlareWing has a sun that never fully sets." Twister said, his eyes trained on the light hiding Father Wing and Princess Yuu from view. "A very long time ago, however, it did. Young Fae like me prefer the way things are now, but

Alexia D. Miller

we aren't opposed to having night and day again. For the elders, however, the thought of another night in FlareWing is a thing of nightmares and bad memories.

"The ceremony is a bittersweet event because it represents a time nearly forgotten until then, and because what happens at its end. Princess Yuu will not live to see the next live. Our Princesses live only to the exact moment the next is born. Without a single choice in the matter.

"Each time a Princess is born, Father Wing turns to ash and is reborn at age close to that of the Princess. He retains his memories from all previous lifetimes, which I suspect to be the heaviest of burdens. This allows him to not only build a kinship with the new Princess but guide her as well.

"You see, we Faeries have nothing directly to do with the process. At least not where development is involved. Father Wing holds all of that burden alone, teaching every new Princess what she needs to know to continue the cycle."
"Does the princess also have these "past" memories?" Phelia asked, "How can Father Wing can take care of her if he is an infant as well?"

"Father Wing has never been reborn the same age as a Princess. Rather, he becomes someone older, yet relatively close in age." Twister clarified. "Considering that he has his memories, Father Wing isn't at a disadvantage when it

Alexia D. Miller

comes to the Princess. His mental capacity doesn't differ. As for the Princess, she has nothing to remember. Father Wing is the same person born anew. The Princess is the daughter of the previous."

"But how can Father Wing come back all of the time? Can't the Princess just do the magic stuffs and stay alive?" Grace asked with a frown. "That's what I would do."

"Alas, it's not that simple." Twister said with a sigh. "Father Wing is the only Faerie in existence that can complete the process. The flower used in the process is a very special flower called the Flare Locus. It is, in part, where the name of our world comes from. Before that, I'm not entirely sure what it was called. Though I suppose there aren't many of us around today that would. Father Wing was born from the man that makes up part of the flower. Or rather, the Faerie."

"What?" Victor said, slowly turning his head to look at Twister. "You're kidding. The flower is a Faerie?"

Twister nodded, closing his eyes. "Or at least he used to be, and he isn't alone."

"I'm not sure I am any closer to understanding how this process works," Phelia huffed, touching her forehead with a sigh.

"Bear with me," Twister said with a chuckle. "His name was Locus, and a long time ago he was a Faerie before he was a flower. He gave his life and magic to recreate the very land we stand on now. At the time, Faeries were dying—killed by the war with the Cursed Faeries. Cursed Fae, as we call them, are Faeries tainted by The Darkness.

"Locus commanded the Faerie Army back then as one of the strongest leaders in our history, but when he faced the Cursed Faerie Army with every intention of destroying them, he failed. Locus refused to fight because the Faerie leading Cursed Fae was Lady Reva. She, like the other Cursed Faeries, originally belonged to our side.

"Lady Reva, you see, had gone missing before the war began. Consequently, Lady Reva was the love of his life, and he'd spent all his time searching for her, so we've been told. Even before he led the Fae against the Cursed. As I understand it, Locus only decided to command the army because it was a greater means to search for her.

"Both Lady Reva and Sir Locus perished together, unable to truly battle. Lady Reva had been with child since her disappearance, unbeknownst to the Fae and perhaps even to Sir Locus. To keep their unborn child from dying, the two of them became the flower that Father Wing calls forth during the ceremony. Whereas Father Wing can be reborn from ashes, the Princess is different.

"Sir Locus had a sibling. A sister named Lily, that became pregnant with a human's child. Unfortunately, only

Alexia D. Miller

snippets of information remain about the human father and his name is lost among the Fae. Both things are very important details because before Lady Lily's death our world still had day and night.

"Even with the death of Lady Reva, we struggled. Cursed Fae were lost and merciless without someone to lead them. We were no match for their emotionless killings. So, Lady Lily, being respected as a strategist and sister of Sir Locus, devised a plan that ultimately saved our world: she took the collective power of her own and several other Faeries with her to meet The Master. The Master is the strongest being where worlds meet, but that is a conversation for another time.

"Together, Lady Lily and The Master were able to overcome The Darkness and the Cursed Faeries, only not without consequence. Somehow, she made it back to our world. Even more astonishing, Lady Lily gave birth to a girl near the Flare Locus before she died.

"It is said that it is a curse cast upon Lady Lily by The Darkness that keeps the Princess from living past her child's birth. As a thank you to Lady Lily and the other powerful Faeries for their sacrifice, The Master shielded our world via the veil. In return, Faeries go to the human world. We wish to pay towards the debt we owe Lady Lily's lover for the birth of the Princess as well.

Alexia D. Miller

"As I mentioned, nightfall disappeared from our world when Lady Lily died, but the Princess symbolizes more than just our history and light. She symbolizes the cycle of life. Furthermore, when the Princess lives, our magic lives as well. When the new Princess is born, a surge of Fae magic disperses, and we are given health and strength. Afterall, every Princess is the result of our magic at its strongest from the original mother Lady Lily, and the Flare Locus which holds Sir Locus and Lady Reva's collective power.

"The Princess balances good and evil just from being here, considering that Lady Reva was flooded with darkness when she became part of our sacred flower. Which is another reason for Father Wing's presence. He was born again and again with knowledge to carry out the process and how to organize the remaining Faeries. We are left to do very little in comparison. We regret our losses and celebrate all else that we can. So, we take pride in going through the veil and doing good work in your world.

"Children and those with the gift of sight tend to see us in the small forms we take there most often, but to the rest we are hidden. Cloaked by the power of the veil which still wards off negativity and evil that may try to force through our world to this day. Although, there always comes a time

Alexia D. Miller

where even those with the gift forget or become closed-minded and never see us again.

"Some Faeries, however, become bitter or other negative emotions let The Darkness slip in, so they are altered and unable to find their way back home. Their abilities weaken because of their betrayal and the veil keeps them from passing through. It is even possible that humans have found them in your world.

"Their physical appearance tends to change, influenced by The Darkness, from their wings to their teeth. The possibilities are almost endless."

"What's happening to them?" Victor asked, interrupting Twister as light encased the crater. Zane willed his eyes to focus on the middle of the light, trying to see through it. Suddenly, Twister frowned with a miserable expression and bowed his head. As Zane looked at the other Faeries, he realized they too lowered their heads, tears skidding down their cheeks.

"Princess Yuu is giving birth to the new Princess. The moment she does, her body will wither away to nothing, forever part of the soil as Father Wing goes through his own rebirth. No Faerie can help but mourn her death. Afterall, Princess Yuu has spent her life balancing the magic in FlareWing and being a beacon of light only to never hold her child in her arms.

Alexia D. Miller

True's voice spoke so softly that Zane had to strain to hear her. "The statue on the fountain then, are them. Yes?" She asked unhappily.

"Yes," Twister said, his voice trembling with emotion. "Sir Locus, Lady Reva, the human father and Lady Lily. The flower symbolizes the cycle, our power, and the passing of our greats. As you can likely guess, the children are Father Wing and the Princess."

"Does that mean that every princess also has the same name?" Phelia asked.

"No. However, only Father Wing knows the name of the next Princess. Each Princess names the next, as any mother would her child. When the next Princess is born, we will know her name as well."

"So, we stay here until the process is done?" Zane asked. He couldn't imagine going through what the Princess did. He couldn't imagine being Father Wing and turning to ash, somehow putting himself back together, only to live his life preparing a Princess to accept her fate—preparing her to serve people she doesn't know and die without ever seeing her child.

"No." Twister said, shaking his head. "The process takes some time. Father Wing will take the new Princess home after he is reborn. Tomorrow, we return to The

Grand Tree for the Princess' unveiling. Then, we celebrate her arrival and her name."

Grace...

Chapter Thirty-Six: Making Sense of FlareWing.

Back at Twister's hut, Grace lay on the floor beside the others. She wondered if Princess Yuu was unhappy when she left The Grand Tree. She wondered if she cried. If Princess Yuu questioned what her daughter would be like or wished she could be by her side when she took her first breath.

Grace even worried about the new Princess. It wasn't that Grace remembered anything about her mother, but at least she knew that she'd existed. At least Grace was sure that at some point she'd been cradled, even if it were only once. The Princess would never know anyone else as family besides Father Wing.

Grace tried to imagine what Father Wing would tell the new Princess about her mother. She wondered if he ever grew tired of explaining to young Princesses why they'd never see their parents. Would the new Princess look like her mother? How would Father Wing take it if she did?

Alexia D. Miller

Looking at Twister's porcelain skin, Grace was reminded of Mirror. Grace was even more aware of the skin on her arm. She was many shades darker than everyone in the room. She hated to bring up differences, especially since all she ever wanted was to fit in, but that didn't stop her interest.

"Twister?" Grace called quietly, not sure how to ask. When he looked over to her, floating gently in the air, she racked her brain for the right words. "Do all Faeries look like you? You know, unless they are Father Wing or a Princess?" She asked, unable to ask her question as directly as she'd hoped.

Twister's small smile comforted her. "There are a lot more Faeries than those living in FlareWing today. Before the war with The Darkness, thousands of us lived here and a surrounding area. Unfortunately, that area was destroyed during the war. Father Wing and the Princess' appearance seems to be the result of the Flare Locus and their parents' characteristics, but I can't say for sure."

"Where did they all go?" Grace asked.

"Faeries find pockets of worlds to inhabit. The distance is sometimes too great to travel on a regular basis, so we are accustomed to meeting our brothers and sisters in the human world. In a way, the human world acts as a short-cut for us. Faeries are simply born the way they are born.

Alexia D. Miller

{308}

Faeries may have different color eyes, wings, hair, and skin. Like humans, Fae also come in different shapes and sizes."

"So, there might be Faeries with skin like mine?" Grace asked warily. "Faeries that look like...me?"

"There's really no "might" about it," He said, crossing his arms. "It is a *guarantee*. There are plenty of us with skin lighter and darker than yours and it makes us no difference." He waved his hand in front of his face dismissively. "What an odd thing for humans to focus on. As if such an insignificant detail makes you an entirely different species."

"It matters somehow anyway." Grace mumbled.

"How arrogant. In our case, a Faerie's hair, skin, and wing color tells you nearly nothing more than where they were born. It isn't even an important aspect of their lineage. A Faerie born in a certain place typically has a natural affinity for that area, which is a base for their abilities, but not always.

"For example, currently a Faerie born with olive skin and blue hair and wings tells you that they come from a generation of Fae currently occupying a mountain. Those of which go by the name Glacier. In other words, they are Glacier-Fae. They may have a water or ice-based ability, but even that is not a guarantee. Every Faerie, however, recognizes that their place of origin is FlareWing."

Alexia D. Miller

{ 309 }

"Why don't other Fae go to the ceremony?" Victor asked, yawning.

"Oh." Twister said, lightly smacking his palm against his forehead. "I forgot to mention that. Some do, but not always. Recall how I mentioned the damage done to FlareWing during the war? Well, FlareWing used to be an entire world of its own.

"Nowadays, FlareWing exists as an extension of the human world, invisible to most, separated by the veil. The veil is connected from one Faerie location to the next, but it cannot be used as a bridge to other Faerie locations specifically There's no linear path from one to the other."

"Other Faerie homes are protected by The Darkness you keep mentioning?" Phelia asked, leaning her head onto Grace's shoulder. "Even though the Faerie world is separated?"

"Yes. Absolutely. Faeries unaffected by The Darkness can easily pass through the veils of each land, even if it takes time to get there. Father Wing and the Princesses, however, are what keeps the balance of them all." Twister explained. "If one Faerie world is damaged or destroyed, they can help restore them. If something happens in FlareWing like the Princess leaving or even worse, perishing, before the completion of the ceremony, the Faerie world will fall apart.

Alexia D. Miller

Our magic will die. Then, the Faerie world will cease to exist."

"Talk about pressure." Zane said, shaking his head. "I'd hate to be Father Wing or any of the Princesses." "It's sad," True said, rolling a flower from Twister's wall carefully between her fingers, "that the Princess can never travel or live outside your world."

. . .

When Grace opened her eyes, she realized she'd been asleep. Beside her, Phelia still sleeping softly. Yawning, Grace looked around the room seeing her shoes in a corner. As quietly as she could manage, Grace slipped on her shoes. In the other room, Grace tiptoed past Zane and Victor. She chuckled, amused by Zane's foot pressing into Victor's cheek as he snored lightly.

Following the sound of low voices out the door, Grace found True and Twister sitting in the grass. Coming to sit beside them, Grace heard an assortment of low sounds in the distance. "Once the others have come to, we'll make our way to The Grand Tree." Twister said extending a small smile in Grace's direction. "I hope you slept comfortably."

"I did," Grace smiled. "I didn't even know I'd fallen asleep!" She said, turning her head to True. Grace wondered

Alexia D. Miller

how she was doing considering yesterday. Although Grace didn't understand why True wanted to hide her face, she was sure it was personal. It wasn't difficult to grasp. If Grace thought that hiding her skin and hair behind a mask and jacket would've saved her the trouble of dealing with people and bullies, she was sure she would do it. Probably without a second thought.

Slowly but surely, Zane, Phelia and Victor made their way outside of Twister's hut. When they did Grace was more than ready to leave. Something delicious, though she wasn't sure what, had been letting her know it existed. Whatever it was, the smell was heavenly, and Grace was ready to find it. Her growling stomach agreed with her.

As they made their way to The Grand Tree, Grace wondered what would await them. Twister mentioned a celebration, but Grace couldn't imagine how Faeries celebrated anything. Of all the things she'd heard about fairies and their mannerisms, no matter if they were truth or fiction, Grace never heard a thing about parties. Would there be music and dancing?

At The Grand Tree, Twister guided them through the crowd to the front line. They were just in time to see Father Wing exit the light shining from the tree bark with a bundle in his arms. Grace clapped along with the Faeries,

Alexia D. Miller

already amazed by what she saw, though she wasn't sure she could call him Father Wing aloud.

Father Wing was no longer the tall man with broad shoulders and large red and white wings. His short hair and angular chin disappeared, although his blazing red eyes remained. Now, his tall frame was replaced by a fragile-looking child's body. His robes pooled around his feet and his short red hair now flowed past his waist behind him. His chin was soft and rounded, and his wings seemed to grow two sizes too big. Large enough that Grace was almost certain he should have been crippled under their weight. She could just imagine them flapping once and sending him skyrocketing through the air by accident.

Today, Father Wing's robes were green and white as he looked down at the bundle wrapped in a gold cloth. Grace was sure she could almost see his eyes sparkle as he smiled and gently pulled back the fabric to reveal the small Princess. The newborn yawned, stretching out her arms and legs between Father Wing's sleeves. Grace immediately recognized the same fiery eyes of Father Wing and Princess Yuu, blinking slowly under long golden lashes.

Slowly, she was lifted into the air for all to see. Like her lashes, the Princess' hair too was golden. Thick strands of golden curls fell against her forehead and neck, her roots

Alexia D. Miller

the color of fire. Grace didn't think she'd ever seen such a beautiful baby in her life.

Turning her over, Father Wing exposed her golden wings. While they were the same butterfly shape Grace saw on every Faerie's back, the Princess' wings were covered in white specks that ran along her spine all the way down her back, eventually shifting to a red similar to her bright eyes. As Grace continued to stare, she could just make out the red flower pattern on the base of her neck.

As Father Wing turned the child around again to face them, Grace's heart jumped; she was completely caught off guard by Father Wing's deep voice. "Your new Princess. Honorable daughter of Princess Yuu!" He roared. "Let her presence remind us that magic still lives and flows through all of our Faerie lands. May she bare another healthy line. May she live in health and be a guiding light. Let us welcome, Princess Aurelia!"

As a series of chants and claps sounded on air, Grace was still overwhelmed by Father Wing's booming voice. She watched in amazement as he bowed his head and lines of colored dust surrounded him and the new Princess. She was mesmerized by Princess Aurelia's small fingers reaching out above her to touch the shimmering dots.

The thrilled shrieks faded only as Father Wing made his way to a brown chair that formed slowly from the ground.

Alexia D. Miller

A chair woven from branches and vines, cushioned by leaves that floated delicately down from The Grand Tree. When he sat down, Princess Aurelia in his arms, Grace almost thought the chair would swallow him whole. He looked as small as Phelia, yet somehow more fragile.

Row after row, Faeries tossed flowers at their feet until he held up a hand to stop them. Almost immediately after, groups of Faeries spread out ahead of them, guiding everyone else to the side. The Faeries, all dressed in earthy brown robes, waved their arms in synchronized motions.

Not too unlike Father Wing's chair, long tables and stools emerged from the ground one after the other. As the tables packed the open space between them a musical humming filled the air. Although Grace couldn't pinpoint where the sound was coming from, she felt a warmth in her chest and a smile spread across her face.

True...

Chapter Thirty-Seven: Father Wing's Pity.

Everything True experienced in FlareWing had been beautiful. From the rolling hills and budding flowers, to the bridge, the bittersweet ceremony, and even the celebration of Princess Aurelia. But the not so beautiful parts of their time weren't far from her mind. Since yesterday, as Twister called it, True had been consumed with sadness and fear. Even sitting at the table with the others and being surrounded by the smiles of Faeries did nothing to bring back her appetite.

True felt more than vulnerable. The very thought of exposing an ankle or a wrist tightened the cramps in her stomach. She wished it had all been a dream. A dream where Twister made her feel comfortable and free just from the air about him. She wished that the words he said hadn't given her hope and that his gentle voice hadn't been so perfect. A dream that everything she felt for those few moments hadn't come crashing down, leaving her to feel exposed, unsafe, and frightened all over again.

Alexia D. Miller

The sudden image of Twister moving across the table in front of her pushed True out of her thoughts. "Drinks," he said, pointing at small liquid bubbles floating to their sides. "I'm sure you can tell which is simply water. The others are fruit and flower blends."

"Like juice?" Grace asked, gently rolling one over to her palm.

"Yes," Twister said with a smile. "Like juice."

True saw the others curiously picking bubbles, between bites of the food on the table. She wasn't sure she could drink something so beautiful. "Are you alright, True?" Twister asked quietly. True watched a small smile cross his lips and his eyebrows crease. Feeling guilty for making him worry, she searched for something to say.

"I'm sorry Twister. I don't have much of an appetite," True replied. She could see his mouth open as if to speak before he closed it again. Instead, he smiled, grabbing a small flower from the table and took a bite. "Then I guess you can sit and watch me eat for the both of us. Can't promise it'll be as satisfying!" He laughed.

"Thank you," True said with a nod. Grateful for his humor. Looking up, True saw Victor's eyes on her. Looking back at him, she could feel her nerves begin to rise.

Since going to the market, she didn't know if she'd made a mistake. Had she been selfish when she prompted

Alexia D. Miller

him to try the flowers from the stall? True noticed that Victor walked furthest behind everywhere they went. She noticed that he hadn't spoken to her or glanced in her direction since, so she couldn't help but wonder if she'd done something wrong.

True did her best to remind herself that Victor couldn't see her from the other side of her mask. It didn't make calming her nerves any easier considering that even if he couldn't see her, she was still peering into his vivid green eyes from across the table. For a moment True was sure that his facial expression changed but the moment she tried to decipher it, he looked away from her.

"We have to find the door and go back," Victor said, taking a bite of a large cube shaped fruit.

"Yes," Phelia chimed in, swallowing another ball of liquid. "Who knows how long we have been away from home."

"I wish we could stay a little longer." Grace sighed.

"It is nice here," Zane nodded.

True knew they should return, but that wouldn't make it easier to leave. FlareWing gave her a break from her world back in Snowville. One she couldn't say she was eager to return to. Even so, True also knew that both of her aunts would be home and they had no way to measure the amount of time they'd already been away. They'd been there for over a day and Twister did say that the Faerie world was situated partly within their own.

True looked around at the Faeries eating merrily and talking amongst themselves. She could just make out surprised eyes and pointed glances in their direction. True questioned if the Faeries in FlareWing were just becoming aware of their presence. Would any of them know where the door is?

True continued to observe the Faeries until her eyes rested on Father Wing. He sat completely still in his overly large chair, his eyes closed, holding Princess Aurelia in his arms. True could make out her slow movement in the cloth and almost hear her coos beneath the river of voices. How could two people be so beautiful?

As True focused on Father Wing's soft features she couldn't help but envision the man he'd grow into all over again. Would he have long hair as an adult, or would it be as short as it had been the day before? Did he grow tired of growing older and repeating the process again and again?

How does he do it? True asked herself. *How does he take care of her all alone? Doesn't he grow tired of playing the same role forever? Twister said he has lived for hundreds of years now.* She liked to think that she could be so selfless, but she wasn't sure. True couldn't help but pity

Alexia D. Miller

him. Even if Father Wing cared for every Princess as much as he had the first, wouldn't he be tired of living?

Slowly, Father Wing's eyes opened and True felt that he was directly returning her gaze. To her surprise, True was unable to look away. She could hear the voices of the others at the table grow further away as seconds passed. Time as she knew it seemed to slow down.

True was flooded with the sensation of moving. Of her stool floating across the grass through the sea of Faeries to the space ahead of Father Wing. Some part of her wasn't sure if she couldn't move or if she simply didn't want to. Even being unsure about her exact position, True could still see directly into Father Wing's eyes.

She could make out the blended reds and oranges with glistening white fragments. She could see the shadow his bright lashes casted upon his eyes and the dark streaks around his pupils. Vaguely aware of her slow blinking, True couldn't tell if she were looking into the eyes of young Father Wing or the older one. Whichever it was, she could feel no hint of a child's air about him.

His deep, pleasant voice spoke, but whether his voice spoke waves on the air or in her mind she didn't know. "I question what I owe the pity of a human who does not know their own fate. Least I've known my path since the dawn I was born into this world. 'Tis only so many ways for a life

Alexia D. Miller

like mine to end. Only a fool wishes for an early death if it means leaving the world he's shaped to fall to ruin. Perhaps, someone ignorant to the purpose of pain would dare wish for more. I am neither, though I will welcome it should it find me."

True apologized, unsure about what was happening. Twister told her that he never knew a Faerie that could read minds, but she was starting to believe Father Wing could— that was if this wasn't all inside her head. "I don't mean to pity you. I just can't imagine your pain. I have felt sorry for myself many times, meanwhile you're responsible for an entire world, teaching the Princess, and the lives of Fae."

"That, child, is worth pity. Your pains are worth no less than that of another. Never compare your burdens. Every life is weighed with its own chains." He spoke. His voice gave True the impression that he was not mocking her inexperience, but rather offering her a push in the right direction. As if he were giving her a piece of some unspeakable wisdom she couldn't begin to understand.

"Your name?" He asked.

"True." She answered quickly, feeling uneasy at the thought of keeping him waiting.

"The door you and your companions seek lies beyond where the Flare Locus seeds. I am quite certain our paths

Alexia D. Miller

will cross again. The next time you arrive in FlareWing, or find yourself lost within reach, seek me."

True didn't know what it meant to seek him out if she was lost within reach, but she knew that she'd been extended an amazing courtesy. As Father Wing's eyes faded out and True became aware of the sensation of floating again, this time back the way she'd came, the voices of Phelia, Grace, Zane and Victor became closer. Louder.

Feeling a hand on her shoulder, True jumped to her feet. "True?" Zane called standing ahead of her with Grace at his side.

"You were totally zoned out." Grace frowned. True looked around, seeing Twister beside Victor and Phelia saying something she couldn't hear. Her eyes shifted to Father Wing. Only to find that he was no longer seated in the chair. Looking amongst the tables she caught a glimpse of him disappearing into The Grand Tree. Realizing that Zane's hand still rested on her shoulder, True took a step back to put distance between them.

"They're leaving?" True asked.

"Didn't you hear? They go into The Grand Tree to rest for ten days after the celebration ends." Phelia said, shaking her head. "You really *were* out of it."

Alexia D. Miller

"Yeah. They've been throwing magic around since last night, so they're probably exhausted." Grace said, emphasizing the words throwing and exhausted with her hands.

"Not throwing, Grace. *Dispersing.*" Phelia corrected. "Well yeah. That." Grace snorted. "Dispersing magic." "Are you alright?" Zane asked again. Had she somehow imagined that conversation? Unsure, True only knew one way to find out. Without a word, True walked off past the tables and happy Faeries. She recalled being told that the door was beyond the crater. Told during a conversation she was *almost* sure she had with Father Wing.

As True made her way past the fountain, she felt a sudden sense of anxiety. She couldn't afford to make up conversations with people she'd never even met. *It had to be real* True thought to herself, vaguely conscious of the others' voices behind her.

She passed Twister's hut then the bridge. Over the bridge she ascended and descended the hills until she could see the crater. Without hesitation she bolted down towards it, turning to go around the side rather than the middle.

"What are you doing?!" The others' voices echoed behind her.

True thought to stop. To try and explain, but her body carried on forward with a momentum outside of herself. When she found herself on the other side, she noticed a

Alexia D. Miller

large indent of pale green grass. She knew she must have been there. Why else would there be a random patch of less healthy grass on the other side of the crater? In all honesty, True wasn't completely sure about her logic, but she was relatively certain the door was there in front of her.

Not giving herself time to catch her breath, True took a step towards the dimpled grass as a swirl of pressure pushed her off her feet. A moment later, light blinded her. True's vision blurred and FlareWing quickly began to fade away before her.

When the space around her was only a heavy nothingness, True could see a fluid looking image of Snowville Temporary Infirmary skyrocketing above her. Panicked and suddenly aware that she was sinking, True attempted to reach out a hand. Only there in the darkness, she didn't feel any of her limbs.

True thought to open her mouth before she suddenly questioned if she still had one. How was it possible she didn't remember? She had to have a mouth. She'd had one in Flare Wing, didn't she? Feeling a rush of pressure unlike anything she'd felt before, her mind clouded and she was unable to think.

When True could no longer see any trace of the temporary hospital, she became suddenly aware of another sensation. The feeling of something wrapped around her legs, dragging her down. As True gave in to the dizzying pressure, she saw a beautiful shimmer swish through the darkness. As it came closer, True registered the two mismatched eyes blinking back at her. Twister?

The longer she fell through the darkness, the heavier the pressure became and the more difficult it was to breathe. Her mind, if she still had one, became mush. If she had seen Twister before, she couldn't see him anymore.

COME. A voice beckoned. COME. COME. COME! It demanded, seeming to shake every ounce of space around her. It hurt. Somehow True could still register the pain she felt. The chills and the agony flooding a body she was hardly aware still existed.

Just as True was beginning to feel numb to the pain that tortured her just moments before, a bright light bolted her way. It smashed into her and flooded her with a warmth she'd almost forgotten. She hadn't registered any pain, but she could hear shrill screams. Were those screams coming from her? True couldn't be sure.

Another flash of light. Another piercing scream. Another and another. Over and over again until the grip around her loosened and she began to feel her limbs again. Soon, the fog in her mind began to lift and she was aware of her own thoughts.

Alexia D. Miller

True could feel her ascension through the darkness even if she didn't know her destination. She felt a sense of relief as the freezing cold faded away, even if she still fought to fill her lungs and sharp pains attacked her head. Darkness diminished around her until she could see the inside of Snowville Temporary Infirmary again. Moments later, True's body dropped against the floor of the building. She gasped as intense waves of pain shot through her.

"True!" Grace's voice cried as she rushed to her side. She could hear the hurried footsteps of the others surrounding her. True pushed herself up as Victor kneeled beside her, Phelia and Zane behind him. "Are you alright?" He asked, offering True his hand. With one hand to her chest True reluctantly took Victor's hand in the other. Slowly he guided her to her feet.

"You went right through the door—the first actually, but were the last to arrive." Phelia said with a frown.

"What happened?" Zane asked quickly.

"Give her some space." Victor ordered as he took a few steps away.

"Okay, but how did you know where the door was?" Grace asked.

"Father Wing told me," True answered without pause. A moment of silence followed and True's eyes flickered across the room. "Where's Twister?" True asked, suddenly feeling lightheaded.

"*Father Wing?*" Phelia asked not hiding her uncertainty.

"Twister stayed behind of course," Zane said looking over to Victor with a concerned look on his face. "You know, in FlareWing. Not that we had a chance to say goodbye with how quickly you went through the door."

True fought the wave of nausea at the back of her throat and the weakness in her knees. She tilted her head in the direction of the wall trying to understand what had happened. She attempted to take a step forward towards the wall, afraid that Twister was still somewhere in the dark place she'd left.

"I'm taking you home." Victor said, lifting her off her feet. "You don't seem well." He said, sliding one arm under her knees. The other she could feel at the base of her neck, putting warm pressure on the other side of her jacket. True attempted to answer, to tell him no or find her way back to her feet. Instead, she was fighting the nerves attacking her stomach and the sick feeling overflowing her body.

True could feel his steps as he descended the staircase, climbed awkwardly out of the window of the building, and out onto the street. She could hear the soft voices of the others as her lazy gaze rested on his face. True

Alexia D. Miller

willed herself to stay awake, opting to focus on Victors face as a distraction.

True voiced some of his features in her head. *Surprisingly, smooth looking skin. Bright green eyes. Black hair pulled back into a ponytail as per usual, if only a bit out of place today.* She repeated, visually tracing a few strands of loose hair down his shoulder with her eyes. When she was tired of repeating that, True focused on the sun high in the sky and the clouds slowly taking shape above them.

True wondered what time it was as she made out the roof of her house and the large black gate posts. Somewhere in the background she could hear her aunts' voices and shuffling back and forth. When she blinked, she saw that she was in her bedroom, but couldn't recall the moment she'd left Victor's arms.

She struggled to sit up and look around her room. Her door was cracked open and her jacket and mask were tucked away into a corner. Her dress had been exchanged for a brown nightgown and a glass of cold water sat on her nightstand. As she continued looking around the room True took notice of fluttering in a far corner.

"Are you alright?" Twister's voice called as he flew over to rest on her shoulder.

"Twister?" True blinked, not completely trusting her blurry gaze.

Alexia D. Miller

"It's me," he said, lightly pressing one of his small hands against her cheek.

"Ugh," True groaned, her head spinning. "But they said—"

"I know," Twister interrupted, "I know."

"Then how...?" True asked, trying to piece together her question through the dizziness in her head.

"Never mind that." Twister said quickly, urging True to lay back against her pillows. "I saw it." He said, his eyes wide.

"Saw it?" True asked, not understanding.

"When the door opened, I saw it pull you in. I couldn't just let it get you! I was afraid I was too late. I-I was afraid that I couldn't save you." He said in a panic.

"Let what get to me? What pulled me in?" True asked weakly. She could hear her heart pounding in her ears. Why was he so afraid? Twister looked at True with a distressed expression, his voice croaking with emotion. **"The Darkness."**

Alexia D. Miller

{ 329 }

Crystal Key Book 1

Part 2:
Darkness Rising.

Alexia D. Miller

Victor...

Chapter Thirty-Eight: Incidents.

Victor stared at his ceiling. He hadn't been able to sleep. His mind compelled him to question everything, even if it meant a sleepless night. For Victor, sleepless hours were a nightmare, let alone a full night.

When he and the others returned from FlareWing, it had been hours since they'd left, much the same as they'd experienced visiting Mirror. The difference in time was something Victor couldn't understand. How could it have been the same day in Snowville when they'd spent days away in Mirror, in FlareWing? Sure, Victor found himself relieved that he hadn't come home to a missing person's report and police at his door, but it didn't make sense. Still, the time-gap or whatever it was hadn't been the only thing that kept him awake.

What happened to True when she went through the door? How was it possible that she'd been the last to get there when she'd been the first to go through? Did only one of them have to wish to go home for the door to open? If not, how had it sprung open ahead of her like that? Why

Alexia D. Miller

was she so confused? Why had she been under the impression that Father Wing told her where the door was when he'd never left his chair? Why did she ask about Twister? Whatever happened on the way through the door was responsible for her confusion, Victor was sure of that.

Frustrated, Victor ran his hands through his hair. Questions were exhausting. Never in his life had he asked so many questions. He couldn't recall a time that he was bothered by *not* knowing a person. So why was this so different? Why was *True* so different?

If he admitted it outright to himself, or worse, if he let the words fall from his lips, Victor knew he wouldn't be able to take them back. Trying not to frustrate himself any further, Victor thought back to his time at the market. To the moment that they'd decided to meet up with Twister and search for True. Victor wondered what he would have done if he'd been able to see the future. If he knew what he was going to see.

When he saw her sitting there, Victor never questioned if the person ahead of them was True. Her relaxed, pale shoulders matched everything else he'd seen. Every single small finger and pale wrist and ankle from Mr. Van-Dayton's classroom. Until that moment, Victor hadn't noticed just how much he observed about her before.

Alexia D. Miller

{ 332 }

Her hair had been glistening under the sun and the flowers in her hair accentuated everything in his sight. In the exact moment he'd found himself in awe, he was overwhelmed with the thought that he was crossing a boundary. He was reminded that True kept every part of her hidden away, and it couldn't have been right—it felt forbidden and altogether foreign for him to see anything ahead of him.

Victor could still recall the pounding in his chest and the warmth flooding his cheeks. He remembered the clenching in his stomach and his sudden struggle to find his natural rhythm. If seeing that much of True was foreign, then everything else he'd felt were a million times more alien. Even his own movement; he'd hardly been aware of moving across the grass in the opposite direction.

When the panic settled and he was able to move again, Victor was surprised by falling behind. More than that, he'd been surprised that he was unable to be any closer to True or the others. He wrestled with the thought of just how close they'd come to seeing True and every possible reaction she could've had to it that his brain could muster.

Victor couldn't escape the thought that he needed to apologize. He felt that they'd been intruding on something private. That they'd stepped over an invisible line and saw something none of them were supposed to see, even if they

Alexia D. Miller

never saw her face. That feeling ate away at him even during the celebration.

As they sat at the table surrounded by happy voices, Victor thought he could apologize, but didn't know what to say. Part of him thought it was better to never say anything at all. Before he knew it, they'd found the door and True disappeared through it so quickly that he was sure she didn't want anything else to do with them.

At least, that's what he'd thought until they were back in Snowville and True dropped to the floor of the building. Victor recalled the relief he'd felt, thinking that True hadn't felt so cornered that she rushed home without a word. A feeling of relief that was soon replaced by a reluctance to get too close to her before he saw her strained breaths and heard her coughs.

It wasn't like I blamed the others for their questions, Victor thought, *I had plenty of them too. But it just felt* **wrong***.* Victor thought, sitting up in his bed. *She was weak when she stood and nothing she was saying about Father Wing and Twister made any sense. Taking her home was the best thing I could think of. Still...lying to her aunts hadn't felt right either.* He thought regrettably.

But what else was he supposed to do? Victor hadn't had a clue what he could tell her aunts and it wasn't as if he offered up any information to his own mother concerning

Alexia D. Miller

the crystals. What could he have told them anyhow? That they'd found magic crystals, traveled to other worlds, and saw things that probably shouldn't exist? That they'd almost been sold off in Mirror and this time around something different happened, but it was still better than being sold off to a slew of gigantic talking animals? *Of course not.*

Even so, it didn't keep Victor from feeling guilty. He didn't like to make a habit of lying. Lying felt too much like a narrow road in his father's footsteps. Feeling disgusted by the thought of his father, Victor turned over on his bed and willed himself to close his eyes. When he opened them at the sound of his alarm, he realized that it had only been five minutes. He had to get ready for school.

. . .

When Victor entered Mr. Van-Dayton's classroom, he saw a group of students huddled around the board. As he made his way past them towards the back of the room, he silently focused his eyes on True's empty seat. Initially, Victor didn't give the class much thought. Obviously, their teacher was running late and the idiots in the classroom had grown bored. It was their laughter, however, as Victor tried to fall asleep that shifted his attention their way, a few minutes later.

Alexia D. Miller

Annoyed, Victor lifted his head from his desk towards the scribbled mess underneath Mr. Van-Dayton's initial warning concerning True. Poorly drawn faces with wiry hair, horns, overgrown teeth, and drooping ears were scattered across the board underneath an emphasized title: "The Many Faces of the ***FREAK***."

Victor thought back to the faces of True's aunts when he brought her through the door. He recalled them scrambling throughout the house to get towels, thermometers, and some personalized emergency kit.

Victor thought about how brave True was to know how many people in the school felt about her and still did her work. To have tried her best to present to the class. How she'd shown a little of her heart in her presentation only to be docked points for something ridiculous. He thought about her going out of her way to help the twins in Mirror and even deciding to help them all return to Snowville. Even if True never showed her face, how did they have the right to call her ugly, to call her a freak, when they'd taken no time to get to know her at all?

Victor made his way to his feet and towards the board. Behind him he could hear a few of his classmates' excited chatter, rooting for him to pick a "version of Freak Face." He scoffed as he grabbed the eraser and grabbed all the markers from the stand. One of which, a girl Victor recognized to be Sydney's groupie, planned to make use of.

Victor swiped his hand across the board, dragging the eraser through the ridiculous looking faces. "Hey!" Sydney's groupie yelled at his back, reaching towards the markers as Victor set the eraser back in its place. "What do you think you're doing?!" She screeched, pushing her weight against him, pointing a marker into his face.

"Get off of me!" Victor hissed.

The girl screamed and her brown ponytail swung through the air past his face. Victor watched as she fell, hitting her head against the corner of the desk as the room fell silent. Mr. Van-Dayton hurried breathlessly through the door and paused at the scene. Victor could see his eyes shifting around the room.

Mr. Van-Dayton rushed to the girl's side. "Maya!" He called, helping her sit up. When she touched the back of her head, Victor caught sight of the blood on her palm. The girl—Maya—looked over to Victor, her eyes wide and screamed at the top of her lungs.

"He pushed her!" Sydney shouted from across the room. "He pushed her!"

The next half an hour Victor lived through slowly. Almost as if time slowed down to a crawling pace to make him suffer. Maya was taken to the nurse's office until her

Alexia D. Miller

parents arrived, Mr. Van-Dayton and Sydney were asked for their statements, and Victor's mother was phoned. Once again, Victor was sent to the principal's office.

To Victor's surprise, Principle Mann had been switched to the high school and some other poor soul his old seat and tacky office. Of course, his luck was so terrible that he'd have to deal with the same guy twice. Victor listened silently as Sydney, another one of her groupies, and a random face from the classroom explained that they'd been playing a "harmless" game on the board to pass time until Mr. Van-Dayton made it to work. He listened to her babble about how at least *they* weren't trying to sleep during class. Sydney emphasized that Victor purposely ruined their game and pushed Maya down.

Victor had been there. He lived through every moment. He didn't remember pushing her down, he didn't remember touching her at all. Yet, the more he heard it described by everyone else, the more he doubted himself. Most of his focus was still on Maya's bloody palm. Vaguely, Victor could hear Mr. Van-Dayton saying that he had no way to know the exact events that occurred and how he'd never witnessed any hostile behavior from him, though Victor did have a habit of falling asleep in class.

Principle Mann's wide frame shifted as he sat back in his chair. "Well perhaps you haven't, but I know this to be at

Alexia D. Miller

least the second of Victor's outbursts." Principle Mann said pointedly, dismissing them as his mother walked into the door. Her face looked pale and her breath was uneven, almost as if she'd ran to the school. Beside her was a thin, short man with bifocals and a messy head of hair. He introduced himself briefly as the vice principle and turned his attention to the principle.

As the man whispered something into Principle Mann's ear, Victor focused on anything and everything he could around the room. He couldn't bear to look his mother in the eyes. Principle Mann's office was full of dark, wooden furniture and ancient looking décor. As far as Victor was concerned, the span of time since he last sat in his office had done Principle Mann no favors.

Today, Principle Mann wore a light gray suit with a neon green tie. His face was still glistening as if he'd just finished a track meet. He'd gained weight since Victor saw him last, and he was almost sure that his nose was even more red than before. The desk, which before seemed to have his waist spilling out at the sides, was now two times larger. Unfortunately, contrary to its size, it didn't have a slimming effect. Attempting not to be rude, Victor turned his attention to the dark green carpet under their feet.

After a few minutes, Principle Mann leaned forward in his chair. As he shifted, the chair let out a long, shrill

Alexia D. Miller

squeak. "Maya Healy," Principle Mann started, folding his hands together, "has since been taken out of school to see a doctor. When the Healy family reports back tomorrow, we will find a suitable punishment for Victor." He shook his head disapprovingly, "Mrs. Gates—"

"Heather, please," Victor's mother interrupted.

"Oh. Well, Miss Heather, then." He corrected with a sigh. "Even if Victor were to give a different version of events, the odds are not in his favor. It seems to me that Victor is starting to develop a pattern. A track record, if you will—and a very serious one at that."

"I hadn't meant to hurt her." Victor added quickly feeling his mother's eyes again. "I'm sorry, mom." He whispered between clinched teeth. He knew that no matter how things happened, he'd hurt the girl—Maya. There was no excuse for that.

"I'm not sure what else you could have meant to do by putting your hands on her, Victor." Principle Mann said pointedly. "Miss Heather," Principle Mann cleared his throat, "It may not be my place to say, but I'm aware that Victor does not have a male figure to look up to in the household. It isn't uncommon for children his age to act out in high school. Specially to do so out of frustration in a *less* than healthy manner."

Alexia D. Miller

{ 340 }

Victor bit down on his tongue as hard as he could manage until he could taste the blood on his tastebuds, and he clenched his fists in his pockets until it hurt. All to fight the rising anger fighting to make its way from the back of his throat. Silently, Victor's mother urged him up from his seat.

"You're absolutely right, Principle Mann. It *isn't your place* to say!" She huffed. "I think we are done here. I suspect you'll give us a call when you hear something. Good day."

Victor knew if he glanced at his mother's face as they made their way through the office doors, he'd hate what he saw. She'd be frowned and red-faced, her cheeks would be full of air as she held her breath, and her lips would quiver as she held back her tears. So, he didn't look. Instead, he let her lead him through the exit doors and past the parking lot without taking a moment to slow down.

The memory of his father drifted to his head as he watched his mother stomp to the street. His father's broad shoulders and pointed chin, his thick brown hair, and the green eyes he hated. Victor could never escape them no matter how much he tried; even though he stopped looking in the mirror a long time ago.

A male figure wasn't what he needed, Victor thought bitterly. If he never saw the man so long as he lived it'd still be too soon. He could never imagine calling him his father

Alexia D. Miller

again. It wasn't long ago that his mother decided not to use her married name, and Victor wholeheartedly supported that decision.

Victor remembered all too well the day he walked into their house to witness a nightmare. He would never forget seeing his father's fist connect to his mother's cheek, sending her to the floor. He couldn't forget seeing her being pulled up by her collar and slid across the countertops. Or the sound of her head slamming against the vase and watching it shatter.

Victor's stomach bent at the thought of it. He remembered the moment his mother's eyes met his and she crawled to her feet in horror. His mother's deafening cries as his father charged at him like a mad bull, ready to rip him apart just for having witnessed it. It had been a night of nothing but blood and tears.

. . .

Victor's mother was still fuming even after they'd made their way home. He didn't know what to say to her, so he told her he was going up to bed. When she didn't stop him, he rushed up the stairs to his room and shut the door. He tried to sleep but memories of his father tormented him, and he managed to re-live every horrible moment—every

Alexia D. Miller

bitter memory of their lives when his father had been around. So, Victor suffered another sleepless night.

The next day, Victor found a note from his mother next to a bowl of soup on the floor. She'd said she was off to work and Maya was relatively unharmed. She didn't have a concussion and didn't require stitches. Victor knew that knowing that should have made things better, or at the very least should have offered a moment of relief, but it didn't.

Another wave of memories resurfaced, and Victor rushed to the bathroom. He coughed until he felt the burning at the back of his throat and emptied the contents of his stomach. When he finished, he wiped his mouth and looked up into his reflection. When had his mother put the mirror up again?

Unable to look at his eyes without seeing his father, Victor slammed his hands into the glass and watched it break apart. He listened to the clangs as chunks of glass fell into the sink. Victor looked at his hands, registering the broken bits in the side of his palms and blood running down his wrist.

He slumped down beside the sink, his eyes burning with tears. He didn't understand. How had she done it? How had his mother worried about him all this time? How had she loved him? How had she looked him in the eyes all these years and not been afraid?

Alexia D. Miller

No, Victor thought clenching his hair through his fists, *No. Half of me came from him, so that kind of monster is inside of me too, isn't it? I don't want to be like him! Mom...are you going to be afraid of me too? There's no way you can still be proud of me now. Not after what I did to her. Everyone will blame you because of me, just like Principle Mann. Mom. I couldn't live with myself if I turned into someone like him. What do I do? Crap, what do I do? I'm afraid.*

Victor pulled his legs to his chest, his body quivering with emotion, and pressed his face against his knees. "I'm afraid," he sobbed, "I'm so afraid."

Phelia...

Chapter Thirty-Nine: Nightmare.

Phelia shot up in bed, feeling beads of sweat on her brow. She could hardly remember it, but she knew she'd had a nightmare. What she could recall wasn't good; a nothingness that made her feel sick to her stomach, an infant suspended in the darkness, a gut-wrenching scream, and red fog. To her dismay, she knew there'd been more but the more she tried to recall, the faster the dream faded away from her. Phelia tried to move past it. Whatever she didn't remember, she wasn't sure she wanted to know.

Surely, she'd had a nightmare before, she tried to reassure herself. Only, she couldn't remember having one. Shaking any more thoughts of nightmares out of her head, Phelia made her way to the floor and straightened her sheets. She went to the bathroom and brushed her teeth before listening at the top of the stairs. She didn't hear their father.

Quietly, Phelia made her way down the steps hearing her brother on the telephone. As she walked into the kitchen, she saw Zane hang the phone on the receiver. He

Alexia D. Miller

sighed as he made his way to the table and sat down. "Are you alright?" Phelia asked walking over to his chair.

"Mhm. It's nothing. I just wanted to check on Victor. Some weird rumors have been circulating around school for the last few days. I finally reached his mom and she said that he seemed to be getting over a cold or something."

"Rumors?" Phelia asked.

"Yeah." Zane sighed again, rolling his crystal across the table under his fingers. Suddenly, Phelia bolted around the kitchen, living room, bathroom and even their father's office. "What's wrong?" Zane called as she zoomed up the steps.

"I don't have my bag, Zane! I didn't realize it was missing." Phelia huffed as she searched under her bed. "It's gone!"

"Maybe it's at the building?" Zane asked.

"Perhaps so." Phelia frowned, looking through the upstairs bathroom. "I recall having it with me around the time we went through the door. Before everything happened with True."

"It's not like you to misplace your things." Zane said thoughtfully. "Well, let's go take a look."

"Okay!" Phelia said. Without missing a beat, she ruffled through her drawers and grabbed a sweater and jeans. She slipped on her socks from the day before and pressed her feet through an old pair of shoes. She didn't bother brushing

Alexia D. Miller

her hair before she raced down the steps, almost running into Zane.

"Stay there." He ordered, glancing her way before disappearing up the stairs. When he came back down, he pressed a hat onto her head. "Grab your coat. It's supposed to snow today."

"Oh. Alright." Phelia said with a nod, making her way back up to her room.

At the temporary infirmary, Phelia and Zane climbed the steps. They'd searched the entire walk from home and even in the broken stair. Upstairs, Phelia was relieved to find her bag on the floor beside the wall. "It's here." Phelia sighed as Zane walked up beside her. She wrapped her hand around the crystal and pulled it out to inspect it.

"Good." Zane said with a smile. "Because I'm pretty sure we can't just get a replacement."

"That's not funny, Zane." Phelia huffed.

"Alright, alright. Sorry. Want some breakfast?" Zane asked, putting a hand on her head.

Before Phelia could reply, a strong light incased them. If only for a moment, Phelia thought she'd been rendered blind by the sudden florescent light. As much as she tried, she could not close her eyes. Phelia could see nothing beyond the blanket of white. Just when she thought to give up seeing anything around her, pale tones lined her

Alexia D. Miller

view. She could see vast open land that gave way to an oversized hill. A sunset filled the space above her, and a slightly chilled breeze blew from behind. Where was she?

"H-how did we?" Zane stammered, stepping up beside her. "What's going on?"

"It's happened before, remember? According to the journal that True had. You read it aloud after all." Phelia said quietly, her eyes still focused ahead of her.

"Yeah, sure...but this is ludicrous. We haven't even been in our own rooms or whatever they are. How did we even end up here?"

"I haven't a clue. Considering that we will have to find the door either way, however, we might as well look." Phelia said, walking towards the hill.

"Don't be in such a rush. We could have ended up in another Mirror for all we know." Zane warned.

Phelia nodded though she made no moves to slow her pace. From what she could tell, everything around them was open land. Miles and miles of greenery. As beautiful and calming as the landscape seemed to be, Phelia wasn't sure what to make of it.

As the two of them continued to walk, Phelia took off her sweater and tied it around her waist. Had the temperature changed since their arrival? Soon, she realized the temperature wasn't the only thing that had changed. The

Alexia D. Miller

grass, which only touched her ankles before, was slowly rising as they decreased distance to the hills. So much so that in a matter of minutes, Phelia had all but disappeared in the large blades of grass.

"It's almost taller than me." She said, parting the grass ahead of her.

"Phelia, get on." Zane demanded, kneeling in front of her, cupping his hands behind his back. Although Phelia wanted to continue on her own, she also wasn't comfortable with the thought of being engulfed in thick pasture. Compliant, she carefully climbed onto his back and wrapped her legs around him.

As they continued further, Phelia realized just how difficult it would have been for her to walk on her own. The grass towered over her height, a hungry beast intent on swallowing them whole. Zane walked cautiously through the grass, pressing his palms to the strands to create his own path forward. To Phelia's surprise, her legs were hidden in the grass even with the extra height her brother provided.

"Oh." Zane said, stumbling forward. "I hit my foot."

"Then the bottom of the hill starts here." Phelia said excitedly. She pushed off Zane's back and plopped down into the grass.

"Phelia!" Zane cried, quickly swiping his arms around the grass to find her. Phelia focused on finding the spot ahead of

Alexia D. Miller

his foot and climbed up the hill until she could look over her shoulder at Zane. The hill was a bit steeper than she'd thought.

"What are you doing?!" Zane asked, shocked.

"Climbing the hill, of course." Phelia chuckled.

Zane didn't look pleased. "Get down from there." He urged.

"You're worried for nothing, Zane." Phelia said dismissively, climbing further up the hill. As she made her way up, her foot slipped and sent her slowly sliding down the hill.

"You call that nothing? Are you kidding me?" Zane's voice called a few feet below.

"It's fine. I'm fine." Phelia nodded.

"Just get on my back. I'll carry you to the top." Zane huffed.

Phelia shook her head, "No. I can do this much." Phelia argued. If he'd said anything else, Phelia didn't know. His voice had been drowned out by her focus. What was wrong with him, anyhow? Phelia thought angrily. *He's always treating me like a baby!*

By the time Phelia reached the top of the hill, Zane was there waiting, peering down at her as she wiped at the beads of sweat on her forehead. Without a word she walked past her brother and descended the hill. Ahead of them a small stream came into view. On either side of the stream were a mess of different sized stones, some almost her height.

Alexia D. Miller

Phelia beamed at the sight of it. She rushed over the rocks towards the stream and stumbled. Her arms moved erratically through the air as she caught her balance. Being more careful, Phelia walked over to the water and dipped a foot in.

A rush of water surrounded her ankle and the sudden feeling of something slithering against the bottom of her shoe sent her straight into the water. Phelia yelped as her body sunk underneath the surface before bobbing back up again. Only moments later she was yanked out by her collar and her back was pressed against one of the large stones. Phelia chuckled through a cough. "It was a lot deeper than I thought it would be."

"Do you think that's funny?" Zane barked, "What's wrong with you today?"

"It was hot, Zane. It felt wonderful in the water, all things considered." Phelia attempted to explain, clearly not to her brother's liking.

"You're being reckless!" Zane yelled. "Look, you even cut yourself and you didn't even notice!"

Phelia looked down at her left leg. The jeans were ripped, exposing her bleeding knee. She hadn't noticed because it didn't hurt. Phelia shrugged as Zane took off his own sweater. He lodged it under a rock and held it in place

Alexia D. Miller

with his foot. He yanked it until it ripped and Phelia watched the shredded gray fabric fall loose.

"It doesn't hurt at all, Zane. You shouldn't ruin your clothes." Phelia sighed.

"If you hadn't been acting so wild, I wouldn't have to do it." He hissed as he ripped a few pieces of the sweater between his teeth and tied it around her knee.

"That's too tight Zane!" Phelia whined.

"Well it's supposed to be tight." He said crossly. "So there."

"This isn't a medical emergency. I'm not in danger of bleeding out or something!" Phelia ranted.

"Don't cry about it. It's just to help you." Zane said, rolling his eyes.

"I am *not* crying!" Phelia said angrily. Without hesitation she took to loosening the fabric herself, before tossing it aside. She pushed herself to her feet and hurried to the far left of the stream.

Why was he treating her like that? If he had a problem with all she did why didn't he just let her be? Phelia knew that Zane was always trying to do everything for her, as if to save her from herself and the entire world, but there was a such thing as too much coddling. He even skipped his date. There were plenty of things she didn't understand as of late. Right now, Zane was one of them. Phelia hated feeling like a burden.

Alexia D. Miller

Zane stepped in front of her. His face flooded with anger. "You're acting crazy!" He said, grabbing hold of her wrist. "We need to find the door and go home. Maybe it's this place that's doing it!"

Phelia pulled her arm away from him. "Maybe it's *you*!" She yelled pointedly. "If you want to go home so badly why don't you just go away? Just leave me be, Zane!"

For the first time in a long while, Phelia felt her age. She felt young and small in comparison to Zane. With her eyes shut tight and her hands balled into fists, she was filled with an overwhelming sense of disgust. "I don't need your help. Stop treating me like a baby! Just. Go. ***HOME***."

There was a long silence as she opened her eyes to see the shock and anger spread across Zane's face. His mouth hung slightly agape. Phelia could see him shaking with emotion as he clinched his teeth. "I'll leave you alone alright." He said, stepping past her. "I'd love to go home!" He hissed.

Phelia walked off in the opposite direction, looking over her shoulder towards the hill to see him disappear on the other side. She continued following the stream kicking rocks into the water. *It's not like we can go home without each other anyhow.* Phelia thought, kicking another pebble into the stream, and watching it fall.

Alexia D. Miller

Phelia looked up to the sky and watched the colors fade. In only a matter of seconds, the sky darkened as if a storm was brewing. The wind picked up, pushing waves of brisk air past her. Phelia fought to keep her hat from blowing away, grabbing hold of the closest large stone she could.

What was happening? Suddenly overcome with unease, Phelia looked around, looking for any sign of her brother. She looked in the direction he'd gone, calling out to him. Only to have her voice masked by the wind. Phelia watched as a whirlpool spun into view in the sky, surrounded by black clouds. Was the wind trying to push her to that thing in the sky?

Just as Phelia was sure that she couldn't hold on any longer, she saw Zane floating to the sky. As if struck by an invisible trampoline, Phelia watched Zane's body bob against nothing, skyrocketing into the vortex. The moment he disappeared from sight, the sky slowly returned to its bright hues and the gusts of wind died down.

Phelia dropped to her knees, completely stunned into silence. What had just happened?? It couldn't be. Had Zane truly been propelled into that thing? Any anger had long ago left her, replaced by panic. He didn't scream—he hadn't reacted at all.

Alexia D. Miller

How? Phelia asked herself, her eyes searching everything she could see. *How do I leave? How do I get home?? Zane!!*

Alexia D. Miller

Zane...

Chapter Forty: A Dream...?

*I*t was dark and empty around him. He couldn't form coherent thoughts. The air was fading, and Zane struggled to breathe. There was a weight on his back, almost as if something were trying to crush him. Moments later, when Zane was sure he had no air left in his lungs, something seemed to grab hold of him. It wrapped itself around his throat and dragged him down. Deeper into nothingness.

Zane opened his eyes, gasping for air, his hand over his throat. His eyes darted around as if searching for a phantom. He sighed in frustration, pulling his covers down from above his head. Of course, he'd felt suffocated. He'd buried himself beneath his sheets.

Zane threw the covers off his bed and sat up as his door creaked open. He recognized his sister's large brown eyes blinking at him through the opening. "Father!" She called, stepping into the room. "Father he's awake!"
"Hey. What's with all the noise?" Zane asked sleepily.

Alexia D. Miller

"You've overslept," his father answered, coming into the room with a cup of tea. "Phelia called me last night, so I ended my shift."

"You did what?" Zane directed at Phelia. "Why would you call him in from work?"

His father put a warm hand to his shoulder. "She said you'd gone out yesterday but didn't wake to make dinner. We couldn't wake you for breakfast or school this morning either. Your vitals were normal. Are you feeling ill?"

Zane frowned. He didn't want his father to worry. He must have been tired. Zane didn't remember hearing their voices that morning. "I'm not sick, dad." Zane said finally, "I guess I must've stayed up too long. Maybe I haven't been sleeping too well lately. I'll go to bed early tonight. I promise."

"Well, you'd better. I'm off the rest of the day and school started a few hours ago. I called and told them you wouldn't be in today." Zane watched his father sip his tea. "I have some paperwork to finish before lunch. Why don't you take a shower? That ought to wake you up."

"Okay." Zane said quietly.

"We'll go on ahead then." His father said, patting Phelia on the head gently.

Alexia D. Miller

{ 357 }

Zane watched as their father shuffled out the door and down the steps. Phelia crawled onto the bed beside him. "I didn't tell father about the crystals Zane. Honest."

"You'd better not tell him anything. You know how he gets. He'd worry." Zane said, squinting his eyes at her.

"Never mind that," Phelia said, placing her hand on his forehead. "Are you sure you're alright?"

"I'm fine," Zane said, shooing her off his bed.

"But how?" Phelia asked, waiting for an answer.

"What are you talking about?" Zane asked annoyed.

"How did you get home? Don't you remember, Zane? You flew right through that vortex or other. I followed the stream to a waterfall and there was a door. I wished to come home and—oh Zane I was terrified something had happened to you! You weren't at the temporary infirmary, so I ran home and found you in bed."

"Ugh, Phelia. Honestly!" Zane huffed, pushing her towards the door. He was too annoyed to listen to her nonsense. He hardly recalled going through the door, let alone a vortex. He did recall their argument and how she'd told him to leave. "I wasn't shot into the sky and I didn't disappear through some hole. I certainly don't remember a waterfall. Clearly, you've been having dreams."

Alexia D. Miller

"You didn't go through the waterfall Zane. *I did.*"
Phelia emphasized. "I haven't been—well I suppose I *have*
been having dreams, Zane, but—"
"No butts." Zane said, shaking his head. "I'm going to take
my shower and you're going downstairs with dad. Then,
when dad goes back to work, I'll do exactly what you wanted
me to do and leave you alone."

Closing his door, Zane went into the bathroom and
turned on the shower. He threw his clothes into a corner
and stepped under the water. He couldn't remember much
after their fight. He remembered walking back towards the
hill and going down the other side. He knew he laid in the
grass and closed his eyes. After that, he wasn't sure. *It
doesn't matter,* Zane thought with a shake of his head. *I've
got that nightmare on my brain. How am I supposed to
remember stuff after that?*

Phelia's words played on a loop in his head. Every
word from their argument fought away any moments of calm
his shower was supposed to offer. He knew now just how
Phelia felt about him. She didn't need his help. For the first
time, Zane found himself wishing Phelia was normal. He'd
never questioned the way she was, even all those years ago.
He knew she was different, but never thought he would be
bothered by it. Some part of him told him that maybe it was
time to stop caring; that he'd cared too much.

Alexia D. Miller

{ 359 }

After his shower, Zane found himself unusually disinterested in spending time with his father. He sat on the furthest couch looking out of the window while Phelia flipped through one of the photo albums on their father's lap. Later, when the two of them picked a movie, time crawled by and Zane felt he was in the movie himself, stuck in slow motion, watching events unfold before him.

At the sound of the phone ringing, Zane rushed to answer it, glad for something to take his attention off of everything else. In the kitchen, he was met with silence on the other side of the line. "Hello?" He called.

"Zane?" Bailey's voice questioned on the other side of the line. "I was just calling to see if you were alright. You umm...weren't at school today. I made you a copy of my notes." She said quietly.

"Oh. Yeah. Thanks. I overslept. My dad ended up calling in for me."

"Oh..." She said, her words trailing off.

"Bailey? Do you want to go on that date today? Maybe just to the park or something?"

"Zane...you know that I didn't call because of that, don't you? I wasn't trying to—"

"I do." Zane said, nodding into the receiver. "I mean, I know. Does that mean you've changed your mind?"

"No!" She said quickly, clearing her throat. "I didn't. Yes. I'd love to. Maybe we could stop by the café too? It's too cold for a picnic."

"Okay. So, how about we meet in an hour?"

"Yes," She chuckled. "Bundle up, okay? It's been snowing."

"Oh. I forgot about the snow," Zane said, peeking out of the window. "Maybe we should do it another day?"

"I'm not worried about a little snow, Zane. See you soon?"

"Mhm. Okay then." Zane said, hanging up the phone.

. . .

At the park Zane was met with Bailey's smiling face. "Zane!" She called, waving at him from a nearby bench. As he closed the distance between them, Zane thought he should offer a smile back but couldn't.

"Hey." Zane said, sitting down beside her.

"Hi." Bailey said with a giggle. "Thanks for asking me. Honestly, I thought you weren't interested. Things...well, you seemed surprised when I asked. And you didn't get in touch the other day."

"I was surprised. I'd never been asked out before." Zane confessed, looking at his footprints in the snow. "I never knew girls asked guys out to be honest."

Alexia D. Miller

"Well, I don't know about other girls, but I did." Bailey said. Zane watched a small smile spread across her lips. "I...I asked but I wanted to wait." She said softly. "I wanted to wait and see if you were interested in me at all. If you could see me that way, but it's been years now."

Zane watched as a pink hue flooded her cheeks and she shot up to her feet. "I guess I got a little impatient!" Bailey laughed and dragged her foot through the snow. Not knowing what to say, Zane frowned. She liked him for years, and he hadn't noticed? He'd always assumed that she was simply friendly. It never occurred to him that she might have been interested in dating him.

"Should we have gone straight to the café?" Zane asked, standing up and following Bailey as she walked further away from the bench.

"I like the park," Bailey said quickly. "Even with all the snow."

"Okay." Zane said, watching her. She scooped up a handful of snow and tossed it in the air. Her yellow coat and gloves contrasted the blanket of white in the park. The snowflakes seemed to sparkle as they fell and melted away on her shoulders.

Zane followed her lead, slipping on his gloves from his pocket, and flung snow into the air. Before long, the two of them were pounding each other with snowballs. Zane ducked behind a slide as Bailey creeped around catapulting snowballs against his back from her coat pockets. As he turned around, a snowball smacked against his forehead and sent him into the snow.

Bailey dropped to her knees and rushed to his side. "I am *SO sorry!* I got carried away and—oh, I'm sorry Zane!" She cried. Zane shook his head, covering his head with one hand and grabbing a fistful of snow in the other. Chuckling, he tapped the snow onto her face.

Bailey gasped as she shot to her feet and flung snow his way, blinding him as he stood. "Oh Zane! You, cheater!" She laughed.

Minutes later the two of them lay with their backs in the snow exhausted and laughing to themselves. "That was so fun!" Bailey squealed breathlessly. "I don't remember the last time I had so much fun—a snowball fight of all things!" She laughed.

"Yeah." Zane said, turning his head and meeting her eyes. As their voices faded, their silence was only penetrated by the cool breeze between them.

Less than an hour later, Zane and Bailey walked into the doors of the café and picked a table. The smell of cinnamon, freshly baked bread and coffee filled their noses. They ordered hot chocolate, sandwiches, and fresh-cut fruit.

Alexia D. Miller

"Today's been amazing." Bailey said, cupping her mug between her palms. "Thank you."

"Well you asked me out first, remember?" Zane said, taking a bite of his sandwich.

"Still..." Bailey said, drinking from her cup. Her voice trailed off as she stared out the window.

"Is something the matter?" Zane asked, following her gaze in the glass.

"I was just wondering if there was any truth to the rumors at school." She said, turning her attention back to Zane. "About Victor getting suspended?"

"Victor getting suspended?" Zane asked, looking up at Bailey from the edge of his cup.

"They're saying a lot more than that. I don't want to say exactly what they've been saying, but something about Victor being cursed because of the new girl. That she's just trouble." Bailey said, picking at her fruit.

"The new girl's name is True." Zane said with a frown. Bailey nodded silently. "And she's *not* responsible for anything Victor does. She's not bad luck." Zane said bitterly, finishing his food and gulping down his drink.

"O-of course not. I was only saying that that kind of thing was floating around school. I didn't know her name, but I think I've seen her around once. It's kind of funny though, isn't it? Her name is True, but she hides her face."

Alexia D. Miller

Zane couldn't explain the rising anger in his chest. He recalled True sitting in FlareWing and the moment that he'd almost seen her face. A moment that continued to plague him. "Or maybe it's because she stays true to herself. Unlike other girls like Sydney and her band of populars." Bailey chuckled. "Maybe so. Sydney and plenty of other girls at school are more than interested in the two of you—not that either of you seem to notice. Technically you're popular yourselves. That's one of the reasons everyone is so bothered with Victor acting so—" She was quiet, thinking. "...different."

"None of you even know him. All this talk about what someone else is up to. Come to think of it, who *do* you spend your time with at school? I mean, you sure are saying a lot of negative stuff for someone just repeating rumors everyone else is spreading around." Zane directed at her. He felt like a tea kettle whistling, ready to boil over.
Bailey shrunk into her seat. "What? N-no I—I'm not saying that I—do you know True? Who do I spend time with?" She stuttered. "You think someone like me could be around Sydney? Would even want to be? Zane I could never—"

"I have to go." Zane said quickly as he rose from his seat. He shifted his eyes to the door, ready to make his escape before the situation escalated any further. Before he couldn't contain his anger.

Alexia D. Miller

"Was it what I said? I really didn't mean anything. I was just—" Bailey stammered, reaching towards him.

"I just have to go, alright?" Zane snapped, taking a step back. "Be careful getting home."

Without another word, Zane went through the doors and out into the chilly air. He walked, not having any place in mind. He thought back to the words Bailey said. Her name. Even after what Zane said in True's defense, he was still bothered. If she were true to herself like he'd said, *why did she hide her face?*

When Zane looked up again, he found himself in front of True's house. Somehow, the house didn't look as intimidating covered in snow. His eyes fluttered over to the gate which stood ajar. In between the gusts of wind, Zane could just make out a voice. Following it, he walked through the gate and to the back of the house. There, he saw a barefoot True walking in the snow.

He could just make out her mumbling as she spoke to herself. So, she was feeling better? As he opened his mouth to speak, he found himself closing the distance between them. With every step Zane felt a deep pulsing rhythm beneath his skin and a warmth throughout his body as if his blood were on fire.

Seconds, minutes, hours later, which Zane wasn't sure, passed by. He could hear his voice coming from his

Alexia D. Miller

lips, but he couldn't understand his own words. True's voice came from below him as the heat subsided under his skin. Zane blinked through blurry eyes, confused.

True lay on the ground below him. She coughed, covered in snow. Her body was shaking, and her fingertips were beet red as she held onto her mask. Zane couldn't understand what was happening. His eyes settled on his own hands. The left pushed pressed against True's shoulder. The right gripped True's mask.

"What's wrong with you?!" Victor's voice called from the space around him. Zane tried to concentrate on it, tried to pinpoint where it was coming from. "What are you doing?!" Victor yelled, sounding closer. Zane looked up attempting to focus his shaky vision as Victor's shape came into view. He watched as Victor got closer and closer, running towards him, just able to make out Grace standing further in the background. What were they doing there?

A sharp pain shot across his face as Victor's voice shouted. "Don't touch her!" Zane had a moment of realization as a screech reverberated through his ears. Victor had punched him—was still punching him. Once. Twice. Three times as Victor continued to yell. His voice like vibrations under water.

Victor accused him of trying to force off True's mask. "No. I wasn't!" Zane argued, struggling to his feet.

Alexia D. Miller

{367}

Why would he ever do that? She was coughing, wasn't she? Surely, he must've been trying to help her. Zane slowly registered the look of pure anger on Victor's face. A look he'd never seen before as he struck him again.

This time, Zane followed up with a blow of his own. Soon, Grace screamed at them as they rolled in the snow. An endless loop of anger, heat, pain, cold and dizziness tortured Zane. Worsening with every second. It wasn't long before Zane could no longer distinguish the voices he heard.

Eventually, the two of them lay in the cold snow suffering through sharp pains and labored breaths. Zane could just make out the jagged pattern of red splashes in the snow. Like the worst abstract painting he could imagine.

The fact that they'd fought hadn't felt real. The feeling didn't settle on him until the pulsating faded and he stood unsteadily on his feet. Not until he heard Grace's shrill cries, ordering him to leave as she cradled True. Not until he dragged himself home angry and confused. Not until he saw his father's panic expression as he looked him over, time slipped away again, and he struggled to fall asleep through the pain.

Grace...

Chapter Forty-One: Leave.

Grace wasn't sure how long she stood there, frozen in True's yard. Even after True crept her way cautiously to Victor, Grace didn't understand. Just an hour ago she'd been on her way to True's, almost compelled to make sure she was okay after all the confusion before. Grace assumed Victor must have had the same idea too, since they ran into each other down the street. Which, if Grace was completely honest, was a good thing. She'd almost turned around when she remembered her last encounter with the house.

When the two of them made their way to the gate, Grace thought it was odd to see it open. When there wasn't an answer at the door, they'd almost left. At least until Victor hushed her, claiming to have heard something. Grace thought that surely Victor had great ears to hear any noise past the howling wind. Nights like this one always made her uneasy. Grace recalled thinking that it felt like a storm had been brewing.

What Grace heard next dropped her heart into her stomach. "I *said* why are you hiding your face from us?

Alexia D. Miller

Aren't we your friends? Do you know what they've been saying about you at school? About us?!" The voice roared. It was a raspy, unnatural sounding voice. A voice so strange and eerie that Grace was almost positive voices like that were reserved for horror films in movies.

Urged on by Victor's bolt towards the side of the house, it was all Grace could do to keep up. She stumbled behind him as quickly as she could, her heartbeat thumping in her ears. As they pressed through the snow, the voice grew louder. Almost loud enough to drown out the wind.
"Prove it! *Take it off!!"* The voice demanded.

To Grace's horror, she made out Zane through the falling snow. He pinned True down into the snow, sending her arms flailing to the side. His right hand quickly pressed against her mask and she pulled her arms up protectively, holding the mask so tight that with every jerk of Zane's hand, she swayed dramatically in whatever direction he pulled.

Before Grace knew it, Victor rushed forward. Without a moment's notice, he'd swung at Zane, his fist connecting with his face. It seemed only seconds passed before the two of them were screaming and leaving heavy imprints in the snow. It made no difference how many times Grace screamed at them to stop. She didn't know if it was because they couldn't hear her over their heated battle or if the wind drowned out her voice, but nothing worked.

Alexia D. Miller

After standing there frozen in mortified silence, the only thing Grace could think to do was make her way to True. To make sure she was alright. Grace could hear her coughs even before she reached her. When she held out her hand, True flinched. It felt like years before True allowed Grace to come any closer, until she let her hug her. Until she let her hold her.

In Grace's arms, True felt small as she shook, coughing and terrified. It made Grace angry. So angry in fact, that she didn't want to see Zane's face. That she didn't want him there at all. So, Grace voiced it. In all her disbelief and anger, with heated tears burning her eyes, Grace told him to leave.

Now, with Zane out of view, Victor wiped blood from his mouth. Even with the snow blowing in the wind and moonlight hardly shining across the yard, Grace could see his face already starting to swell. "True, I'm sorry." Victor swallowed. Grace could hear the tremors in his voice as he spoke. He lifted a hand towards True who immediately shrunk further into Grace's arms again. "I won't come any closer." He said, trying to reassure her.

"It's alright," Grace said softly, sniffling. "It's alright." "I don't know what he was—I don't understand why he was here or why he was...I don't have any explanation. I can't believe he even—Are you alright?" Victor said, stumbling

Alexia D. Miller

over his words. Grace could see his hands balled into fists at his sides as he shook his head. "Grace, please make sure she gets inside," He said, looking over his shoulder as he walked back the way they'd came. "I'm sorry."

Grace got to her feet, wanting to say something. Wishing she knew what would make things better as she saw Victor disappear around the side of the house. She turned her attention back to True and slowly helped her to her feet. In that moment, Grace thought that if True hadn't trusted anyone before, she was sure she would trust even less now. Maybe she couldn't make things better right now, but she could at least do what Victor asked.

Slowly, Grace led True to the front door, being patient every time she had to shift her hand and made True jump, and through every coughing fit until she stepped into the house. In the doorway, True turned around to face her. "I'm sorry, Grace. I think I need to lay down."

Grace wanted to argue. She wanted to tell her that she was going to help get her to bed and stay with her even, until she wasn't afraid anymore. But she couldn't. She felt the weight of True's words, almost like a heavy mallet pushing her out of the door. Instead, she said the only thing she could muster. "Make sure you get warm, okay?"

"Thank you." True's small voice said as she closed the door.

Alexia D. Miller

Grace stood there waiting to hear the bolts lock into place before she made her way down the porch steps. Normally she'd have been afraid of walking around at night, but she had a million more questions tonight.

Her mind had been so confused that it didn't have room for fear. What happened to Zane? The voice she'd heard carried over the wind hadn't sounded like him—hadn't sounded human at all. It had been crazed, breathy and cold. So much so, that even thinking about it brought chills down her spine.

Grace knew that she had more to learn about the others. She knew that she didn't know any of them well enough to make judgements, but Zane and Victor had been best friends for years. Nothing about their friendship had pointed to arguments and fist fights, as best Grace could tell. Would things be alright?

Alexia D. Miller

True...

Chapter Forty-Two: Progress.

$\mathcal{F}$or the second time, any progress True had felt seemed to disappear. All the confidence she'd spent reconstructing since their time in FlareWing, in between recuperating, seemed nonexistent. True never thought Zane could do such a thing. Even Victor had been shocked. She didn't know what to worry about more: The perplexing emotions she'd seen in Victor's eyes, or Zane's actions.

She felt sick. Worse than before. Her body wasn't nearly as calm as her brain. It betrayed her at every turn. Every moment she'd wanted to accept Grace's care or soothe Victor's worry, it acted of its own accord. Even now she was shaking, and it had very little to do with the winter air seeping through her window.

To think that just an hour or two ago she'd followed Twister outside after days of hearing him tell her that she needed to get fresh air. Even if she weren't feeling well enough to go to school, he'd said, she couldn't lock herself away from everything and make her aunts worry even more. Considering what had just happened, True was relieved that

Alexia D. Miller

her aunts hadn't returned home yet. Even after what happened, True didn't blame Twister, or herself for taking his advice.

As if her thoughts were a beacon, Twister reappeared, breathless and worried. "I'm sorry True. I had no idea." He said quickly.

"It's alright, Twister. I doubt there was much you could have done." True said, climbing into bed. She pulled her legs to her chest and laid her head against her knees, feeling anxious and dizzy thinking back on what happened. "I don't understand. Why fight? Why did Zane...?"

"You didn't see it?" Twister asked, fidgeting.

"See what?" True asked cautiously.

Twister's face became solemn as he spoke. "I wasn't sure about it at first, you see. I didn't know where it was coming from—why I felt it. There was an aura." He tried to explain.

"An aura? Energy?" True asked.

"Sort of—I suppose that's not the right word." Twister said, shaking his head. "Like a shadow. Something looming and dark when the two of them started fighting. It was like The Darkness was here somehow."

True's heart raced the instant he'd said it. She didn't understand the full scope of The Darkness. She didn't understand what It was or how horrible It could be outside of anything Twister said. She didn't know if The Darkness

Alexia D. Miller

could destroy their world like It had done to FlareWing, but she knew she never really wanted to find out.

She'd felt It's grip on her. She'd felt Its empty, icy claws around her when she was alone in that nothingness. She'd been surrounded by Its uncomfortable deep stillness. A feeling almost like It would wrap Itself around her like a blanket and seep into her skin. As if everything she felt would take hold of her and her mind would never piece it together.

Twister had saved her. Even now his presence offered almost an immediate relief from her negative thoughts and the fear she felt. She couldn't imagine what would have happened if he hadn't been there to rescue her. She never even thought to bring it up to him. But now, hearing what he'd said, she wondered if she should have. Should she have asked more questions? True didn't know what they would do if The Darkness truly made Its way to Snowville. If it had, was it her fault?

"Will you tell the others that you're here?" True asked. She doubted fighting made things any easier. For them, or Twister.

"I think that's for the best," Twister said with a sigh. "I thought I'd have had the chance to do so already. Considering what happened, I'm not sure what approach to take."

Alexia D. Miller

Crystal Key: Door to a New World

Alexia D. Miller

Victor...

Chapter Forty-Three: Lavender Waves.

Victor lay in bed, once again staring up at his ceiling. He couldn't recall the last time he'd felt so helpless. Between the thoughts of his father making him sick, his fight with Zane, and his mother's worrying, Victor was losing even more sleep.

More and more, he found the thought of facing himself in the mirror to be impossible. There seemed to be endless reasons to compare himself to the man he hated. Victor knew that his father had been a sorry excuse for a husband, ex or otherwise. A horrible father; the worst type of human being. Ironically, his father had been a teacher, and one of the students' favorites, according to his mother. Someone who was supposed to help others excel and a person who others sought to be like. It was laughable. Except when it wasn't.

Victor recalled the first time his father struck him. He remembered how his father said that he'd disappointed him when he failed a test. How he'd told him he was the

Alexia D. Miller

reason teachers felt the need to cheat the system, and how he was lucky that he was perfecting a system to ensure he succeeded. Of course, at the time Victor couldn't have thought his father was talking about the list. Even if he could have, it had yet to exist.

At one point or another, Victor even thought he was better off for what his father did that day because he never failed a test again. Not ever. Victor was sure he could have written it off, that he could have truly believed his father had done him a favor, if only it ended that day.

It wouldn't have mattered if Victor had known his father would strike him again for days, months, years. There would have been nothing he could do about it. All the times his father yelled or lashed out in his anger. All the times he meticulously tortured him and taught him to cover up his wounds, Victor never imagined that his mother was also a victim.

In fact, Victor recalled being outrageously naïve. He'd thought to himself on more than one occasion that if he didn't complain to his mother, if he silently accepted his father's words and fists, somehow each blow that hammered away at him would never reach her. It was so naïve that Victor was ashamed.

He didn't know at what point his naivety turned to blindness. Or stupidity. He used to think that perhaps if his

Alexia D. Miller

mother made one less excuse on his father's behalf, he would have understood. But even that was only a justification for what he didn't see in front of him. So, the day that he walked home from school with knots in his belly and pounding in his ears, truth met him at the door.

As he turned the knob on the front door Victor could hear his father's incoherent shouting. Victor could hear his mother's voice straining to speak, shaking and terrified as he walked down the hallway, past the smiling family photos he hated on the walls. Those pseudo smiles mocked him with every step towards the kitchen. Almost as if they knew what was on the other side.

The moment Victor rounded the corner he saw his father's fist send his mother to the floor. He heard her cries as he yanked her up into the air before she could stand and dragged her face across the countertops. He jumped with every plate and mug that smashed against the tiled floor. And again, when he smacked her head against the vase and it shattered, sending a trail of bloody droplets to the floor.

Victor tried not to picture it, to re-live any more of what had happened that day, but nothing he tried worked. Even when his tears stung against his broken skin from the fight he'd had with Zane, Victor found no relief. As if he was in the past, he saw his mother fall to the floor, sobbing.

Alexia D. Miller

Victor could never forget the heat skyrocketing through his veins. For all he knew, he could have sprouted wings and flew his way over to his father. He'd never remembered how he made it across the room, or if he'd said anything as his fists pressed against his father's face. It only mattered to Victor that he'd gotten him—that it hurt. It wasn't long, however, before his father wiped the blood from his nose and slammed him against the wall. It wasn't long before he met eyes with his mother as she reached out to him. He couldn't understand the words she said. He could only hear her awful sobs.

It was his father's turn to strike. And strike he did. One fist after the other until Victor felt numb. Until he could barely feel the shaking of his body against the wall. When his father's thick hands wrapped around his throat and forced the air out of his lungs, he'd hardly understood what was happening. When he did piece it together, Victor's only thought was that his father's evil face would be the last thing he saw.

His lightly sun-tanned skin, his stupid beard, and gold-rimmed glasses. His light brown hair and bright green eyes that he was sure held the doors of hell between them, if there ever was such a thing. Eyes just like his own. The same, at least, if darkness had slithered there like a snake. The only thought worse than dying by his hand was the fact

Alexia D. Miller

that his mother would be there all alone after he was gone. Alone to face his father's wrath and there was nothing he could do about it.

Victor hadn't been aware of the tears running down his cheeks or of his vision starting to fade before his body fell to the floor. He had, however, felt the dry heaves as his lungs filled with air. From his crooked vantage point on the floor, he could just make out figures struggling and shattering noises echoing from the cold tiles against his cheek.

A moment later, a pair of teary eyes blinked at him. His mother sobbed and Victor struggled to hear her apology. Determined to fight the dizziness in his head, Victor reached out to his mother. She kissed his hand, mumbling more apologetic words he could hardly understand before wrapping her arms around him and slowly steadying him onto his feet.

They didn't have time, his mother said. They had to hurry. So, Victor leaned into her as they stepped over broken glass, spilled drinks and a slew of slushed food on the floor. Eventually, they would step over his father too. He laid motionlessly on the floor, blood seeping into the patterned tiles, and his glasses lay halfway across the room. Before Victor could ask, his mother shook her head. No. His father wasn't dead. He was alive.

Alexia D. Miller

Crystal Key: Door to a New World

His mother led him to the steps and sat him there with instructions to stay put. Victor watched her disappear up the stairs and stared down the hall as his head cleared. Victor glared at the photos on the walls. He could almost hear them laugh at him, at his mother. Filled with rage all over again, Victor stood up shakily and made his way down the hall.

At every picture he hurled it to the ground and watched it shatter. With every broken photo he felt a slight burst of relief and a feeling akin to happiness. At every step he ripped another photo from its place and shattered it. One after the other until there was nothing left to break.

By the time he was finished and out of breath, his mother was there at the end of the staircase, silently watching. The two of them shared a long glance before his mother rushed him out of the door. They'd left that night with nothing but two bags and his mother's purse. Victor recalled wondering how he'd ever been afraid of his father when they'd stepped out onto the porch and walked down the steps.

As sad as it might have been, Victor was afraid—still afraid. Even after the divorce, even after moving and the restraining order, he hadn't escaped his father. He saw him every time he looked in the mirror. He'd felt the dark, violent side of him during the incident with Maya and his

Alexia D. Miller

{ 383 }

fight with Zane. Weren't the eyes enough? How close was he from turning into the man he despised?

He couldn't trust himself. Not even around his supposed best friend. Someone he'd only fought once since they'd met because of something as childish as money in an envelope. Someone that helped him find himself when he was lost and surrounded by nothing?

So, what about her? Was he protecting True or had he used her as an excuse to lash out? Had he been focusing on her because he was being controlling? Victor didn't want to notice the soft patter of her feet. He didn't want to recognize her presence from down the hall. Couldn't he have handled things differently with Zane? How long before it got worse? How long before he lashed out at True? At Phelia? At Grace? At his mother?

He didn't know anything. Victor didn't know that he'd feel like his room was trying to suffocate him with his thoughts and he'd rush out of the house. He didn't know that he'd go to True's and catch a glimpse of Grace's thick red hair coming closer. He hadn't known that before he could explain what he was doing there that Grace would take hold of his sleeve and pull him along. He hadn't known what they'd find hearing the voices in the wind or that he'd see a rage behind Zane's eyes he'd never witnessed before. Or that Zane wouldn't stop until they struggled in the snow.

Alexia D. Miller

For the next hour Victor racked his brain. He still wanted to see him. He wanted to understand Zane. Just as much as he wanted to know that True was alright, that she hadn't shut herself away from everyone. Only, he didn't know how. So, Victor listened to the wind whistling past his window until he heard a knock at the door.

When he sat up to answer it, however, Victor realized he wasn't in his bedroom anymore. He'd been sprawled out on a large, flat stone feet away from a cabin he'd never seen. Victor looked up at the sky. He saw a swirl of blue and pink and light cascading down around him. He couldn't make out clouds or a sun.

Swallowing his panic, Victor stood upright and listened. He heard no voices, music, or birds. Only the distant sound of water, so he followed it. He walked past the cabin and a large tree with looping vines with cream colored berries. A few steps past the tree, Victor realized was the end of a cliff. A cliff that had a stairway jutting out the side which looked over lavender colored water.

Victor watched as the lavender waves rushed up the bottom of the cliff. Not daring to venture down the staircase and any closer to the water, Victor turned around and headed back towards the cabin. When he circled it, he found no one. Instead of people, he saw a small shed and a stone well.

Alexia D. Miller

{ 385 }

With nothing else to do, Victor made his way to the door of the cabin. He knocked and waited, but there was no answer. He tried again. Nothing. When he placed a hand to the door handle, Victor discovered that it was open.

Alexia D. Miller

Phelia...

Chapter Forty-Four: Different.

*J*ust yesterday, Phelia had been relatively happy. Although she was still shaken by going through the door. She knew what Zane said, that she'd been having dreams. It was true that Phelia couldn't be certain she hadn't dreamt up the vortex. Afterall, her nights seemed to begin and end with a nightmare as of late. Even still, her father's gentle hands and loving presence kept all those thoughts at bay.

After Zane spoke to their father and left, they finished their movie and decided to go shopping. Phelia was pleased to find a wonderful black fountain pen with curves etched in gold and a handmade leatherbound book. Which her father bought for her before she could say she was interested. Her father walked her down the stretch of road past nameless shops and people, gently humming to himself as they went. Eventually they stopped by the bakery and left with their arms full.

It had been such a blissful number of hours that Phelia had nearly forgotten her fight with Zane. That was, until they made it home. They'd managed to cook dinner

Alexia D. Miller

and even make an apple pie from their mother's recipes—even if it was a terrible attempt. When Zane walked through the door, Phelia had been determined to meet him with a smile. She'd wanted to let him know that they were likely just having a rough week.

Only, Zane had no interest in dinner or pie. He'd stumbled in the door out of breath and freezing from the cold. His eye was dark and swollen. Which Phelia realized as her father examined him, wasn't very different for the rest of him. It looked to Phelia like Zane had survived a beast attack through the sharpest bundle of thorns.

Even when prompted he didn't speak and was soon treated and shuffled off to bed. When they tried to wake him for dinner, he didn't respond. Phelia wanted to force him awake and demand answers, but her father told her that they needed to give him space. That sometimes boys got into fights.

Even if that was true, Phelia didn't agree. She wanted to tell her father that Zane never got into fights. That whatever boys her father was describing was nothing like her brother. Still, she didn't argue with her father. Even when Zane didn't wake up again for school and her father said he'd call the school to excuse him.

Now, Phelia couldn't believe that she had been so unbothered the day before as she sat upstairs in her room,

Alexia D. Miller

talking in hushed tones to Grace. She couldn't believe what she had been hearing. The fight that Zane had gotten into had been with Victor. Even worse, from what Grace told her, Zane had been attacking True? What Grace described didn't sound anything like her brother.

"Have Zane and Victor ever fought before?" Grace asked.

"Well, I suppose they have once, but that wasn't anything like what you've just told me. Or at least, that wasn't how Zane explained it." Phelia said thoughtfully. She thought back to a conversation she'd had with her brother years ago. A conversation about how he and Victor became friends. "When they were first getting to know each other they fought," Phelia nodded.

"What happened?" Grace asked. "I just couldn't even imagine them fighting. They seem so close."

Phelia nodded again. Yes. They *are* close. So close, in fact, that Phelia had been certain she understood what true friendship was supposed to look like by watching them. Could there really be a clue to Zane's behavior from such a drastically different story? She was uncertain, but it couldn't hurt to think about it.

"As my brother put it," Phelia began, "It was only a couple of years after we moved here that Victor and Zane met. We'd been living here in Snowville a year when mother

Alexia D. Miller

died. It wasn't long before father took Zane and I on a vacation. We left Snowville for almost half the year, traveling around and seeing mother's favorite places. Father told us stories and bought us little trinkets.

"We couldn't stay away forever, of course. Father had work and we needed to go to school. Zane said he was sure the vacation was father's way to escape. To protect us from all the voices whispering as we walked by or left the house—all the people we saw were talking about mother's death. I imagine that it could have been as Zane said, but I also wondered if it was because father was too sad to stay in our home after mother was gone. So, we came back to Snowville. Only, everything was sad here and---well, it was almost a year before Zane went off to school.

"I went to a daycare center but that didn't quite work out. Father was able to enroll me into school early and before long that wouldn't work out either. In any case, the important thing here is that Zane went back to school. When he did, he met Victor.

"Brother said that Victor hardly spoke to anyone and wouldn't answer the teachers no matter how upset they got with him. If I recall correctly, Victor had become a new student there while we were away on vacation with father. Apparently, a girl name Sydney was pestering Victor in class,

Alexia D. Miller

so Zane told her to "get lost." From then on, Victor greeted him back when he said hello in the mornings.

"I don't know that it was much to celebrate, but Zane had seemed happy about it at the time. Some weeks later, Victor knocked at our door. He'd been going around, it seemed, asking to do yard work or odd chores for money. Anything he could do to help his mother. As I understand it, he'd been brushed off by the neighbors.

"Zane told father that Victor was a boy from class and father offered to let Victor come over to pick up sticks and trash in the yard. When Zane realized there hadn't been anything for Victor to find, he spent days collecting sticks and breaking them up in the yard. When he thought father wasn't looking, he even took trash from the house and tossed it around. Then he'd go about sighing the rest of the day saying 'Oh I *wish* **someone** would pick up all the litter in the yard! Dad, why don't you pay Victor to come clean up?'

"Of course, father would leave the trash around until Victor made his way back to the house and diligently picked up the mess. Soon enough Victor started to come inside too and clean. They'd sort out the trash together and go about like maids through the house.

"On Zane's birthday, he invited Victor over to celebrate. When practically everyone had gone home, Zane tried to give Victor the money he'd gotten in his cards. He'd

Alexia D. Miller

stuck it in one of the envelopes and put it in his hands. Before long they were shoving the envelope back and forth until they were fighting, and father had to separate them."

Phelia chuckled. "I was so confused. I didn't understand why they'd been fighting at first. Until I realized it was because they were simply caring about each other. It had only been a few minutes before Victor fell asleep in the corner and Zane got upset and woke him up. By the next day, they apologized to each other and a couple weeks later, Victor started talking to us.

"It always seemed to me like they'd been friends forever, but I realize that it has only been a few years since they met. Somehow, one can't guess it by looking at them. I remember being fascinated by that. They were so close to each other, almost as if they were brothers. Surely, they got along just as well as Zane and I and we are truly related. Zane has been cheerful since they met, and Victor didn't look so far away anymore. Although little can be said for his ability to fall asleep at a moment's notice. I'm not quite sure he'll ever stop doing that."

Grace smiled. "I've never heard of a nice fight before, but I imagine that could count as one." Phelia watched her sigh and flop onto her back. "It definitely doesn't sound anything like what I saw. I'm telling you Phelia, something was weird. Something was *different.*"

Alexia D. Miller

Phelia didn't know what to say. She hadn't been there. She hadn't seen things for herself, but she couldn't imagine that Victor and Zane would fight. Or that they'd truly hurt each other. As the phone rang, for the third time that day, Phelia got to her feet.

"Your father lets you pick up the phone?" Grace asked surprised, jumping up from the bed as Phelia went to the doorway.

"Yes, of course." Phelia nodded with a sigh. "Only, I wish I didn't have to. It's probably her again."

"Her?" Grace asked, following her down the stairs.

"Yes. Bailey. I met her a few times before. She was here that day for brother's birthday. A few times as well for some project or other last year. Every time I answer, she seems miserable."

Zane...

Chapter Forty-Five: Voice.

Laying on his bedroom floor, Zane was sure he was going insane. All night he'd tried to rest to no avail. His thoughts were constantly drowned out by a voice in his head. The voice was furious. As if it were soaked in a hatred for everything and everyone. In the briefest of moments, he'd been able to recall all the horrible acts he'd done. Only, it hadn't seemed real.

Every moment that he played back in his mind seemed far away. As if he were suspended in air at a distance, watching and listening through a glass he couldn't break. His arguments with Phelia hurt him, but not nearly as much as what he'd done to True, or what happened with Victor.

Zane wasn't sure who he was anymore. He didn't even know if he'd have friends once he left his room. If he could change things, if he could go back to the way things had been before—Before what? He didn't know when things had started to take a turn for the worst.

Alexia D. Miller

When Phelia knocked on the door and mentioned Bailey calling, Zane made no attempt to respond. He could almost feel himself sinking through the floor. His disbelief in the things he had done was nothing compared to the guilt he felt. Not just with Phelia, True and Victor, but with hurting Grace and Bailey. Even worse, his guilt couldn't compare to the hate boiling inside of him. It was like nothing he'd ever felt before.

Zane recalled once how Victor mentioned hating his eyes, how he wished he could look in the mirror and not hate what he saw of his father. He'd never questioned him about it, never truly knew what happened aside from the rumors he heard. He did know, however, that he wished he only hated a single part of him in that moment. How easy it would be to hate a leg or a foot instead of every fiber of his being.

WHY HATE YOURSELF? The voice echoed through his mind. YOU SHOULD BE BLAMING THEM FOR WHAT THEY'VE DONE TO YOU! IF ONLY PHELIA—Zane screamed as loud as he could in his skull, hoping to drown out the voice inside him. He knew how irrational it seemed to yell at himself, even more so in his head. Still, he needed to do *something*. Anything to get the voice inside his head to stop speaking. To stop the pounding at the corners of his skull if only for a moment.

Alexia D. Miller

Grace...

Chapter Forty-Six: A Rare Night.

MaryAnne and Duke were gone, apparently on some trip for a friend's birthday. Which was strange. As far as Grace knew, MaryAnne and Duke didn't have friends. Sure, they had business partners, the occasional stay-at-home wife who shared her recipes, and anyone else they invited at random to a holiday party or celebration, but Grace didn't think they were friends. Of course, she knew she didn't always understand adults, and her days at school certainly proved they knew even less of her, but she was almost sure most of the people her foster parents interacted with didn't even like them.

Grace could hear their mockery, which her foster parents always excused as jokes, and saw their snickering when their backs were turned. She'd even told them once, only to be locked away as if she was the one in the wrong. After that, Grace learned to make note of the worst ones in her head and steered clear of them any time they were around.

Grace supposed none of that really mattered for now. What mattered in that moment was that her foster parents would be gone for a few days and she was determined not to get in trouble. Not with the neighbors, with Eustis, or anyone else at school. Though, if Grace were being honest, the best thing about being home alone was the bath. She could take the warmest, longest bath she wanted. There'd be no timer and no one forgetting her towel. She could bury herself in the water until the moment it got cold.

So, she did. Grace ran herself a steaming hot bath. It was so hot that Grace couldn't climb in at first, so she sat on the toilet, wrapped in her towel, and dipped her toes in the water to test it. Each time it stung her she laughed; a kind of joyful cackle that might have scared her neighbors if they'd heard her. Like a mad witch celebrating the perfect brew.

When she finally found herself in the water, Grace spent a great deal of time nervously checking the timer on the other side of the bathroom. Nearly convinced that it would start ticking away the seconds and MaryAnne would barge in, shrieking about her next punishment for not following the rules. To combat her anxiety, Grace buried her head under the water, watching her thick curls float over her face, and held her breath.

When she closed her eyes, she felt a warm, familiar tingle in her chest. A kind of warmth that spread to the rest

Alexia D. Miller

of her body. A different kind of warmth warmer than her bath. Grace knew she'd felt it before even if she couldn't remember where. She tried to probe the feeling, tried to home in on everything she felt. The moment she tried, however, it faded away.

Unable to hold her breath any longer, Grace pushed herself through the water, sending rushes of warm water spilling down her back. She wondered if the warmth she felt had anything to do with the crystals. If it did, what did it mean? What were the crystals anyhow? How did it take them to other worlds? Why didn't the freakin' things come with instruction manuals? Where did they come from? What about Brilla and the others who supposedly had the crystals before them? What happened? Where were they?

Between the steaming bathroom and the thoughts buzzing around in her head, Grace was starting to get dizzy. The truth was, Grace had no idea how to get answers to any of her questions. She wondered if she were as smart as Phelia if she could figure it out. Phelia, her first friend, who seemed to be a genius.

Grace felt lucky to have met her. She figured that she would have been all alone if not for Phelia. More than that, being around her made Grace feel understood. Maybe best of all, Phelia had never seemed ashamed to be with her.

Alexia D. Miller

Victor...

Chapter Forty-Seven: Your Friend.

Victor closed his eyes with a sigh. He'd searched around the small cabin and hadn't seen any evidence that someone had been living there recently. Aside from a bed separated from the rest of the cabin by a simple wall and general kitchen items, the only thing of interest was the letter he found by a stack of papers and pens. A letter Victor struggled to read from the very first sentence. Save for some details, Victor almost felt he could have written it himself.

For U,

I hope that this doesn't sound as cruel as it does in my head, but since I met you my life has been confusing. The day after we met, I was full of questions, most of which haven't been answered. Then, I found the crystal and somehow that led me right back to you.

Before long, I needed to know you. Regardless of everything the others think at school. It doesn't change anything. By now, I have forgotten how long it's truly been since we met, although I am sure it couldn't have been as ancient as it feels to me now.

Alexia D. Miller

*Even odder still, I can recall the exact number of
freckles on your face, and the number of times you
brought a new book to read instead of your math book
because you said math didn't interest you. How can
someone say that and still ace every test?*

*I remember your favorite pair of reading glasses and
how you step into the largest of puddles after it rains
or the snow melts, as if compelled by some unknown
beckoning even without your boots. How strange is
that? Me, of all people, who can't recall the color of my
teacher's hair or my mother's birthday.*

*I'm almost sure I should feel guilty about it, but I don't.
The way things are now, I find myself thinking of every
moment we've had together—moments altogether too
short, I realize. Of the seconds we've shared, even
though I cannot count them. With things as they are
now, I didn't want to regret not telling you these things.
Still, I don't know if I can muster such courage when
you look at me. Because in your gaze my world shifts
and I am altogether too knowing. When you laugh with
someone else, I am filled with the most ridiculous of
joys and bitterness all at the same time. Happy, to see
your smile and disappointed that your smile is not
directed at me. And when you lay in the grass and look*

Alexia D. Miller

up at the sky, humming sweet songs to yourself, I wonder if I could ever be there beside you.

I don't know if you recall, but the two of us held hands once. I was so distracted that I still can't remember what excited you enough to slip your hand in mine and stroll me along. Since the moment you let go, it has felt unbearably empty there. As if some part of me detached and went away with you and never returned to me.

I haven't a clue if it is alright for someone like me to entertain the thousands of selfish thoughts that run through my head. So yes. Since I met you my life has been utterly confusing, but it has been many more things too: it has been the most hilarious, sad, enduring, exciting, and most beautiful thing that's ever happened in my life. I've never been as proud or as ecstatic as I am now.

I don't want this to be goodbye. So, I'll do whatever it takes. And perhaps one day, after all this strife and battling comes to an end, perhaps there will be another kind of adventure awaiting us. Perhaps we can walk again, hand in hand, without worry that there's more to be done. Perhaps we should be so lucky to laugh again without burden. With no dangers in sight.

Alexia D. Miller

Undeniably Yours,

Mathew.

Victor cleared his throat, feeling embarrassed and ashamed of his curiosity. It dawned on him that this letter meant that Mathew had been there however long ago. Which obviously also meant that Victor had been whisked away through the door. His door? Or theirs? It was too confusing to think about.

Whatever the case, Mathew expressed things in his letter that Victor couldn't imagine putting words to. He couldn't have written it. Not just because he had no clue what True looked like, or because he'd never so much as had a deep conversation with her, but because whatever Mathew had experienced seemed altogether different, even if it felt familiar.

There were plenty of things to question in the letter if he let himself. Like what possible dangers he was speaking of, if the burden he mentioned had been the crystals, why the letter was there of all places, and what he meant when he said it didn't matter what others said at school. *Great.* Victor thought. *I'm starting to sound like Grace,* he said to himself, amused.

Not knowing what else to do, Victor gently placed the letter back where he'd found it and plopped down onto the bed. It seemed only an instant later that he saw a flash of

Alexia D. Miller

light and the dark wooden ceiling faded away, replaced by a yellow flat surface above him. His nose filled with the smell of dust and he sat up, uncomfortable.

Victor cautiously swung his legs around the side of the bed. He looked at the rows of beds to his right and the large table and broken chairs to his left. He recognized the boxy machines and the fireplace in the corner. Making his way to his feet, Victor quickly dusted himself off, shaking his head in disbelief.

What was he doing there? How had he gotten to the abandoned hospital building? A gentle moonlight glow shined through the broken window where the sheet board should have been. Had he been dreaming? Sleepwalking? Victor didn't have a clue.

He climbed his way through the window and to the outside. He felt the cool air ruffle his hair and swat the branches of nearby trees. As he placed the board against the window, he noticed he wasn't even wearing shoes and the snow had already began to melt away.

Victor pushed away any panicked thoughts in his mind and focused on walking. It wasn't long before he was making his way past True's house and stopped. The gate was closed and there wasn't a light to be seen. He wondered what time it was. Had everyone gone to bed or was True

Alexia D. Miller

somewhere inside the dark mansion alone and afraid to come out again because of his fight with Zane?

Just as he turned to continue walking, movement in the yard caught his attention. Following its direction with his eyes, Victor made out a white glossy face with dark eyes peeking from behind a tree. A mask? "True...?" Victor asked cautiously, untrusting. It was possible that he was seeing things. Afterall, he'd somehow managed to get from his bedroom all the way to Snowville Temporary Infirmary without noticing—and without shoes.

"Victor." Her small voice said as she stepped around the tree. In his mind, Victor told himself not to waste the chance to speak to her, to see if she was alright, but standing there in the night just yards away without any shoes, he didn't take a step forward. *Speak for crying out loud,* Victor thought cross with himself. *Don't just gawk at her like a creep.* He demanded, shifting his gaze down to his feet.

His lip quivered as he looked up, seeing True only feet away now. Another second later, he felt her hand in his, leading him through the gate. His mind turned over the letter he'd read—or at least was almost certain he'd read. When she let go of his hand, would it feel empty there too? How were her hands so soft and warm?

True led him to a plush blanket on the porch in front of the door and when he sat down beside her with his back against it, he could feel the heat wafting up his back. He wanted to ask her what she was doing outside but was still swallowing the lump in his throat in the silence between them.

"Victor?" True's voice called from beside him.

"Yeah?" Victor managed finally.

"Are you feeling alright?" She asked, pressing her head to her knees. "You're not wearing any shoes."

Victor chuckled. She was one to talk. He looked over at her pale feet, her dainty toes visible from the end of her dress and jacket. How did she manage being barefoot all the time?

"I'd rather ask how you're doing," Victor said truthfully. "I'm sorry," Victor said, having found his voice again. "I'm sorry about Zane and the fight. You must have been terrified. What he did—what *we* did wasn't right." He said quickly. "I don't know what's going on lately."

"Thank you," True said softly, "for protecting me. Even from your best friend." Victor nodded, not knowing what to say. He'd found that happening a lot lately. In the moments that he actually wanted to speak he was at a loss for words. As another silence faded in between them, Victor wondered what True was thinking. He wanted to understand the thoughts that went through her head as if they were his own. He wondered if his father started out that way, thinking the way he did.

Alexia D. Miller

{ 405 }

"Are we friends?" True asked suddenly, taking Victor by surprise.

"I—I don't know. Crap. I mean—I didn't know if you—I don't even think I'd be a good friend to anyone the way I am now."

"The way you are? You're Zane's best friend, aren't you?" She asked without hesitation.

"Well, yeah. Although I'm not sure if he hates me now or not. I hope to talk to him if he'll let me. I don't really have friends."

True nodded. "I decided that maybe it's okay to try again. One more time. Things could be alright."

Victor wanted to ask her what she meant. He wasn't sure if she'd been talking to him or talking to herself. "It isn't just my decision though, is it? You can't force someone to be your friend. It has to be mutual or it isn't really friendship." Victor tried to explain. He wondered how True lived before coming to Snowville. Did she leave her friends behind? Did she have any?

"I'd like to be your friend." True said warmly. "The way you are. However, you are. I'd like to try." Victor didn't know when he'd began to hold his breath, or when his heart started to pound in his ears, until he closed his eyes. He exhaled slowly as quietly as he could manage. He looked off to the side, clearing his throat and scratching the back of his head awkwardly.

"I don't know that I would be a good friend to you, but I would like to try. If that's alright with you." Victor said nervously. He wasn't sure it was a good idea, but the thought of turning her down bothered him much more than the horrible thoughts swirling around in his head. It was possible that he'd never get the chance again. Of all things, True had been the one to ask *him*. He only hoped neither of them would regret it later. Maybe it was possible to be friends with her but keep his distance all at the same time.

"You're shivering." True said, standing.

"Oh." Victor said, his voice trailing off as he followed her lead and got to his feet. "I guess I am. I should go." He said, feeling his teeth clatter as he spoke.

"We can warm up inside." True said, rolling up the blanket and opening the door.

"You shouldn't just invite guys into your house." Victor said quickly.

"Why not? I'm inviting *you*." True said dismissively.

"Well I'm still a guy." Victor said self-consciously. "Are your aunts here?"

"No. They're gone until morning." True said, taking Victor's hand again and leading him in the door. Victor watched her close it behind them and toss the blanket in a corner.

Alexia D. Miller

"Uhm...okay. We can sit in the front room and as soon as I'm warm enough I'll go, alright?"

True nodded and Victor followed her to the living room. He remembered the last time he'd been inside, carrying True. She seemed steadier on her feet than yesterday and he didn't hear any coughing. Maybe there wasn't as much cause for concern, but a part of him wondered if Zane bruised her. He remembered the marks on her arms the day they met. From what he could tell, Zane had been rough with her.

When True began to light the fireplace, Victor offered to help. True shook her head, wanting to do it herself. When she was finished, she asked Victor if he wanted tea without waiting for an answer. Before he knew it, she'd disappeared down the hall and he could just make out a pale light cast against the floor from the kitchen.

Victor had half a mind to search the living room and the halls for cameras. What an abnormal turn of events. The other half of him wondered if he was sleepwalking, dreaming an impossible dream. As the fire flickered on behind the grate, Victor could feel the warmth filling the room although he was also aware of a slight chill wafting down from the stairway.

As True made her way back to the living room, Victor found himself still staring up the dark staircase.

Alexia D. Miller

"Aren't you lonely being left in such a big house by yourself while your aunts are away?" Victor asked somberly.

"It's alright. I'm not alone." True said, passing Victor a cup of tea from the tray she placed on the coffee table. "The old souls are probably lonely too. Most of them are nice ghosts."

What did she say? Victor thought with a frown. *What does she mean?* "Ghosts?"

"Mm-hm." True nodded, taking a sip of her tea.

Phelia...

Chapter Forty-Eight: Crawlspace.

Phelia had been more than happy to hear from Grace. Even more, she was overjoyed at being invited to her house. She'd never had anyone invite her over before. In school, Phelia recalled that many children had parties often. As if it were some big secret, Phelia would listen to their whispers. "Don't invite her" they'd say. "She isn't going, right?" "She's too weird!" "She's a know-it-all. She'll ruin everything!"

When she was going to school with the older students, they joked about having to deal with police for kidnapping a baby or some similar phrase Phelia thought to be in poor taste. The harsher ones, Phelia let herself forget, though the feelings never left her. For all their secret planning and jokes, Phelia always knew when one of the parties ended. Both the younger and older crowds had a habit of going on and on about them the days following during class.

From the sound of it, Grace wasn't having a party, but she'd still been invited over. And when Grace called her over the walkie talkie to ask her if she wanted to come, Phelia didn't hesitate to say she'd be there. She sat on the other side of Zane's door knocking away until he answered an hour later. She had to beg him to walk her there, but he'd agreed.

It didn't bother her that his face was still bruised, at least the swelling had gone down. If anyone made faces or whispered while they walked, Phelia heard none of it. Even if someone looked down on them, surely something as small as Zane's bruised face meant little in comparison to her family's years hearing ridicule and rumors about her.

Looking up at him, Phelia saw that her brother's brown hair was grossly unkempt. His blue eyes seemed duller even in the daylight and his movements were awkward and stiff. He was paler than she'd ever seen him, and he had a dark patch on his cheek. Phelia wanted to ask if he'd finished his soup from breakfast, but she decided against it. He hadn't been talkative. In fact, he hadn't said anything. Even earlier that day Zane only nodded, threw on his jacket and shoes, and waited for her to get dressed before they left.

Phelia unfolded the piece of paper in her pocket and handed it to Zane. Grace had given her directions, which she took the liberty of writing down, but Phelia already committed it to memory. She watched him read over the notes silently as they walked. Eventually, Phelia took hold of

Alexia D. Miller

Zane's hand expecting him to say something or to get upset, but he did neither. In fact, Phelia was almost sure he never even noticed.

Soon, Zane saw Phelia off at the white picket fence. She stared into the large heart carved into one of the boards, something Grace said she couldn't miss. Phelia stared at the pale-yellow two-story house. She silently took in the gray and white trims, the wavy designed shutters, and the heart shaped window on the front door.

Before Phelia could finish knocking, Grace swung open the door, smiling from ear-to-ear. Grace nodded to Zane as he disappeared down the street. Just vaguely, as Phelia's eyes shifted to the nearby houses, she could make out blinking eyes and random fingers watching through their curtains. "Don't mind them," Grace said with a frown. "They're always peering like that—watching me like vultures."

Phelia wanted to ask what she meant. Why would the neighbors be so focused on one child every time she came and went? Instead, she let Grace lead her into the house. She saw the plain white walls and large wooden furniture. The hall gave way to a kitchen on the left with a four-seat table and pots and pans lining the countertops. What most struck Phelia as odd were the locks on the cabinets. A red wired lock on the fridge open.

Alexia D. Miller

"Why are there locks on all of your cabinets?" Phelia asked with a frown.

"Oh!" Grace chuckled, "I think MaryAnne and Duke are worried I'll eat up all the house."

"Is that so? Well what about the one on the fridge?"

"Normally they'd be worried about late-night snacks, I guess. But MaryAnne made some sandwiches and put them in the fridge for me while they are gone. Cookies too, on the table." Grace smiled, pulling Phelia further down the hall.

When they entered the living room, Phelia realized just how cold it was inside the house. Cold enough to see their breath. It felt warmer outside, as if Grace's home hadn't been heated for days. Seeing the fireplace, Phelia went to start it.

"W-we can't!" Grace said quickly, jumping in front of her. "I'm not allowed to use the fireplace. But uhm! If you're cold there is a heater and blankets upstairs. Just wait here." She said, rushing out the room and across the hall to the stairs. "MaryAnne and Duke's rooms are upstairs, and they wouldn't be happy about us being up there. The bathroom is right down the hall if you need it!"

Phelia nodded, though she didn't understand. How strange that the entire house was freezing but she wasn't allowed to heat it. And the upstairs being off limits? Not wanting to upset Grace, Phelia said nothing about it as Grace

Alexia D. Miller

{ 413 }

returned. For all she knew, it could be normal. She had no way to know. She'd never had friends to find out.

Phelia took a moment to look at the photos on the walls. The largest of the photos showed a young Grace wearing a ruffled gray dress holding a stuffed monkey. She was smiling widely beside two people who Phelia could only assume were her foster parents. The man was tall and thin, dressed in an expensive looking blue collared shirt. His glasses matched the dark hat on top of his head, and he was—as best as Phelia could tell—smiling. Both corners of his mouth slightly faced upwards but looked more like a disturbing grimace.

The woman wore her hair tied in a loose bun with strands falling visibly around her neck. There was no mistaking her large red-lipstick smile that clashed with her lime green and grey stripped dress. Somehow, Phelia found her smile to be even less comfortable to look at than her husbands.

The other photos were smaller and easier on the eyes. In each one they dressed in matching outfits, but this time without the smiles. In these photos, however, Grace's hair was tied to the back of her head or covered with a scarf. One photo of the group intrigued her.

This time, Grace sat on a brick wall in the middle of her foster parents. Each one of them dressed in cream and

Alexia D. Miller

gold. Grace's hair was tied in pigtails with golden ribbons and MaryAnne wore the same bright red lipstick as she did in the ones before. Phelia could make out a body of water on the other side of the wall as MaryAnne and Duke turned their heads to look. Grace's gaze, however, seemed distant and forlorn as she looked past the camera.

"Would sandwiches be alright for lunch?" Grace asked, throwing the cover over the couch.

"A sandwich sounds perfect," Phelia said, offering a small smile.

"Then I'll be back in just a moment." Grace smiled as she checked the heater before sprinting off towards the kitchen.

Not sure she wanted to look at any more photos, Phelia walked out of the living room and down the hall, taking notice of an angled, discolored area against the wall. Leaning down to get a closer look, Phelia noticed a small knob and a latch. A door? Unable to move past it, Phelia unlatched the lock.

Upon pulling it open, she realized the door was iron and had been painted to match the wall. Towards the top of the door there was a small diamond shape opening that she could hardly peek through. On the other side of the door, bitter air pressed against her face.

It was so narrow when she first crawled inside that Phelia had almost been convinced she couldn't fit. Until it

Alexia D. Miller

widened. Even then, Phelia's head was skewed against the ceiling at an uncomfortable angle. Just when Phelia thought to turn around, she saw dark spots on the floor. As she bent down to get a closer look, she realized that they were leading further inside.

There was no light inside or candle holders along the walls to light her way. Deciding it was best to continue on her knees, Phelia delved deeper. She realized that the floor was made of concrete, explaining why it was almost unbearably cold. This was made even more unpleasant as a sour, stale smell drifted to her nose. Reaching the end of the space, Phelia knocked into a tin bucket, which she quickly found to be the source of her anguish.

She struggled to turn around and rush out the way she'd come. On the other side, she heard Grace's voice calling her name. Phelia made her way to her feet, feeling queasy as she dusted herself off. As Grace made her way down the hall, Phelia watched her stumble, eyes wide, almost dropping the plates in her hands.

"P-Phelia! Did you...go in there?" Grace asked, her voice shaking with emotion.

Phelia looked down at the painted iron door. As much as she wished she hadn't, she had ventured through the door and witnessed something horrible on the other side of it. As she looked at Grace's horrified face, Phelia's voice dissolved

Alexia D. Miller

inside her. She felt an acute sense of panic and guilt. Surely, she'd found something she hadn't been meant to see.

"Please tell me you didn't." Grace whined, her eyes brimming up with tears. "You can't go in there. You can't!" Grace yelled.

"I'm sorry Grace, truly I am," Phelia said quickly, "but...what is this room—this crawlspace?"

Alexia D. Miller

Zane...

Chapter Forty-Nine: Today.

Yesterday, when Zane made his way back to Grace's house to pick up Phelia, she'd been quiet—too quiet. She'd hardly said a word on the way home or during dinner. When their father took them shopping for matching sweaters, Phelia didn't have any suggestions.

Zane mentioned it to his father, who wrote it off as the burden of tomorrow. He did think that going to their mother's grave could have been responsible for upsetting her, but somehow it had seemed more than that. Even so, he couldn't bring himself to ask. Every time he thought to do so, the voice in his head told him to stop worrying about her, to stop being so ridiculous.

Today, Zane thought that it was a day worse than any other. He looked at the light blue sweater decorated with a slew of falling holiday stockings, candy canes, stars, and snowflakes, feeling anything but jolly. When Zane took his shower, he found himself relieved at the silence in his head. Downstairs a few minutes later, he saw his father double-checking the items in his bag.

Alexia D. Miller

As the three of them walked out of the door and onto the porch, Zane was surprised to see Victor, Grace and True walking towards them. What were they doing there? MAYBE THEY CAME TO EXTRACT THEIR REVENGE. MAYBE VICTOR IS HERE TO RIP YOU IN TWO THIS TIME. YOU SHOULD END THINGS HERE WHILE YOU HAVE THE CHANCE, BEFORE THEY TELL LIES TO YOUR FATHER, the voice hissed from the back of his mind. So much for thinking it had left him in peace.

Zane took in Grace's red dress and candy cane stockings, Victors and his green sweater and stereotypical elf hat, and True wearing her usual jacket, this time wearing a smiling reindeer mask. As much as he wanted to be amused by the mask's cartoony face, he found it more unnatural than the masks she normally wore. YOU'D FEEL BETTER IF YOU RIPPED IT OFF HER FACE, I PROMISE, the voice echoed in his head. *Shut up*, Zane demanded. Only to be met with a dark laugh at the back of his skull.

"What are you guys doing here?" Zane asked, looking at Phelia. She silently stared in Grace's direction, not looking up to meet his eyes.

"It's an important day," Victor said, sliding his hands into his pockets, "so I figured we could all go together."

"We wore festive outfits!" Grace smiled, showing off her dress.

Alexia D. Miller

{ 419 }

Zane looked over to his father who glanced over to Victor before turning his attention to the others. "We could always use the company. I'm sure I packed too much food again this year anyhow." He said, walking down the steps and stopping in front of True. "I'm sorry, I don't believe we've met."

"Her name is True," Victor said quickly. "She's a bit...shy. The mask stays on."

Seemingly unbothered, Zane watched his father reach out a hand with a smile. "I see. It's a pleasure to meet you True. You make a wonderful reindeer."

"Thank you," True said softly, shaking his hand. "I wore brown."

Zane raised an eyebrow, looking at the same black jacket he'd always seen her in. Even her shoes were black. Where was the brown?

"You don't say," his father said with a nod.

. . .

It wasn't long before they stood in front of their mother's stone. Zane remembered casting their handprints into the tombstone as if it were yesterday. He remembered how they struggled to pick hearts instead of angels and the unbearable weight of heartache. "In loving memory of a

Alexia D. Miller

wonderful mother, a gentle and caring soul. For the most amazing wife. May she rest peacefully in wait of her loved ones." Phelia read quietly.

Zane watched his father go into his bag and take out his camera and a bundle of colorful flowers. "Honey, not much feels like it's changed since you left us." His father said, huddling them all together for a photo. "The world still feels a lot less bright without you in it. The world still turns, work still calls, almost as if you'd never left it. Still, I have the children and I—we—still breath every day.

"I'm sure things are changing a little every day. The kids and I are struggling a bit, I think. Judging by the state our son and Victor are in, I think things are complicated. I'm going to be patient and wait until they can tell me as best I can, but I hope you're watching. I hope you're happy and we're making you proud. We miss you." He finished, turning around to face them with a smile.

Although his father was composed, Zane found himself exceedingly emotional. As he began to cry, he was surprised to see tears falling down Phelia's cheeks and hear Grace sobbing behind him. In that moment, it took everything he had not to tell his father everything. About the crystals, about Mirror and FlareWing, and his fight with Victor.

Alexia D. Miller

WHO KNEW YOU WERE SO EMOTIONAL the voice said with a hint of mockery. *Great,* Zane thought bitterly. *I can't even grieve on my own.* OF COURSE, YOU CAN. GREIVE AS LONG AS YOU'D LIKE. I *LOVE* THE TASTE OF SALTY TEARS. ANGUISH, HATRED, AND DISPAIR ARE WONDERFUL. Zane worried that the voice inside his head was a sadist. Was he always hiding that part of himself?

"Things have definitely been changing, Honey." His father continued with a small smile. "Some of the proof is right here after all. This year, the children have a few friends to add to the family. I'm sure this year's photo will be your favorite too." As Zane and Phelia hugged their father, Grace hobbled her way over and joined them, still sobbing loudly.

"Why don't you go ahead and stretch your legs while I set things up here?" Their father said quietly. Zane knew what that meant. Silently, he urged the others away from their mother's tombstone.

"Shouldn't we help?" Grace asked unsure.

Phelia shook her head. "If father mentions us getting exercise, he needs time alone with mother. It's best if we leave him be."

"He probably doesn't want the two of you to see him upset." Victor spoke, stepping around a tombstone.

"It's lonely, living without someone you love." True said softly.

Alexia D. Miller

"Zane?" Phelia started, "Where do you suppose people go when they die?"

Zane contemplated his answer. "People have different answers for it, but I'm not really sure. But mom couldn't have gone anywhere bad. Mom was a Saint if anyone's ever known one. Dad agrees."

"I wish we could see for ourselves." Phelia sighed.

"I'm sure that pretty much everyone does." Victor nodded.

"Uhn-Uh." Grace said crossing her arms, "I don't like anything dead. No way."

"You're not the *least* bit interested?" Phelia prodded. "Ghosts are scary, Phelia. Even if I *am a teensy bit* curious, there's no way." Grace said, shaking her head. As she spoke, a strike of light skated across a nearby tombstone caught their attention. "Oh *no*," Grace groaned as the cemetery began to sway, folding in on itself. Where they being pulled through another door? Zane thought nervously. What about their father?

Alexia D. Miller

Grace...

Chapter Fifty: The After Land.

From the moment Grace saw the light shimmer and expand from the tombstone, she knew her crystal was reacting to something. She didn't know how the crystals worked, but she was terrified. Where else could a door in a cemetery lead expect to the land of the dead? How'd they even go through a door when they weren't in the abandoned building anyway?

She felt the familiar nothingness and knew she was surrounded by darkness. *Nope. No way. I'm not going to look*, Grace thought defiantly. Even after an unfamiliar voice called out to Jennifer. "JENNIFER!" They called. "Where are you, Jennifer?"

Grace could feel the sweat on her palms and her heart pounding away in her ears. *Don't look. Don't look.* Grace thought nervously. *What will I see if I open my eyes? Who the heck is Jennifer?*

The sudden feeling of a hand on her shoulder made Grace's heart jump in her chest. Afraid, Grace screamed.

Alexia D. Miller

"Grace! Grace, it's me." Zane's voice called as Grace slowly opened her eyes. Looking into Zane's blue eyes, feeling relieved, Grace immediately took refuge in his arms with a dry sob.

"Uhm...look, Grace. You don't have to forgive me for what I did. I don't expect you to, but--" Zane said, shifting his feet.

Grace rolled her eyes, pressing her palm to his mouth, cutting him off. "Zane, you have *horrible* timing." Grace said dryly. Zane raised his eyebrow and Grace quickly removed her hand, apologizing.

As she turned away from him, she looked about. They were still in the cemetery. It looked darker than she remembered. Were they back already? The world of the dead had simply been filled with nothingness and disembodied voices? *No wonder that guy couldn't find his Jennifer*, Grace thought. Still, it didn't make her feel better about the future if that's what she had to look forward to. It was creepy in its own way.

"Oh well," Grace said, "let's go find Phelia and the others, your dad too, I'm hungry." Grace said quickly. Zane pressed a hand to her shoulder, stopping her midstride. "What is it?" Grace asked, watching him shake his head. "Grace we aren't in Snowville. At least not...our Snowville I think." Zane said with a frown. "I went to mom's grave

Alexia D. Miller

already and it didn't look right. Dad wasn't even there. Besides, look around. Everything is so gray or something."

"Of course, it's gray, Zane. Almost all the stones are in the cemetery!" Grace said defiantly. "I-it's just getting dark is all." Grace stuttered, feeling her resolve slipping away. She tried not to take another look around, but she couldn't help herself. He was right. Everything around them was covered in a gray-blue hue, as if she had a piece of film over her eyes.

Grace looked at her arms, surprised to find that she didn't look like everything around her. In fact, she looked no different than normal. Looking at Zane and realizing that he was the same, Grace had chills down her spine. What should have been a relief only made her more afraid. *I said I didn't want to come here*, Grace thought nervously, *and yet, here we are.*

"So, if we aren't in Snowville, but in some strange no-man's-land, then where are the zombies, or ghosts or whatever?" Grace asked Zane.

"Now's not the time for jokes, Grace." Zane said. "We should go back to mom's grave. Phelia's bound to meet us there if anywhere."

"Okay." Grace said quietly, letting Zane lead the way. She tried not to be bothered by the fact that they'd been split up like a bad horror film. Grace didn't want to die. She didn't

Alexia D. Miller

want anyone else to die either, especially with things so awkward with Phelia since she found *That* room.

Grace could explain away the other things as MaryAnne and Duke's strict rules of house, but she couldn't even open her mouth to explain the horrible room away. So, after she regained some semblance of her composure, she changed the subject. They talked about the ugly décor in her bedroom, school, and any other miscellaneous thing Grace could think of. Before long, Phelia was gone and Grace hardly had the strength or words to say goodbye.

At their mother's grave, Grace understood what Zane had meant. The flowers they'd placed in front of the stone were gone. The blanket and the Doctor were nowhere to be found. The air wasn't particularly cold nor warm, but Grace was aware of a distinct airy feeling surrounding them, like a sneaky low breeze. Even the words on the tombstone seemed strange, almost like Grace had her eyes open underwater.

After what felt like an eternity, Grace heard Phelia's voice calling out to them. Beside her was Victor. As Grace and Zane met them in the middle, Grace frowned. "Where's True?" She asked.

"Why is it she always ends up by herself somewhere?" Zane asked with a sigh.

Alexia D. Miller

"Do you think she got lost? I don't think she's ever been to the cemetery before." Victor chimed in.

"Who's lost?" True's small voice cut in from behind, startling Grace for the second time that day.

"True!" Grace called, trying to calm her racing heart. "Where've you been?" She asked, watching her point off to the right. Grace could just make out a bright shimmer some feet off in the distance.

"I was following that dog. Jewel." True said.

"Dog? Jewel?" Zane asked. She nodded, saying that it was on the dog's collar. How could that blob be a dog? Grace wondered, not sure what to say. Not particularly to her surprise, Grace watched as Phelia started off in its direction.

"We should follow her." Phelia said without hesitation. "Maybe it knows where it is going."

Until they were closer, Grace had no more reason to question True. Through the light surrounding her, Grace could make out a shaggy dog. A darker gray than everything else around them, with pale blue eyes and silver streaks in her hair. "How's she glowing like that?" Grace asked. She looked at True, almost expecting an answer. When she was silent, Grace figured True had nothing to offer.

Jewel slowed her pace as she walked, looking over her shoulder at them as if to let them know she was aware of

Alexia D. Miller

their presence. Grace listened to the dog's light snorts as she trotted forward and led them out of the cemetery. Soon, they were passing main streets that Grace knew, but couldn't read the blurred signs. Before long, they reached Phelia and Zane's home. Jewel stopped, looking at them expectantly.

How did the dog know its way there? Grace watched Zane rushing up to the porch and when she looked back down, Jewel had disappeared. Grace followed the others up the steps and into the house. Inside, they saw the same muted gray hues. Only, Dr. Brand was nowhere to be found.

"What is this?" Zane asked, looking frustrated. Before anyone could open their mouths to respond, the sound of overlapping voices nearby stole their attention. They walked to the living room to peek out the window. Grace could make out a group of men and women as pale as the rest of the place seemed to be. They had heavy iron chains around their ankles, practically dragging across the ground.

They had scrapes, bruises, and open wounds. It looked so painful that Grace couldn't stand to look at them and she shut her eyes. The sound of their wails, sighs, and sobs filled the house as their chains rattled. Whatever and whoever they were, she wished she didn't see them at all. Almost wished they didn't exist.

Alexia D. Miller

The sound of the door creaking open forced Grace to open her eyes. Just wide enough to see Victor walking out the door with True on his heels and Zane's mouth opening in protest. Grace shared a worried glance with Phelia as she quickly took hold of her hand. "Together." Phelia said, giving Grace's hand a light squeeze.

Grace wanted to tell her that they didn't have to go. That they could stay safely inside, but she knew that they couldn't let any of them go out there alone. She knew that they'd have to follow them. Out of habit, Grace watched Zane walk ahead of them and she shut the door behind them. *I guess I can't really call this no-man's-land after all,* Grace thought to herself as they slowly walked off the porch.

As the wave of people passed by, Grace wondered if the people she saw could even be human. They didn't seem to notice them watching. They didn't even seem to be in control of their cries. More unsettlingly, their feet seemed to skate across the ground at an unnaturally fast pace that the rest of their bodies couldn't match, almost so quickly that their feet moved forward in a blur.

"What are they?" Phelia asked, tilting her neck forward almost as if she were looking for something specific. All Grace wanted to do was get as far away from them as possible.

Alexia D. Miller

{ *430* }

"I don't like them." Victor said, stealing the words right out of Grace's mouth.

"Can't we help them?" True asked, dejected.

"I don't even want to try." Zane said.

"There's nothing you can do for them, children." An almost musical voice called from behind them. As if in sync, they all turned around to see a tall, shimmering woman with unusual features. She had almost translucent white skin, a short bunch of black curls, and dark cream-colored eyes Grace had never seen.

"Who are you?" Phelia asked without hesitance.

"A guide." The woman answered gently. "My name is Life."

"How ironic. We just came from a cemetery." Grace said aloud, immediately feeling like she should apologize.

"Even more so when you consider that you've stumbled into the Land of the Dead." The woman chuckled. Grace didn't like being right one bit. Couldn't they have ended up somewhere nicer? Even more than that, what was so amusing? Grace thought, worried and perplexed. She had no idea why them being there was even remotely funny.

"Did you say Land of the Dead?" Phelia asked.

"Well, I would say it is more specifically The After Land. Something that you may call the afterlife, but it is a matter of preference. Of course, this isn't all there is. This is only the beginning, a first step if you will."

Alexia D. Miller

Grace looked back over her shoulder against her better judgement. She saw the moaning people in chains fade into a black mass and was relieved to see them go. Still, something told her that beyond the black mass lay something dark and endless. She didn't want to ask, and she hoped they wouldn't find out for themselves.

"Why can't we help them?" True asked quietly, turning Grace's attention back to the others. Grace was sure that this woman—this Life—was radiating the light around her, almost as if it were coming from deep inside her body. "There's simply nothing to be done for them. They are past the point of return and they understand the extent of damage they've caused." What does that even mean? Grace wondered.

"But where did they go?" Phelia asked, looking in the direction they'd vanished.

"To a place they will not return." Life said, shaking her head slowly.

"What have they done?" True asked, looking even more pained than before. Grace didn't know how she could look past their looks enough to feel sorry for them in the first place.

"It's not one thing in particular. It is never quite so simple. No one is more aware of the things that lead them here than they are themselves. It would be altogether too complicated to explain." Life said simply.

"Sorry but all of this gives me the creeps. I just want to get out of here!" Grace cried.

Zane nodded in agreement, "She's right. We left my father. Do you know where the door is?"

Life looked at them silently for a moment before speaking again. "None of those who visit The After Land who are of The Living World do so without reason. If you've come here, it is to accomplish something—to learn something."

"Do you know why we're here then?" Victor asked.

Life smiled, a small smile that almost seemed like pity to Grace. "I have no such knowledge. You are likely to know when it is time for your departure."

There was an uncomfortable silence. As if everyone was stuck inside their own heads. A silence that only ended as the shaggy bright dog Jewel suddenly reappeared. Grace watched as the dog quickly made her way to Life's feet. She barked and panted, wagging her tail from side to side. "Hello little one," Life said, bending down to rub Jewel's dark gray fur. "Have you found him?" She asked.

In response, the dog jumped up on her hind legs and turned around in a circle before dropping down to the ground. She continued to spin excitedly, and Grace wondered then if dogs ever got dizzy. It was dizzying just

Alexia D. Miller

watching her. "Well, let us meet him then." Life said patting Jewel's head as the dog closed her eyes. As she did so, Grace saw a small spark of light appear between them for an instant.

As Jewel trotted slowly off to the right, Life offered them a warm smile. "Come. Let us witness a reunion, children." Her musical voice chimed brightly. Before Grace could take a full breath, they stood on a corner, not far from the abandoned hospital, as if they'd teleported there. As she tried to find a way to voice her surprise and wonder, she saw a man crossing the street. His skin was the same blue-gray hue as everything else around him, but for some reason elsewhere seemed to have more color. He was an elderly man with silver hair, one leg, and a cane. His face was full of sadness and even from across the street, Grace could make out the man's heavy sighs.

Without so much as another look in their direction, Jewel rushed to the other side of the street, barking loudly. She jumped against him with such force that he stumbled to the ground. They watched as the man sat up with Jewel in his arms. She licked his face; her tail was hardly more than a blur of motion. He laughed and when he parted his lips, he spoke silent words Grace couldn't hear.

A few moments later, the man was on his feet, petting Jewel, and walking towards a swirling bright mist.

Alexia D. Miller

"Where's he going?" Grace asked curiously. She recalled the dark mass the wailing people in chains disappeared in. Why was it different?

"He is going to where he belongs. A place he will spend an eternity. He, like many others, must be led into his resting place." Life said, waving her arm gently ahead of her.

"You said you were a guide," Zane said, "so why did Jewel show him?"

When Life rested her hand at her side, small balls of light appeared before them, like budding flowers. In them, Grace could see different people with lively, bright eyes but their bodies were still tinged the same horrible blue gray they'd seen every time they looked around. Some of them called out random names. One young boy led an elderly woman to another misty light, and in another, a teenage girl followed behind a middle-aged woman with her cat in her arms. No matter which one Grace stared into each person was smiling.

"Yes, I am." Life smiled, "However, I never said that I was the only. Some guides are specific to a person. For the lost children, I can particularly be of use. The young, typically cross over the elderly, and some may cross over by the help of a loved one or a pet. There are those lost and wandering, and even poor souls who may not yet know they've expired."

Alexia D. Miller

"Were you one of these people once?" Victor asked.
"No." Life said, "I've never lived in the sense that you say so."

"If you've never lived, how can you exist?" Phelia asked.

"Phelia, that sounds rude." Zane said, shaking his head.

Life seemed unfazed. "It's perfectly alright." Life said as Grace watched the balls of light fade away. "I exist in much the same way as most beings in existence. To not have lived does not mean one has not been created—been born---at all.

"The sun of your world does not live in your world and yet it was created, just to exist in a different way than you. Your trees do not speak. It does not have a heartbeat, and yet it grows and lives. Its purpose lies both in conjunction and independently of humanity in your plane of existence. All the while, it tends to offer the same in other worlds. My life is much the same in many ways."

Grace couldn't say she completely understood. She felt that she knew just enough to make sense of her words but couldn't do anything to piece together exactly what she meant, or what Life was. For all intents and purposes, Life looked enough like a human to pass by first glance. It was when Grace had enough time to study her, however, that she felt grouping Life with humans would be a mistake.

Alexia D. Miller

It wasn't just her skin that seemed void of veins, or her unnatural yet somehow beautiful cream eyes. It was the carefree yet formal way she spoke. It was the sound of her voice, the light a whimsical echo shadowed every word she spoke, and the light beaming around her that didn't hurt when you stared.

Before Grace managed to ask the question burning on her mind, True walked off down the street. She didn't speak as she sped up and her bare feet glided across the pavement. Grace had no time to ask where they were going, but she wondered if True had somehow managed to find the door again like she'd done in FlareWing. Grace followed her with the others close behind. Effortlessly, Life glided by her side, as if she were used to chasing quick young women on the way to the unknown.

It didn't take long for Grace to recognize True's house. The large iron gate looked almost perfectly preserved, even though Grace knew that it hadn't been in Snowville. There were no water spots or tiny scrapes of rust to be seen. As they made their way closer, Grace was filled with worry. The air surrounding the house was cold and uninviting. She could almost hear the voice inside her screaming that danger was waiting for them with open arms. A voice that told her that she needed to turn away and run back, in any direction that would lead her far away from it.

Alexia D. Miller

"He went inside." Victor said from her left.

"Who did?" Grace asked. What were they talking about?

"The little boy." True said quickly. Grace hadn't seen anyone. Not even when they opened the gate. Had they been following someone?

"Let's go in," someone said to Grace's dismay.

Grace looked around them for any sign of Life but didn't see her. What was it about people in other worlds leaving them behind? She'd disappeared, much like Jewel, without a word. She was sure that whoever prompted them to go inside the house hadn't been her. Grace didn't know what was best to do. Should she give herself time to think about it? Should she tell them about the voice inside screaming that they shouldn't go in?

Grace wasn't sure if she was just afraid. She didn't know if she were being irrational or if her instincts were on full alert and could be trusted. She wanted to ask the others if they knew where Life had gone, but the others had already started up the stairs to the porch. Not feeling like she had much of a choice, Grace hurried to mount the stairs behind them. There was absolutely no way she was going to be left out there on the street alone. As True's hand wrapped around the doorknob, Grace wondered if anyone else was shaking.

Alexia D. Miller

{ 438 }

True...

Chapter Fifty-One: Secrets.

True paused for a moment as she walked through the iron gate and admired the mansion. She looked at the mix of geometric shapes and its dark black paint with plum accents. Her eyes traced the arched window trims and the oversized wooden porch. It was the same house, in a different world. Only, it felt much less like the house at home. It felt dark and menacing. As if it was swallowed by a gigantic blood-thirsty beast when they weren't looking.

Still, True was sure that he'd entered her house: the boy with the shining blue eyes. As it had been at Zane and Phelia's home, her door was unlocked. She knew it hadn't been when Victor and Grace picked her up before they went to the cemetery. Would the house look the same?

Inside, True saw the peach and grey patterned rug on the floor. In the living room she saw the large fireplace and the little trinkets from her childhood perched on the top just as they'd been earlier that day. The brown couch still sat in its usual place, adorned with an army of decorative pillows and the blanket she'd used to cover Victor when he fell

Alexia D. Miller

asleep barefoot after tea that night was still folded there undisturbed.

The dining room still had the handwritten chalk sign nailed above the doorway and her Aunt Rose's flowers were in the vase on the table. They'd lost all their color and shine, as if they were behind the screen of an old movie. How was that possible? True recalled that somehow, even Phelia and Zane's house had been more colorful than the world outside their door. As True made her way to the kitchen, she recalled her conversation with Victor.

"So, you mentioned uhm...ghosts?" Victor asked, taking a drink from his glass.

"Yes." True nodded, "I don't see them, but I feel them here." True remembered looking at his brilliant green eyes as he sat silently in thought beside her. How she'd watched the light from the fireplace flicker through his eyes and waited to be told she was insane.

Victor chuckled, "I used to think that if I were quiet enough, I could hear them talking." In that moment True realized she'd hardly heard him laugh. Only a few times since they'd met, like when he raced Zane down the hills in FlareWing only to be beaten by Grace. She had also found herself relieved that he hadn't made fun of her. She'd wanted to ask him about his life, but instead responded to his comment.

Alexia D. Miller

"It feels similar." True said honestly. "What I feel is like that. Like a whisper but in your body instead of your ears. With people sometimes too."

"I can't imagine what being in Snowville feels like to you then. Or worse, school." Victor said. True didn't want to think about the things she felt at school or in the town, so she changed the subject.

"Twister. I really have seen him." True said quietly, not sure what his response would be. She remembered the look on the others' faces when she mentioned him after she made it through the door. "He's been staying here most of the time, though I don't know where he's run off to now." She tried to explain. It was something Twister did for some reason. Without Twister she didn't exactly have proof of him being there.

As Victor looked in her direction, True noticed, as she often did, that she couldn't read the expressions on his face. His face didn't often tell what he was thinking. With her Aunt Trina and Aunt Rose, True could almost always figure it out. "I figured you'd seen him," Victor said finally, finishing his tea. I thought about that day a lot."

He had? "You believe me?" True asked in disbelief. She'd never expected him to say that. For some reason, it didn't feel like he was lying, though True didn't know at the time if she could be sure.

Alexia D. Miller

"Well, yeah. If you say you saw him—if you say he's been freeloading around here—I believe you. I just don't know why he would be." Victor said with a yawn.

"Why? Why do you believe me?" True asked him, unable to push the question away.

"We're friends, aren't we?" He asked with a shrug. "That's one reason to believe you. Then there's the fact that I'm pretty sure you haven't told me a lie before either. Like with the crystals. So, I'm not going to assume you are now either."

True had felt truly touched by his words that night and what seemed to be some sort of trust he had in her. When she'd started to try and explain what happened on the other side of the door, he gently rested a hand on hers.

"Don't. We have time later. Don't push yourself." His voice had been so soft and gentle True wondered if that was how her mother spoke to her as an infant. With a careful and caring tone.

His apparent trust in her was something she'd never experienced outside of her family before and she didn't take it lightly. Still, this time around it hadn't been just her. He'd seen the boy too. This time, there hadn't been any need for proof.

"Are you alright?" Grace asked her, peeking around from her right side as she stood in the corner of the kitchen.

Alexia D. Miller

True could feel her body shaking. Was she cold? True tried to reassure her with a nod.

"It looks the same." True said.

"He's going up the stairs." Victor called quietly, ushering them towards the staircase. "Or at least he was going up? He disappeared."

"I still have yet to see anyone." Phelia said, and Grace and Zane nodded in agreement. True wondered how they could have missed him.

"Elevator or stairs?" True asked, feeling a little impatient. She wanted to find the boy.

"You have a friggin' elevator in your house?" Grace exclaimed, dropping her hands from the air as she spoke. "Of course, you do."

"Can we take it?" Phelia asked.

Grace shook her head. "Have you not seen what happens in a horror film elevator scene? Or worse, a horror film that takes place *entirely* on an elevator?" Grace asked in disbelief.

"We aren't in a horror film, Grace." Phelia chuckled.

"Sure, we aren't at some ancient hotel with fifty floors, but it still applies. Besides, I don't know about *you* but I'm living a freaking living nightmare." Grace said frustratedly.

Alexia D. Miller

"Alright. Alright. We take the stairs." Zane said, not looking any less anxious than Grace. "For the record, I don't like this either."

"Thank goodness!" Grace sighed.

At that, True quickly rounded the handrail and made her way to the second floor. "This floor," True explained, "has the old ballroom and a number of bedrooms with baths."

"But there's like a *million* doors." Zane said with emphasis.

"They all lead to the ballroom, on the left." True said, walking to one of the doors.

"I'm already running out of room to be surprised," Grace sighed again.

True remembered the first time she'd seen the ballroom. It was labeled with a large golden cursive sign, had a polished marble floor and enormous double windows. There was a beautiful golden chandelier on the ceiling and buffet tables and chairs were pushed off in a corner. There was no sign of anyone inside or that anything had been moved.

Slowly, they made their way through the rooms until they'd checked them all. "I guess there's nowhere to go but up," Victor said, sliding his hands into his pockets. As they made their way back to the stairs, True saw movement ahead of them, zipping up the staircase.

Alexia D. Miller

"There he goes again." True said, rushing up the stairs.

She'd seen him again. Only for an instant, but she'd seen him. She made out his light gray suit and those bright blue eyes. The others followed close behind. The boy flashed in and out, leading them up the stairs and disappeared on the fourth floor.

"Do we have to go up there?" Grace whined.
"I'll go first." Victor said to True's surprise. His brows were creased, and his lips faced down in a tight frown. In that moment, True felt what she had outside more acutely. With every step, True felt an overbearing heaviness around her. Almost as if they'd stepped in the jaws of the invisible beast who'd swallowed her house—as if they were helping it eat them by sliding down its throat.

On the fourth floor, the boy stood in front of a door True had never seen before. "There are no blue doors here." True said quietly. A moment later the door swung open and he disappeared. True could hear Grace's gasp.
"Was that the little boy?" Grace asked nervously.
"I saw him too," Zane said in disbelief.
"Even I." Phelia agreed.

"We have to follow him." True said, slowly making her way to the door. Victor stopped her, stepping in front of her.

Alexia D. Miller

"I'm going first, remember?" He said through another frown. True conceded with a nod. She watched Victor's back as they made their way through the door which led to another stairway. Was that door something that only existed there, or had there been another door in their house before?

The stairs led to a small A-shaped room. Inside, the boy sat in his gray suit, holding a feathered pen and a piece of paper. His large blue eyes blinked at them and he put a finger to his lips. "Shh." He laughed. "Mother's going to find me." The boy said, telling them to hide. True could just make out an accent when he spoke.

"Can he—is he actually talking to us?" Grace said, her voice shaking.

His legs were crossed as he scribbled on the piece of paper and folded it away, tucking it into his suit jacket. The boy stared from across the room, giggling as he looked from one of them to the other. Eventually, his eyes rested on Grace. "How odd." The boy said, tilting his head to the side. "'Course I am," he said, shaking his head. "'Less there's anyone else to talk to. What a strange houseslave."

Grace's eyes widened and if Victor hadn't been quick to grab her, True was sure she would have lunged at him. "*Special* **house slave***? Do I look like a* **slave** *to you?!"* Grace yelled as Phelia slapped her palm against Grace's forehead.

Alexia D. Miller

"Oww! That hurt, Phelia! Why'd you do that?" Grace shouted.

"He's just a little boy, Grace. He's from a different time. He doesn't seem to know any better." Phelia chided. Grace scoffed, but she seemed calmer than before.

"We all look odd to you, don't we?" Zane asked.

The boy shrugged. "Like the circus." He sighed.

Grace rolled her eyes. "Of course, we do. Meanwhile you've turned blue, so what does that make you?" She asked pointedly.

The boy quickly looked down at his arms, stretching out his legs and pulling up his pantlegs. "I am not!" He argued. He couldn't see it. True shook her head, "What's your name?"

The boy, having recovered from Grace's pointed statement, smiled. "Chester. I'm Chester Eintracht. Mother calls me rooster but that's only a nickname—only mother can call me that."

Victor's face fell somber. "True, that boy is from The Death House. He—"

"I know." True said, looking back to the boy across the room. This Chester had to be the little boy that went missing in her house all those years ago, but what was he doing there? Chester shushed them again.

Alexia D. Miller

"Darn. Mother's found me already. You were too loud." He huffed, squinting his eyes at them disapprovingly. True imagined that the boy was trying to shoot rays from his eyes to show them how upset he was or punish them even. It was a simple childish gesture she'd witnessed often as a child.

A few moments later, the stairs creaked with weight. Grace cupped her hands over her mouth, looking petrified. As the figure began to emerge from the other side of the door, True realized that perhaps Grace felt it too. True was dizzy feeling the brooding vibrations in the space around them.

The face that peered through the doorframe was not a woman, but a man. He was a tall man with broad shoulders and thin dark hair True didn't think matched his face. He smiled as he came towards them with a cup in his hands. "Father," Chester called as he crawled towards the man. "Is mother with you?"

The man shook his head. True noticed his expensive suit and the matching handkerchief folded in his breast pocket. "She'll be joining you in a moment, I'm sure." The man said. True didn't like his voice. It was grating, like a serrated knife against pavement. "What are you doing?" He asked, not coming any further into the room. It was a small

Alexia D. Miller

space and True couldn't imagine the man being able to stand upright if he came all the way in.

"I was talking with the strange people," Chester said, "while waiting for mother to find me. They were so loud father, so I thought that perhaps you were mother coming to catch me."

The man seemed unfazed. As if he didn't notice their presence in the room. When his eyes shifted around, he looked through them. "Strange people, huh? Well, here." He said, handing Chester the cup.

Chester thanked his father politely and gulped down the beverage. "Father...the end-bit tastes odd." He said, wiping his mouth with the back of his sleeve.

"It's just a little medicine, Chester, to keep you from catching cold." His father said with a smile, ruffling his hair as he retrieved the cup. "Why don't you stay here until your mother comes to get you?" He suggested.

"Okay!" Chester beamed. "You were right father; it will take ages for mother to find me here." He laughed.

"Yes." His father said, kissing his forehead. "So, you'll have finally become the champion of the game by the end of it." He said, disappearing back down the stairs, taking the cloud of heaviness with him.

To True's dismay, within seconds Chester lay on the floor, sweating, coughing, and foaming at the mouth. They

Alexia D. Miller

all stood there in horrified silence as Chester's body convulsed until he didn't move at all. Phelia and Grace rushed into Zane's arms and Victor stood ahead of True to block her view.

As soon as True's heart had stopped racing and Victor and Zane hurried them to the door, Chester sat up on the floor screaming. "FATHER DID IT! FATHER DID IT! FATHER DID IT!" His voice echoed at their backs after they bolted out of the room and down the stairs. They ran as fast as they could and True found herself chasing the faint sound of music.

She dashed through the ballroom doors, only stopping when she heard them closing behind her. Only after she'd began to catch her breath did it occur to True that there shouldn't have been any music playing at all. Looking up, True could see guests splayed face down across the marble floor.

Food and drink were wasted on the tables, candles burned almost down to the wick on the walls, and the buffet tables were turned on their sides. True couldn't say a word as they bolted back out of the ballroom, down the stairs, and to the living room.

Without time to catch their breath, the sound of glass breaking in the kitchen drew their attention. Slowly, they walked back to the hall and closer to the kitchen. True could hear Grace's voice complaining, not wanting to look. The kitchen they saw ahead of them was not one True could recognize. The moment True tried to focus on the differences, however, the screams were too distracting.

A woman with blonde hair and the same bright blue eyes as Chester's cried, pushing the man True recognized to be the boy's father away. "No!" She screamed, beating on the man's chest with her fists. "*No!* What did you do? What did you do, Fredrick! Tell me...please tell me you didn't!" "It was the only way, Jess. It was the only way!" He shouted angrily. "Look what you've done! You're spilling it. **Drink it!**"

He shoved the drink towards her mouth, holding her in his arm. The woman struggled against him, making him spill some of the liquid on her dress. As the cup fell to the floor and shattered, the woman's face fell pale. Looking terrified, she turned to them, reaching out her arms as if begging them for help. Could she see them, like Chester had?

Victor, clearly upset by the scene in front of them, demanded that Fredrick unhand her.

"He's trying to kill her!" Grace cried.

A moment later, both Jess and her husband disappeared and, in the distance, True could make out the sound of her sad, fearful pleading. It took mere seconds for Victor to race off up the stairs. As if he'd forgotten they'd

Alexia D. Miller

ever witnessed anything terrifying just minutes before. Before she knew it, they'd chased after Victor to the master bedroom.

Again, True couldn't recognize the room ahead of her. Not the large wooden bedframe or the hanging silk drapes. She had never seen the vanity in the corner or the floral wallpaper on the walls.

Using the overhang on the bedframe, Fredrick was pulling his wife up by the neck, attempting to hang her even through her tears. Her cries didn't seem to affect him. "No! I won't leave him! I've done nothing. My rooster. My baby! My Sweet Chester!" She shrieked. "Please!" She called out, frantically pulling at the fabric around her neck. "Don't worry, Darling. We'll be with him soon." Fredrick said, sporting a dark smile. "He's waiting for you."

What followed was the most painful cry True had ever heard. It echoed through the room, shaking the space around them. True watched as Victor launched himself across the room at Fredrick. He slammed against him so hard that the two of them flew across the room to the wall. True didn't understand. How could he touch him? Hadn't Fredrick and his wife died?

They crashed into the wall with so much force that it cracked behind Fredrick's large frame. As Victor started to stand, Fredrick disappeared and reappeared on the other

Alexia D. Miller

side of the room, seemingly suddenly away of their presence. True was tense as Fredrick's face contorted and he began to growl almost like a wild animal. Realizing that his attention was focused on Victor, True began to step forward worried for his safety, only stopped by Zane stepping ahead of her. "I don't know what you are, but you aren't gonna hurt him!" Zane yelled, "Not without going through me first, you monster!"

True was sure Fredrick's eyes changed color as he turned around and took a step towards him. In a blink of an eye, Chester's mother stood tall in front of Zane. She stretched out her arms protectively as her entire body came into color. Her blonde hair brightened, almost as brilliant as her blue eyes. Her dress shimmered purple and her skin tanned.

"*NO.* She said harshly.

As she spoke, the room began to shake. Unable to stand any longer, True dropped to the floor. The room broke apart piece by piece. "Victor!" Zane yelled, crawling on the floor towards him on the other side of the room. "Victor!"

Once True was sure that they would all crumble away like the room around them, the room began to fix itself. As if someone had pushed rewind on a remote. By the time the room was in the same condition as it had been

Alexia D. Miller

before, there was someone else in the room. Or rather, some thing.

Something with the arms and legs of a man, the chest of a large furry animal, and wings of a broken bird towered over them. Its eyes flamed a deep red and black steam circled the corners of his eyes towards its frog face. It held out one of its mismatched arms and a chain appeared in its palm. Silently the massive hybrid swung the chain above its head with such force that the air circled the room with every rotation.

With a flick of the wrist, the hybrid sent the chain flying across the room. It wrapped around Fredrick's neck as a black ring swirled against a wall. From the ring, True could make out the sound of voices from the other side. With no effort, Fredrick was dragged away into the dark circle and it shrunk until it vanished.

Jess stood off to the side staring towards the wall where her husband disappeared. She had no hint of emotion on her face, almost as if nothing had happened and she was staring off in her own thoughts. By the time True looked away from her, Life stood in the middle of the room. With her presence, True couldn't feel the dark weight she felt in the house before.

True and the others crawled to their feet. "Poor children." Life said giving them a look of pity, "The things you've seen. You must be here to learn the truth, as horrible as the truth may be."

Grace's face flooded with anger. "You *left* us! And you knew what was here! Didn't you?"

Life gently touched her head and True watched Grace's anger fall away. "I have known souls to reside inside, but I have no way of knowing what you children know. Nor what you are meant to experience, or why." Grace opened her mouth to speak, but Life shook her head. "The being you saw is in charge of the souls you witnessed when you first arrived."

"That's not an answer." Phelia said looking upset herself.

"You must understand, children, that your language is very limited. Such beings are not so easily explained by your terms." Life said tolerantly.

"Then you must at least tell us what's happened!" Phelia demanded. "What was all of that?"

"You're very aware of what happened, child." Life said, shaking her head, gesturing to Jess. "You understand what matters, but I suppose I can explain what you don't. "

Life spoke quietly, as if to avoid disturbing some unknown audience. "Chester's father poisoned his son, countless other unaware souls, and his wife as well. He was— by your definition—a man addicted to gambling and living a life that meant choosing between his addiction and the way

Alexia D. Miller

his family lived. Although I cannot quite say all that led to his ruin was so simple. He lost his..." Life's voice faded off as she tapped her chin in thought.

"Oh yes." She said finally, snapping her fingers. "He lost his currency, his money, to his addiction and kept it a secret from his family. Meanwhile, he never stopped spending it. He became stressed about it, as most humans do, and eventually blamed his family. He blamed his wife's spending and his son's needs more than he did his addiction or extravagant lifestyle.

"He never took responsibility himself. In poisoning the richest adults in the town, he felt powerful and as if he was ridding himself of the standards and lifestyle he felt were also to blame. This was also an excuse of course, to keep others at bay after he selfishly ended his son's life. Fredrick realized too, that his wife's grief would never leave her and he himself was riddled with guilt. Perhaps most important, he could not undo his mistake.

"It should come as no surprise that he negatively impacted the generations that followed as well. Even though Fredrick spared the lives of any other children at the party due to his remorse, the damage was done. After their deaths, both Jess and Chester have been unable to move on because Fredrick held them captive. They endlessly relived the worst day of their lives, unable to reach each other. That is, until

Alexia D. Miller

today. Until you broke the loop and found out their truth, setting them free.

"But in town, people said—" Zane started.

Life shook her head again. "Over time, the truth often fades, for all things. Humans, other beings, animals, and spirits alike. It is the nature of humans to forget and the ignorant to fill holes to satisfy themselves. What you were told is just that. You have witnessed truth for yourselves.

"What now then?" Victor asked, looking exhausted.

Life gave them another small smile. "Chester and his mother will be able to find each other again. They will be guided to their resting place. For you, it seems you are near the end of your journey."

"Near?" Phelia asked, still looking unhappy. "Why must you speak so vaguely? Can't you be more direct?"

Life chuckled amusingly. An instant later, the five of them were outside of the house, near the gate. True almost expected Life to disappear again. She still had so many questions. If a parent could murder his child for money and pride, she wondered what else a parent could do. What a nightmare. *If my mother had been a person like Fredrick, I could have been in a horrible predicament. But she wasn't. She loved me and my aunts love me too.*

Maybe Chester had been lucky too, in a way. He had a mother that loved him so much, she fought to live. He had

Alexia D. Miller

{ 457 }

a mother that didn't leave his side even though they were separated and continued searching for him while re-living her worst nightmare. Jess endured. She waited and endured some more. Just so that they could be together again.

Even So, they'd suffered for so long. She imagined that at some point even Fredrick suffered alone. True looked over at Victor silently. If he hadn't intervened, how much longer would Jess and Chester have suffered? Would the two of them have ever been free? True didn't want to think about it, but even what was done didn't change the reality. The two of them and all the others would never live again.

True wanted to ask how Chester and Jess were able to see them. She wanted to know what was different. When she was ready to ask Life her questions, however, Zane's voice distracted her. "B-Bailey?" He muttered, rushing to the gate. True was sure she recognized the girl from somewhere. Had they met?

"Bailey?? What are you doing here?!" Zane yelled as Victor made his way beside him.
"What's going on?" Grace asked, looking at Phelia. "Is that girl the same Bailey you told me about?"
Phelia nodded. "That's her."

True watched the girl flash in and out, like a channel with a loose antenna. "Zane...?" Bailey called, seeming

Alexia D. Miller

disoriented. "It's really you, isn't it? I was so worried about you. I called and called you know."

"Bailey." Zane said shaking the bars of the gate. "What are you doing here??"

"Do you hate me now, Zane?" Bailey asked, fading out again and then shaking back into view. The more it happened, True realized Bailey had no idea that it was happening at all.

"Hate you? No. I don't hate you." He said, kicking the gate door. He turned his attention behind him towards Life. "What are you doing? Let me through! Open the gate!"

Life closed her eyes. "I've done nothing. There's nothing I can do."

"That's Bull!" Zane yelled insolently. "Bailey!"

"I was just walking around. It looks like home, but it isn't home at all." Bailey said, shaking her head. "What a *strange* dream."

"Did something happen to you?" Victor asked warily.

"Are you—you can't be...**dead?**" Zane asked, his voice shaking with emotion as he looked back at Life again.

"Dead...?" Bailey repeated the word as if she didn't know what it meant.

A flash of light skated across the top of the gate as Life spoke again. "Now, children, seems to be the end..."

Alexia D. Miller

AN INTERVIEW WITH THE AUTHOR:

1. *What charities are readers helping support?*

Great Question!! A portion of each book sale is donated to several charities. This would be after publication and printing costs, of course. Unfortunately, these fees are not optional and are taken from book sales automatically. These charities include SPIDR (Suicide Prevention Initiative and Depression Research Foundation), DAV (Disabled American Veterans), The National Coalition for the Homeless, Campaign Zero, The NAACP Legal Defense and Educational Fund, Pride at Work, The Grameen Foundation and ACORE (American Council on Renewable Energy). I'd love to donate to more as book sales increase.

2. *Before now, I've never heard of an author directly donating from their book sales. Why do you do this?*

To put it as simply as I can, it is important to me and the people who receive services from these charities. Regardless of our personal opinions, the world is full of a myriad of different people who live different lives. All of them deserve to live a better life, no matter who they are.

Alexia D. Miller

I have personally faced a number of challenges that charities like those listed [above] help, although I have never received help from any myself. However, that doesn't mean that they are not helping the people you pass every day. No one knows everyone's story and no charity is/can be omnipresent. If my donations will mean that even **ONE** more person gets the help they need, then I will continue to donate to any degree that I am able. My readers, however, make that possible.

3. *Why are the teachers and other staff so horrible?*

I realize that in the first book, there is a lot of negativity surrounding teachers. Although, growing up I have had a few teachers who hurt my feelings, this was not my overall experience at school. It is important to remember that one, this story is fiction and conflict makes the world go round. Two, there are plenty of times that even teachers become desensitized to things going on in the classroom. It could be because that teacher is having a rough week, perhaps their students don't listen/seem to respect them, or maybe that person just isn't fit to be a teacher. Three, Snowville is a very small town. If you've ever been in one you realize that a lot of people have the same/similar views.

Aside from this, there are also staff members that are genuinely trying to do their jobs the best they know how, even if students don't always understand that. Principle Mann is a great example of this, although we realize he has his own flaws and

Alexia D. Miller

opinions like any person does. In his case, however, he doesn't particularly voice his concerns in the most sociable manner. I am happy to say, however, that we do get to see a wonderful side to several teachers/figures throughout the book series. We have already gotten an indication of this within this book.

4. *What do you want readers to gain from reading your story?*

I hope my readers take away many things from Crystal Key and any book that follows it. I want my readers to walk away with the understanding that everyone around them has their own story and we won't know it unless we ask the meaningful questions in life. I want my readers to recognize that life is messy and full of scary things, but there are also wonderful things waiting beyond what we think is endless.

We must often face hardship(s) to see the value of life and to recognize that the best packages can come in any form--including friendship(s). It was also important to me to highlight what real acceptance looks like. Each character has to learn what that means for themselves and weigh it against a scale from society that they may otherwise ignore. Which isn't much different than what everyone else must do.

We have to care about someone else to accept them just as much as we have to find a way to care about ourselves and shape our own self-acceptance/self-esteem. Of course, it helps when you have other people around that are willing to help you along the way.

Alexia D. Miller

For some, however, the reality is that they will have to build that bridge for themselves. It is a difficult thing to do, but those people will be stronger for it in the end.

5. *Do you have a favorite character?*

As Cliche as it sounds, I really don't. I find all my characters fascinating. Every main character, for example, has something very powerful about their personalities that could be mistaken for weakness until shown otherwise. Even a supporting character's involvement, like Bailey, adds something to future books in the series.

Throughout the book, I try to highlight different aspects of each character. Especially the things that will be important in a following book. So, if you're paying attention, you could probably even figure out some of the main events in the next book!

6. *Why don't their parents know what is going on with the crystals?*

In truth, this question has a pretty simple answer. Adults are busy. Even doting parental figures can't be around every minute of the day. It isn't that the parents aren't paying any attention. It is simply that they are noticing *different* things with divided attention, which is not by choice.

Also, the difference in time in Snowville and other worlds plays a large part in the children "getting away with" disappearing.

Alexia D. Miller

Now that I think about it...there is a third answer to this question as well: plot. Haha. I can't tell you exactly why, but this question becomes more important to conflict later.

7. <u>*Why do the crystals take them to other worlds?*</u>

Since this is answered in book two, my answer is because they (Phelia, Zane, Victor, True and Grace) **must** travel to other worlds.

8. <u>*Don't you think that what happened in The Death House is a bit...controversial? Couldn't you have told it a different way?*</u>

It is my opinion that most things an author writes will be controversial for one reason or another. The Death House's story had to be told because it is central to move the book along and explains a lot of unanswered questions, we don't get answers to otherwise. It is difficult on the main characters as well, but I wouldn't change much about it.

Often, people forget that there are plenty of places/times in human history with a dark/unfavorable past. Some just as disturbing as what occurred in True's home, and others much worse. A lot of the time we must be uncomfortable to learn lessons in life and there were plenty of take-aways embedded in that chapter.

Alexia D. Miller

9. *How did you come up with the characters in the book?*

The same way that I come up with every character from any of my stories, I guess? I sit down with an idea. I find out what kind of people matter/are central to the story. Then I figure out what their personalities are and how they look.

Most times, these details are very specific. Like how tall they are, their eye color, and how long their hair is. I ask questions like... are they an emotional person? What ticks them off? What are their strengths? After that, I come up with their names and add a back story. With the Crystal Key series, even the adults have a backstory. In their case, of course, there is some overlap with their loved ones (like their children).

10. *What inspired you to come up with this story?*

This story was something I had a few details written down about, but I didn't plan for it to be my first published work. I had a list of other stories to choose from that I'd been working on. So, it kind of felt like the book forced me to publish it. Haha.

Aside from that, I liked to develop my own backgrounds surrounding "beings" whose existence we already question every day, while having the freedom to make up more creatures and the like. I had so much fun integrating a different concept of "Fairies"

Alexia D. Miller

from another book I started years ago. So, I guess I should say that I was inspired by everything and nothing at all.

11. *Do you think that someone can become a writer if they don't feel emotions strongly?*

This is a **SUPER** interesting question!! Yes, I do believe that someone can become a writer even if they don't feel emotions as deeply as other people!! I think that a person in this situation may have an easier time writing certain kinds of books like Mystery/Suspense and Scifi which don't have to focus heavily on emotions, but it is more than possible!

To write a book that is emotionally intensive, like a romance novel for example, I think it would be easier if you research popular books to model your writing after and have another writer help you find any weak spots in your book. After all of that, finding someone to edit your book as a precaution would probably be the best course of action.

If you do want to write a book with a lot of emotion, *don't give up*! It will take time to learn, but it **can** be done. You'd be surprised how many emotional cues you can already pick up on, even if you don't feel them as much as the next person. Being able to pick them out will make all the difference in your writing.

12. *What Is Book Two About?*

Alexia D. Miller

Crystal Key: Door to a New World

Book Two is called Crystal Storm. It focuses on answering questions like what happened to the other crystal key holders, Grace's past, what's happening to Zane, Why Bailey was seen in The After Land, and mysteries surrounding FlareWing. I'm not going to spoil all the fun, but there's plenty reason to be excited!

What a fun interview!! I look forward to your reviews (feel free to put your next interview questions there).

Please look for the next book in the series in the coming months!

Alexia D. Miller